A TALE OF TWO SISTERS

Also by Rachel Terry

<u>The Guardians Duology</u>

Lightbringer

Flameseeker

<u>Atlas Sea</u>

The Phoenix and the Crown

A Tale of Two Sisters

A TALE OF TWO SISTERS

RACHEL TERRY

PHARUS PRESS

For information, contact: https://www.rachel-terry.com

Cover design by Rena Violet

www.coversbyviolet.com

Map made with Inkarnate

ISBN: 978-1-960519-10-8

10 9 8 7 6 5 4 3 2 1

To anyone who has ever wondered about the story that came before.

INDRIS
Brisban
ALARA
Palace

Palace
DAERA
ATLAS SEA
The Pirate Haven
AMBERLEIGH
Erlohn Monastery

PROLOGUE

They say tragedies come in threes. For one family on the edge of Alara's southern coast, it came in the form of their two daughters. Each had their mother's red hair, but that was the only way in which they resembled her.

Calida was born first and her parents knew at once that they hadn't been spared their worst fears. Her fate was determined the moment she'd been born. The witch-mark was proof enough of that, shaped vaguely like an anchor on the top of her left foot. It would be easy enough to hide, but it didn't matter. The girl's mother knew well enough what awaited her daughter.

Neither of Calida's parents were themselves witches, but it ran in the family on her mother's side. Her mother had been spared that fate, the inheritance having skipped a generation, and she vowed to do everything in her power to ensure that her own children would not be witches either.

Calida's father was not a witch, nor did he have any history of it in his family. Calida's mother sought him out specifically for that reason, though she had come to love him in his own right.

But it had all been for naught. Their first daughter hadn't been spared.

Neither would the second.

Thalia came a year later, the mark on the small of her back, also easy to hide, but her parents knew what the consequences would be if their deception were discovered.

Their mother was beside herself with grief. In a moment of madness, she suggested they take the children down to the river and drown them. In her mind, it was a kinder fate than what awaited them. A life of servitude, she argued, is no life at all.

She had seen it happen to her own parents and knew how Calida and Thalia's grandparents had been sent away to the Erlohn monastery to be trained by elder witches. Their powers would be determined, their particular gifts established—and exploited.

They would be able to have their own families, of course, but they would be forced to marry fellow witches, to ensure the best chance of the genes passing on to the next generation. They would never be free to choose their own destiny, as she and her husband had done.

For in Alara, witches were little better than slaves, forced to use their gifts—more a curse—in whatever way most benefited the kingdom. So had it been for centuries and so would it continue to be. There was no sign that anything would change and that life would be any different for Thalia and Calida.

Every child born in Alara was registered and when they turned twelve years of age, they were examined by emissaries sent by the crown, to see if the parents had been honest about whether or not their children bore a mark.

Calida and Thalia's parents hadn't lied when they registered the girls. They knew if their deception were discovered, they would both be killed and their children would be taken away regardless.

And so it was that they bid a tearful goodbye to Calida the fateful year she turned twelve. They would not see her again until after she had graduated, released from the monastery's hold—and only then if she chose to visit or had time and provided they were still alive. Neither parent truly expected to see either of their daughters again.

A year later, Thalia followed her sister. For the parents, still grieving their first loss, the second goodbye was no easier.

CHAPTER 1

Calida peered out of the carriage windows at the scenery passing by. She had never ventured beyond her small village and she was eager to see the town. She could see children, about her own age, chasing each other through the cobbled streets, shrieking as they went. Though there was nothing physical that set them apart, she knew they were not like her. If they were, they would have been riding in the coach too.

One of the adults, an emissary from the palace, leaned over and yanked the curtains back over the window, plunging the coach into semi-darkness and hiding the town from view. Calida frowned at him, undeterred, but he said nothing. None of the palace emissaries had said anything since they instructed Calida to bid her family a hasty goodbye and climb up into the coach.

The coach rumbled over a particularly uneven patch of ground, rocking Calida into the child seated next to her. Most of the others were likewise silent, not daring to look at each other. One boy babbled incessantly, about what he thought the monastery would be like, what he was most looking forward to, what kind of witch he would be. How one person could talk so much, Calida didn't know and she had long since tuned him out.

None of the other children were dressed in fine clothing, having come from the same area of Alara as Calida, which was typically poor and dedicated to farming. Calida wore her best dress, a blue rough spun smock. Her mother had insisted that her daughter look her best when she arrived at the Erlohn monastery.

Calida couldn't care less what she looked like. On the rare occasions she'd been permitted to wear it, she'd never been able to keep her dress clean. It would get dirty soon enough, only this time, Mum wouldn't be there to wash it for her.

At that thought, Calida felt tears prick her eyes and she blinked rapidly to be rid of them. She wasn't going to cry, especially not like this, in front of the palace emissary and the other children. She mustn't let them think her weak. There was no place for weakness at the monastery. More than anything, she wanted to make the family she would never see again proud of her.

Still, one of the other children wasn't so lucky. Tears began coursing down his cheeks, leaving tracks in the dirt on his face. He let out a whimper and was immediately told to hush by the emissary.

Calida turned away, facing the wall if she couldn't look out the window. She didn't know what to expect at the monastery; neither of her parents had ever gone there. But she wasn't entirely clueless. She knew that none of them would likely see their parents again—the source of her sadness. It would be best if she didn't allow herself to think about it.

She pictured her sister, Thalia, eleven, who would follow her to the monastery a year from now. That might be the hardest part, doing this without her sister beside her. They had always done everything together, but Thalia wasn't here now.

Calida glanced down at her foot, just visible poking out the end of her skirt, at the worn leather shoe that concealed the proof of why she was there. The witch's mark, her parents had called it. Proof that she was different.

Rather than being sad about it, Calida tried to feel cheer at the thought. She was something special, different. Those children running about in town had no idea of the things she was capable of. And neither did she—until they reached the monastery.

She glanced at the other children out of the corner of her eye, searching for their marks, but none were visible that she could see and she wondered where they were. Were they in the same place as hers, on top of her left foot? Were they the same shape?

Time passed slowly without any scenery to look at or the sun to tell what time of day it was. The emissaries had come for her early that morning and they were still traveling. The constant rocking motion of the coach was uncomfortable and it grew stiflingly hot inside. Calida felt sweat covering her skin, clinging to the roots of her hair, taking a bit of the natural curl out of it, but she didn't complain.

They didn't stop to pick up any more children. The coach was full as it was, which did nothing to help the heat.

One of the girls complained of hunger and was told they would be fed once they reached the monastery. Calida hadn't had anything to eat since breakfast, but she ignored the discomfort. She wanted to sleep, not because she was tired, but because the trip might pass faster that way.

At last, she felt the coach begin to slow and she sat up straighter as the emissary stirred, a thrill of excitement bolting through her. As the coach rocked to a halt, the emissary stood and opened the door, instructing the children to file out orderly, one by one.

Calida was on the far side from the door and she waited impatiently for the others. Her legs were stiff from the long ride as she shuffled toward the door, finally stepping out into the open air, breathing deeply. It was much cooler out here than it had been inside the coach.

They stood in the middle of a forest, sunlight filtering down through the thick canopy of leaves. From the height and size of some of the trees, Calida knew they were quite old. The sun had begun lowering in the sky, its long slanted rays stained orange, but there were still a few hours of daylight left, hopefully time enough for them to get settled in and explore.

Through the trees, Calida glimpsed a massive stone complex of buildings, rising up into multiple levels. The Erlohn monastery resembled a stone keep, with smaller buildings nestled within the outer walls. The roofs were thatched and a central courtyard stood in the middle. Within the courtyard was a well, some garden plots, and trellises stood propped against the walls, covered with flowers and vines. Everywhere Calida looked, there seemed to be plants.

Stone steps led up to the various levels and at the very top of one of the towers, she spied a bell, silent and still for the time being. Somewhere, she could hear a river babbling nearby, but it remained out of sight. There was a slight breeze that might have been carrying the sound from much further away than it seemed.

Her immediate impression of the place was one of peace and beauty. This was to be her home for several years. Just contemplating the amount of time she would spend here was hard for Calida to fathom. It seemed like an unspeakably long time. She would be a completely different person by the time she left, departing through that main gate.

"Do we have time to get them sorted?" the female emissary asked her companion, jolting Calida out of her thoughts.

This second emissary had ridden on the outside of the coach, with the driver, while the taciturn male had kept the children company.

"We should," he replied. "Let's get them to the headmistress and be off."

Together, the group of children were herded forward, beneath the great stone arch that housed the main gate, and into the middle of the courtyard. As she passed, Calida glanced at each of the buildings within the complex, wondering what they were for.

They approached one of the towers, taking the outer stairs that had been carved into the side of the building, climbing up to the top to what Calida assumed must be the headmistress's quarters. One of the emissaries knocked on the door and then stepped back.

"Enter," a voice called from within.

The door was pushed open and the children ushered inside. "The last of the first years, headmistress," the female emissary announced.

"Thank you," the headmistress replied. "You may go."

The emissaries bowed briefly and departed, shutting the door behind them.

The headmistress was a tall, thin woman, with dark skin and dressed in white robes, her hair carefully braided and pinned up. She was quite beautiful, in a striking way, and Calida found herself intimidated by this woman in a way she hadn't been by the palace emissaries, with their scarlet and gold livery.

"I am Headmistress Anise," the woman explained, clasping her arms behind her back. "Welcome to the Erlohn monastery. As you likely already know, you are here because you have been born with special gifts. It is our job, at the monastery, to teach you how to use these gifts to best serve your kingdom. In order to determine which gifts you have been given, we will perform a simple test."

The headmistress sat down behind a table in the center of the room, an open ledger before her. In front of the ledger sat a small potted plant and a bowl of water. Individually, the headmistress gestured for them to come forward.

While she waited her turn, Calida glanced about the rest of the room. Aside from the wall with the door, it was completely surrounded by arched, crosshatched windows. Above her head, plants were nestled in the rafters, their long vines sprawling out across the ceiling. Every spare inch of space seemed to be taken up by book shelves.

Calida watched from her place in the back of the group as the test took place, not quite understanding what she was seeing. The girl in front of her was shaking slightly and her anxiety only seemed to grow worse as they drew closer to the front.

"What's your name?" Calida whispered. They were the first words she had spoken since leaving that morning.

The girl turned to her, hazel eyes wide. She had a plump, round face, a faint smattering of freckles across her nose. "Lorelei."

"I'm Calida." She glanced at the table, still not knowing what awaited them there.

Lorelei followed her gaze. "I wonder what sort of test it is."

Calida had taken tests, in the short amount of time she had gone to a normal school, learning to read and write and do basic math. But it hadn't been her destiny and so she hadn't stayed long. Something told her this wasn't that sort of test.

"I'm sure you'll do great," she told Lorelei.

The other girl smiled and turned back to face the front.

Calida was the last to be called and she approached the table with trepidation.

Headmistress Anise looked up from her ledger. "Name?"

Calida gave it and watched the letters as they were inked into one of the columns, the headmistress's quill scratching across the parchment.

The woman set her quill aside. "Now, Calida, for our little test, I'd like you to concentrate on each of these separately." She motioned toward the potted plant and bowl of water. "See if you seem to have a connection to either of them, if either one calls to you. If you can make them move."

Move? Was that what she was supposed to be able to do?

Her mother hadn't told her much of what to expect. When Calida had asked, over dinner one night, the subject had seemed to upset her and so Calida hadn't pressed, but now she wished she had. None of the ordinary children at school had known she and Thalia were witches, but she'd heard them talking about the monastery.

The other children had made it sound like a mysterious place, somewhat creepy and strange, where witches learned to do things like make the earth split apart and call down lightning. Calida had thought them ridiculous—she'd never heard of anyone calling down lightning before—and her impression of the other children was made all the stronger by the way they spoke of witches, as though they were little more than freaks of nature, all the while blissfully unaware that there were two such individuals in their midst.

Calida had been so insulted that she'd wanted to fight the boy telling the story. She'd wanted to break his nose and knock him into the dirt, to wipe that smug smirk off his face. Her father had shown her how to throw a punch, teaching her to fight until her mother had found out and put a stop to it, saying that Calida would never need to use her hands in a fight. The lessons may have stopped, but Calida remembered what she'd learned.

The only thing that had saved that boy's nose and Calida from being expelled that day had been Thalia. Quiet Thalia, pointing out the obvious, asking what the point of it would be. Her logic had cut through Calida's fiery temper and brought her back to herself.

Thalia, a year younger and in many ways, so much wiser.

Thalia, who wasn't here.

Calida swallowed, pushing the memories aside, and focused on the test set before her. The plant or the water. Which would be the better power to have? Calida had always loved the water, playing in the creek back home, and so she chose to focus on the bowl first.

Make it move, the headmistress had said. How was she supposed to do that without touching it? Was she supposed to blow on it? But that seemed stupid; anyone could do that. It had to be something that an ordinary person couldn't do.

She was tempted to shout at the water and order it to move, but she felt foolish doing that in front of the headmistress, who was watching her with intense dark eyes.

A few of the other children before her had attempted something similar, but it hadn't seemed to achieve any results. She wished she'd paid more attention before it was her turn, instead of talking to Lorelei. She wished she'd been able to see better.

"Try the other one," the headmistress suggested after several long moments of Calida staring at the water to no avail. "It's all right if you don't get either in your first try. Not everyone does."

But I want to, Calida thought, beginning to feel frustration boiling up inside of her.

She turned her angry gaze on the potted plant, as if she could scorch it with a look. That didn't happen. The plant did not blacken and wither, but it *did* slowly begin to grow, snaking upward a good five inches, its leaves spreading.

Calida let out a gasp and took an involuntary step backward. She'd never seen a plant move on its own.

"Well done," the headmistress was saying.

No, not on its own, Calida realized. *I did that.*

The headmistress scribbled something else in her ledger beside Calida's name and then rose to her feet. "Follow me.

I'll escort you to the barracks, where you'll meet up with your fellow earth witches."

Earth witch. Is that what I am?

Calida followed the headmistress back down the winding stairs to one of the outbuildings.

"The barracks," the headmistress explained. "The male and female dormitories are separated, of course."

The other students were already inside, getting settled. The headmistress led Calida to the female dormitory. The building was long and narrow, with a low ceiling. Bunkbeds stood in rows. In the dim lighting, Calida spotted Lorelei. All of the girls that she could see were wearing identical tunics—either blue or green—that were long in the front and back, and shorter on the sides, which hung down over a pair of trousers that narrowed as they tapered down to the ankle.

"I saved you a spot," Lorelei murmured as Calida approached, gesturing to the bunk above hers.

"Thanks." Calida reached up, pulling down her own uniform and quickly changing into it since the others had already done so.

It was a kind thing for Lorelei to do and Calida wondered why she had made the gesture. Had she managed to make a friend in such a short amount of time? She'd never really had friends at the normal school she and Thalia had gone to. She hadn't bothered, knowing there was no point. The two of them wouldn't be staying.

From the dormitory, they were escorted to the mess hall, Calida's stomach growling. At the prospect of finding out what type of powers she had, she had momentarily forgotten how hungry she was, but that was over now. They filed into the massive dining hall and stood in line until it was their turn to pick up a tray holding only a slice of bread and a lump of porridge.

It didn't look like much, but Calida was too hungry to care at that moment. She and Lorelei quickly found a table and dug in, though she could hear some of the other students complaining about such small portions.

"I hope they let us eat some of whatever they grow in the orchards," Lorelei said quietly.

"Don't get your hopes up."

Calida looked up from her porridge. The boy sitting across from them had spoken. He wore a green tunic like them, and he appeared to be a few years older, perhaps fifteen, with a thatch of brown hair.

"They don't let us eat any of it?" Lorelei asked, clearly dismayed.

"Oh, they do, but not very often," the boy warned. "Mostly, you get to eat what you grow, so the better you are at it, the more you get to enjoy."

Calida studied him. "What year are you?"

"Fourth year." He gave her a wry smile. "Only four more years to go."

They entered when they turned twelve and didn't graduate until they were twenty.

Eight long years. Almost as long as Calida had already been alive. Unfathomable.

"What's your name?" Lorelei asked. "I'm Lorelei and this is Calida."

"Daniel."

Lorelei fidgeted nervously. "What if you're not good at growing anything?"

"You still get to eat," Daniel reassured her. "It does them no good to starve us. But it's more like what we're having now. It's our incentive to try our hardest. But don't worry. That's only if agriculture is what you're best at. If you're to be a soldier, obviously they don't expect you to know how to grow crops."

Lorelei visibly paled. "I don't think I'd make a very good soldier."

Daniel shrugged. "It's not about what you want, though, is it? It's about what you're good at. How we can best serve our kingdom and all that."

"What are *you* good at?" Calida asked.

Daniel grimaced. "Agriculture. At this rate, I'll end up supervising crops somewhere after I graduate. It isn't what I imagined for myself, but that's the way it is sometimes."

Calida tried to imagine herself in charge of growing plants for the rest of her life and couldn't. No, that wasn't what she wanted for herself and she'd try her hardest to make sure it didn't happen.

Being a soldier sounded exciting and important, but she would wait to hear what other options there were before deciding what she would try to commit herself to.

She glanced around the room suddenly and saw what looked like a sea of green. There were only a handful of blue tunics among the crowd.

"What kind of witch are they?" she asked Daniel, nodding toward the blue robes.

"Sky witches," he replied, with a tinge of something she couldn't identify in his voice.

"There aren't that many of them, are there?" she remarked.

"There never are," he answered. "Sky witches are pretty rare."

"What can they do?" Lorelei asked, staring at the nearest blue tunic, eyes wide.

"They control the wind and waves. The strongest can create storms and I've even heard they can call down lightning in a storm."

So it was true. There were witches who could call down lightning.

Calida felt a sudden flash of envy, wishing she had been a sky witch. It seemed so much more impressive than being able to control plants. What use was that?

"They're almost always soldiers," Daniel added. "Though the weaker ones are often assigned to crops, too. Make sure they get enough water."

That only made Calida more jealous. If she wanted to be a soldier, she would have to compete against people who could summon storms. What was anything she could do when compared to that?

But there must be earth witches who were soldiers too. She would find a way to make it happen, no matter how hard she had to work or how creative she had to be.

"What about them?" Lorelei asked suddenly, nodding toward a student dressed in a gray tunic. Looking around, Calida spotted one or two more that she hadn't noticed before.

As usual, Daniel had all the answers. "They haven't passed the placement test yet. The one you just took. Until they can pass one of the tests, they can't be sorted into either group. They'll get a color when it's known what kind of witch they are."

Calida frowned. "Is that normal?"

"There's always a few every year that take longer than the rest. It doesn't bode well, though. Late bloomers almost always get the most menial assignments at graduation."

Calida cast another glance at the gray tunics, thankful she had been able to pass, even if she was an earth witch instead of sky.

At least she didn't have to wonder, even if her type wasn't the one she wanted. There was some consolation in that, she supposed.

Dinner ended soon after, the headmistress coming to collect them and usher them back to the dormitories.

"Try to get some sleep," Daniel told them before they parted ways. "We're up at first bell. Breakfast is served at second bell, so don't be late or you'll miss it. First lesson at third bell. Whatever you do, don't be late for that. Tomorrow will be a big day."

"Why's that?" Lorelei asked as they began shuffling through the crowd.

Daniel grinned. "You get to choose your familiars. Or rather, they choose you."

"Familiars?" Calida asked, but Daniel was already gone.

Dusk had fallen across the monastery and the air had cooled considerably as they stepped outside. The headmistress stopped briefly at their dormitory before moving on to the other, imparting a few last words.

She reiterated the bell system that Daniel had spoken of. "The washhouses and bathrooms are over there," she said, pointing to another outbuilding. "Freshen up there every morning and then head straight to breakfast. Are there any questions?"

No one said anything. There were plenty of questions that Calida wanted to ask, but the headmistress wouldn't be able to answer them so she stayed quiet.

The headmistress nodded. "Very well. You will see less of me from now on. I will supervise your overall education and training while you are here, but starting tomorrow, you will begin training with teachers who are the same type of witch as you. They will evaluate your abilities and begin to see where your talents lie. Even so, know that my door is always open. I wish you all good luck and good night."

Lorelei and Calida ducked inside the dormitory and found their way to the bunks they had chosen. Calida was about to begin climbing up into the top bunk when Lorelei grabbed her arm.

"Look," she whispered.

Calida followed Lorelei's gaze. There were animals moving about and settling down beside some of the other students. Everything from owls and foxes, dogs and cats, tiny pigs, lizards and snakes.

"They must be the older students' familiars," Calida whispered back.

Lorelei nodded wordlessly and crawled into bed.

Calida clambered up into her bunk, trying to follow Daniel's advice. She knew tomorrow would be a big day, their first full day of training, and she doubted it would be easy. They were here to be shaped, molded into whatever the kingdom needed them to be. Those who were the best in their fields were given the best positions and the best futures.

No matter how friendly everyone else in the room with her may be, at the end of the day, she was still competing against them for the best positions. Even Lorelei.

But Lorelei doesn't want to be a soldier, Calida reminded herself. *You do, so there's no conflict there.*

Still, she was too excited, too many thoughts swirling through her mind, to allow sleep to come. She thought about all the animals that were in the room with her and which one she would like to choose.

But which one would choose her?

CHAPTER 2

First bell came abysmally early. Used to working on her family's farm, Calida didn't mind too much, but she heard some of the other students grumbling as they stumbled about in the dark. Lorelei was one of them.

"Why do we have to start so early?" she muttered as she followed Calida toward the wash house. It was just past dawn, the first rays of sun beginning to lighten the trees.

The wash house wasn't large enough to accommodate the entire dormitory at once and so those that arrived late had to wait their turn. Calida and Lorelei were among the first to arrive and they tried to be as quick as possible so that others could have their turn.

Breakfast in the mess hall was much the same as dinner had been the previous evening. They were greeted by trays of the same bland porridge, but there was an egg or two on the side this time. Not having met any of the other students yet, Calida and Lorelei sat across from Daniel again.

He nodded to them. "How are you settling in?"

"Well enough," Calida replied. She didn't want to admit how little sleep she had gotten.

Lorelei gave an enormous yawn. "I'm afraid I'm going to fall asleep in my porridge."

Daniel smirked. "You get used to it."

"Really?" Lorelei asked dubiously.

"No, not really."

After breakfast, at third bell, the first years filed out of the mess hall, following headmistress Anise. She led them over to another of the outbuildings and stopped before the doorway, fixing them all with a somber gaze.

"Ordinarily, you would be in your first class at this time of day, but there is something that must be done first. The selection of the familiars."

Calida heard excited murmurs break out behind her and felt a little thrill go through her at the prospect of finally getting a familiar of her own.

"For those who don't know, familiars are animals who share a special connection to a witch. You will be able to communicate with your familiar as easily as I am speaking to you now. The stronger your bond, the deeper the sense of communication. One day, with the proper training, you may even be able to link their vision to yours."

Calida had no idea what that meant, but it sounded impressive.

"This is not to be taken lightly," the headmistress warned, her dark eyes raking over them, her expression the gravest Calida had yet seen. "Every witch will have a familiar, regardless of the type, and each witch gets only one familiar. Your familiar will choose you, not the other way around. Their fate is directly tied to your own. If you die, so does your familiar. If your familiar dies, you, however, will continue living, but you can never again form another bond with such a companion. Otherwise, your familiar will be with you for your entire life, unless they should choose someone else. This bond is not to be taken for granted. Like any relationship, it can be broken or lost. Are there any questions?"

There might have been, but everyone was so excited to get inside the building that they didn't dare risk dragging it out any longer by asking questions.

"Very well," the headmistress said, stepping aside. "Enter. Take your time. You'll know the connection when you feel it. And remember, regardless of what familiar you would like for yourself, there's no point in arguing over one. The familiar makes the choice, not you."

But Calida wasn't listening anymore. She had rushed inside, followed closely by Lorelei. *Please let me get a good familiar.* She didn't know what a bad familiar would be, but she didn't think the snake she had seen last night in the dormitory would be particularly useful. What might one need a familiar to do?

Inside, the air was filled with the earthy scent of all manner of animals. Despite what the headmistress had said, Calida ignored the animals she was uninterested in and went straight for the more exciting ones.

She stopped before a fox, admiring its orange coat. It stared back at her with keen, intelligent eyes, but she felt nothing that she thought could be considered a connection. Disappointed, she turned instead to the mink, but felt no different staring at it than she had the fox. What was she supposed to be searching for?

She looked up and froze. There was a hawk perched further down the line and curious, she made her way toward it. It wasn't quite fully grown yet, but already it was a beautiful bird, its plumage a mixture of brown, orange and white.

Slowly, as if her movements were not her own, Calida felt herself drawn toward the bird, her feet stepping forward. It did not look away but met her gaze directly with yellow-orange eyes, blinking slowly.

"Hello," Calida said, feeling slightly ridiculous, but also knowing that this was what she was supposed to do.

"*Hello*," the bird replied. Its beak had moved but she heard a voice rather than any normal sound a hawk might make.

"I'm Calida," she introduced herself. "What's your name?"

"*My name is whatever you would like to call me.*"

And Calida knew then that this bird had chosen her. This was her familiar.

"Calida!" Lorelei rushed breathlessly up to her. "Look at my familiar."

A small monkey perched on her arm, all legs and tufts of dark fur. It peered up at her with a round, pale face.

"It's cute," Calida replied.

"Have you found one yet?"

Calida turned back to the hawk. "Horus," she said. "This is Horus."

She held out her arm and the hawk nimbly leapt from his perch. The weight of the animal surprised her, but even more surprising was how gentle Horus was, despite his talons. She could see how sharp and wicked they looked in the dim lighting, but his grip was so light, there was no chance of them hurting her.

She reached out, softly stroking his feathers. She had never been so close to a wild animal before and certainly had never touched one.

Wings, she thought. Horus could be her wings. She might have been stuck at the monastery, but he needn't be. He could go anywhere and tell her of the things he saw.

Far better than a fox could ever be.

* * *

Training began in earnest after that, the young witches accompanied by their familiars nearly everywhere they went. Calida and Lorelei trained with the earth witch masters, each one in charge of teaching a specific discipline. They saw little of Daniel, being several years above them and already having determined which skillset he was best at.

"What are you going to try for?" Lorelei asked nervously their first full day. "I want to stick together."

"I was hoping for soldier," Calida admitted, knowing how Lorelei felt about that.

Her friend's face fell slightly. "Oh. Well, I think I could be a soldier."

Calida was touched by her friend's loyalty. For the earth witches, combat was taught by a gruff, middle-aged witch name Kallias, who seemed impossibly old to Calida. His hands were covered in white, ropey scars and he bore another scar on one side of his face, from the temple to the corner of his mouth. It had healed poorly and it pulled at his mouth, always making it look as though he were sneering.

Many of Calida's fellow first years wanted to be soldiers. She surveyed the group of them that had gathered and was silently impressed.

She had thought Kallias would have been pleased with the amount of students expressing an interest in his subject, but she was wrong.

His lip curled as his gaze flicked over them, pacing back and forth, hands clasped behind his back. "There's a large group of new recruits every year that think they want to be soldiers. Hoping to avoid a less interesting placement, eh?"

His eyes shot to Lorelei, who quickly looked away, but Calida didn't flinch, even though his assumption was correct.

"By the end of the year, over half of you will be gone," Kallias continued. "You either have what it takes to be a good soldier or you don't. And only the best will be chosen to serve in Alara's military."

Over the course of their lessons, he explained what an earth witch could do and how those abilities could be utilized in combat. Earth witches, naturally, could control the earth. Plants, dirt, the ground itself. But they could also talk to animals other than their own familiars and persuade them to do their bidding. Sky witches, for all their dramatic flair, were limited to communicating with only their own familiar. Calida felt a certain sense of satisfaction at that.

"You are limited only by what your specific powers can do," Kallias instructed. "The rest is up to your imagination. Get creative. This is no place for narrow-minded thinking. It makes your attacks too predictable, too easily countered."

He demonstrated how their particular skillset might be utilized in such a way. Roots could be called upon to immobilize an opponent. Trees could be toppled to block roads or crush enemy soldiers. The ground could shake beneath their feet or give way completely to swallow them whole.

They emulated such attacks on training dummies that had been set up in the combat area. Calida had no trouble copying the skills, but she wasn't foolish enough to think it would be as easy with a living target as it was with the dummies.

Lorelei, on the other hand, struggled. She knew what needed to be done, but it was as if her magic refused to comply, almost as though it was incapable of carrying out the actions.

"I can't do it!" she exclaimed one evening when they were in the dormitory together. "I'm way behind the rest of you. If I can't catch up soon, Master Kallias is going to drop me from the class."

"I'm sure it won't come to that," Calida tried to reassure her. "You're not that bad."

"You heard what he said. Only the best. We either have what it takes or we don't."

Calida snorted. "That's rubbish. I'm sure you can learn to do anything. It just takes some people more time than others."

Lorelei shook her head. "That's not what Daniel said."

"Oh, really?" Calida said, slightly annoyed. "What did Daniel say?"

"He said we don't have a choice over what we're good at and what we're not. We're either earth witches or sky witches, but there's always going to be one thing we're best at doing, whether we like it or not. And that's what our placement will be when we graduate. That's how we're going to best serve our kingdom."

"That's stupid," Calida retorted, but she had a sinking feeling that Daniel might be right. She had heard other students and even some of the teachers say something similar, but she hadn't wanted to believe it.

She wanted to believe that if she yearned to be a soldier badly enough, then that was what she would be best at.

"I don't know," Lorelei murmured. "I think it might be true. Why else would Daniel's placement be agriculture? Do you really think tending crops was something he would have chosen for himself?"

Calida didn't reply; she knew the answer well enough. The thought that a good placement might be out of her reach no matter how hard she worked, because her particular magic was better at something she didn't even want, made her angry. Why couldn't she do what she wanted or enjoyed? Why did it always have to be about whatever best benefited the kingdom as a whole?

For the first time, she understood why her mother hadn't wanted to talk about the monastery. Why she had seemed almost fearful of what awaited her daughters there.

Calida shook the thoughts away. She had to get a good placement. She had to. She was damned if she was going to wile the years of her life away, tending crops in some backwater just because she could make plants grow.

And Lorelei was going to get a good placement too.

But her friend had been right. She and a few other students were soon culled from the class by Master Kallias, leaving Calida on her own. With every student that was removed from the class, competition only grew fiercer for the remaining spots and Calida was determined to keep her place.

Lorelei began focusing more on the other classes that were available to her: healing, agriculture, and the care of animals. Calida had all of those classes too, but she barely focused on them, so intent was she upon attaining a position as a soldier.

Kallias taught them how to wield physical weapons as well as magical, telling them that although a witch never hoped to have to rely on any weapon other than their own magic, there may come a time when such knowledge would be useful.

The swords, shields, and longbows were all too large or heavy for Calida to wield, even though her body had become stronger under Kallias's training. She settled for a dagger, dissatisfied with its performance and lack of application when compared to some of the other weapons. But there was nothing she could do about it.

Her magic was what mattered and despite what Kallias said, she never intended to rely on anything else. It was her magic that would land her a placement in the military, not her skills with a blade.

She and Lorelei saw Daniel every day in the mess hall and he made sure to stay apprised of how well they were doing.

"Caring for the animals is going really well," Lorelei told him. "I like it."

"That's good," Daniel said. "It's always nice when your natural talents also happen to be something that you enjoy." He hid it well, but Calida still caught a trace of bitterness in his words. He himself hadn't been so lucky.

"Calida's doing really well in healing," Lorelei added.

Was she? She'd hardly noticed, her complete attention devoted to Kallias's lessons.

"Maybe you could be a medic in the army," Daniel suggested.

"I don't want to be a medic," Calida told them stiffly. "I want to be a soldier. Kallias is going to start the duels soon."

She hadn't wanted to think about it. Every time she did, her stomach seized up and she felt an uncomfortable lurch in her chest, about where her heart would be.

She could go through the rotation of skills on the training dummies in her sleep, but dueling her fellow students was something else entirely. Dummies couldn't fight back.

Still, she needed to pass this part of the class and knew that if she didn't, she would be dropped like Lorelei had been.

The morning of the first day of duels, Calida felt so nervous, she thought she might throw up. Lorelei tried to convince her to eat some breakfast, knowing she would need the energy, but she didn't dare.

"You're taking this very seriously, aren't you?" her friend remarked as they filed out of the mess hall to their first classes of the day.

Calida whirled on her. "Aren't you?"

Lorelei stopped short. "Well, of course I am, but—"

"You know what this means, don't you? What's at stake? How well we do here will determine what will happen for the rest of our lives. I don't want to be stuck on some farm forever, tending to crops or cows!"

Lorelei blanched and Calida knew she'd said the wrong thing. "What's wrong with any of that? The kingdom still needs people to do those things, even if they're not as glamourous as a soldier's life."

"You're right," Calida sighed. "I'm sorry. They are important. It's just not what I want for myself, that's all."

"I don't know what I want for myself," Lorelei said softly. "Do you ever wish we could just be normal?"

"Normal? You mean, not be a witch? Like everyone else?"

She nodded.

Calida had never really thought about it before. There was nothing exciting about being ordinary. She had very little idea what sort of lives people led outside of the Erlohn monastery, but the other children in her old school hadn't been witches. They'd been normal and hadn't seemed like anything special. Certainly not something she would want to be.

"What's so great about being like everyone else?"

Lorelei shrugged. "I don't know. I think it would be nice not to have this sort of pressure. Kids our age are out there playing, not a care in the world. They're not worried about their futures or what they're going to be doing for the rest of their lives."

"Maybe."

The third bell rang out, startling them both.

"I gotta go or I'll be late!" Calida called out and took off running for the training grounds.

"Good luck!" Lorelei shouted after her.

Calida ran for the gate, toward the training grounds where the students gathered outside the keep walls. Her strides were almost leaping bounds, stretching out as far as she could, her steps eating up the ground beneath her feet, in a desperate attempt to avoid being late. The wind tore through her red curls, tugging at her tunic.

In the distance, she could see the vineyards and fields, orchards and bee hives, the pastures for cows, sheep, and goats. All part of the monastery, each one a potential placement.

Calida shuddered, though whether from dread or excitement, she didn't know, her heart racing faster than her thoughts.

In the end, she was late anyway, which did nothing to please Master Kallias. He chose her to be one of the first in the dueling ring, which meant that if she wanted to make it to the end, she would have to fight more opponents than anyone else in order to get there.

Calida sighed, straightening her shoulders, trying to slow her breathing and recover from her frantic flight.

There was nothing she could do about it. She'd just have to make sure she won.

She had studied her fellow students over the months they'd trained together and knew which skills they struggled with and which they favored. An earth witch's abilities were far more physical than that of a sky witch and the best way to defeat your opponent was to take them down as quickly as possible. She would have to use certain skills on them before they had a chance to do the same to her.

It was fast and vicious, but it needed to be. With every opponent she defeated, Calida knew she wasn't making any friends, but she couldn't stop and think about what she was doing. A good soldier didn't think in the heat of battle, they simply acted. They did what needed to be done and so did she.

Her favorite move, and the one that seemed to work the best, consisted of summoning thick roots to wrap around her opponent's leg, yanking them backward off their feet so that they fell face first onto the ground, and then quickly wrapping the roots around them so that they couldn't move.

It caused more than one bloody nose from the fall, but it was effective, moving her up the ranks. Until she came to the more experienced students, who had caught on to what she was doing, and refused to let it happen to them.

Calida began to tire, feeling the effects of being in every fight, her reactions slower, sweat running down her face, sticking to her scalp. The uncomfortable sensation was all she was aware of, breaking her focus, distracting her. The sun was now directly overhead and they fought in the full heat of the day.

Still, through sheer force of will, she made it to the final round, until there was only one more opponent left. One more person standing in her way.

A boy named Arin, whom she had taken a disliking to from the outset. He was full of himself, though not without reason. He was one of the most talented students in the class and the biggest threat to her ambition. Calida curled her hands into fists, eager to take him down, remembering how her father had taught her to throw a punch and how Thalia had stopped her years ago.

Thalia wasn't here now, but Calida still wished she were able to see it.

Arin didn't give her time to summon any roots. Immediately, the ground beneath her feet trembled, so violently that she pitched forward, onto her knees.

A bramble snaked upward, lashing around her calf. Calida cried out as the thorns cut into her skin, drawing blood. She looked up and saw Arin smirking at her. This was all a game to him. This was easy. He was enjoying this, Calida realized. And he wasn't the only one.

Among the spectators were some of the students Calida had previously defeated. They watched eagerly, almost with glee, waiting for Arin to finish her and avenge their own failures.

Anger surged through Calida. He was just toying with her now. She had been on the ground for several seconds, with the bramble still wrapped around her leg. Arin could have chosen to end the duel any time he chose, but still, he waited.

"How does it feel?" he asked.

No one else had managed to land much of a hit on her, much less get her on the ground. Arin must have expected her to give up when faced with actual competition.

If so, then he was a fool.

Calida glanced over at Horus, where the hawk was perched on the sidelines, watching the match. It was forbidden for familiars to interfere in the fight, but they were earth witches. They could communicate with animals other than their familiars and get them to do their bidding.

A group of crows had gathered in the trees as if they, too, were watching the proceedings.

It was all Calida needed.

She reached out to the crows, too angry to form a coherent command, but the birds must have picked up on her fury and the source of it, because they understood what it was she wanted.

With a raucous cry, they sprang from the trees and within moments, they were upon Arin, clawing, pecking, shrieking and beating him with their wings. He cried out, throwing up his hands to shield his face, and the bramble around Calida's leg fell away.

"Enough!" Kallias called. "Enough!"

Reluctantly, Calida let the birds go. Arin had fallen to the ground, folded in upon himself to present as small a target as possible. But she could see the bloody scratches on his arms.

"Calida is the winner," Kallias announced.

Now it was her turn to smirk at Arin as he got to his feet, unable to hide the pride she felt. Against all odds, she had done it. She had defeated every opponent that stood between her and victory, proving herself worthy.

Arin's eyes were murderous and she knew that this wouldn't be the end of it. She had just made a very powerful enemy, but in that moment, she was too high off her own victory to care.

"You cheated," he growled.

"What Calida did was completely within the rules," Kallias said, walking up to them. "It showed the ingenuity we look for in a soldier. Get yourself to the infirmary and have those scratches seen to."

Arin scowled and stalked away.

Kallias turned to Calida. She was still panting, adrenaline fading slowly, sweat pouring down her brow, clinging to her tunic. "I'm glad you changed your approach. Things were getting a bit predictable there, though the greater tragedy is that so few of the other students managed to exploit that in their favor. Still, you fought well. It is a victory well-earned. The ruthlessness you demonstrated and the willingness to do what it takes is precisely what we look for in our candidates."

Calida flushed at his praise. "Thank you, sir."

"Your task is not yet finished," Kallias warned. "You may have bested your fellow earth witches, but I'd like to see how you fare against the sky witches."

Her heart sank, the feeling of euphoria fading, burning out almost as quickly as it had come. "Oh."

She was good and more importantly, she knew how good she was, but she didn't think that would extend to defeating a sky witch in combat. She had limitations and as much as she hated to admit it, Arin could have probably beaten her then, if he hadn't been so arrogant and simply taken the chance when it presented itself.

She had been tired and hadn't expected the earth to shake so violently that she lost her footing. It had been luck just as much as it had been skill. Next time, she might not be so lucky.

"Don't worry," Kallias added, seeing her expression. "You and Arin will have a place in the class next year, regardless of the outcome of your duel with the sky witches. It's a long way off, so you'll have plenty of time to prepare. Still, I expect to see your best effort. If I feel you are slacking off because I told you that you are guaranteed a spot, I will reconsider your place in my class. Is that understood?"

"Yes, sir," Calida nodded, feeling slightly relieved.

Of all the students who had joined at the beginning of the year, hoping to become soldiers, she and Arin were the only earth witches deemed good enough.

The rest of Calida's classes passed in a blur. She couldn't stop thinking about her victory. She had done it! And she couldn't wait to tell Daniel and Lorelei.

At the end of the day, before dinner, she went to the wash house to clean up, cleaning the dried blood off her leg. She had considered going to the infirmary earlier, but hadn't wanted to encounter Arin there. He was the one who needed a healer, not her. She refused to be seen as weak.

The mess hall was buzzing with conversation when she arrived and for a fleeting moment, she thought maybe they were all talking about her and what she'd done to Arin. Then she reminded herself not to be so arrogant. That was what had cost Arin his victory, after all. It so easily could have gone the other way.

"Calida!" Lorelei waved her over. "Have you heard?"

"Heard what?" Calida asked impatiently. She wanted to tell them her own news. She thought she might burst if she had to wait a moment longer.

"The Daeran queen gave birth to a son. It's a prince!"

Daera, the kingdom to the north. Known for the lumber from their vast forests, ore from deep within their far mountains, and fish from their cold, gleaming, silver rivers.

Why on earth should any of them care about what happened in Daera, unless they suddenly decided to declare war on Alara? It was all so far away. Other than the little she had learned in school, Calida knew almost nothing about the northern kingdom.

Thinking about it now, it didn't feel like a real place at all. Somewhere she had never seen and would never go to.

"Oh," Calida said. "Guess what? I won the duels! Kallias said he will accept me next year."

"Congratulations!" Lorelei exclaimed.

Daniel nodded. "Looks like you were meant to be a soldier after all."

Calida felt a rush of pride. It wasn't uncommon for a student to take longer than a year to determine their future placement, so long as they had it by year three. But Calida had done it before the end of her first term. She was well on her way to making her goal a reality.

The Daeran prince was all anyone could talk about and conversation soon turned back to that, but Calida didn't mind too terribly. She had done it and nothing could take that victory away from her.

CHAPTER 3

A year later, Thalia came to the Erlohn monastery. The students in her group comprised one of the smallest the monastery had ever seen and she would later catch a few of the teachers muttering about how fewer and fewer seemed to arrive all the time. But none of that concerned her.

She was only interested in being reunited with her sister. The past year had been very strange at home without Calida there. They had always done everything together, but her sister's sudden absence had forced Thalia to become more independent. She relied more on herself and had to make her own decisions about what she wanted to do, without consulting anyone else first.

Her parents had doted on her, though the list of chores had never grown any smaller. With Calida gone, it fell to Thalia to take up the remaining slack at the farm. Mostly, she didn't mind too much, but there were a few times where resentment had crept in. She never blamed her sister; Calida had no say in whether she went to the monastery or not, just like Thalia herself would have no say in a year's time.

It was the system itself that she resented, that made witches out to be little more than slaves, in her mind. Always at the mercy of the kingdom's whims, forced to do whatever benefited it the most. Those who ruled Alara weren't even witches themselves. They had no idea what it was like to be singled out, but they were more than happy to take advantage of the "gifts" of others.

When it came time for Thalia to take the test in the headmistress's office, she stared down at the potted plant and bowl of water, unsure which to try first.

"What type of witch is my sister?" she asked instead.

The headmistress blinked at her. "Your sister?"

"Calida."

"Ah, yes. I should have known, with that fiery hair of yours. She tested as an earth witch."

That settled the matter for Thalia. She focused on the potted plant and tried to force it to move as she'd been instructed. But nothing happened—not so much as a leaf quivered.

Glaring at the plant, Thalia turned to the bowl of water. Was she to be a sky witch instead, different from her sister? It wasn't what she really wanted, but she had lived the past year apart from Calida, and so it didn't bother her as much as it might once have.

The two of them were bound to be different now, after all. Calida would not have remained unchanged by her time spent at the monastery. Thalia wondered how her sister's training was coming along and what she was now capable of.

Thalia looked levelly at the water and willed it to rise. The surface rippled and the water sprang up to do her bidding, as if it had suddenly transformed into a fountain.

The headmistress looked slightly taken aback. "That's very impressive, Thalia. Most first years are lucky if they can cause a ripple."

Thalia felt a rush of satisfaction. She was not only a sky witch, the rarer of the two, but she was apparently a powerful one, too. Or at the very least, she had the potential to become so.

She fell in with the other students from her year as they were given a tour of the grounds. In the barracks, she found a blue tunic waiting for her and she put it on eagerly, looking around at her fellow students as she did so. Among the first years, hers was the only blue tunic. The rest were either green or gray.

It only furthered her sense of pride. She truly was unique.

They made their way to the mess hall, where the older students were already gathered. Thalia scanned the crowd eagerly, searching for her sister. Calida's bushy, bright red hair was hard to miss and Thalia headed for her table.

Calida sat with a plump girl about her own age, with hazel eyes and brown hair that framed her face. The boy sitting across from them was a few years older, with dark hair. All three of them wore the green tunics of earth witches.

Calida leapt to her feet upon seeing her. "Thalia!" She rushed forward, wrapping her younger sister in a hug. Thalia laughed and returned the embrace. It had been so long since she had felt her sister's arms around her, heard her laugh.

Calida released her and stepped back, taking in her appearance. "You've grown."

"I'm almost as tall as you now," Thalia said proudly.

"Not even close!" Calida retorted, then hesitated. "You're a sky witch?"

"The only one in my year."

Her sister smiled. "I'm happy for you. You'll do great." She turned back to the girl and older boy. "This is my little sister, Thalia. Thalia, this is Daniel and Lorelei."

Thalia felt a flicker of irritation at being introduced to these two strangers as Calida's *little* sister, when she was probably more powerful than both of them, but she nodded politely. If these were her sister's friends, she would like them on principle, but she wasn't here to make friends herself. She was just happy to see her sister again.

"What placement are you going to try for?" Lorelei asked as Thalia joined them at the table.

For the first time since arriving, Thalia felt unsure. "I don't know."

"She just got here," Daniel admonished. "She doesn't know what all of the placements are. She doesn't even have a familiar yet."

"A familiar?" Thalia asked, confused.

"You'll see," Calida promised. "You'll get one tomorrow. You can meet Horus when we get back to the dormitory."

"What placement did you pick?" Whatever Calida had aimed for, Thalia wanted them to do it together.

"I'm training to be a soldier," her sister replied and Thalia didn't miss the note of pride in her voice. "One of only two earth witches deemed good enough. We could do it together. You're a sky witch and Daniel said sky witches are almost always soldiers, so you should have no problem getting in."

Daniel nodded in agreement.

A soldier. Thalia had never given much thought to what she wanted. It would be hard to know until she learned what all the placements were. During the past year, she had mostly found herself wishing she were ordinary. If she and Calida hadn't been born witches, they would have never been separated.

But they were here together now and if Calida wanted to be a soldier, then Thalia would do her best to become one as well.

She nodded. "I'd like that."

Upon returning to the dormitory, Calida and Lorelei showed Thalia the familiars they had mentioned. Lorelei's monkey held little interest for Thalia, but she stared up at Horus in wonder as the hawk allowed her to stroke his feathers.

"And you can talk to each other and everything?" she asked.

"Yes."

Calida had chosen the bunk above Lorelei's so Thalia had to take one across from them. She thought about her sister's hawk as she lay in the darkness, waiting for sleep to come. Tomorrow she would have a familiar of her own and she wondered which animal would end up choosing her.

Despite her longing for an ordinary life, perhaps she could get used to being a witch after all.

* * *

The next morning, after breakfast, Calida wished Thalia good luck and they went their separate ways. Being a year ahead of her, Calida wouldn't see much of her sister except in the dormitories and the mess hall, until they each moved up into the advanced combat class, where the best students were trained together.

Thalia accompanied the rest of the first years to the building where the familiars were held. The floor was covered in a thick layer of straw, the only light filtering through the slanted windows near the ceiling. It took a few moments for her eyes to adjust and when they did, she took in the vast array of animals before her.

She had quizzed Calida and Lorelei the night before about familiars and the selection process. They had stressed to her that she didn't choose the familiar; the familiar chose her. But how did you know when one had chosen you, she had asked.

Their answer hadn't been particularly helpful. You just knew, they'd said. But it was all she had to go on.

Thalia strolled through the rows of animals. She didn't have anything particular in mind that she would like to have as a familiar. A snake would be impressive, she thought. She had always loved snakes. Calida had tolerated them, but their mother had been deathly afraid. She had shrieked once when Thalia had come up to her with a snake wrapped around her arm and threatened to send her to bed without supper if she didn't go put it back right this instant.

Thalia felt herself smile at the memory. But looking at the snakes, she felt nothing different than she had when facing any of the other animals. She turned away and moved along, until her feet came to a sudden stop. She looked up, wondering what had made her pause.

A fox sat before her, the vibrant red of its coat nearly matching her own hair. She looked into its yellow eyes and *knew*. She could sense the connection that she hadn't felt before, suddenly there, quiet but unmistakable.

Thalia named the familiar Jade and it accompanied her to her first lesson, which was combat. The teacher for her class was different than the one Calida had told her about, since she was a sky witch.

Though Thalia had been the only sky witch in her year, Ayani, the combat instructor, was not going to teach her separately. And so Thalia was thrown into a class with the second year sky witches. It was a baptism by fire, of sorts. She would either keep up and learn quickly—twice as fast as everyone else, who had a whole year's advantage—or she would be crushed beneath the demands being placed upon her.

She had wanted to be a soldier with Calida and so she knew there was only one option.

Ayani was a harsh teacher and put each of her sky witch pupils through their paces daily without exception or respite, regardless of the weather. Under her guidance, Thalia learned how to control the water, forcing it up into great waves that could be used to flood villages and sink vessels on the sea.

But it was the air itself that Thalia found most useful. She couldn't conjure water out of thin air; she was forced to manipulate that which already existed and unless she found herself near a body of water to wield, it wasn't all that practical. But the air itself was always around them, ready to be called upon at a moment's notice.

A sky witch could summon powerful winds, strong enough to knock a man off his feet and send him flying. They could lift heavy objects into the air. Ayani showed them how they could force the air out of their opponent's lungs, causing them to fall unconscious or suffocate entirely. Thalia was the only one in her class who managed it and she felt a thrill go through her at the sheer power that was hers to command.

She had never felt that way before, aware of her own potential, and she never wanted to lose the feeling. Now that she knew what she was capable of, she could never again go back to what she once was. The knowledge would always stay with her, along with the power itself.

Sky witches could also manipulate the weather, summoning or controlling storms. Ayani told them that the strongest sky witches could call lightning down from storms, but no one in the class was yet able to do that. Thalia wasn't bothered by her inability to call lightning or summon storms. She was already the most powerful sky witch in her class, and though Ayani never said as much, Thalia had glimpsed the surprise on her face at seeing just what she was capable of.

It was the same reaction that headmistress Anise had demonstrated, the evening Thalia had tested as a sky witch. Thalia didn't mention it to any of her friends, not even Calida, but she knew deep down that first year students, sky witch or no, weren't supposed to be as strong as she was.

Instead, she kept it a secret, reveling in the knowledge. The only one who knew were Ayani and her fellow sky witch students.

Her classes were far more limited than Calida's and the other earth witches. Thalia couldn't help grow crops until she mastered manipulating the weather and she wasn't as good with animals as they would be, but she still tried to learn.

For a little while, everything was fine and Thalia found herself happier than she could remember since Calida had left. But her presence did not go unnoticed and she began to wonder if she had drawn too much attention to herself, flaunting the fact that she was the only sky witch in her year and if rumors of her power had spread.

No doubt it would cause no small amount of jealousy among those less gifted.

It wasn't long before she found herself the target of a second year earth witch, a boy called Arin. Calida had spoken of him a few times, boasting of how she had bested him in the duels last year to become one of only two earth witches allowed to move on.

The two of them had formed a mutual hatred of each other and Thalia's arrival at the monastery provided Arin with an opportunity too good to ignore.

One afternoon, as Thalia was on her way to the mess hall, Arin cornered her outside of the wash rooms. They were situated on the far end of the courtyard. Thalia glanced around as Arin approached, but there was no one else in sight. They were likely already in the mess hall, where she herself should be, if she hadn't wasted so much time.

There were two others with Arin, a boy and girl, standing slightly behind him. Thalia knew from their expressions to expect trouble, but she refused to be cowed. She wasn't going to run away.

She balled her hands into fists and glared at him as he approached.

"If it isn't Calida's little sister," he sneered. "What are you doing out here all alone?"

Little sister. Again that annoying phrase that instantly reduced her to nothing more than Calida's shadow.

"Who says I'm alone?" Thalia retorted. But she was alone. Jade was waiting for her back in the dormitory. She didn't even have her familiar by her side.

Arin snorted, ignoring her comment. "I've been hearing a lot about you. They say you're the best in your class, despite being an entire year behind everyone else. Very impressive."

The two students behind him snickered as if he'd said something amusing.

Thalia kept glaring at him. "What do you want?"

"See, here's the thing. Master Kallias says we have to duel the sky witches. I've worked hard to get where I am and your sister already cost me the top spot in my class. So do me a favor and stay out of my way."

"Maybe I'll just beat your arse instead," Thalia snapped.

Her father would have spanked her good for using such language, but he wasn't here now and it felt good to taunt Arin, to see the look of rage cross his face.

Her feeling of satisfaction didn't last long. Arin moved with surprising speed for an earth witch and before she knew what had happened, his fist had connected with her cheek, sending her reeling from the blow. Thalia sprawled in the grass, tasting blood.

She gathered her arms beneath her, preparing to rise. Already she was beginning to gather the air toward her, either to blast back outward and throw Arin off his feet or pull the air from his lungs, she hadn't yet decided.

But then she stopped, her anger melting away as quickly as it had come, replaced by icy fear, as something dawned on her. Arin had already heard about how powerful she supposedly was and he and the others expected just such a response from her.

They viewed her—and her power—as a threat and had singled her out, intending to eliminate the threat she posed before she eliminated them.

If she hadn't flaunted her skills with such callous disregard, they wouldn't have sought her out. They wouldn't have even looked at her twice. Instead, she had made herself a target.

What good was power if everyone *knew* you had it? Wasn't it better if no one knew just how strong you really were? The one who was constantly underestimated, who was seen as no threat, was the most powerful one of all.

People looked at obvious power and knew what they were up against, knew what to expect. But from an unknown factor, a dark horse, there could be no predicting. They expected you to be exactly as you appeared, the image you portrayed, weak and helpless, and when you chose to finally reveal the truth, there would be no time to react.

Thalia realized her mistake. She didn't want anyone knowing exactly how strong she was or what she could do. Wasn't that why she had kept it a secret from her friends, even her own sister? Why, then, was she still showing off in class?

She hadn't concealed her hand as carefully as she should have, and she was paying for it now, but there was time to reconsider. There was still time to fix it.

And so she released her hold on the air and lowered herself back down as if defeated, spitting blood out of her mouth.

"What?" Arin taunted. "That's it?"

He landed a vicious kick to her ribs and Thalia wondered if he hoped to bait her into fighting back. She ignored the kicks and jeers, the test they set before her, knowing what they expected her to do. She wasn't going to do what was expected. Her greatest strength lay in being unpredictable.

At last, Arin let out a sound of disgust and stepped back. Thalia didn't think she had convinced him of her helplessness yet, but she also wasn't stupid enough to think he was done with her.

"Let's go," he told his friends and they loped off toward the mess hall like the pack of wolves they were.

Thalia glared at them as they walked away. *Just you wait.* The bell rang out, signaling the end of lunch. She had missed it and would have to go hungry the rest of the afternoon.

She picked herself up, dusting the grass and dirt off her tunic. She didn't see Calida until dinner that evening and by then, her cheek had already darkened nicely into an obvious bruise.

"What happened?" her sister demanded upon seeing her.

Thalia debated within herself whether or not she should tell the truth and then decided she had nothing to lose. "Arin and a few of his lackeys cornered me outside the wash house on my way to lunch."

"We wondered where you were when you didn't arrive earlier," Lorelei said, her gaze full of concern. "You should have gone to the infirmary. That looks like it hurts."

Thalia shrugged. "It doesn't, really."

Not nearly as much as the blow to her pride or the chilling realization that she had painted a target on her back.

Calida's storm-gray eyes burned with anger. "I hope you gave him a good thrashing in return."

Thalia didn't want to tell her that she had decided not to fight. She didn't think her sister would understand. Skilled as Calida undoubtedly was, she hadn't done anything to make people view her as a threat—or covet her skills with a fierce jealousy.

Jealousy that someone might one day decide to do something about.

"There were three of them," she said instead. "I was outnumbered."

Calida placed her palms flat against the table and made as if to stand up. "Where is he—?"

"Don't!" Lorelei reached across the table for her wrist. "You'll get into so much trouble."

"She's right," Thalia said. "He's not worth it."

Calida let out a slow breath and sat back down. "If he touches you again, the beating I gave him in the dueling ring will look like nothing."

Thalia was touched by her sister's loyalty, but she didn't want her getting into trouble on her account. She vowed to avoid Arin as much as possible, but she doubted it would be that easy. Arin would seek her out again, if only as a means to get back at Calida.

And when he did, Thalia was determined not to fight back, not to reveal the depths of the power he had heard so much about. And the more she refused to fight, the more Arin would come for her, recognizing easy prey. He would come to forget the rumors and eventually disbelieve it entirely, seeing only what she wanted him to see.

A quiet, timid girl, who was too weak one way or another to fight back.

And then, when the time came, Thalia would unleash a tempest upon him, the likes of which he had never seen and could never fathom.

Go on. Underestimate me. It'll be your undoing.

* * *

Training continued and Thalia no longer tried to show off in class. She did the bare minimum to get by and avoid being dropped, nothing more. Perhaps the others would attribute her first few lessons as a fluke, beginner's luck, and that now she was only demonstrating a level of skill appropriate for a first year.

But she wasn't even doing that.

More than once, Ayani held her back after class to ask what was the matter. Thalia had no answer to give her. She couldn't explain what she was doing. They wouldn't understand and it would defeat the purpose.

Arin continued to harass her, usually whenever he found her alone. Thalia never told Calida about the beatings, and when she could, she went to the infirmary to hide her injuries. But there were times she couldn't keep them hidden and she saw her sister's gaze darken with anger and the promise of revenge.

The next time, Arin made a mistake when he cornered her.

"Well, well," his voice spoke from behind her. "If it isn't the witch with no powers."

Thalia spun around to face him. She had been down by the river, watching the little fish in the shallows. Few of the other students liked to come down here and Thalia was fond of the solitude. But now Arin was here, intruding on what she had come to think of as her special place.

"Go away, Arin," Thalia warned. "I don't want to deal with you."

Jade was with her this time, and hearing the anger in her mistress's voice, the fox let out a growl, hackles rising.

"Don't want to?" Arin taunted, adjusting the pitch of his voice to mock her. "Don't want to? Well you're gonna, whether you like it or not." He pushed her, but not too hard, and Thalia took a step back. "What are you gonna do about it? Are you gonna use your sky witch powers against us?"

The boy and girl that always seemed to follow him around laughed as if on cue, like trained seals.

"Never go anywhere without your lackeys, do you, Arin?" Thalia retorted. "You don't have the courage to face anyone alone. Even a witch with no powers," she added, throwing his earlier words back in his face.

"Maybe you're not a witch at all." Arin shoved her again, harder this time. Thalia lost her footing and toppled backward into the river, landing with a splash and sending the small fish scattering. She gasped at how cold the water was, soaking through her tunic in seconds.

Jade lunged forward, teeth bared, but she wasn't yet fully grown and even if she had been, she wouldn't have presented much of a threat to Arin. He laughed. Jade yelped as he kicked her to the side.

There was something about seeing her familiar mistreated that snapped inside of Thalia. Arin and his cronies could bully her all they liked, but Jade? That was going too far. She glanced down at the water beneath her. The entire river was right here for her to use, however she wished.

She could feel the power in that cold water as it brushed through her fingers, calling to her, urging her on. Through the trees, she could see the sky, essential to accessing her power. She could smell electricity in the air, feel the hair stand up on the back of her arms.

Thalia didn't know what she would have done in that moment, but she never had to make the choice.

"Leave her alone!" a boy's voice shouted.

She looked up and Arin turned to see a first year boy striding toward them. He wore the green tunic of an earth witch. Thalia had seen him before but paid him little mind. His black hair hung lank over his brow, his skin so pale it almost looked sickly, as though he never spent any time out in the sun. He was painfully thin. Arin practically towered over him.

"Looking for a beating too, are you?" Arin growled. "If not, I suggest you move along."

If possible, the boy paled even further, but to his credit, he didn't back down. "It's not right, what you're doing."

"Not right? We're all competing against each other here, or haven't you noticed? This entire monastery is nothing but a competition. The strongest witches get the best placements and that's all there is to it. Alara wants only the best witches. There's no place here for weaklings."

"And I said to leave her alone."

"Who's going to stop me?" Arin challenged. "You?"

He reached out, grabbing ahold of the boy's shoulders and pushed him into the river as well, landing beside Thalia, but not before a small brown-bodied creature had crawled out of the boy's sleeve and onto Arin's hand.

It was a rat, Thalia realized, and as she watched, it sank its teeth into Arin's hand.

He let out a shriek and with a flick of his hand, threw the rat to the side. "It bit me!" he cried to his friends. "Kill it!"

Thalia almost laughed in amusement as the other two stomped their feet desperately, trying to squash the rat, but it was too fast and scurried back to its master. The boy held it in his hands and Arin turned to them, his eyes promising murder.

She didn't know what he would have done—likely abandoned his fists altogether and turned to magic—but he never got the chance. A bird's shrill cry split the air and a moment later, Horus swooped down, raking his talons at Arin's face. He cried out, throwing his hands up to shield his eyes as the hawk beat his head with his powerful wings.

Jade jumped back into the fray, sinking her fangs into the calf of one of Arin's friends. Calida stepped into view, not far behind her familiar.

"Call it off!" Arin screamed at her, still trying to duck away from the hawk.

Calida did no such thing, standing there impassively. "I'll call him off when you learn to leave my sister alone."

With another cry of frustration, Arin took off running, his two companions trailing behind. Horus followed them a short distance and then returned to Calida, perching on her shoulder.

Stiffly, Thalia got to her feet. She was soaking wet and chilled to the bone by the freezing river. She turned to the black-haired boy beside her and offered him a hand.

"Thanks," he murmured as she pulled him to his feet.

"Why did you do it?" she asked softly. Their hands were still clasped, his skin clammy against hers, but she didn't let go and neither did he.

"Arin's been harassing me, too, ever since I got here," he muttered. "I'm in the same placement, one year behind him."

"Combat?" Thalia asked.

The boy nodded. "My father wanted me to be a soldier—bring honor to the family, he said. But I don't know if I'm strong enough. Arin certainly never misses the chance to convince me I'm not." His voice was bitter.

"I'm Thalia," she said, finally releasing his hand. "What's your name?"

"Mordred," Calida answered, nodding to the boy. "Isn't it?"

"That's right." Mordred turned back to face Thalia. "I thought maybe the two of us could have taken him." He blushed. "Stupid of me, really."

"Well, two certainly have a better chance than one. It was a brave thing you did," Thalia told him. "Thank you."

Mordred's face broke into a grin and Thalia was startled by the depth of his feeling, elicited by her words alone. She knew words carried their own sort of power, but it was interesting to see the instant effect they could have on someone—whether spoken in truth or not.

"Maybe we could…look out for each other," she suggested.

"I'd like that."

Calida said nothing more during the exchange, waiting until they were done before confronting her sister.

"Why didn't you fight back?"

Thalia sighed, not wanting to have this conversation now, if ever. "I didn't want to get into trouble." The lie slipped easily from her lips.

"You wouldn't get in trouble for defending yourself."

"You don't know that. Arin would spin the story in his favor and he'd probably be the one who's believed, not me."

The fight seemed to go out of Calida then, unable to argue with her sister's reasoning. She came to sit on the riverbank,

Horus hopping off her shoulder to perch beside Jade, and Thalia joined her. After a moment's hesitation, Mordred did as well.

Thalia glanced at the hawk, his talons stained red. "You shouldn't have used him like that, you know," she added softly. "You need to be careful. The elders could have him taken away."

"They won't," Calida said, with more confidence than Thalia would have felt. "A witch only gets one familiar, after all, and that bond can't be broken."

Thalia looked down at her own familiar. Jade waited by her feet and Thalia scooped her up. "Are you all right?"

"*I'll live,*" the fox replied, her voice audible only to Thalia's ears.

Calida sighed and stood, restless. "Come on. We should be getting back."

Thalia waited until her sister had disappeared from sight before calling the air to dry her tunic. Only then did she follow.

CHAPTER 4

The day that Calida had both dreaded and anticipated finally arrived—the day she and Arin were to face off against the sky witches. Thalia was excited for her sister and eager to watch.

Given her dismal performance of late, she hadn't thought Ayani would select her to be one of the sky witches in the dueling ring, but her instructor must have remembered the power she had displayed upon first arriving.

"Me?" Thalia said in surprise when Ayani informed her that she wanted Thalia in the ring.

Ayani nodded. "I think it will be a good challenge for you. Perhaps it'll be just the push you need."

Thalia swallowed down her dread. "But one of the earth witches is my sister."

"All the more reason. In the course of your career, you'll be called upon to do all sorts of difficult, unpleasant things, but do them you must. Do I make myself clear?"

Her dark eyes glittered as she regarded Thalia. She was a severe-looking woman, her features sharp, her dark hair pinned into a bun at the back of her neck.

Usually, all it took was a single look to silence noisy students or get them to comply with the orders that were given. Looking at her now, Thalia could understand why.

"Yes, ma'am."

"You're both here because you want to be soldiers, but you must earn your place like anyone else. You'll only be able to succeed if you want it badly enough."

But Thalia wasn't sure what she really wanted anymore. She did want to be a soldier with Calida, that much hadn't changed, but she wasn't sure she was willing to do what it asked of her.

She couldn't tell Ayani any of that, of course, and when the fateful day arrived, she dutifully followed the rest of the sky witches to the dueling ring.

* * *

Calida glanced across at Arin out of the corner of her eye. They stood around the ring that had been assembled, the ground covered in sand, as the sky witch contenders filed in. She and Arin had been studiously ignoring each other, but there was no ignoring the fact that they were the only two earth witches here. The only green tunics in a sea of blue. They would have to fight each of the sky witches in order to get to the end, the same way Calida had done to beat Arin.

That didn't bother her; she had done it once. There was no reason why she shouldn't be able to do it again. But she wondered how well Arin would hold up. And this wouldn't be the same as fighting her fellow witches, whose abilities she knew well because they were her own. This time, they had no idea what to expect and that made the sky witches all the more dangerous.

Calida looked up and felt herself stiffen at the sight of familiar red hair in the crowd of sky witches. Thalia was here. Calida frowned. She hadn't thought her sister was performing well enough in class to make it into the ring. Surely they wouldn't ask such a thing of a first year anyway, making her go up against second years.

Arin had noticed Thalia as well. He smirked. "I can't believe they let her in." He turned to Calida, leaning in close.

"I'll make sure she regrets it and this time, there's nothing you can do to stop me."

Calida said nothing, glaring at him, hoping she could intimidate him into reconsidering. If he used this tournament as an excuse to hurt Thalia, *he* would be the one to regret it.

The cuts Horus had inflicted on him had long since healed, but neither of them had forgotten it and when she looked at him, she still remembered the image of him screaming, trying to shield his face with his arms.

She focused on that image, holding it close, as she stepped into the ring. Let her anger make her stronger. Let it be taken out on her opponents.

It did not go as she intended.

Just as she was unfamiliar with sky witch abilities, they were as unfamiliar with her own. She managed to land a few hits on some of them, and even to best the first two, more through sheer dumb luck than any superior skill.

But that was where any such luck ran out.

It was as though the sky witches could summon their powers and execute their will faster than Calida ever could. She could call roots or vines to her at a rapid speed, but the air already surrounded them and took no time to respond.

She was blown off her feet and gasped as she landed hard on her back. It did nothing to incapacitate her, the way being wrapped in vines would, but each time she struggled to her feet, the sky witch across from her simply knocked her back to the ground again.

Clenching her teeth, determined not to give up, Calida forced herself to rise again and again, only to be sent back to the ground. She felt heat rush up the back of her neck at the sound of Arin's mocking laughter, but there was nothing she could do.

She was outmatched in every way.

Just wait. You'll be in here next and we'll see how smug you are then.

She lost count of how many times she struggled to her feet before she finally accepted the futility of it all and did not try to rise again. Her muscles ached, trembling with exertion, her breathing ragged. Only then did the sky witch instructor, Ayani, call the match and Calida exited the ring, burning with disappointment and fury at her performance.

What did you expect? You knew they were better fighters. You knew this wouldn't be easy.

But she hadn't appreciated just how hard it would be. She knew she should have been proud, really. She had managed to best two of them, which was better than none at all, and Master Kallias had already told her that she would keep her place in his class so long as she made an effort. She had definitely done that.

At least you didn't have to fight Thalia. Maybe they wouldn't make her sister fight after all.

Calida's hopes plummeted as she came to stand beside Master Kallias and turned to face the ring. Arin had already taken his place within, flexing his fingers, and across from him, looking impossibly small in her blue tunic, was Thalia.

This is your chance, Calida silently urged her sister on. *Show him what you're made of. Make him pay for everything he's done to you.*

Calida wanted to call out all of those things to her sister, but spectators were forbidden to communicate with anyone in the ring. All she could do was clench the material of her tunic in her fists and wait.

* * *

I might have known I'd be facing him, Thalia thought bitterly. She half wondered if Ayani had heard of her feud with Arin and set her up on purpose, hoping Thalia might be forced to use her powers to their full extent again. She would either reveal just how powerful she was to everyone gathered here or be humiliated in front of them.

And oh, was she tempted. How satisfying would it be to unleash all her rage on Arin, to send him to the ground, watch him crawl, to reduce him to nothing more than a pathetic display of helplessness.

But then the world would know the extent of her power, the threat she could be. And she hadn't taken all those beatings from Arin just to throw away her strategy now.

Thalia took a deep breath and the fight began. She made a paltry effort this time, as opposed to doing nothing on the other occasions she had been confronted by Arin. She summoned a weak breeze and sent it at him, but it didn't so much as make him stumble.

He laughed. He wasn't allowed to speak to her during the match, but he could still find ways to taunt her.

At least it was over quickly. Thalia thought he might toy with her, dragging the fight out unnecessarily for the pure sadistic pleasure of it, but he didn't. In a real fight, a good soldier wouldn't waste time on such things. You needed to best the enemy quickly and efficiently, and to his credit, he did.

A tree root snaked out, lashing around her ankle and yanking hard. Thalia fell face-first to the ground and before she had a chance to fight back, the root had released her and wrapped around her arms, pinning them.

Arin was triumphant. He had gotten to embarrass her in front of everyone. But it didn't last long. Thalia was the only sky witch he managed to best.

Even though neither earth witch had managed to advance very far, Calida had still performed better than he had. The only opponent Arin had managed to beat had been a student a year younger than him who was hiding her powers. Thalia hoped that fact rankled.

Once the tournament had ended, Thalia wanted nothing more than to retreat back to her place near the river, but Master Ayani held her back for a moment after the other students had been dismissed.

A feeling of unease settled in the pit of her stomach as Thalia approached her teacher.

Ayani's lined face was graver than usual. "I do not like to say such things, Thalia, but your performance in the ring left much to be desired."

Thalia looked down, unable to meet her gaze. "I know."

"This is not the talented young sky witch who first came to my class. What's happened? Is there something wrong?"

For a moment, Thalia had the horrible urge to confess everything to Ayani, so desperate was she to confide in someone. It was a terrible thing to have to keep hidden, but she knew she couldn't do it.

How could she tell Ayani that she wanted to be something more? That she knew her power was strong enough to make that dream a reality?

She was no longer content to be a mere soldier. Not with power like hers. There had to be something more for her out there, something worthy of such a gift.

Ayani was part of the system. She was a teacher at the Erlohn monastery, where children went after being torn from their families, in order to train gifts only they possessed so that they might better serve their kingdom.

Thalia's power belonged to her and her alone. Not Alara.

She had to give Ayani an answer and so she said simply, "I don't know."

Ayani sighed. "I'm disappointed and I know you must be, too, but the fact remains that I can only keep the best students in my class. I've tried to be patient with you, to give you time, and I think I've been more than generous. Yet nothing has improved. I'm sorry, Thalia, but I'm forced to remove you from my class. Combat is not your placement. I trust you will find your true calling elsewhere, but it does not lie with me."

She was being dropped. This was it. There would be no more combat lessons after this. Her ambition of becoming a soldier with Calida ended here.

Thalia swallowed. She knew she shouldn't feel disappointed and yet she was. She'd known that her choice would eventually lead here. She had only done the bare minimum to scrape by in Ayani's class and that was no longer good enough.

"I understand."

Ayani jerked her head. "On your way, then."

Ignoring her next scheduled class, Thalia headed for the river. Calida trailed after her, as she somehow knew she would. She would demand an explanation and Thalia would have to tell her that she had been removed from combat class.

Thalia pretended not to notice she was being followed. She sat down on the riverbank, tracing small patterns in the air with two of her fingers. The water responded easily, copying her movements as it swirled up into the air, defying gravity.

It was so simple. Thalia squeezed her eyes shut for a moment, so tight it was almost painful. She could have destroyed Arin if she'd wanted to. She could have made him pay. She could have made him bleed.

And she hadn't.

Calida sat down beside her. "Why didn't you fight back?"

Thalia still didn't want to explain it to her. "You wouldn't understand."

"So help me understand."

Thalia opened her mouth but couldn't form a reply for several long moments. She lowered her hand and the water's surface stilled. "I—don't want to hurt anyone," she said at last, the lie leaving a foul taste on her tongue. Bitter, like blackberries that weren't yet ripe.

"We're going to be soldiers, Thalia," Calida pointed out. "Sooner or later, we're going to have to hurt someone."

"Not anymore," Thalia said. "Ayani removed me from her class."

Her sister stiffened beside her. "What?" She rose to her feet. "I thought we were going to do this together."

"Maybe I don't want to be a soldier."

"Then what do you want, Thalia?" Calida demanded. She sounded angry now but Thalia didn't look at her for fear Calida might see the lie in her eyes.

"I don't know," Thalia snapped, suddenly angry with herself, also getting to her feet. "Not this. But it doesn't really matter, does it?"

"What are you talking about?"

"It doesn't matter what I want, what any of us wants. I could want to be a soldier more than anything in the world, but if my gift lies somewhere else, then that's what my placement will be. We don't get to choose. We didn't get to choose any of this."

"You knew that already," Calida said quietly.

"Doesn't mean I have to like it."

Calida snorted. "You're being childish. Of course you don't have to like it, but that doesn't change anything. It's always been this way and it always will be."

"No, it won't," Thalia insisted. "Nothing lasts forever." She looked around, her voice lowering to a whisper. "Not even this place."

Calida shook her head in disgust and turned away.

* * *

Calida was forced to continue with her own combat classes knowing that, one day, Thalia would not be joining her. She didn't understand her sister's attitude toward what had happened. What did she want? In a way, Thalia's answer made sense. It didn't ultimately matter what she wanted and

Calida had to admit that there were times when it felt like their fates were already decided for them.

But Calida knew what she didn't want and she didn't want to end up performing a menial task for the rest of her life. If Thalia didn't feel the same, well, that was her problem.

One morning, Master Kallias took her and Arin over to the stables where the horses were kept. Calida had spent some time with them during the classes on how to care for animals, one of the few that she bothered to pay attention to outside of combat training.

One of the horses gave her a friendly nicker, recognizing her, and Calida reached up to stroke its muzzle, smiling. She thought she much preferred animals to people, sometimes. They were easy to understand in comparison.

"Those who will become soldiers will learn how to ride," Master Kallias explained. "Those who will not will simply learn how to care for others' horses. The two of you are here to learn the former."

Calida felt a little thrill shoot through her at the prospect of learning to ride. The horses were quite large and she felt slightly intimidated by the height, but she refused to let it show in front of Arin.

They were shown how to saddle their own horses; even though this wasn't something they would typically be expected to do on their own, a good soldier was always self-sufficient, should the need arise. Out in the pastures, they put the horses through their paces, growing comfortable at all gaits until they worked their way up to a gallop.

Calida loved every moment of it. On horseback, she felt the freest she had since arriving at the monastery, the wind flowing through her hair, brushing against her cheeks. She wanted to urge the horse on faster, ever faster, until its hooves barely touched the ground.

For a moment, Thalia's words came back to her and she wondered what life might be like if fate had been kinder. If she had just been an ordinary girl riding her horse. But this horse wasn't hers and there was more expected of her than simply riding. She wouldn't be able to go out and do this whenever she liked.

Calida slowed the horse to a halt, pushing Thalia out of her mind. If Thalia had worked harder, she might have been there right now, learning to ride as well. Calida wanted to share the experience of what it felt like to ride with her sister, but words were not enough to convey her feelings and Thalia would likely never know herself.

As Calida turned the horse back toward the stables, she only hoped that whatever placement her sister ended up with, she would be able to find some happiness in it.

* * *

After the tournament had ended and Thalia removed from Ayani's class, Arin seemed to have lost all interest in her. He harassed her on occasion, but nothing like before. Perhaps he was wary of being set upon by Calida's hawk again or perhaps he no longer viewed her as a threat now that she had no chance of becoming a soldier.

She should have been disappointed that the choice had been taken out of her hands, but she wasn't. She had made a different decision, one she thought better, and she had to live with that.

That didn't mean Thalia had given up on her power. Every chance she got, whenever she was alone and had time between classes, she snuck down to the riverbed and practiced there, testing the limit of her power. It was a good place to be, with the sunlight filtering down through the trees and glinting off the water's surface. The small fish shimmered like silver coins and there was always a pleasant breeze, stirring the leaves as if they were whispering to her.

But her secret didn't remain so for long.

Thalia spun around as she heard footsteps behind her, letting the water she had lifted out of the river slam back down with a splash, hands clenched.

She expected Arin, finally stumbling upon her secret, or Calida, prepared for yet another confrontation.

Instead, Mordred stood behind her, his dark eyes wide, his rat perched on one shoulder. "Wow," he breathed. "You can really do that?"

Thalia exhaled heavily. "I just did, didn't I?"

He stepped closer. "But they kicked you out of the combat class."

"Don't remind me," she muttered, turning away and moving closer to the river.

Mordred followed. "But why would they do that if you can do all this?"

"Because they don't know that I can. I've been hiding my powers so no one knows how strong I really am." There was no point in denying it now that he'd seen the truth for himself. She glanced at him sharply. "Don't tell anyone."

"I won't." He hesitated. "Do you think…that you could train with me?"

She looked at him, raising one eyebrow.

Mordred flushed and glanced away. "I—I'm not doing very well in my own class. I'm not sure that I'm meant to be a soldier and Master Kallias says that if I don't show some improvement soon, I'll be dropped."

Thalia cocked her head. "If it's not your talent—"

"I know, I know. Then it won't be my placement."

She considered the scrawny boy standing beside her. He didn't look anything like a soldier, though she knew what mattered most was the strength of his magic, not his body. "Is being a soldier what you want?"

"You know that doesn't make any difference."

"No, but if you want it for yourself, then I think it might make you try harder."

"My father wanted me to be a soldier. Get a good placement, don't dishonor the family. But the more I think about it… Yes," Mordred said, his voice firm. "I do want this. Will you help me? We could train together and no one would ever know."

She looked him in the eye and saw the hope reflected there and beneath that, the steel. Here was someone who would also be a target for bullies, though not for the same reason she had been. Here was someone who was hungry, desperate to improve. And she had to admit that learning to fight against an earth witch might prove very beneficial.

"All right," she agreed. "We'll help each other. But we'll swear an oath. Make it binding."

Thalia knew it was all show with little substance. There was nothing she could do if Mordred decided to go back on his word, but she thought it would add more gravity to the situation and maybe help drive home its importance.

She cast about for a stone until she found one sharp enough and ran it along her palm until the skin split and blood welled forth. She instructed Mordred to do the same and then they clasped hands.

They wouldn't breathe a word of this to anyone else and together, they would survive the Erlohn monastery.

CHAPTER 5

The year was nearly half over. Soon, there would be more of it behind than there was ahead and Calida's second term would become her third. But just as the duels at the end of the previous year had been a test to see who advanced and who did not, Master Kallias had another trial planned.

He fetched Calida and Arin one evening, after the other classes had ended for the day and the students had a few precious hours to themselves. He led them outside of the keep, beneath the entrance arch and past the walls, out into the forest where a coach waited, much like the one that had brought Calida here over a year ago.

A sky witch stood outside of the coach, waiting as they approached. When they stopped before it, the witch rapped roughly on the door. It swung open and a few other witches stepped out, dragging two men with them. Calida's eyes widened at the sight.

Their clothes and skin were filthy, as if they hadn't bathed for some time, their hair lank, faces unshaven. Their wrists were manacled, though their ankles remained free. Both of them were blindfolded and they stumbled out of the coach clumsily.

"What is this?" Arin asked, voicing the same question Calida had.

Master Kallias turned his back on the two men, facing his pupils. "This," he said softly, "is your next task. These two are prisoners sent from Brisban."

The capitol of Alara.

"They are brothers," Kallias continued. "Both convicted of murder. Your task is to carry out their sentence and execute them."

At a signal from Kallias, one of the other witches removed the men's blindfolds. The brothers squinted and blinked in the fading rays of sunlight, taking in their surroundings.

Calida locked eyes with one of them, unable to look away, as she stared into the face of a killer. A man she was expected to kill.

She had been asked to do a lot of things in the course of her training with Master Kallias, but never had she been instructed to kill another human being. Arin did not look the least bit surprised by this revelation.

She stared at the condemned man in shock, unable to decipher the emotion flickering in his dark gaze. Fear? Anger? Remorse?

"At my signal, they will be released," Kallias warned. "I expect they will try to flee."

Calida opened her mouth to protest but had no idea what she would even say.

Master Kallias stepped back, nodding to the witches. They released their hold on the prisoners.

One of the brothers seized his chance and took off at a run. It was awkward with his hands still bound in front of him, but he fled with the desperation of a man who knew his life was on the line.

Arin didn't hesitate. He stepped forward, raising his hands. The nearest tree root shot out, lashing around the fleeing man's ankle. He cried out as he tipped forward and fell painfully on his arms. Slowly, the root pulled back, dragging the prisoner closer to where Arin stood.

Calida didn't want to watch. She glanced down at the other man, the one meant for her. He hadn't fled and he wasn't looking at her either. He was watching his brother, his face pale beneath the grime. Reluctantly, Calida returned her gaze to Arin, wondering how he meant to finish this.

One of the nearby trees had been nearly choked by vines. They spiraled up around the trunk, splaying out across the branches. Looking at them, Calida had a sudden idea of what Arin had planned and hoped she was wrong.

She wasn't.

One of the vines that had wrapped around a particularly thick branch snaked down and wound itself slowly around the man's neck as he whimpered in fear. Calida clenched her teeth at how slowly the vine moved, wending its way almost lovingly in a caress that was anything but.

At last, it stopped moving, coiled back on itself around the man's neck. Arin gave an almost casual flick of his fingers and the vine yanked upward, snapping taut. The prisoner jerked, lifted off his feet, and hung suspended from the tree branch as though hanging from a noose, his neck bent at an unnatural angle. He squirmed for a few uncomfortable moments, feet twitching, until he finally hung still, his body swaying gently in the evening breeze.

It was an oddly fitting end for a murderer and showed more imagination on Arin's part than Calida would have given him credit for, but she felt ill just watching. Her pulse thudded painfully hard in the sides of her neck and gooseflesh had erupted over her arms. She could feel the others' eyes on her, waiting to see what she would do.

Calida turned back to her prisoner and he looked back at her, eyes wide and glassy with fear. He didn't speak a word. Perhaps he realized that begging for his life was pointless.

She screwed her eyes shut, not wanting to look at him, trying to dredge up the courage to do what needed to be done. But behind her eyelids, all she could see was the moment the vine had pulled taut. She fought down a fresh wave of nausea.

Come on! she screamed at herself. *This man is a criminal. A murderer! He deserves it.*

As a soldier, in war, she would be expected to fight and kill enemy soldiers and they were guilty of nothing more than being on the wrong side. They hadn't committed whatever heinous crime this man had. Killing this man should be easy compared to what would ordinarily be asked of her.

She opened her eyes and raised her hands, hating the way they trembled before her. The man flinched as if she'd already struck him and shrank back. A grown man, cowering in fear before her. She was thirteen. She had no idea how old he was or what he might have seen and done in the course of his life, what might have led him to this moment. She was a child and yet this man was afraid of her.

But regardless of what he had or hadn't done, she couldn't kill him. She couldn't be the one to end his life.

Calida lowered her hands and looked away, unable to bear looking at any of them. She couldn't bear to see the disappointment in Master Kallias's eyes.

"Calida?" he asked softly.

"I can't," she murmured, hating how weak her voice sounded to her own ears.

"Can't or won't?"

"I don't know." Was there even a difference at this point?

Out of the corner of her eye, she saw Kallias gesture to Arin, who stepped forward. Tree roots erupted out of the ground, swiftly wrapping around the remaining prisoner, from shoulder to ankle. Slowly, they constricted, wrapping tighter. The man cried out as he was crushed to death and Calida winced at the sound of bone cracking.

This time, she didn't look. But that did nothing to shield her from the sound and her own imagination.

At last, it was over and silence descended over the forest once more.

Master Kallias clasped his hands behind his back. "Arin, return to the keep."

He wants to speak with me alone, Calida realized as guilt flooded her. *You should have just killed the prisoner like he ordered you to.* Whatever method she would have chosen would have been kinder than what Arin had done to him.

She waited until the sound of Arin's footsteps faded before daring to look up at her instructor. His expression was unreadable.

"You chose to show mercy," he murmured and for a moment, Calida thought perhaps he approved of her decision after all.

She nodded. Showing mercy was a much kinder way of saying that she had been too weak to carry out the order. Maybe that was what he meant, but it still sounded better.

"Did you not think he deserved to die? I told you he was a killer."

Calida suddenly wondered if that was even true, though she saw no reason for Kallias to lie. Unless it was a test of their loyalty and how well they followed orders. *Blindly and without question, the way a good soldier should...*

Calida could think of nothing to say to that.

Kallias sighed. "I need my soldiers to be creative in their attacks and quick on their feet. But I also need them to obey orders when they are given and you did not obey the order I gave you. I need soldiers who will do what needs to be done and sometimes that requires the taking of life. If you are unable or unwilling to do so, this is not the path for you."

"No!" Calida cried, looking up in alarm. "Please—" She wanted to say that she would prove herself to him, that she would make up for her mistake, but she wasn't sure it wouldn't be a lie.

He might make her go through the same test again. Either way, eventually, she would be expected to kill someone.

"One day, Calida, your life will be on the line and you will have to make a choice. Or if not your own, then someone else's. Your fellow soldiers need to know they can count on you. You will trust the soldier beside you with your life and I will not have soldiers that cannot be trusted. I'm sorry, Calida. I had high hopes, but I think it best if our journey ends here."

Calida couldn't believe this was happening to her. She felt the watery sting of tears and tried to blink them back. She could no longer see Kallias clearly, his form nothing more than a blur.

"Can't I have another chance?" She despised how pathetic she sounded, reduced to begging, but what else could she do?

Surely everything she had done up until that point had to count for something. Hadn't she proven herself in other ways?

Kallias shook his head. "I'm sorry, Calida, but being a good duelist doesn't make you a good soldier. It's only one small part. My decision is final."

The tears spilled forth then and there was nothing Calida could do to stop them. She choked back a sob, feeling Kallias's hand on her shoulder, which only made her cry harder.

"Don't be too hard on yourself," he said gently, his kindness at odds with his appearance. "Some people are meant to be soldiers and some aren't. There's no shame in it. Your calling lies elsewhere. You'll find another way to bring glory to Alara."

Calida was barely listening. All she could think about was that she had failed and all her hard work had come to nothing. All of it had been undone in the span of one ill-fated evening.

She was relieved when Kallias dismissed her. She turned away from him and ran beneath the entrance arch, back onto monastery grounds.

It had all been for nothing. All the time she had put forth, ignoring her other classes, the surety she had felt that she was on the right path, that this was what she was meant to do. She'd been so certain about her placement and now she found herself cast adrift in an unknown sea, uncertain of her future, and forced to consider other placements she had previously ignored and looked down upon.

Stupidly, she thought of her horse and how she would never get to ride it again. Instead, she would be a squire, one of the people tasked with caring for the animals of others, but never getting to ride. Never again would she feel so free.

It's not your horse! she reminded herself furiously.

Calida ran blindly, tears streaming down her cheeks, unable to see where she was going but no longer caring. She wished she could keep running, beyond the borders of the monastery and never stop. But where would she go? There was nothing for her out there, no place she belonged outside of these walls.

If only she had just killed the prisoner like Master Kallias wanted. Then all of her problems would have vanished and she wouldn't be in this mess. She would still have been a part of his class, on her way to achieving the placement she had wanted.

It was nearly dusk, the light dimming further as the sun sank lower in the sky. Calida yelped as she tripped over an unseen tree root and fell forward, scraping her hands. She barely felt the pain beneath the tumult of emotions raging inside her.

She pushed herself up and kept going, only slowing as she neared the river at the edge of the monastery. She was no longer sobbing, but she couldn't seem to make the tears stop. Impatiently, she reached up and wiped them away with the heel of her palm.

Calida froze. Over the faint sound of the river, she could hear voices up ahead. She crouched down low and crept forward through the underbrush. All thoughts of the prisoner fled her mind at the sight before her.

Thalia stood barefoot in the water, Mordred on the opposite side of her. As Calida watched, Thalia lifted her arms and the water responded to her command, rising up into the air as if weightless. She heard Thalia speaking, explaining what she was doing, but the words barely registered.

Thalia urged Mordred to reach out toward the tree roots visible along the riverbank, to feel for them. Mordred stretched out his hands toward them tentatively and they broke free of the dirt, snaking forward.

Calida retreated further where she could watch but not hear what was being said.

Thalia was secretly giving Mordred lessons. Calida's first reaction was one of hurt. Why hadn't Thalia confided in her? They could have worked together. And Calida was an earth witch, like Mordred. She could have helped him more than a sky witch ever could.

But that feeling quickly gave way to something else. Thalia was clearly stronger than she'd let on that day in the dueling ring. Stronger than she'd led everyone to believe, including Calida. She could have beaten Arin easily, but she hadn't. Why not?

Calida had never seen her sister use her power to this extent, almost as if she didn't want anyone else to see. But that didn't make sense either. She hadn't told her own sister but she willingly showed Mordred?

Calida clenched her scraped hands into fists, ignoring the pain. Thalia could have stayed in combat class if she had wanted to. She belonged in that class in a way that Calida clearly didn't and yet she'd thrown it all away.

It wasn't fair for someone like Thalia to have such power and not take advantage of it, when Calida would do anything to be as strong as her. She would have given anything to have a second chance, to get back into that class, to be rid of the uncertainty, the fear of what the future held for her now. Whatever lay ahead, it wouldn't be easy since she had devoted all of her time and focus into being a soldier, a door now closed to her.

Thalia faced the same problem, but she was a sky witch and that made nearly everything easier for her. The best paths were open to her in a way that they never would be for Calida.

She turned and left before either of them knew she was there. She wouldn't say anything for now. Calida made her way back toward the dormitories, hoping her eyes weren't too red or blotchy. She didn't want to have to answer any questions from Lorelei.

Luckily, her friend wasn't in the dormitory when Calida arrived. She sank down onto her bunk, grateful for the darkness. Maybe she would wake up tomorrow to find that this entire evening had been nothing more than a bad dream and everything would go back to the way it had been. All she wanted was to forget it had ever happened.

But the two prisoners followed her into her dreams and she woke the next morning feeling no better than she had when she went to bed. Nothing had changed—and yet everything had. She would have to get up and attend her classes, this time with one less, and try to find where her true calling lay.

She thought about what Thalia had said, about how it made no difference what they wanted for themselves. Thalia was right and Calida would never doubt the truth of it again.

CHAPTER 6

The morning after it had happened, at breakfast, Calida told the others about her expulsion from Kallias's class. It was not a task she relished, but she knew the rumors would begin swirling soon enough and she'd rather they hear it from her than anyone else.

Lorelei had been in the dormitory the previous evening when Calida had initially been called away and so she knew something had happened. "What did Master Kallias want? I meant to ask you when I got back, but you were asleep and I thought it could wait."

Calida picked at her porridge, not wanting to look at any of them. Much to her annoyance, Thalia and Mordred were also present. Thalia seemed to have taken to the boy the way one would a lost, helpless puppy. Calida hated to admit her failure in front of them both.

She sighed. Better to get it over with, like pulling out a thorn. "He expelled me."

Lorelei gasped, her hazel eyes wide. Even Daniel, usually unflappable, looked shocked. Mordred had blanched considerably, though Calida didn't know how that was possible since he always looked like that. Thalia's expression was impossible to read.

"What happened?" Lorelei asked.

In as few words as possible, Calida told them about the two prisoners and that she and Arin had been ordered to kill them. "Arin made it look so easy," she said, with a mix of bitterness and revulsion. He hadn't even hesitated and she felt fairly certain he'd never done such a thing before. It shouldn't have been that easy.

That's just because he has what it takes and you don't.

"I had no idea they gave tests like that," Daniel muttered. "I've never heard of it before."

"That's awful!" Lorelei exclaimed, earning a few looks from nearby tables. "I can't believe they'd ask you to do something like that."

Calida shrugged. "We're supposed to be soldiers, Lorelei. And besides, they were both killers. They deserved it." And yet that hadn't helped her go through with it.

"There's a difference between soldiers and murderers," Lorelei said firmly. "Deserved or not, this wasn't on a battlefield. Neither of them were armed. It's not right."

"I'm sorry," Mordred ventured. "I know how much it meant to you."

Calida glanced at him and Thalia. Her sister had yet to say a word. *I know what you two are doing.*

"What do you plan on aiming for now?" Daniel asked.

"I don't know." She was passable at growing crops, decent at caring for animals—that one hurt too much to think about right now.

"You're good at healing," Lorelei offered. "At least, you're better than me."

Calida hadn't given it much thought. Was she meant to preserve life instead of take it, to heal wounds instead of inflict them? She wasn't sure if that was what she wanted. It didn't seem nearly as exciting as the life of a soldier.

But it wasn't about what she wanted and she could certainly do worse.

Daniel had once suggested that she could be a medic in the army. She had responded hotly at the time; it hadn't been what she wanted. But now, it might be a way of salvaging some small part of that dream.

She'd just have to go about it a different way.

For the first time, Calida was forced to pay attention in her other classes. The vineyards, orchards, and fields of crops were all tended by her fellow earth witches, coaxing the plants to grow and ideally ensuring a bountiful harvest. They got to enjoy the fruits of their labor each day at the mess hall, adding mangoes, papaya, and grapes to their meals, as well as vegetables from the gardens and bread made from the wheat in the fields.

Calida was decent enough at it, but the plants she had an affinity for seemed to be the herbs, which were used to add flavor to meals and also in the infirmary by the healers. Still, she hoped that tending to crops would not be her placement. The assignment she dreaded most upon graduating was to be sent to the island of Indris and assist in the growing of sugarcane.

Life on Indris was far from pleasant.

Calida continued to care for the animals, but she wasn't as good at it as she was with the herbs and a future in agriculture seemed increasingly likely. At the infirmary, she learned the basics of healing. Witches had no means of magically healing wounds, but under the care of some, injuries did seem to heal faster than normal. She learned the correct way to apply bandaging and splints, the names of the herbs and their functions, how to grind them up and make a poultice.

It was boring work compared to combat class. There was nothing flashy about it. Irjah, her instructor, stressed to each of her pupils the importance of the art of healing. Deep down, Calida knew she was right. It was important work and far smarter to want to learn to heal wounds than have the skills to inflict them. She tried to be satisfied with that, but it was hard after what she had given up.

Lorelei excelled at both healing and caring for the animals. One of the horses was heavily pregnant and Lorelei tended to the animal each day, eagerly anticipating the foal's arrival. Calida was happy for her friend. Whichever placement Lorelei received, she would certainly have no trouble with it.

One day, while Calida was helping Irjah sort through the bundles of herbs the first years had brought in, Thalia came into the infirmary, a gash in her forearm.

Irjah glanced up, taking in the sight of blood and determining the severity of the wound. "Why don't you handle this one, Calida? I'll finish up here."

Calida glanced at her uncertainly and then slowly rose to her feet, setting the herbs aside. She grabbed her medicine kit and led Thalia over to where the cots had been assembled, separated by thin partitions. Thalia sat down on the edge of one of the cots and Calida set her kit down beside her.

She surveyed the gash, wondering how her sister had come by it, relieved that there would be no need for stitches. "What happened? Did Arin do this?"

"No," Thalia said quickly. "I got careless. I fell and scraped it."

Calida frowned, realizing all at once how it must have happened. It was a result of one of her secret training sessions with Mordred.

"You're a terrible liar," she said as she began to clean the wound. She thought about revealing what she knew, but decided against it. Let Thalia know she didn't believe her explanation and wonder at how much she knew.

Moving quickly and efficiently, she applied a poultice, bandaged Thalia's arm, and sent her on her way, instructing her to keep the wound covered and dry.

She sighed to herself and went back to helping Irjah sort the herbs.

* * *

The day after Calida had seen to her arm, Thalia stood beside the river as the sun set, waiting for Mordred to appear. He was already late, which wasn't like him. Usually, he was the one already present, waiting for her, eager and impatient to begin. Thalia looked down at the bandage around her arm and wondered if he would show.

It had been an accident, what he'd done to her arm, but he might not see it that way. She had glimpsed the guilt on his face as she tried to reassure him that it wasn't anything serious.

The undergrowth rustled and she looked up as Mordred walked down the slope toward her.

"I was starting to think you weren't coming," she called.

He made a face. "I wasn't sure I wanted to. Not after—" His eyes darted to her arm.

"It's just a scratch, Mordred." She quickly changed the subject. "Are your classes improving?"

He joined her, standing on the small outcropping of rocks and pebbles that protruded from the water. A tree stood on the bank to the side, towering over them, its roots poking through the sandstone where the water had eroded the ground. Behind Thalia, the sides of the bank gradually rose, until it seemed as though the river was framed by sandstone cliffs.

Mordred nodded. "I'm not at the bottom of the class anymore and you can be sure Master Kallias has noticed. I can tell he's wondering what changed, but he has no complaints." He hesitated. "I know this is what I want, but after what Calida said…I don't know if I have what it takes. I'm good enough in class, but that can only take you so far. I don't want to hurt anyone."

Thalia suppressed a sigh. She wanted Mordred to succeed, but his near-constant need for reassurance wore on her at times. It was tiring, always having to search for something new to say to alleviate this newest round of self-doubt.

"It's not about hurting someone. It's about protecting those that others want to hurt, the way you did for me when you stood up to Arin, the day we met."

There, that sounded good, didn't it?

"I suppose I could do that."

"Good. Then let's keep at it."

It was true that Mordred had shown marked improvement ever since they had begun training in secret. Thalia no longer had the guidance of a sky witch instructor to help hone her skills, but she had paid attention in class and remembered all she had learned.

Though she wasn't sure what good it did her. She still didn't have a placement and her options were limited. She could care for animals, but there were plenty more gifted at it than her. Her only other options would be to find herself on a merchant vessel one day, shielding it from the weather or any marauding pirates that might wish to plunder it—or as a manipulator of weather.

Both of those appealed to her and overlapped a little. She had allowed herself to show a modicum of what she could do in class, hoping she would be selected for it. The thought of pirates didn't scare her the way it did some of her fellow students. It may not have been as exciting as being a soldier, but the idea of living a life on the sea somehow appealed to her.

She had never seen the sea before, but she desperately wanted to. To see more of the world than their little corner of Alara. Perhaps she could convince Calida to take her one day. She hadn't seen much of Calida lately and she wondered if her sister was avoiding her.

* * *

In between her other classes, Calida practiced strengthening her bond with Horus. They already knew how to communicate and Calida could give commands, but they hadn't yet completely mastered the art of linking their vision. She attempted it in her spare time, as she lay in the darkness of the dormitory when everyone else was asleep.

She had sent Horus out into the night, instructing him to fly beyond the borders of the monastery. It felt like so long since she had seen something outside of the keep, even though it hadn't yet been two full years, and she longed to see if the outside world had changed.

One of their teachers had told them that the stronger the bond with a familiar, the further they could physically be apart and still maintain a connection. Calida wanted to test those limits and see how far Horus could go.

They were limited to verbal communication since no witch could communicate telepathically and so she couldn't speak with Horus while they were apart. But they could occasionally pick up on each other's emotions.

Tonight, Calida could feel the hawk's exhilaration to be out beyond the grounds, stretching his wings, as if it were her own. Perhaps he felt as constrained here as she was starting to feel.

She rolled over in her bunk, sighing softly. It wasn't yet time to try linking her vision with his. She needed to give him time to reach the nearest town first.

Every day here was the same, exactly like the one before it, and tomorrow would be no different. The same classes, the same people, the same chores, meals, and expectations. The thought of spending another six years here was enough to make her want to scream.

Calida felt an emotion shift within her—Horus's, not her own. It was something akin to awe and she wondered what the hawk was seeing to inspire such a reaction. Quickly, she closed her eyes, reaching out toward him in her mind and trying not to think about her current surroundings.

They had managed it only a few times before, for a few moments, but this, if it worked, would be the longest connection they had yet achieved.

All at once, the darkness behind Calida's eyelids was replaced by what her familiar was seeing. She nearly gasped aloud and forced down her excitement, for fear she would sever the connection.

She was looking down at a town at one of the docks, where Alara met the sea. She could see the wood of the dock and the storefronts that lined the street. It was too dark to see what they sold, but they no doubt catered to sailors. The windows below were lit warmly in the darkness and she spotted a few dark silhouettes as people went about their business.

But it was the ships anchored in the harbor that caught Calida's attention the most. They were massive, their tall masts stretching into the night sky. Most of the sails had been furled, but what little canvas remained flapped gently in the breeze. Beyond, the Atlas Sea stretched out far as the eye could see, the water shimmering in the moonlight.

Calida wanted to stare at it forever, but eventually, Horus turned around and began heading back toward the monastery. She opened her eyes, the connection severing, and found herself in the darkened dormitory once more.

What would it be like to be an ordinary human, enjoying a night on the town? What would it be like to climb aboard one of those magnificent ships and simply sail away, into a new life free of responsibilities and preordained destinies?

The thoughts followed Calida into sleep, but she vowed that she would know at least one of the answers.

There was no one else to share such things with, that she thought might understand. Except perhaps Thalia, who might just be as unhappy here as Calida was beginning to be.

She thought the time had finally come to confront her sister over what she knew.

Calida approached her in the late afternoon, before dinner, careful to wait until after Mordred had left. Thalia was just leaving herself, climbing up the bank of the river. The two of them always left separately to avoid being seen together.

She started as she looked up and saw Calida. "What are you doing here?"

"Looking for you," Calida replied. "Let's see if we can catch some fish."

Thalia looked at her suspiciously. "Why? It's almost time for dinner."

Calida grimaced. "You and I both know that the fish will be better than anything they feed us in there."

Thalia smiled at that and relented. "All right." She turned, heading back down to the river and Calida followed. "What, exactly, do you plan on catching them with?"

"Bare hands. I suppose I could try to convince a few of them to throw themselves up on dry land."

The thought was gruesome, using her power to persuade the animals to participate willingly in their own destruction.

"Do you think that would work?"

Calida had been joking, but Thalia sounded interested. She really didn't know if her power over animals extended that far. "I don't know."

The two of them sat down on the rocks in the middle of the stream. Calida looked down at the small fish slipping by and tried ordering them up out of the water with no success. She supposed she couldn't order an animal to do something directly opposed to its own wellbeing.

"It was worth a try," Thalia remarked. "Just imagine if it had worked."

"You could use the water to catch them, you know," Calida said casually.

Her sister stiffened. "I don't know…"

The time had come. "I know you can do it," Calida told her bluntly. "I've seen what you can do. I know you're training secretly with Mordred. That's what happened to your arm, isn't it?"

Thalia looked at her in alarm. "Who else knows?"

"No one, so far as I know. I haven't told anyone."

"You're not going to, are you?"

"Why would I?"

Her sister visibly wilted with relief.

"You know I wouldn't have told anyone," Calida added softly. "Why didn't you tell me?"

Thalia shrugged, not meeting her eyes. "You don't need any help with combat training."

"Not with that part, anyway," Calida muttered, somewhat bitterly. "But neither do you. You're good enough to have stayed in that class, so why didn't you? Why did you let them kick you out? You must have known that was going to happen sooner or later if you didn't try."

"I know."

"Then why?" Calida exclaimed. "Why did you let them bully you? You're twice as strong as any of them, maybe more. They targeted you because they thought you were weak and you gave them no reason to think otherwise."

Thalia turned to her then, her dark blue eyes reflecting the sun off the water. "Let them think I'm weak. I'm always being underestimated. And that's why I'll win."

"Win what?" Because in Calida's mind, it seemed her sister had only lost.

Thalia didn't answer, her gaze far away.

Calida sighed. She didn't understand and in other ways, she did. "Do you ever wonder what it's like to just be normal? To not have any of these responsibilities?"

It was the same thing Lorelei had asked her, all those days ago. Then, Calida had felt such a question foolish. Why would she want to be like everyone else?

Now, she wasn't so sure.

"Why?" Thalia challenged. "Normal people are nothing special. Not like us. We're destined for something greater."

Calida didn't feel like she was destined for anything that could be considered great, but she could see how her sister had to believe that, in order to make life at the monastery bearable. Perhaps she had once believed it herself, but now she didn't know what she believed.

"We're destined for whatever the kingdom says we are. Nothing more."

"For now," Thalia murmured and Calida wondered what she meant. Her sister stood abruptly. "Come on. I thought you said we were going to catch some fish."

Shaking off her bad mood, Calida stood and waded into the river, getting the ends of her tunic wet. Bending over near the surface of the water, she waited, bare hands poised, ready to snatch at any fish that got too close, missing every time and sending water flying.

Thalia shrieked as the water splashed her and soon the fish were forgotten as Calida targeted her. It was a lost cause. Thalia, in a rare display of her power, simply summoned a wave that doused Calida from head to toe and nearly swept her off her feet.

When the bell rang for dinner, they both climbed out of the river soaking wet.

"How are we going to explain this to the headmistress?" Calida asked, gesturing to her sodden tunic. It clung to her and was far heavier than she would have expected.

Thalia waved her hands, summoning a strong gust of wind, and within moments, their tunics were dry. "Explain what?"

Calida gave her sister a playful shove. "I'll race you to the mess hall."

"That's not fair! You're taller!"

But Thalia's words were lost behind her as Calida took off running. Neither of them had caught any fish, but she wasn't disappointed. It had been more of an excuse to approach Thalia than anything else, and besides, they would have had no way of cooking the fish if they'd even caught any.

Still, she thought she had likely been right in that the fish would have been better than what awaited them in the mess hall.

CHAPTER 7

The rest of the year seemed to pass slowly, but before any of them knew it, it was over and they were on to the next one. By the time Calida's second year had come to a close, each of them had already found their placement. Daniel's, as ever, was in agriculture. Lorelei had found her place as a result of caring for the animals. The time had come for the horse to give birth and Lorelei regaled them all in the mess hall with stories of how she had assisted. The foal had been facing the wrong way and Lorelei had helped turn it, ensuring a successful delivery.

Mordred had retained his place in Kallias's class, well on his way to becoming a soldier. Calida wondered what he would be expected to do in order to keep his place.

Thalia had found a spot in weather manipulation and hoped to one day find herself aboard a ship, ensuring that it made good time and that no trouble befell it. Calida was still training with Irjah, learning the finer points of healing, but she had not forgotten the view of the docks at night and still yearned to venture out into the wider world.

She voiced her plan to the others one day, while they lounged by the river, eating the berries that grew there. The fruit was guarded by sharp thorns and more than one of them had pricked themselves trying to get to it, but it was worth the risk.

All of them seemed to be growing rapidly and the food from the kitchens never seemed like enough. Before long, they may have to make good on Calida's suggestion and go fishing.

They had amassed quite a pile, stuffing the berries into the pockets of their tunics and depositing them in a great heap in the grass. Calida lay on her back, staring up at the tree branches swaying overhead, the dappled sunlight falling on her face. Thalia had warned her that spending so much time in the sun would give her freckles but she didn't care.

She reached over, popping another handful of berries in her mouth, savoring the way the juice exploded with flavor and made the back of her jaw tingle.

She sat up slightly, propped on one arm. "What do you guys think about going into town?"

The others looked at her as if she were crazy. "What do you mean?" Mordred asked, his chin stained with berry juice.

"I want to go into town. It's so boring being stuck here all the time. Don't you want to see what the docks look like? The ocean?"

"I *would* like to see the ocean," Thalia said warily, but Calida could tell she was interested.

"We're not allowed to leave!" Lorelei squeaked, looking scandalized. "We could get into serious trouble if anyone catches us."

Calida grinned. "Best not get caught then." She sat up fully, holding one arm out and Horus swooped down, landing lightly. "Horus can keep watch."

"If anyone sees him—"

"It won't matter," Calida said quickly. "He looks ordinary enough. No one would know he's a familiar just by looking at him, not like some of the others. There are plenty of ordinary hawks about."

"It would be risky," Daniel murmured.

"It will be *fun*."

"But we can't go out dressed like this," Lorelei said, grabbing her green tunic. "They'd take one look at us and know."

"She's right," Mordred agreed. "And we don't have any other clothes."

Calida frowned. "There must be something we can do."

The dress she had worn upon arriving at the monastery was now too small and she was willing to bet the same was true for Thalia and Mordred. The students that had been assigned a gray tunic had since passed the test and there were no gray tunics large enough to fit any of them.

"We could try the laundry," Thalia suggested. "There may be something there we could use."

"I don't like this," Lorelei muttered.

"You don't have to come," Thalia snapped.

"I think it's worth the risk," Calida declared. "I want to go to the tavern and taste some ale." She knew the teachers at the monastery brewed alcoholic drinks, but never let the students have any. "Thalia and I will see what we can find at the laundry and then we'll meet back here. If we can find clothes that will work, we'll sneak out under the cover of darkness and be back before dawn. No one will ever know we left."

"I think someone will miss their clothes," Lorelei said, but no one paid her any mind.

The next time she was assigned to laundry duty, Calida surreptitiously rifled through the piles of clothes. There wasn't much to choose from. Most of the teachers always wore tunics of their own and would still be too conspicuous out in the general public. The teachers seemed to spend all of their time on monastery grounds, as if they never ventured out either, and Calida doubted that they ever did. Not only did they live a completely self-sufficient life at the monastery, growing or making anything they could possibly need, but witches were supposed to live different, separate lives.

But for once, even if only for a little while, she wanted to know what it felt like to be ordinary.

She managed to find a few sets of clothing that looked as if they were worn when engaging in dirty, manual labor that magic wouldn't be able to help with, like mucking out stalls. They were far too large, meant for fully grown adults. Daniel, now seventeen and nearly a grown man, might be able to fit into them without any trouble.

Calida folded up the clothes as tightly as she could and smuggled them out beneath her tunic, stashing them down by the river in a hole that had been hollowed out, partially concealed by roots, where no one would ever find them.

Thalia reported marginal success when it was her turn for laundry duty and she added her finds to the cache.

Calida waited several hours after they had all turned in for the night, until the sounds of snoring and heavy breathing told her that most of the others were asleep.

She swung down from her bunk, moving quietly but unhurried. If anyone happened to see her, they would merely think she was headed to the wash house and hopefully, they would fall back asleep before she returned so they wouldn't notice how long it took her.

She crept down to the river. Daniel soon joined her and together, they waited in the darkness. It was agony, waiting for the others to arrive, but they had agreed that they shouldn't be seen leaving together.

Fortunately, the sky was overcast, concealing the moon. Unfortunately, it was so dark that she could barely see her hand in front of her face.

Calida looked up as she heard a muffled swear and Thalia joined them, Horus perched on her shoulder. Calida hadn't wanted to be seen leaving with her familiar, so the hawk had followed her sister out the door, as if needing fresh air.

"Tripped on a tree root," Thalia grumbled, rubbing her foot. "It's black as pitch out here."

"It'll be brighter in town."

Mordred joined them a few minutes later, his rat peeking out of one sleeve of his tunic.

"Why did you bring him?" Daniel demanded. "We agreed that the only familiar coming with us was Horus."

No one in town would have a rat on their person and if anyone noticed Mordred's familiar, they would know at once.

"I don't like leaving him alone," Mordred protested. "He's so small."

"Go put him back, this instant, before Lorelei arrives," Daniel hissed.

"It's fine," Thalia cut across him. "Just keep him hidden inside your clothes."

When Lorelei at last joined them, Calida moved to where the stash of clothes had been hidden and began passing them out. It was hard to see what was what in the darkness, but it would have to do.

"They'll probably be a little big," she warned. "But it was the best we could do, so put them on."

"Now?" Lorelei whispered.

"Yes, now," Thalia said, voice tinged with impatience. "We won't look and it's too dark to see anyway."

Lorelei huffed and for a moment, the only sound was that of rustling fabric as they stripped off their tunics and changed into the workers' clothes.

Calida found herself wearing an enormous white shirt, and trousers, the legs of which reached well past her ankles, pooling on the ground.

"All ready?" She turned to face the others, who were similarly dressed.

Daniel's fit quite well, as expected. He had grown over the past year and put on some muscle, filling out his clothes better than any of the rest of them. Mordred looked positively dwarfed, the shirt falling to his knees and giving him the appearance of wearing a nightshirt. Thalia had knelt down and was rolling up her pant legs until they reached the middle of her shins, securing them with a thin piece of rope.

She reached into the pocket of her discarded tunic and pulled out some more. "I nicked some twine. Thought we might need it."

"Good idea," Calida said, taking some. The end result looked a bit ridiculous, but at least she could walk. She stuffed the overlong shirt into her trousers, tucking it in. "Everyone ready?"

They nodded. Horus hopped onto Calida's shoulder and they set off, skirting the edges of the monastery grounds, keeping close to the shadows cast by the keep walls. Calida held her breath, fearful that at any moment, they would be caught, but no one cried out in outrage. No one demanded to know where they thought they were going. No one stopped them.

She sighed in relief as they passed unhindered beneath the stone archway.

"Which way?" Lorelei whispered.

Forest surrounded them on all sides, no sign of civilization to be found.

Calida turned to Horus. "Is it far?"

"*No,*" came the answer.

"Lead the way."

Moving quickly, they followed the hawk through the darkness, mindful not to trip on anything. Calida didn't know how far they'd gone, but it felt like it must have been miles. It certainly hadn't taken Horus this long the night she'd linked vision with him, but he could take to the air while they were limited to traveling on foot.

At last, the lights of the nearest town came into view, twinkling in the darkness, and Horus launched himself higher, out of sight, so he couldn't be seen by anyone who might be watching.

"The ocean," Thalia breathed.

And there it was, laid out before them. They stood at the edge of a cobblestone road, leading deeper into town. The docks stretched out on their left, the water lapping at the wooden piers. The buildings had steep, gabled roofs, their sides dark, windows lit. Calida inhaled deeply, breathing in the scents of salt, brine and fresh sea air.

The ships docked at the harbor were even larger than they had appeared when she had looked down upon them from above. Despite the late hour, there were people bustling all over, mostly sailors, moving from the ships to some of the buildings and back again.

"Well, we're here," Lorelei murmured. "What now?"

"Let's find the tavern," Calida suggested, moving forward.

It wasn't hard to find. Drawn by the sounds of loud voices, boisterous laughter, and the smell of food, they soon made their way there. A man stumbled out as they reached the other side of the street. He took a few steps in the opposite direction before falling face-first to the ground. He didn't move again and Calida knew he must be drunk.

"Are you sure you want to go in there?" Mordred asked. "Won't someone notice a bunch of kids together and get suspicious?"

"We're not kids," Calida retorted, striding forward. "Not anymore."

If nothing else, she had ceased to be a child the moment she'd been instructed to kill someone.

"But Calida—" Thalia called.

Calida ignored her, pulling the door open and stepping inside. Her first instinct was to stop and stare at everything, taking it all in, but she knew that would only draw unwelcome attention, and so she walked in as if familiar with the place. There was a table in the corner that was unoccupied and she chose it, thinking it best to have a solid wall at your back so that nothing could sneak up on you, leaving you free to survey the rest of the room.

They filed in around the table and only then did she allow herself to look around. Through the window, she could see that Horus had landed on a nearby post and was keeping watch. He would give them a signal at any sign of trouble, but until then, they were relatively safe.

"What if one of the teachers likes to come here?" Lorelei asked softly, her voice nearly lost in the other sounds of the pub.

"Don't be stupid," Mordred chided. "They don't leave the monastery."

The inside of the tavern wasn't much of an improvement from its exterior. The lighting was dim, lit lanterns hanging from the ceiling. The air was thick with the smell of unwashed bodies and tobacco smoke, but beneath that, something was cooking and it smelled delicious. Calida couldn't remember the last time she'd had any decent meat. At the monastery, meat was rare and usually chicken. She thought, if she stood up slightly, that she could see an entire boar roasting over a spit in one of the back rooms.

There was no need for a fire in this tropical climate, but there was an unlit hearth in one corner all the same, the mounted head of some deer hanging over it. Calida glanced up at the rafters above their heads. On the opposite side of the bar, separated by a wall, a flight of stairs came down, which must have led up to a second floor. A few people ascended as she watched.

All of the patrons she could see were older than her. Some didn't appear to be much older than Daniel, but the rest were grizzled men, unshaven, their faces tanned and weathered. Their arrival had attracted a few looks from the other patrons, but no one had said anything or approached them.

One of the women moving between tables, taking orders, glanced at them and Calida thought she would turn away and ignore them, but she moved in their direction.

"Can I get you lot anything?"

Calida opened her mouth to say that she would like some ale, but Thalia nudged her under the table and leaned in close, lowering her voice.

"Calida, we don't have any money."

Oh. So that's what her sister had been trying to tell her before they came in. She hadn't even thought about it, but it was true. They had no money and so they couldn't possibly enjoy any of the things the pub had to offer.

"An ale," Daniel spoke up, glancing at Calida.

She wondered briefly if everyone else thought they were all his younger siblings, even though they looked nothing alike.

"Just the one?" the barmaid cocked her head to the side.

She was wearing a low-cut white dress with an apron tied over the front.

Daniel's eyes flicked momentarily to her plunging neckline and then he looked away, reddening. "For now."

The others looked at him in surprise. "You have money?"

He swallowed uncomfortably. "A little. My father gave me some before I came here and there's nothing to spend it on at the monastery, so I've been saving it."

"You don't have to buy us anything, you know," Calida said hurriedly.

He shrugged. "I want to. Like you said, it gets pretty boring back at the monastery. I want to have a little fun before I resign myself to a life of growing crops."

"Well, as long as you don't spend too much."

Secretly, Calida was pleased. She was finally going to taste ale after all.

The barmaid returned shortly, placing a pint of ale on the table. Daniel passed her a gold coin, a griffin stamped on one side, the symbol of Alara.

He passed the tankard to Calida. "You first, since you're so keen."

She took it and swallowed a large mouthful of the liquid inside. The taste wasn't exactly to her liking, but the act of rebellion she was committing just by being there, drinking it, was infinitely more appealing. The second swallow wasn't as bad as the first and she thought she could almost grow to like it. Perhaps it was an acquired taste.

The tankard was passed around the table, shared by all of them, until it was gone. Lorelei in particular seemed fond of it, despite her reluctance to be there at all.

"Do we have time for another one?" Calida asked Daniel.

He glanced down at the small leather pouch in his lap that contained his coins. "I think so."

"Forget that," Thalia said. "I want some of whatever they're cooking."

Calida had to admit that it smelled quite tempting. But Daniel was the one paying. "Your call," she told him.

He hesitated. "I was going to suggest saving some for next time, but there might not be a next time."

He had a point. They all knew they'd gotten lucky in sneaking out once. No one had caught them, but that didn't mean their absence would go unnoticed. Even now, the monastery might be in an uproar, teachers searching for them.

"You're right," Lorelei nodded. "We're here now. May as well enjoy it while it lasts."

Calida cast a quick glance out the window. Horus still perched on the post, keeping an eye out. So far, there'd been no trouble. The sky remained dark, dawn still hours away.

"All right, then," Daniel concluded, waving the pretty barmaid back over.

They all ordered some of the food and more ale for everyone. When it arrived, they dug in greedily. The meat was warm and fresh, with a side dish of fruit Calida had never seen before. The bread was a bit stale, but she didn't mind when compared to everything else. It was far better than anything they'd ever had at the monastery, except that which they could pick and eat the very same day.

The barmaid returned, asking if everything was to their liking, and Daniel, perhaps bolstered by the ale, struck up a conversation with her, though none of the others paid the two of them any mind.

Calida ate until her stomach felt full to bursting and still she wanted more, but eventually the plates were picked clean. Calida slumped back in her seat, feeling stuffed but content. There was a pleasant warm feeling inside of her, courtesy of the ale, and it was hard to think about much of anything. All she wanted now was to curl up and go to sleep. Her previous thoughts about life at the monastery now seemed far away.

Daniel glanced out the window at the night sky. "We'd better get going if we want to get back in time. Still have a long walk ahead of us."

Calida didn't want to move, but she knew he was right. Moving stiffly, she forced herself to her feet, staggering slightly.

He reached out, gripping her by the elbow. "I think someone's had a bit too much to drink." He sounded amused but Calida barely heard the words.

The air outside was much fresher than it had been in the stuffy tavern and she took a deep breath as they stepped out into the night. It was always slightly humid in Alara, but a nice, cool breeze flowed in off the sea and the ships bobbed slightly as the waves stirred against them.

While she waited for the others to step out after her, Calida walked toward the dock, staring out at the sea beyond. Horus flew up to land on her shoulder, the hawk feeling unnaturally heavy. Calida blinked, trying to make her eyes focus, but it was hard.

Somewhere out there, though she couldn't make it out, lay another land mass, and she struggled to recall the name of the island from her lessons in school.

Amberleigh. The pirate haven.

Calida had never met a pirate. They were the sworn enemies of Alara, but she found herself wondering what it would be like to live that sort of life instead of being a witch. To live by no one's rules but her own and be able to go anywhere she wanted.

Of course, there was no sign of the northern kingdom, Daera. It was too far away, even farther than Amberleigh. Looking out over the endless sea, she found it hard to believe that it was really out there at all and not just something someone had made up.

Thalia's voice spoke behind her. "Ready to go?"

She turned away. "Yes."

On unsteady feet, she followed after the others on the long walk back to the monastery. They needed to be back before dawn. The return trip seemed to take far longer than the first time around. More than once, Calida stumbled and nearly fell. She noticed a few of the others similarly struggling, but not as badly as her. They must not have drunk as much of the ale.

The forest was alive with the sounds of insects, monkeys, and other animals Calida couldn't name. Briefly, she wondered if there were any dangerous predators out here that might try and pick off a few teenagers, but the thought didn't last long. All the racket was giving her a headache, making it hard to concentrate.

At last, the archway came into view and they slipped back onto monastery grounds, heading for the river. It wasn't yet dawn; the sky hadn't even begun to lighten. They'd made good time.

They found their tunics where they'd discarded them and stripped off the stolen clothes, once again slipping into the tunics. *Back to being witches*, Calida thought with a twinge of regret. It had been nice to be someone else for a little while, to feel a sense of normalcy, even if it was only pretend.

"What do we do with these?" Lorelei asked, gesturing at the clothes they had taken from the laundry.

It had been a risk taking them in the first place and trying to put them back might be an even bigger one. They could be caught trying to replace them when they otherwise might never be found out.

Calida bent, gathering them up. "We'll keep them hidden here. For next time."

Lorelei frowned and Calida knew what she was thinking. There may not be a next time. Getting away with it once was one thing, but to push their luck again seemed foolish. Still, Calida already knew she would go back, even if none of the others wanted to go with her.

She put the bundle of clothes back in the hiding spot beneath the roots. She would need to find a blanket or something to wrap them in, to shield them from the weather, but it would do for now.

Daniel hung back as the others went ahead, returning to their dormitories, and Calida fell into step beside him. "You intend to go back, don't you?" she guessed.

He nodded. It was too dark to say for certain, but she thought he blushed slightly. "I want to see Elle again."

"Is that her name? The woman at the tavern who served us?" Calida hadn't caught her name, if she'd introduced herself, which she must have done at some point if Daniel knew it.

He nodded again. "She asked if I would come again and I said I would."

"Just be careful not to tell her anything important," Calida warned. It felt strange, warning someone who was several years older than herself to be careful, as though it should have been the other way around.

She should have been the one doing something foolhardy, putting herself at risk, and he the one to warn her. But then, they would both be doing something foolish by going back at all.

"I won't," Daniel promised, but under the influence of too much ale, there was no telling what one might say or do.

Daniel was one of the lucky ones, in that his witch-mark wasn't in an obviously visible place. Calida glanced at him, wondering where, exactly, it was. She had seen some of the students who had half their faces covered with one, or their hands. They wouldn't be able to pass as normal out in society, the way either of them could.

Regardless of what transpired between Daniel and Elle, Calida hoped he knew better than to get too deeply involved. No one had spoken to them yet of such things at the monastery, but she knew they were expected to find a fellow witch to marry and have children with, ensuring that their powers would be passed on to the next generation and that Alara never lacked for witches.

Nothing about our lives is our own, Calida thought bitterly, grinding her teeth together. *Not even who we are to marry.*

The thought stayed with her as she and Daniel parted ways and she returned to her dormitory. She had to be very quiet now, to avoid waking the others, who might remember seeing her leave hours ago, and demand to know where she'd been. But with a belly full of ale, that was easier said than done.

Somehow, she made it back to her bunk and climbed up, feeling a bit sick. She supposed she could always use that as an excuse for her absence if anyone should ask. She'd been at the wash house, sick.

But no one asked and Calida fell into a fitful sleep.

* * *

It felt like only an hour had passed when the first bell rang out, jolting her awake. Sunlight streamed through the dormitory windows, searing her eyes and Calida groaned as she sat up. The mild discomfort of last night had only worsened, not improved. Her body ached and her head stabbed with pain at the slightest of movements.

Her gluttony last night had been a mistake and she was paying for it now. Calida wanted to lay back down and skip her classes for the day, which was only allowed if they were violently ill or seriously injured, of which she was neither. There would be no reprieve for her. She would have to power through the day and bear it, somehow.

She stumbled her way to the wash house to find Thalia already there, splashing water on her face. Her hair was still damp from a bath, turned a darker red by the moisture. She looked tired from a night of little sleep, but not as bad as Calida felt.

A bath helped revive Calida a bit, but she didn't feel like eating anything in the mess hall, doubting she would be able to keep it down.

"You need to eat something," Daniel said, setting a plate of scrambled eggs and a piece of toast in front of her. "Trust me."

"How do you know?" Calida grumbled, nibbling at the toast.

"Because I've seen this happen before," he said.

She believed him and forced herself to eat the toast, but couldn't bear to touch the eggs. She gave them to Thalia instead.

The sunlight that had seared her vision that morning didn't stay, the skies turning overcast, and within the hour, it was pouring down rain, adding to her misery.

"Can't you do something about the rain?" Calida complained to her sister at lunchtime. She could hear it, still drumming on the roof of the mess hall. "I thought you were practicing weather manipulation."

"I'm not that good yet," Thalia retorted. "Besides, it's good for the crops. They need it."

Calida grunted noncommittally.

"You could get something from Irjah for your headache," Lorelei suggested helpfully.

But Calida didn't want to raise even a whiff of suspicion about what might have happened and so she went without. Luckily, the weather cleared late that afternoon, the tropical storm vanishing almost as quickly as it had come, leaving everything dripping wet and the air filled with the earthy smell that only existed after a downpour.

Calida met Thalia at their spot down by the riverbed, wanting to relax. She hoped the stolen clothes hadn't gotten too wet from the rain. It was so oppressively humid that it was taking the curl out of her hair as she sat next to Thalia. As unpleasant as it was, it would only be worse inside.

Wordlessly, Thalia handed Calida a small packet.

"What's this?"

"Poppy seeds, from the infirmary. In case your head still hurts."

"You didn't—"

"I told Irjah I had cramps," Thalia interrupted. "Don't worry; your secret is safe."

Calida marveled at her sister's generosity, at her cleverness. Why hadn't she thought of that excuse? She probably would have, if her brain had been working properly. If this was the effect ale had on her, she didn't care how nice it tasted, she would never touch the stuff again.

The two of them lapsed into silence, sifting through the pebbles at the edge of the river, looking for any unusual shapes. Calida was just about to ask Thalia if she thought one looked like a heart when they heard voices nearby.

Both of them froze and flattened to the ground, hoping the tall riverbanks would hide them from sight. They weren't doing anything wrong by being there, but neither of them wanted anyone else to know about the spot. The fewer people they had to share it with, the better, and the less chance there was of the stolen clothes being discovered.

"Arin has done very well in his training."

Calida recognized Master Kallias's voice.

"He has a nasty temper," replied a female voice that she didn't know. It must have been another teacher.

"He's gotten far better at controlling his emotions since he arrived. He'll make a good soldier one day."

"I'm pleased to hear it. But it's not enough. You passed on only one earth witch student this year, Kallias. I know the crown prefers sky witches, but I'm afraid we may have to be more lenient in the future. Perhaps you should give Calida another chance. I've seen what she can do in the ring."

Calida couldn't see either of the teachers and she hoped that meant they couldn't see her or Thalia. She imagined Kallias shaking his head as he answered.

"What she can do in the ring is of no use, Ayani, if she's too squeamish to take life in battle."

"Disposing of one prisoner is hardly battle, Kallias," Ayani's voice was thick and wry. "In the heat of the moment, when it's kill or be killed, you'll find most willing to take life in defense of their own."

"It's not worth the risk," Kallias retorted. "We must have only the best as soldiers."

"I agree, but I still think we'll have no choice but to expand the ranks of those we accept." Her voice dropped slightly. "I hear they're putting more than one sky witch on our merchant vessels now. Daera has already suffered heavy losses and when their merchantmen do arrive here in port, they've sometimes suffered heavy damage. And they don't have the benefit of witches the way we do."

"Pirates?" Kallias asked.

"The sea wolves are growing bolder. It's not enough to have just one sky witch on board to protect the ship anymore. With so many being called away to serve in the navy, we'll need to accept more earth witches in order to fill the ranks on shore."

"It's too late for Calida. I've heard she's already found a placement with Irjah and so much the better. We may have need of her services if it's as bad as you say."

"Well, just so you know for the future. We're at peace with Daera, but that may change. And if it does…" Ayani let the sentence trail off without finishing.

Nothing more was said and Calida assumed they must have left. She wasn't angry about the dismissive way Kallias had spoken of her. She'd already made peace with the idea that she was to place as a healer instead of a soldier. The sting and bitter disappointment surrounding her expulsion from his class were gone, though she knew better than to think about it for too long.

Even feelings believed long buried could be dredged to the surface again.

She waited several minutes, in case they hadn't quite left yet, before standing fully.

"It's clear," she told Thalia and her sister stood as well.

"Pirates," Thalia murmured. "I didn't realize they were such a problem."

"They won't be for long," Calida said darkly.

They were, after all, just ordinary men and women. There was very little they could do against both the might of Alara's navy and the witches they had on board.

CHAPTER 8

Life continued at the Erlohn monastery much as it always had. Thalia went about her duties, including waking up abysmally early to milk the cows, a task she loathed. It seemed more like a job for an earth witch to her. She saw signs of strain among the teachers, though they did their best to hide it.

Occasionally, she accompanied Calida and Daniel back into town and eavesdropped on the local gossip, though more often than not, the two of them went alone and she stayed behind. Ever since the first outing, neither Mordred nor Lorelei went with them.

Despite Calida's prediction, the pirates continued to cause problems. There was some talk at the tavern that the crown was considering a raid on Amberleigh, to burn the place down and drive the brigands out, but nothing ever came of it. Rumors swirled around the monastery of the possibility of early graduation, that students would be pushed through and out into the real world more quickly than before, per the crown's wishes.

Thalia would have liked nothing more than to graduate early and she threw herself into each task that was appointed to her. In her weather manipulation class, she no longer held herself back the way she once had. Stormy days were her favorite to practice on. The instructor would have her draw the storm nearer to them until it was right on top of them or push it away so that it passed them by.

By the end of her second year, she had succeeded in calling down lightning, though she took care not to do it again after that. She had proven that she could do it and that was enough. Though the look on the other students faces, ranging from fear to awe to envy, was enough to make her want to do it again. She was careful not to give in to that temptation. She had to remember what the end game was.

Sometimes, she found herself thinking about her parents, wondering if they still missed her and Calida. But as time went on, she thought about them less and less. There was no point in missing them. They were a part of her life that she'd had to leave behind and life at the monastery was something they couldn't share.

* * *

The more time that passed without anyone discovering her absences from the monastery, the less Calida began to worry about it, the fear fading away. She wasn't stupid enough to become cocky or careless, but the choking, breath-stealing fear that had accompanied sneaking beneath the stone archway no longer trailed her steps whenever she snuck out.

Daniel always went with her. Sometimes, he went alone, but each time she went, he was there making the trip beside her. He had long since run out of money to pay for anything at the tavern, but Elle was quite fond of him and she would give him an occasional drink on the house, placing it on the table before him and then walking away with a wink, his eyes watching the sway of her hips.

Calida didn't mind missing out on the food, even though it had been good. It was information she came for now and the tavern was an excellent source of it. Liquor loosened men's lips and made them eager to talk. No one paid a thin fifteen-year-old girl any mind.

She was now in her fourth year, Thalia in her third. Daniel was eighteen and had only one more year before he would graduate and leave the others behind. Calida would miss him when he was gone. She asked him once, on the way into town, what he thought about the possibility of graduating early.

He had shrugged. "I'm in no hurry to get to my placement, Calida. Besides, I don't think I'm good enough for it."

She had looked across at him. The moon was out, allowing her to see him. They no longer cared about sneaking out beneath overcast skies. If it rained, they wouldn't go, but that was the only concession they made.

Calida wouldn't have thought it possible, but he had grown even more. He was at least a foot taller than her now; she didn't even come up to his shoulder. He was muscular from long days of hard labor, his skin tanned from the sun, and he had grown a short beard, making him look older than his years.

She had to admit that he was very handsome and it was no wonder that Elle thought so too. Calida couldn't see herself paired with him for the rest of her life, however, even though she was supposed to look among her fellow witches for a life partner. No doubt he thought of her only as a younger sister or at the very least a friend and nothing more.

She didn't know what man would be interested in her anyway. She was too skinny, with few curves to speak of, lean and angular where a woman should have been round and soft.

It's a long way away, she reminded herself. *You don't have to worry about that now*. Still, it remained a nagging thought in the back of her mind that she knew she would have to confront one day.

Daniel knew which days to go to the tavern, when Elle's shift ended early and she was free. She walked up to their table and Daniel rose, following her up the stairs to the second floor.

At first, he had asked Calida if she minded being left alone. She assured him that she didn't. She was used to it, though she wished that Thalia would come with them more often. But Thalia had said that their red hair drew too much attention and that someone might remember having seen them.

So Calida sat alone at their table, watching Daniel leave with Elle. She worried about him. The very thing she had feared might happen clearly had—he obviously had feelings for Elle but Calida couldn't see it ending happily for either one of them. Perhaps they weren't as serious as they appeared and she worried for nothing.

She would leave before Daniel returned and make her own way back, alone except for Horus. She hadn't lied; she didn't really mind, but she did feel lonely sometimes.

One of these days, he's going to stay too long and not make it back in time. One of these days, he's going to get caught.

She had told him as much once and he had shrugged it off. There were moments when Daniel seemed in low spirits and Calida wondered how he faced each day, staring down such a bleak future and coped with it. Maybe Elle was the answer. Maybe she reminded him of the excitement of what it felt like to be alive and their time together was what he looked forward to.

Calida pushed the thoughts away with a sigh, picked up the discarded tankard of ale on the table and drained the last of it. Fifteen was too young to feel the way she did about the world.

"Is this spot taken?"

She looked up over the rim of the tankard to see a young man standing beside her table, looking down at her. He was a few years older than her, but not quite as old as Daniel, she thought.

He had auburn hair and warm brown eyes, a few freckles standing out against his tanned skin. He wore a loose-fitting white shirt and brown trousers. He had no shoes.

How does he walk about with no shoes? His feet must be as tough as cow leather.

"No," she answered his question, setting the tankard down. "It's not taken."

He grinned, sliding into the seat beside her. "I've seen you here a few times."

"Spying on me, are you?" she asked, giving him a wary look.

"I'm a regular and so are you. That's all. Kind of hard not to notice that hair of yours. Like a brand of fire."

Calida glanced at the hair that fell down her shoulders and draped over her chest. It was slightly curly, thick and unruly. It could be frizzy at times and humidity wreaked havoc on it. She'd never been fond of her hair. Not even the color. Many times, she'd wondered why it couldn't have been a nice blonde like some of the other girls.

But the way this boy spoke of it made her almost proud of it. *A brand of fire.* She liked the sound of that.

Thalia was right. The hair is memorable.

"I'm Calida. What's your name?"

"Jeremy. Jeremy Lussard." The boy held out a hand and Calida shook it. It was rough and calloused.

"Well, Jeremy, what are you doing here on such a fine evening?" Calida had been surprised to see someone so close to her own age in the tavern. Despite his claim to be a regular, she didn't recall having seen him before. But he must have been, if he recognized her.

He smiled easily. "No better place I can think of to be."

He hadn't really answered her question. So he had secrets? That was fine by her. She had secrets she didn't intend to give up either. Her thoughts strayed to the witch-mark on top of her left foot as she kicked that very foot under the table.

Jeremy glanced at the empty tankard. "You want some more?"

"Not really," Calida lied. What she wanted didn't matter when it came to having no money to pay for it.

"I'm buying." He plopped a leather bag down on the table. She heard the coins shift inside and wondered how much was in there.

She side-eyed him for a moment and then shrugged. "All right, then, if you're buying. Why not?"

He grinned and hailed a passing barmaid. "I'm always pleased to buy a pretty girl a drink."

She felt like rolling her eyes at his obvious flirting, but she flushed despite herself. "And you make a habit of that, do you?"

He met her gaze. "I'd like to."

Her stomach suddenly felt as though it had flipped inside out. Damn it, what was happening? Quickly, she decided that she didn't care. He had offered to buy her a free drink and it would be both rude and stupid to refuse.

Soon enough, their orders arrived. Jeremy had ordered food for himself, proclaiming that he was starving, and asked if she wanted anything. Calida had wanted to try some of the fish and as soon as it was set before her, she knew she'd made a wise choice. It smelled heavenly.

"It's fresh," Jeremy said, nodding to it. "Just caught today."

"How do you know?" she asked, digging in. "Are you a fisherman?" Was that how he earned all that money?

"No," he replied.

It was hardly a detailed answer, but it seemed like the truth, at least.

Still… "If you're going to buy me food and drinks, I think we ought to get to know each other, don't you?"

He hesitated mid-chew. "All right. What do you want to know?"

"What do you do for a living?"

"Living? Who says I do anything?"

Calida crossed her arms. "You got all those coins somehow."

"I'm independently wealthy."

His appearance didn't speak of someone who came from a wealthy family, but then again, maybe it was a disguise, allowing him to sneak out without being recognized. Like her own attire.

"What about you?" he asked. "What do you do?"

"I don't…have much of a living," she admitted. They weren't paid during their time at the monastery. The top of her left foot suddenly itched.

"Is your family poor?"

She admired his boldness for asking. Most people would have made the assumption and not confirmed it aloud. Then again, she was the one who insisted they get to know each other, so perhaps she'd brought this on herself.

"Yes." Her family had been poor, working on their farm, and with both daughters now away, she couldn't imagine the workload had become any easier for her parents. What difference her power would have made if she'd only known how to use it at the time.

"My parents are dead," Jeremy said, taking another drink of ale. "I'm my own man now, free to do as I please."

"You're lucky," Calida murmured, then, realizing how that sounded, quickly added, "Being able to do as you please, I mean." How desperately she longed to know what that felt like.

"Suppose I am," he agreed.

They lapsed into silence, finishing their meal. Calida glanced out the window at Horus and pushed her chair back, getting to her feet. "I should be going."

Jeremy also rose. "Can I see you again?"

Calida hesitated. This boy was nice enough and he had given her free food, but she wasn't sure it was wise to get any further involved. She thought briefly of Daniel, still upstairs with Elle. They had a secret to protect, after all. She wondered if he had slipped up and told Elle what he was or if he had done so willingly.

"Come on," Jeremy pleaded, seeing her hesitation. "I don't have many friends and it's not every day I meet a girl like you."

"Like me?" she asked, fearing that he somehow knew. *But that's impossible! How could he know?*

He cocked his head to one side. "Kind. Pretty. Mysterious."

For some reason, it pleased her to know that he thought of her as mysterious. But most of all, pretty. No one had ever thought her pretty before. Or if they had, they hadn't bothered to tell her.

She bit her lip. "Well, I guess it would be all right." So long as she was careful and she was always careful.

He grinned and her stomach did that weird flipping thing again. "Great. I don't know when I'll be here next, but when I am, I'll keep an eye out for you, firebrand."

She nodded, inordinately pleased, and hurried out the door, fetching Horus. She'd stayed longer than she meant to, but she hadn't planned on eating a meal. Still, she would make it back before Daniel.

Lorelei stirred as Calida crept back into the dormitory. "You're late," she whispered.

"I got sidetracked," Calida replied, leaning close so Lorelei could hear. "Go back to sleep."

"Your breath smells like alcohol. I thought Daniel didn't have any money left. How did you get the drinks?"

"Never you mind," Calida retorted, climbing up into her bunk.

"Fine." Lorelei rolled over. "Keep your secrets."

But holding onto her secrets, Calida thought, might be very difficult around a boy like Jeremy Lussard.

She knew it was dangerous to meet with him again, but she had given her word and she intended to keep it. She supposed she couldn't fault Daniel for his sojourns into town anymore; she was hardly better herself.

But there was something thrilling about having a friend outside of the monastery, who had no idea who or what she was, and accepted her anyway. Accepted her as if she were normal. She would just have to be careful not to tell him anything, tempting though it may be.

The first chance she got, Calida sought Thalia out. She wanted to tell her sister about the friend she had made, but didn't want anyone else overhearing. This was something they could share between the two of them. She might tell Lorelei later, but she doubted her friend would be very approving.

Thalia was back on laundry duty, hanging up the wash on the lines that stretched between two of the outbuildings. If any of the teachers had been outraged by the theft of clothes, they hadn't blamed her for it.

Thalia glanced at her, standing up on her tiptoes to pin the clothing to the line. She was as tall as Calida now and for some reason, that made it hard to think of her as the younger sister.

"Why do you look like the cat that got the cream?"

"I went into town last night," Calida replied.

"I know you did. I saw you leave." Thalia gave her a sharp look. "I heard Daniel got back late last night. Someone noticed. He's shrugged it off for now, but he needs to be more careful."

Fat chance of that, Calida thought. *He's infatuated with Elle*.

"Never mind about Daniel," she said. "I met someone at the tavern."

Thalia hadn't lost the wariness in her eyes. "Who?"

"A boy named Jeremy. Jeremy Lussard."

"And what's his claim to fame?"

"I don't know what he does. He didn't tell me. He said his parents were dead and that he's independently wealthy, so I assume he's living off of whatever inheritance he got and doesn't have to work." Calida shrugged. "He bought me dinner."

"And I suppose that was just out of the kindness of his heart," Thalia muttered.

Calida frowned. "Why do you have to be so cynical about everything?"

She sighed. "Isn't it obvious? He wants something from you, Calida. People aren't just nice for no reason."

"Why not? Why can't he just be nice? But actually, you're right. He did want something."

"Whatever it was, I hope you didn't give it to him."

"He wants to be my friend and to see me again. I told him I would." Calida crossed her arms. "You don't have to be like that. If you met him, I think you'd like him. He was nice."

Thalia sighed again. "Maybe I would. Just…be careful around him, all right? He may seem nice, but you don't know anything about him. And whatever you do, don't tell him what you really are."

"I don't need a lecture," Calida snapped. *Especially not one from my little sister.* What did Thalia think she was, stupid? "I just thought you'd like to know, but obviously I was wrong."

She spun around and stalked off, leaving Thalia to finish hanging up the laundry, where she would then blow it dry with the wind.

Despite her confidence, Thalia's words lodged stubbornly in her mind, the niggling doubt refusing to go away. What if her sister was right and Jeremy had only been kind to her because he wanted something? What if this was his way of charming her, patiently waiting until she came to trust him and let her guard down? Would he want to know who she really was or was there something else he was after?

Calida wasn't exactly naïve. She knew how some men could be and that there was only ever one thing that sort wanted from a woman. She hoped Thalia was wrong about Jeremy, but if she wasn't and he did want something from her that she wasn't prepared to give, she'd put him in his place and never see him again.

Her doubts didn't keep her away. The next time Daniel snuck into town, Calida went with him. Nearly a whole week had passed since they'd last gone, Daniel having abandoned his previous schedule that coincided with Elle's shifts.

"I didn't want to push it," he explained as they walked. "After what happened last time."

"What did happen? Thalia told me a little, but not all of it."

Daniel grimaced. "Arin caught me as I was coming back. I told him I'd been at the wash house, but I don't know if he believed me. I think he knew I'd been gone for a while."

Damn that Arin. "He needs to mind his own business," Calida growled.

"*I* need to be more careful," Daniel admitted. "I'm sure he'd like nothing more than to catch me sneaking out—or back in."

"He didn't see you leave this time, did he?" Calida asked, slightly alarmed. She cast a glance over her shoulder but could see no one.

Of course there wouldn't be anyone. She didn't think Arin the type to follow after them out of curiosity to see where they were going. As soon as he saw them leave, he'd run straight to the headmistress's quarters and rat them out.

"*No one saw us*," Horus murmured to her. She knew the way into town by heart now and there was no need for him to fly ahead, so he rode on her shoulder.

"No," Daniel answered. "He was sound asleep when I left."

"With all the traveling we do at night, it's a pity you're not an owl," Calida added to the hawk. He ruffled his feathers indignantly. She turned back to Daniel. "I wonder if I could mix up a concoction of herbs to drug him with. To make sure he stays asleep."

"You could always try."

The idea had a certain appeal and Calida couldn't claim that she wasn't the least bit tempted.

The tavern came into view and her pulse quickened in anticipation. Would Jeremy be there? Was he waiting for her right now?

She had told Daniel about him, of course, but Jeremy hadn't met Daniel. She followed him over to their usual table and Elle soon came over to join them. Elle chastised Daniel for not coming sooner and he gave her some excuse as to why he had been unable to visit, but Calida wasn't listening. She craned her neck, scanning the tavern for any sign of her new friend, but couldn't spot him in the crowd.

Her heart sank. Perhaps he wouldn't be here. Maybe he wasn't as eager to see her as she had thought.

Elle brought Daniel a drink and he offered to share it with Calida, but she didn't want anything. The idea of traveling into town simply for a drink had lost its appeal. She wasn't here for that. Soon enough, Daniel retreated upstairs with Elle, leaving Calida alone.

Why would she think Jeremy would be here? Why would he come back for someone like her?

"Why the long face?"

She looked up and suddenly he was there, smiling down at her.

"There you are!" she exclaimed. "I didn't think you were coming."

"I just waited for your friend to leave," he said, nodding toward the stairs Daniel and Elle had taken. "Truth be told, I wasn't sure *you* were coming. I kept an eye out for you the past couple nights, but you never came."

"Sorry. My friend—" Calida had been about to say *got a little careless*, but that was coming too close to the truth of what they were. It would sound strange. "We always come together," she amended quickly. "And I was waiting for him."

Jeremy looked at her strangely. "Your friend…there's nothing between the two of you, is there?"

Calida flushed. "What? Skies, no." The idea was absurd. "You just saw him leave. He's infatuated with that barmaid."

He laughed, a pleasant sound, and immediately Calida wanted him to do it again. "Well that's one way to put it." He sat down next to her. "Can I get you anything?"

She wanted to try some dessert this time around and ordered a slice of peach pie. It was easily the most delicious thing she had ever tasted and she forced herself to eat slowly, savoring every bite.

Calida pushed her empty plate aside, wishing she could enjoy such food every night. "You spoil me, Jeremy Lussard."

He grinned. "My pleasure." His smile faded and he stood. "Come with me. There's something I want to show you before you have to go."

Warily, Calida pushed to her feet, Thalia's words of warning ringing in her ears. "Where are we going?"

"For a walk. Just down to the docks."

"All right."

She had been down to the docks briefly herself, the first night they had ventured into town. How dangerous could it be to go with him? She had trained to be a soldier after all, and he was ordinary, not a drop of magic. She should be able to handle him easily enough, should it come to that.

Still, she kept her wits about her, aware of her surroundings as she followed him outside into the humid night air. Horus glanced at them from his post as they walked by and followed, sticking to rooftops, but always somewhere nearby.

Jeremy strolled along confidently, as if he owned the place. She noticed he moved with an odd, flowing kind of gait. She had never had cause to notice it before, since they had always been sitting in the tavern.

Calida had to admit that Alara at night certainly was beautiful, with palm trees swaying in the wind, the windows glowing with warm light, and the heat of the day having fallen away.

Jeremy followed her gaze. "It's beautiful, isn't it?"

Slightly startled that he'd noticed her staring, she nodded. "I don't often get to come here."

"Neither do I," she said.

He looked at her with those brown eyes and she quickly glanced away, looking at the ships along the dock, all of varying sizes.

Jeremy stopped suddenly, standing before one of them. "Here we are."

"What is it?" Immediately, Calida felt foolish. It was a ship, but she didn't know why he had wanted to show it to her.

Fortunately, he seemed to understand what she meant. "This is what I wanted to show you. My ship. The *Sea Witch*."

The name felt oddly appropriate, she thought, given the circumstances, although it suited Thalia better than her.

"I like it," she said. She didn't know much about ships, but she thought it was a schooner, with two masts. She liked the look of it, at any rate.

"Well I say 'my ship', but it's not mine. I'm just part of the crew."

She turned away from the ship to face him. "So you're a sailor, then?"

"That's right." Jeremy inhaled a deep lungful of the salty air. "One day, I'll be captain of my own ship, just you wait and see. But for now, I'm just a younker."

"A what?"

"The youngest of the foremast men."

"I don't know anything about sailing," Calida confessed. "What's it like?"

"The greatest thing you could imagine," he said softly, a reverence to his voice. "Unless you've actually done it, there's no way to know what it's like. There are no words to describe it. If I could, I'd take you with me, so you could see for yourself, but I don't think my crew would approve."

Calida wanted so desperately to go, she almost begged him. But what would she tell the others? What would they think if she just disappeared? She couldn't do that to any of them. She couldn't leave Thalia.

"Why not?" she asked instead.

"Well, practically speaking, you don't know anything about sailing and so you'd just be underfoot and in the way. Plus, you'd be another mouth to feed. On the not-so-practical side, sailors tend to be a superstitious lot. Bad luck to bring a woman on board."

"That's not true!" she exclaimed.

Jeremy held up his hands. "I didn't say I believed it." But she could see the laughter in his eyes and knew he understood she wasn't offended by him.

"Some of the sky witches on board Alaran ships are women," she pointed out.

She nearly added *My sister will be one of them someday*, before catching herself.

The amusement faded from his expression. "Aye. That's what I mean."

Calida didn't know what he meant, but she thought it best not to press him. The topic had already strayed into dangerous waters.

He shoved his hands in his pockets. "Well, this is my last night in port. At dawn, we shove off."

"Where are you going?"

"Wherever the wind takes us." He shrugged easily. "It's not up to me. But I wanted to tell you that I won't be back here for a while."

"When will you be back?" The thought of not seeing him made her chest ache.

"I don't know. I wish I could give you a better answer. I will come back, but I don't know when and I don't expect you to wait for me."

"Of course I'll wait for you." He was her only friend and connection outside of the monastery. There was no way she'd let such a precious thing slip through her fingers.

He smiled. "I'm glad to hear it. The food at sea isn't nearly as good as it is here. When I come back, we'll eat better than the king himself."

Calida laughed. "I'll hold you to that."

Jeremy stepped closer, reaching out to tuck a stray strand of hair behind her ear. "There's something about you, firebrand, that I can't put my finger on. You're a mystery to me."

A little thrill went through her at how true his words were, at how much he didn't know. A reckless, irrational urge came over her to confess what she was this very moment. To tell him.

She fought it down, but that didn't make the temptation go away. It remained, beneath the surface, gnawing at her. She wondered how long she would be able to resist.

"I'll think about you," he murmured, "while I'm away. Counting the days until I can see you again."

"I'll be here," she breathed.

Jeremy lifted her hand to his lips. "Until then."

He turned and walked up the gangplank onto his ship. He gave her one last glance over his shoulder and then he was gone, vanishing below decks, leaving her standing on the dock, already missing him.

You're a fool, some sensible part of her mind warned her. But if this was what it felt like to be foolish, then Calida never wanted to be anything different.

She looked up at the *Sea Witch*'s rigging, stretching far above her head, the furled sails all but motionless in the breeze. She took in every detail, wanting to remember it, and then turned away, heading back toward the monastery.

CHAPTER 9

Days turned into weeks as Calida waited for Jeremy to return. Weeks became months and still he did not appear. She tried to be patient, reminding herself that he had warned her that he hadn't known how long he would be away or when he would come back. But the longer time stretched on, the harder it became to wait—or have faith that he would return at all.

The trips into town that she had grown to look forward to lost all their appeal. Each time she went, Calida told herself that this would be the one. She would walk through the door and there he would be, but it never happened. Eventually, she kept looking, but without any real hope that he would be there. And he never was.

She wandered down by the dock, scanning the ships moored there for any sign of the *Sea Witch* but did not see it. Laying in her bunk at night, her mind imagined all sorts of horrible fates that could have befallen him and the ship, preventing him from returning.

What if the *Sea Witch* had run into a storm and sunk and he had drowned or at the very least, was shipwrecked somewhere, on a desolate island that no one knew about? What if he had been attacked by the pirates that continued to plague Alara? What if he had fallen victim to some illness and was never coming back to see her?

The worst fears she preferred not to think about at all, but they still managed to creep up on her in the middle of the night, the more time went on.

What if he had lied to her and he was never coming back?

What if he had somehow learned what she really was and was repulsed or afraid of her? That one, she knew deep down, was ridiculous, but that didn't stop her from wondering and worrying.

By the end of her fourth year, she had all but given up on Jeremy Lussard.

Slowly, she didn't think about him as much as she used to. Calida put him out of her mind and went about her other tasks. When she wanted to be alone, she climbed the trees down by the river and lay among their branches, watching the sun go down and ignoring anyone calling for her.

It was Daniel's last year at the monastery. At the end of that year, when they all moved up, he would move on to his placement and they would likely never see him again. All of their spare time seemed to be spent together.

When she couldn't fall asleep, Calida sent Horus out into the world and practiced linking her vision with his, wanting to be able to see farther.

He made it all the way up to the palace itself, perching on a window sill, peering within. It was hard to see much of it at night; the curtains had been drawn and everywhere were forbidding stone walls, meant to keep people like her out. But occasionally, through Horus, she glimpsed someone walking by, dressed in silk finery more elegant than anything Calida could have imagined. Any conversations that took place within were beyond her hearing, but she eagerly took in all that she saw, a window to another world.

What she wanted most was to catch a glimpse of the king or queen. Or perhaps even the prince, who was supposed to be close to her own age, but she saw none of them on any of Horus's visits.

The longer the journey, the stronger his wings and their connection became. One night, Calida began sending him out to search for the *Sea Witch*. It was a fool's errand, she knew. The Atlas Sea was vast and Horus couldn't traverse its entirety in the span of one night, never mind the fact that he would be forced to stop and rest at some point and out on the open sea, there was no place to land.

He went as far as he dared, but there was no sign of the ship that Jeremy Lussard had been so proud to show her.

Calida remembered standing at the dock, looking out over the sea, and wondering about Amberleigh, the pirate haven just out of view. What must such a place look like? She knew better than to go there herself—if such a thing were even possible—but the hawk could, under the cover of darkness and then she could see it for herself.

It seemed a better plan than sending her familiar back up to the palace or out to search for the *Sea Witch* again. The open ocean became quite dull to look at after a while, in the dark.

Calida closed her eyes and lay in bed, waiting, watching as Horus approached the island. Slowly, it grew larger until it wasn't so small in the distance and details began to come into view.

Even after dark, the island was a flurry of activity. Wooden or brick buildings lined the streets and alleyways. The windows of the buildings and lanterns on the ships were lit golden. Calida wished she could hear and smell everything that Horus could. She found herself imagining what it must smell like—probably something like the port town that she so often snuck off to, but somehow wilder. And for some reason, she imagined that there was music playing somewhere.

It didn't seem like such a strange assumption when Horus spotted a few people, arm in arm, twirling in circles in the street. It didn't look at all as lawless as she had imagined it would. The people that she could see looked ordinary enough, like someone she could walk past in town.

There was a much greater variety of ships docked at Amberleigh. Where there were mostly merchantmen at the harbor in town, here there were all sorts. Schooners and sloops and even a few frigates. None of them flew a pirate flag and if they weren't docked at Amberleigh, Calida wouldn't have known they were pirates at all, though she guessed that was kind of the point.

Her gaze swept over the ships hungrily, taking in the dark hulls and furled canvas, raking over the block and tackle, counting the masts. Any one of them could have taken her anywhere in the world.

Horus suddenly stopped looking around, as if he had spotted something, and he banked sharply, pulling Calida's attention away. Her heart seized in her chest and she thought it might stop altogether when she realized what she was looking at.

The *Sea Witch* was one of the ships anchored along the dock. What was it doing, here, in the very last place she expected to see it? Had her fear been true, that the crew had been attacked and the ship captured by pirates? Was the *Sea Witch* now a sea wolf?

It looked exactly as it had before, but that was no indication.

Horus flew up to the foremast, perching on one of the furled sails, peering down at the deck below. A few men remained on board, sitting together, playing cards, but they weren't familiar to Calida. She couldn't say whether they were members of Jeremy's crew or not. She had never met any of the crew.

The hawk looked up at one of the buildings near the dock as the door swung open. Warm light spilled out and a group of men stepped into the night. Calida didn't recognize any of them.

Or so she thought.

Suddenly, there he was. Jeremy Lussard followed after the other men, one arm slung around the shoulders of another young man beside him. From the way they walked, she could tell they'd been drinking. But rather than looking frightened to be in the company of pirates, Jeremy seemed at ease. He was laughing, judging from his expression.

He's one of them, she realized, watching the group board the *Sea Witch*. He'd told her that he was a sailor, when he was really a pirate. Although, she supposed he hadn't lied. He just hadn't told her the whole truth.

Calida opened her eyes, severing the connection, not wanting to see anymore. A pirate. Her friend was a pirate, a scourge on the kingdom that she would be expected to serve and protect upon graduation.

Part of her felt hurt that he hadn't told her, though she knew why. He was a criminal and his crime carried a death sentence if he were caught. Hanging. She wouldn't wish that on him—the Jeremy she knew was too kind for something so cruel—but she was beginning to wonder if she really knew him at all. Or was the Jeremy she knew merely a façade?

And to think she had been tempted to tell him that she was a witch. As a mark of trust and a sign of friendship, she had *wanted* to confide her most important secret to him. The only secret that mattered, really.

All this time, he had been hiding an equally deadly secret from her. *Well, perhaps his secret is the more deadly one.*

Now Calida understood why he hadn't returned. She wasn't sure how he had ever come to be in town to begin with. It must be a great risk for a pirate ship to pull right up into an Alaran harbor. What if someone recognized it?

She squeezed her eyes shut, but didn't try to reconnect with Horus again. She felt tears stinging behind her eyelids. No doubt the hawk was already on his way back, having felt the whirlwind of emotions now battering Calida.

Thalia was right. Jeremy hadn't been who she thought he was.

* * *

Her newfound knowledge didn't stop her from continuing to venture into town with Daniel. She still searched for Jeremy each time, now with a mixture of anticipation—which she found both puzzling and annoying—and dread of what would happen if she did see him. What would she say to him? What would he say? The fact that some part of her still wanted to see him, even knowing what he was, irritated her.

She decided she wouldn't mention anything about what she had seen. In fact, she wouldn't mention pirates at all. If she told him that she knew he was a pirate, that would require explaining how she had come by such information and that was an explanation she couldn't give him.

Her fifth year was now halfway over. Calida was sixteen and no longer all angles the way she had once been. She just wondered how long it would take her treacherous heart to stop yearning for Jeremy to come back, how long it would take before her thoughts no longer strayed in his direction.

"Have you squared things with Elle yet?" Calida asked as she and Daniel made their way into town one night.

At the end of the year, he would have to leave and likely wouldn't see the barmaid again. It would be cruel to simply run off and abandon her without telling her something. At the very least, even though he couldn't tell her the truth, he needed to find some way of bringing their relationship, or whatever it was, to an end.

He grimaced. "Not yet."

"Do you love her?" Calida asked bluntly. What even was love and did anyone truly know? She certainly felt like she didn't.

Then again, she had always said that Daniel was infatuated with the barmaid, which hardly implied anything lasting and serious. She was beginning to see that she had allowed herself to fall into the same trap. She hadn't known Jeremy well enough to truly fall in love with him.

She had been infatuated by the attention, the excitement of meeting someone new. Such a thing had never happened to her before and she hadn't known how to react or what to make of it. In the moment, it had seemed like something so much more than it was, but now, in hindsight and with months of separation to look back on, she saw more clearly.

"I like her," Daniel replied. "But I don't know if I love her."

"Then you don't," Calida said. "If you loved her, you would know."

He swallowed, looking away. "I'll end things with her tonight, then. I planned on waiting until the end of the year, but you're right. There's no point in delaying the inevitable. We have no hope of a future together anyway."

"I guess you won't be coming back after tonight, then."

"No." He looked at her. "Will you?"

"I don't know," Calida said honestly.

Perhaps it would be best to leave things the way they were. Her time with Jeremy, short as it was, had been fun. She wanted to remember their relationship as it had been and not risk ruining it. But at the same time, she wanted…

What did she want? Answers? An explanation?

All she knew was that she wanted something she didn't currently have. Something that was missing. And she would likely keep on wanting it until she did something about it.

They entered the tavern and Elle came straight over to their table, the same as always. Daniel got to his feet, taking her hands in his, and led her upstairs. Whatever conversation they were about to have, and however it went, it was something to be done in private. Calida didn't think it would go well and she felt a pang of sympathy for Daniel. He had done this to himself, but then, she knew a little something about what that felt like.

She glanced up and froze. Jeremy Lussard was walking toward her, meeting her gaze. He was even taller than he had been all those months ago when they had first met and there was stubble along his jaw. His auburn hair was longer and it fell in waves to his shoulders. In a way, she barely recognized him, but the eyes and easy smile were the same.

"There she is," he said, taking a seat beside her. "The firebrand. I didn't think you'd be here. It's been so long."

"It has," Calida said. Her hands shook and so she hid them beneath the table, in her lap. "I said I would wait for you."

"And here you are. I'm sorry it took so long. It wasn't safe for me to come."

If she hadn't sent Horus to Amberleigh and linked vision with him, Calida would have had no idea what that statement meant. But now, she had a pretty good idea. *I'll bet it wasn't safe.*

"Well," she said weakly. "You're here now."

"I'd hoped you would wait." He reached into his pocket. "I have something for you." He withdrew a small box, offering it to her.

Calida took it slowly, easing the lid open. Inside lay a blue stone. Even in the dim light of the tavern, it shone darkly, glinting like blue fire.

She lifted the stone out. "What is it?"

"A sapphire."

A real sapphire. This small stone was more valuable and expensive than anything her family had ever owned. And Jeremy was *giving* it to *her.*

"Where did you get it?" she asked, thinking she likely knew the answer, but she wanted to hear what he had to say.

Jeremy hesitated. For a moment, she thought he might try to claim that it had belonged to his family and was part of the inheritance she had once believed he had. *Independently wealthy indeed.*

"I acquired it," he said, with an easy shrug. "I have my ways."

Some of Calida's disappointment must have shown on her face. She had hoped he would admit the truth on his own. She placed the stone back in the box.

He frowned. "You don't like it?"

"I don't like being lied to."

He raked a hand through his hair. "I want to tell you the truth, Calida. I wanted to tell you the last time I saw you, but I didn't know if I could trust you. You waited for me, when it didn't seem like I would ever return. You waited when most people would have given up. You trusted me to come back when you had no reason to think I would, other than my word. I think that's worth some trust in return."

Calida held her breath. Was he about to tell her the truth after all?

Jeremy stood. "But not here. Come with me."

Calida closed the box again and took it with her, warily following him outside. They made their way along the docks again, past the rows of ships, until they came to the *Sea Witch*. The ship looked exactly the same as it had every other time Calida laid eyes on it, but it was somehow different looking at it now, knowing what it was.

Jeremy stopped, looking up at his ship, hands in his pockets. "I haven't been completely honest. The *Sea Witch* isn't a merchantman. She's a pirate and so is every man on board. Including me."

Calida released a breath. She'd been breathing shallowly without even realizing it, waiting to hear the fateful words. She took a deep breath, the tension easing out of her.

He had told her the truth, of his own volition, when he didn't have to. He had trusted her enough to impart such dangerous information, trusting that she wouldn't run off to the nearest magistrate or royal guard and turn him in.

Did his faith in her deserve some trust in return?

She made a decision. "I know," she said softly.

Jeremy looked stunned. "You knew? How?"

With a quick glance around to make sure no one was paying them any mind, Calida reached down and slipped her left shoe off, revealing the witch-mark on the top of her foot. She whistled, holding up one arm, and Horus launched himself off of one of the nearby rooftops, soaring over to land on her arm.

From the look on his face, she knew she didn't have to say the words aloud, but she did anyway. "I'm a witch. This is Horus, my familiar. I sent him to Amberleigh because I wanted to see what it looked like. I linked my vision with his, allowing me to see what he sees. And I saw you."

"Ah," he said, voice quiet.

Calida slipped her shoe back on, shaking slightly, feeling as if she were naked in front of him. Was that all he had to say? She had expected… Well, she didn't know what she had expected exactly, but it wasn't this.

"Are you…" she started to ask, but her voice trailed off, unsure of how to finish the question. *Are you afraid of me? Angry? Repulsed?*

Already, she regretted confiding in him.

She tried again, her voice nearly a whisper. "What are you thinking?" *Say something!*

Jeremy exhaled softly. "I'm not fond of sky witches. No pirate is. The kingdom sends them out on board their warships. They can sink our ship from a distance, without a fair engagement."

"I'm an earth witch," Calida said. It was the first time she felt a little bit proud not to be a sky witch. "My power is useless at sea. Earth witches can only use their power on land, but all a sky witch has to do is be able to see the sky. It's not fair. Nothing about any of this is fair."

"You live at the Erlohn monastery?"

She nodded.

He cocked his head to the side. "You were taking quite a risk, then, whenever you snuck out to see me."

She felt herself blush slightly, heat rising to her cheeks. "Yes."

"And this last time, despite my long absence and the fact that you already knew I was a pirate, you came anyway."

"I've never met a pirate before. I've heard a lot of things, but I can't judge all pirates based on you. And I also can't judge you based on all pirates."

"Well, then I suppose I shouldn't judge you based on other witches."

"I'd still like to be friends," Calida said. "If you want to."

Jeremy hesitated. He must have realized that anything more between them would be impossible because he said, "I'd like that."

Calida sighed in relief.

He grinned. "I knew there was something different about you, firebrand." He sat down on the edge of the dock, his legs dangling over. "Tell me about life at the monastery."

And so she did, explaining that none of their destinies were their own, the various gifts that each of them had and how they were expected to use it for the betterment of the kingdom.

In return, he told her of his life as a pirate. Calida listened to every word, imagining for a moment that such a life were her own.

When it came time for them to part ways, Jeremy got to his feet and helped her up. "Are you sure I can't convince you to run away with me? Life at the monastery sounds horrid."

"It can be," Calida replied, not wanting to admit how tempted she was by his offer. "But I don't think my sister would come with me and I can't leave her."

"I understand." He released her hands. "Will you still come into town?"

"Yes. I'll keep coming until I can't anymore."

He smiled at her. "Good luck."

Calida glanced over her shoulder at him as she walked away, knowing in the back of her mind that this could be the last time they saw each other. She could be caught sneaking out of the monastery at any time and there were too many dangers out at sea to name.

Part of her still felt strangely giddy. He knew what she was and he hadn't cared. He still wanted to be friends and accepted her as she was. Still, there was no way she could tell her friends what she had done. They would think her foolish.

They each knew the other's deepest secret now and would take it with them to the grave.

Daniel was waiting for her outside the tavern when she returned. "Ready to go?"

She nodded.

"Where have you been?"

"By the docks," she answered, not wanting to elaborate. She changed the subject. "How did things go with Elle?" Jeremy's sudden appearance had nearly made her forget Daniel was supposed to be ending things with Elle.

Judging from the red mark on his face, she guessed Elle hadn't taken too kindly to the news.

"She's upset. And confused, as you can imagine."

"You didn't tell her the truth, did you?"

"No. I couldn't. It's better for her this way."

Calida wasn't sure she agreed. It would have been better for Elle—for both of them, really—if they'd never gotten involved with each other in the first place. But it was too late for that now and it would be callous to point it out. What was done was done and there was nothing for it now but to move on.

"Maybe it's cruel," he murmured as they set out, "but I'm glad that I got to know her."

Calida hoped that Elle would come to feel the same one day.

CHAPTER 10

She continued to see Jeremy, though Daniel no longer went into town with her, and the times that Jeremy was in port were few and far between. When he did appear, they spent nearly the whole night catching up on everything that had happened since they'd last seen each other.

A few of the other students at the monastery had graduated early, pushed through, no doubt, at the insistence of the crown, but Daniel wasn't one of them. He had to finish out his final year, waiting until the last day before he would leave the monastery behind forever. But that day, far off as it may have once seemed, crept up on them slowly.

Two weeks before he was set to graduate, Lorelei proposed an idea that shocked Calida.

"I think we should have a picnic," she declared. "A sort of going away celebration."

"Where are we going to get the food for that?" Mordred asked.

"I thought we could take it from the kitchens," Lorelei confessed. "And anything else we needed, we could take from the vineyards or orchards."

Calida looked at her friend in surprise, but it was Thalia who said what she'd been thinking.

"Stealing?" Thalia remarked. "I wouldn't have thought you had it in you."

Lorelei blushed. "Normally not. I wouldn't suggest it for no reason. But we don't have much time left together and I want to make it special."

Calida turned to Daniel. "What do you think?"

Not having gone into town, he hadn't been able to enjoy the food there in quite some time. Calida wouldn't have been able to either, but Jeremy had given her some money, to be spent sparingly until he returned. She felt slightly guilty about spending it, knowing it was most likely stolen, but if he had taken it from Alaran ships, she was just giving it back to the Alaran people, so she didn't feel *too* bad.

The first few times she had returned to the tavern without Daniel, Elle had shot her looks of contempt and refused to serve her table. Calida hadn't done anything to her, but Elle remembered her association with Daniel.

"You don't have to go to all that trouble," Daniel answered, breaking into her thoughts. "But if you want to…why not? There never has been much here to enjoy. Let's make the most of it."

Under the cover of darkness that night, when the kitchens would be deserted, Calida and Lorelei snuck out of the dormitory. They had decided that the fewer people who went, the better. Any more and they might be noticed. They would be quick and efficient, grabbing whatever they could find, and getting out.

"It's so dark," Lorelei murmured, letting out a muffled curse as she rammed her toe into a chair leg.

"We can't risk a light," Calida whispered, though she didn't know why she was whispering. There was no one to hear. "Someone might see. What are we looking for?"

"Anything that might be good for a picnic." Lorelei began rummaging around in one of the cupboards. "Look at this!"

She pulled out a large bundle and in the dim light, Calida saw it was a block of hard cheese.

"That'll be perfect."

"Why didn't we think of doing this before?" Lorelei asked, speaking to no one in particular. "We could have eaten like royalty long before now!"

Calida silently agreed. It wasn't that the food they were served in the mess hall was bad; they just didn't get enough of it at one time and for growing teenagers, that was a problem.

They found a loaf of bread and some jam, a few slices of ham, apples, and a sausage roll. Lorelei let out a gasp from the other side of the room and Calida rushed over to her side.

"What is it?"

She gasped herself as she saw what Lorelei had found. The best yet. It was a pie of some sort—impossible to tell what kind in the dark—and only one piece was thus far missing. It was nearly entirely whole.

"It's almost as good as a whole pie," Lorelei said, picking up the dish.

"You're taking the whole thing?"

"Of course. I don't do anything by half-measures."

In the vineyards the next day, when the instructor wasn't watching, Calida pocketed as many grapes as her tunic would hold—without causing the pockets to bulge conspicuously. Last night, after leaving the kitchen, she and Lorelei had stashed the pilfered food down by the river, leaving Horus, Jade, and Lorelei's familiar, Penny, to stand guard and make sure no other animals or thieving humans took any.

By the time evening arrived, everything was ready. They spread an old blanket on the bank of the river and sorted the spoils.

Everything was delicious, possibly made all the more so by the fact that it had been stolen and they had gotten away with it. But they couldn't entirely forget the reason they were here and a somber mood fell over the little party.

"Does anyone want the last piece of sausage?" Mordred asked, fidgeting uncomfortably. They could all feel the change in mood and no one particularly wanted to address it. And yet, they couldn't ignore it forever.

"Go ahead," Lorelei answered, reaching for the pie. "I hope this is as good as it looks."

She had only taken three bites before she let out a sob and tears started rolling down her face.

"Does it really taste that terrible?" Thalia asked.

"It's not that," Lorelei sniffed. She turned to Daniel. "I'm going to miss you when you've gone."

They all would, Calida thought. This small group were all the friends she had at the monastery and it would soon be even smaller. Life at the monastery wasn't easy, skies knew, but the group of people around her had made it a little bit brighter.

"I don't want to stay here forever," Daniel admitted. "But I can't say that I'm terribly excited to be moving on to my placement either. I'll miss you all, of course, but we all know that nothing can stay the same forever."

"Maybe it won't be as bad as you think and you'll be happier than you are here," Mordred suggested.

"I hope so."

"I'm happy for you," Thalia said. "I can't wait to leave this place behind."

"That day seems like it will never come," Daniel remarked. "But it arrives faster than you think, trust me."

He was right, of course, and in fewer than two weeks' time, the Erlohn monastery saw another year of its students graduate and Daniel was gone. Calida and Lorelei were now the oldest in their group, both seventeen.

Another year had come and gone.

* * *

Thalia found herself increasingly bored at the monastery. She had never liked Daniel overmuch, but things were undeniably—if it were possible—even more dull without him. She knew Calida still snuck off to town on her own and while Thalia didn't approve, she knew it provided a much-needed diversion from the monotony of life at the monastery.

Sometimes, she wished she could sneak away too, but she had no friend waiting for her in town. Calida hadn't spoken of the boy she had met after the initial conversation they'd had about it, but Thalia assumed she must have still been meeting with him. Why else would her sister go? What was waiting for her in town that she hadn't already seen a million times? Things changed there about as often as they did at the monastery.

But she knew better than to go into town or do anything that might risk her place. The excitement could come after she graduated. Until then, she just had to be patient no matter how hard it was. Her instructor had told her that she was well on her way to graduating a year early and she would do nothing to jeopardize that.

There was one thing, however, that kept nagging at Thalia and refused to go away no matter how hard she tried to ignore it. She wanted to achieve a placement on board one of the naval ships, protecting it from harm. A life on the sea was what awaited her, but other than the brief glimpse she'd had the night they'd all snuck into town, she had no idea what the sea looked like.

It was one thing to know what it looked like and another entirely to know what it felt and tasted like. Thalia wanted to go down to the beach and if her sister was willing to sneak into the same town time and time again, why shouldn't she be willing to go along with Thalia's idea, which seemed so much better in her mind?

The first chance she got to mention it to Calida, Mordred wasn't with them, but Lorelei was. That irritated Thalia slightly; she would have preferred it to be just her and her sister, but she couldn't bring it up without Lorelei also hearing and so she would be forced to invite her along as well.

Never mind. It will be a girls' night out at the beach.

"You want to go to the beach?" Calida asked. From her tone, it was impossible to know what she thought of the idea.

"Yes," Thalia replied. "I don't see why we shouldn't. We can all go, just the three of us, and make it a girls' night out."

"That does sound fun," Lorelei admitted. "Other than the night we all snuck out together, I've never seen the sea before. I grew up miles away from it."

"It's no more dangerous than you sneaking into town," Thalia told Calida. "In fact, it's probably safer. There are loads of people in town, what with it being so close to the harbor. There won't be anyone at the beach at night."

Calida hesitated for a few moments before finally coming to a decision. "I guess it wouldn't hurt." She said it casually, but Thalia could tell that she was just as excited by the prospect as the rest of them.

It didn't take as long to reach the Atlas Sea as it did to reach the town, giving them more time to enjoy themselves. They crossed the river where it ran shallow at their favorite spot, making their way through the woods until it began to thin, sand appearing beneath their feet. Breaking free of the tree line, Thalia stepped out onto soft white sand, stretching out before her until it met the sea. There was no one that she could see; they had the place all to themselves, just as she'd predicted. The only sound was the breeze in the trees and the ocean as its waves rolled lazily ashore.

"It's beautiful," Lorelei murmured. "It looks like it goes on forever."

It's powerful, Thalia thought. She could feel the water stretching out before her, vast and unknowable. Calm for now, but easily incited to wrath.

She reached down, slipping her shoes off, and ran down toward the water, her bare feet sinking into the wet sand. She scurried back quickly as the wave approached before stepping forward again, a dance only she and the sea knew. It sang in her blood, unlike the others, forever bound to the earth.

The next time, she didn't step back, allowing the warm water to wash over her feet.

She'd never seen so much water in her life. The wind tugged at her hair, whispering to her, the sky clear overhead. Never had she felt so powerful, in awe of the world and her place in it.

Thalia inhaled deeply, wanting to be out on the sea instead of stuck on land. This was her power. This was where she belonged.

The familiars—Horus, Jade, and Penny—had remained on land, but the others had taken their shoes off as well and Lorelei hiked up her leggings, splashing through the surf. The water was so clear, Thalia could see the bottom for a good distance before it was finally obscured by the depths.

Calida walked up to her, the ends of her tunic trailing in the water. "Remember that time we played in the river?"

Thalia smirked. "You mean the time you said you wanted to go fishing?" It seemed liked forever ago.

"I still think I could have caught some."

"I don't think so," Thalia said haughtily.

"Oh, really?" Calida scooped her hand through the water, playfully flicking it at her.

"Are you sure you want to play this game?"

"I think I could win."

"Oh, really?" Thalia replied, throwing her sister's words back at her.

There was no need to pretend here, with just the three of them. Thalia gave into the urge, calling upon her power, feeling it rush through her, as the water around Calida tossed and writhed. Calida threw herself to the side, avoiding the wave that tried to sweep over her. She was reduced to striking the water with her arm in order to splash Thalia, but she wielded it with surprising precision.

"Ugh!" Thalia gasped, spitting water out of her mouth. "It tastes awful!"

It was so salty that, in a way, it no longer tasted anything like salt. There were no words for it.

Calida cackled. "Got you!"

Thalia pushed the wet strands of hair out of her face and lunged toward her sister, which wasn't easy with water around her knees. Calida shrieked and took off running, occasionally turning around to send a splash back at Thalia.

Thalia followed for a while, amused by the chase, but Calida was quickly overcome, disappearing beneath a wave that washed her back up on shore where she lay, soaked to the skin and panting.

"All right, I think that's enough."

Thalia glanced at Lorelei. The other girl had watched them for a time, then turned her attention to the various shells that washed up on shore, picking through them and pocketing the most attractive ones.

She waded out further into the water, peering down at the bottom. "That one's really pretty," she pointed.

Thalia followed her gaze. A small shell winked back up at her, the moonlight reflecting off its unusual blue and green coloring. It was as if the color of the sea itself had been painted onto it and Thalia had to admit that it was pretty.

"Go get it, then."

Lorelei frowned. "I can't swim."

Thalia turned back to the shell. It was clear that Lorelei fancied it and Thalia couldn't resist the opportunity to show off, having kept her power mostly a secret all the years she'd spent at the monastery.

The water swirled around the shell, dislodging the sand at the bottom and pushing it to the surface. Lorelei reached down and snatched it up, looking at Thalia in awe.

"Thank you."

Thalia shrugged. She'd done something that neither of them could ever do and Lorelei knew it.

Lorelei's monkey, Penny, had waded a little way into the surf, eager to see what her mistress had found. Lorelei walked back and leaned down, showing the shell to her familiar.

"Isn't it pretty?"

Penny nodded enthusiastically and reached for it.

Lorelei handed it to her. "Here. You keep ahold of it for me."

The monkey let out a screech of what must have been joy and jumped along the surf. Jade yipped and bounded after her, the fox easily keeping pace. Horus, wanting nothing to do with the water, soared above them in lazy circles, no doubt keeping an eye out for any potential trouble.

Suddenly, Thalia wanted something of her own to remember the evening by. She began searching for something as lovely or interesting as the shell Lorelei had found, but nothing caught her eye and she started to regret giving it to her.

They kept walking, picking up whatever caught their eye, leaving footprints in the sand. Thalia had no idea how long they'd been out or what time it was when Horus suddenly let out a shriek of warning.

Thalia turned to Calida, unable to hear what the hawk might be saying.

"He said there's someone up ahead," Calida answered the unspoken question.

Lorelei clutched her shells. "But you said there wouldn't be anyone here!"

Thalia bristled at her accusing tone, as if the intrusion were somehow her fault. "It's probably just a couple, out for a romantic stroll. Come on." She strode forward.

"What are you doing?" Lorelei exclaimed.

"It wouldn't hurt to take a look. But you can run back to the monastery if you're scared."

Lorelei frowned. "I'm not scared."

"Then come on."

They were witches, after all, and they each had their familiar with them. What was there to be scared of?

The earth curved inward up ahead and they couldn't see what lay around the bend, but Thalia assumed that must be where the intruder was, or else they'd have seen each other before now.

Thalia headed back into the tree line. Where the ground curved, the palm trees nearly met the sea, blocking their view of anything or anyone who might be on the other side. The trees would also provide them cover, concealing them from whomever was down there.

Distantly, Thalia could hear voices as she inched closer, aware of the others behind her. She stopped, nearly at the tree line once more, and peered around at the scene before her.

"That's not a couple," Lorelei whispered.

A group of men had rowed a longboat onto shore and were busy unloading it. She watched them carry the crates, wondering where they were taking them and what they contained. Beyond the longboat, anchored out on the open sea, was a larger ship with three masts. On either side of the ship, stretching out, was the shore, forming a natural cove of sorts.

The men ranged from thin and gangly to stocky and muscular. Most wore thin, loose cotton shirts—though a few wore no shirt at all—and trousers. None of them wore shoes.

The moonlight glinted off the weapons at their belts, daggers and cutlasses, and Thalia glimpsed more than a few pistols.

Calida stared out at the ship anchored in the cove. "It's not the *Sea Witch*," she murmured to herself.

"What?" Thalia demanded, but Calida ignored her. They watched as the men climbed back into the longboat and shoved off, rowing back to the waiting ship.

"I think we should go," Lorelei whispered. "They're pirates."

"How do you know?"

"What else could they be?" she hissed. "What kind of reputable, honest sailor unloads cargo on a deserted beach in the middle of the night? They're storing the things they've stolen."

"I think Lorelei's right," Calida murmured. "We should go before they come back."

"All right," Thalia grumbled, irritated that her night had been cut short.

Lorelei turned to go back the way they'd come and stopped short, letting out a scream, the sound splitting the night. Thalia whirled around and saw several of the men right behind them. One had his pistol drawn.

"Look what we 'ave 'ere," said the one with the pistol.

"Aye," said one of his companion, leering, one of his teeth chipped. "Not every day you see such fine lasses."

His hand snaked out, latching onto Lorelei's arm. She opened her mouth to scream again—little good it would have done—but the man with the gun pointed it at her. "Now be a good girl. We'll 'ave no more of that."

Another man reached for Calida. "I always did like redheads."

In an instant, Calida commanded the tree roots to wrap around his legs, rooting him in place, but he glanced down, snapping them as if they were nothing.

"A witch," he growled, yanking a dagger out of his belt and striding forward. Calida let out a yelp, staggering back.

Horus shrieked and swooped down, raking the man's face with his talons. The pirate screamed and jerked back, blood pouring into his eyes. "I can't see!"

Before Thalia could move, several things happened. The man with the gun turned the barrel toward Calida. The pirate holding Lorelei threw her to the ground and reached for his belt. Lorelei's eyes widened in horror.

Penny, her familiar, leapt onto the man with a screech, sinking her teeth into his arm. He cried out. The man with the gun swung around, aiming it at the enraged familiar. Fire flashed from the muzzle as he pulled the trigger, the report deafening, drowning out Lorelei's cry.

Thalia's ears rang. If Lorelei's screams hadn't attracted the attention of the men on the ship, the gunshot surely would. And the other pirates would return, regardless, for the men they'd left behind. They needed to act quickly.

The pistol had fired its only shot. It was no longer a threat and it would take time to reload.

Thalia called upon her training and this time she didn't hold back.

The wind sprang up from nowhere, pushing her hair back from her face. The air smelled of electricity, the hair on her arms raising.

She forced the air around the pirates violently back, sending the men flying like rag dolls as the wind threw them from their feet, slamming them against the trees. Dazed and senseless, they slumped to the ground. All but one remained there, motionless.

It was the pirate who had tried to attack Calida. He wiped the blood from his eyes and staggered to his feet. Dispensing with the dagger, he yanked the pistol from his belt and cocked the hammer.

Lightning would have been quicker, and Thalia could sense it, brewing, waiting. But calling down lightning would have made it obvious that a witch had wandered where they weren't supposed to be.

Thalia thrust a hand forward, clenching her fingers into a fist. The pirate's mouth opened in a silent gasp and he stumbled, grasping his chest. She had sucked all the air out of his lungs. The gun fell from limp fingers as he fell to his knees, face turning an unnatural shade of red, the strain obvious.

Briefly, he looked up, meeting her gaze. She saw the hatred in his eyes, but beneath that, the fear. He was afraid of her, of what she could do. If anything, she clenched her fist tighter.

He slumped forward, eyes no longer seeing anything at all.

Only then did she loosen her grasp.

"Y—you killed him," Lorelei stammered. She still lay on the ground, stunned.

Of course I killed him. He tried to kill my sister.

Thalia didn't bother replying. She hauled Lorelei to her feet. "Are either of you hurt?"

Calida shook her head, gray eyes still wide and frightened.

Lorelei turned to where Penny had fallen, a hole in her side from the pistol shot. She let out a wail, reaching for her familiar.

"Leave her," Thalia instructed. "There's nothing you can do. And if you bring her back to the monastery, there will be questions. Come on. We have to leave now, before the rest of them wake up." *If they're even still alive.* Some of them had struck the tree trunks quite hard.

Still reeling from what had happened, they hurried after Thalia, anxious to be away. Thalia didn't think either of them truly relaxed until they had crossed back onto monastery grounds, but for her part, she felt no fear.

She had been afraid for a brief moment at the beginning, frozen by shock. But then she remembered herself. She knew what she was capable of, but those men hadn't. They had underestimated her, believing a mere girl couldn't possibly possess such power.

They guessed wrong and she had won.

She paused outside the dormitory, stopping both of them. "I don't think I need to say this to either of you, but don't tell anyone what happened tonight."

"What about the body?" Calida hissed. "Someone could find it."

"There's nothing about his death to suggest it was anything other than natural." She shrugged. "His heart gave out, that's all."

"But Horus attacked him. Someone might wonder how he came by those particular wounds."

"And what about Penny?" Lorelei whimpered. For a horrible moment, Thalia thought the girl might start crying again. "How am I supposed to explain why I have no familiar?"

Thalia closed her eyes for a moment. If anyone did come across the scene, the monkey's body would be the most incriminating thing. She wished she had the ability to control fire instead of water. Then she could have incinerated any evidence that they had ever been there at all.

"If anyone finds my familiar there, I could be—" Lorelei trailed off. None of them truly knew what would happen to her.

"Then for your sake, you'd better hope that doesn't happen," Thalia snapped. "Or else take the risk of going back to bury her. There's nothing else we can do about any of it now. Now go to bed and don't say a word to anyone."

It had been a mistake to go down to the beach, a temptation she should have treated as such, but she had given in. That wouldn't happen again. Thalia vowed not to leave the monastery again until she graduated.

It simply wasn't worth the risk.

She didn't think the other two got any sleep that night. Thalia herself certainly didn't. She lay awake thinking about what might happen if anyone discovered that they'd snuck out. The event itself didn't bother her overmuch.

Clearly, that wasn't the case for the other two. After dinner was over the following day, Calida told Thalia to meet her and Lorelei down by the river. Thalia didn't particularly want to talk about what had happened, but she met them there anyway.

When she arrived, Lorelei looked as though the tenuous hold on her emotions might snap at any moment. "I've been asked about Penny. I told them when I woke up, I found her dead, that I didn't know what must have happened to her, and that I buried her in the woods. It's a flimsy excuse, but it's all I could think of. I just hope no one asks any more questions."

"You could always say that she ate something she shouldn't have and it poisoned her," Thalia suggested. "I'm sure there are any number of plants around here that are dangerous to animals."

Lorelei nodded. "I could try that."

Calida looked at her sister miserably. "How are you all right with this?"

"What do you mean?" Thalia asked, jerking her tunic straighter.

"You just killed a man like it was nothing!"

Thalia recalled the task her sister had been given before she had been expelled from Kallias's class. He had instructed her to execute a criminal and she had balked, unable to do it. *How was what I did any different from what she was asked to do? Pirates are criminals and this was definitely self-defense.*

She shrugged. "It was me or him and I chose me."

"You make it sound so simple," Lorelei breathed.

"It was. Stop making it more than what it is."

"But weren't you scared?"

"Not for myself. I knew I could handle it."

"I wish I had your confidence."

"What did it feel like?" Calida asked softly, tugging at a piece of grass. "To kill someone?"

Thalia hesitated, wondering what her sister wanted her to say. She closed her eyes briefly, picturing the look of fear in the pirate's eyes right before he died.

"I've never done something like that before," she said carefully, "so I don't know what it's supposed to feel like. But it wasn't hard."

In fact, it had been all too easy. And Thalia knew exactly how it made her feel.

It had felt good to wield her power. To be feared.

* * *

That night, Calida snuck back into town. She didn't really want to leave the monastery again, conscious that danger could lurk anywhere. What if one of those pirates was in town and recognized her? The thought made her shudder. It had been foolish of them to go down to the beach and the last thing they needed was to risk another scene. This time, if something happened, there would be plenty of witnesses.

But she needed to see Jeremy. She wanted to tell him what had happened and she prayed that he would be at the tavern when she arrived.

Instead of heading straight for her usual table, Calida stood just inside the doorway, rapidly scanning the room for any sign of him, her heart thudding uncomfortably. If he wasn't here, she would be straight out the door again, high-tailing it back to the monastery as fast as she could go.

She was aware of the looks she was attracting, standing there so conspicuously. Were any of the men looking at her from the beach? She hadn't gotten a good look at their faces so she couldn't be sure, but the longer she stood there, the more convinced she became that at least one of them was.

Jeremy was a pirate. If he came here, why shouldn't any of the other pirates?

Calida was about to turn and flee when she saw him stand, having seen her, and began making his way over to her. She thought she might collapse in relief. Her legs shook beneath her.

Jeremy touched her on the arm. "What is it, firebrand? What's wrong?"

"I need to speak with you. Not here."

He frowned and led her outside, heading along the dock to where the *Sea Witch* sat anchored. Without hesitating, he climbed up the gangplank and after a moment, Calida followed him.

One of the men at the helm, who must have been left behind to guard the ship, scowled upon seeing her, but Jeremy preempted him. "She's with me," he said firmly.

The man said nothing and with a fearful glance at him, Calida followed Jeremy to the bow of the ship.

"Wait here," he said and disappeared briefly below deck.

Calida felt vulnerable, exposed on the deck, the ship rocking gently beneath her. This wasn't a place meant for her. She belonged securely on land, with the earth firm beneath her feet.

Jeremy returned, carrying a bottle of wine. He uncorked it and handed it to her, taking a seat on the wooden deck, cross-legged. "You looked like you could do with it."

"Thanks." She took a sip of it and sat across from him. It was much better than ale.

"Now what's happened?"

In between sips of wine from the bottle they passed back and forth, Calida told him about sneaking down to the beach and being beset by pirates. She left out nothing, adding that one of her friend's familiars had been killed and that her sister had killed a man.

Calida still shuddered to think of it. The look in Thalia's blue eyes had been wild and fierce, like a storm rolling in, beautiful and deadly in equal measure. She had killed a man with cold efficiency and hadn't batted an eye. It wasn't the sister she knew. Calida hoped that Thalia was just as horrified by it all as she was and that she was merely hiding her feelings, as she always did so well.

Jeremy listened to her story without interrupting. When she had finished, he said, "Most pirates are bad men. Some are criminals who can't remain on shore. Others are in it solely for the profit. Men like that are dangerous."

Calida felt slightly better having unburdened herself to him and the wine had warmed her nicely. She managed a small smile. "And what are you in it for, Jeremy Lussard?"

He grinned. "Freedom. Adventure. I suppose you could say I have a wanderer's soul. I never feel at home for very long, anywhere I go. The only place I've ever belonged is on the *Sea Witch*. The sea is my home and she's how I live there."

Calida sighed, leaning back against the railing. "I wish I could just run away."

"Where would you go?"

"Daera, maybe. They treat witches better there. Or at least, I haven't heard that they treat them badly."

Indris was too lawless to consider and Amberleigh—out of the question.

"If I could convince my sister to come with me, could you take us on your ship?"

"I don't know," Jeremy replied. "The *Sea Witch* is a pirate ship, not a ferry. But do you think she would even agree to go?"

"I don't know, but I have to try. If I stay there any longer, I feel I'll go mad."

* * *

The next time Calida was alone with Thalia, she brought up her idea. "We should run away. To Daera. My friend Jeremy can take us on his ship."

She didn't mention he was a pirate. Thalia still didn't know about that and it would be difficult enough to convince her as it was. They would cross that bridge when they came to it, but for now, her sister didn't need to know.

"Run away?" Thalia said scathingly. "And do what? We don't know anything about Daera."

"Why not?" Calida challenged, suddenly feeling foolish.

Thalia, being younger, had a way of doing that. She had a way of making anything Calida said seem unreasonable and that their roles in the conversation should have been reversed. It should have been the younger Thalia suggesting such a thing and Calida calmly and reasonably talking her out of it.

It made her angry.

She crossed her arms, adding, "It's better than staying here."

"You're seventeen," Thalia pointed out. She made it sound like it was no better than being eight years old. "Do you really think you can make it on your own in an unfamiliar kingdom, out in the real world, when all you've ever known is the monastery?"

"So you're not coming, then?"

"Of course not. Whatever I may have planned for my life, running off to Daera isn't it. I'm not going to do anything else to put that at risk and I suggest you don't either, Calida, if you know what's good for you."

"What does *that* mean?" Calida demanded, but Thalia had already walked away.

* * *

Calida avoided Thalia for a while after that. There was no chance of persuading her and Calida couldn't leave without

150

her, so they were right back to where they started. Nothing ever changed.

Or at least, nothing good.

Lorelei's classes had been suffering ever since the night at the beach. She could no longer practice in classes focused on strengthening and building the bond between a witch and their familiar. The fact that she no longer had a familiar set her apart from the other students, making her a sort of pariah.

Arin took every opportunity to pick on her because of it, painfully reminding her of her loss. Calida was happy to take her anger out on him, but he had continued with combat training while she had not. He was the better fighter now in every way that mattered and he made her pay for her interference.

Calida picked herself up off the ground after he'd left, nursing a split lip and an eye that would probably turn a nice shade of black.

She turned to Lorelei beside her and helped her up. "Are you all right?"

Lorelei nodded. "He didn't really do much to me. He was too busy hitting you. You shouldn't keep getting up, you know. Just stay down."

And let him think he broke me? I'd rather die.

"I'm a healer. I can take care of it."

Her friend took a deep breath. "I've decided I don't want to work with animals anymore. They remind me too much of Penny."

"But if that's what you're best at—" *Then you don't have a choice.* She broke off, refusing to finish the tired, old line.

"I've decided to train to become a midwife. I've dealt with enough animal births it shouldn't be too hard to switch and I already know a bit about healing. My instructor said it shouldn't be a problem."

If that was the case, Calida was happy for her. It wasn't often that someone got what they wanted. She knew things hadn't been easy for Lorelei. She'd often seen her sitting at the base of a tree, crying, when she thought no one would see.

The loss of a familiar, the severing of such a powerful bond, must have been devastating, made all the more so by the knowledge that Lorelei would never have another such companion again. A witch only got one familiar in life and once lost, that bond could never be replaced or regained.

Calida never wanted to know what that felt like.

CHAPTER 11

For her part, Calida continued to pay visits into town to see Jeremy, though she was always aware, in the back of her mind, of the fear she had been introduced to the night at the beach. It made her more cautious than she otherwise would have been, but perhaps that was no bad thing. There was no way of knowing, but maybe that fear kept her from being caught.

On one particular night, she went into town with a heavy heart, hoping more than ever that Jeremy would be there. There were only a few weeks before it would be time for her own graduation and then she would be off to her placement. It wouldn't be impossible for them to see each other again but Calida wasn't going to leave anything to chance.

If she never got another opportunity to see him, she needed to let him know what was happening, where she had gone, and why she wasn't coming anymore.

She let out a breath of relief as she spotted him and he came over to join her table. They caught up with each other's news as always and then Calida came straight to the point.

She kept her voice low, not wanting any of the others to overhear, but the tavern was boisterous and she didn't think it likely. "I graduate from the monastery soon. I'll be sent off to wherever I'm assigned. I don't know if I'll be able to come here anymore."

Jeremy turned his tankard slowly atop the table. He was a grown man now, tall and muscular. He'd cut his hair back to its normal length; it no longer reached his shoulders. "So this might be goodbye, then? Well, if I never see you again, I'm glad to have met you, firebrand."

"And I you." They shook hands briefly, smiling, Calida trying to swallow down the tears she could feel forming at the idea that this might truly be the last time she ever saw him. "I'll try to visit, every chance I get, and then I can tell you all about my new job."

"I'd like that. Gets a bit boring, hearing about the monastery all the time," he joked, nudging her with his shoulder.

"Not as dull as living there," Calida replied.

But if she were honest, there was a part of her that was scared to leave the monastery behind. Boring and predictable though it was, it also meant safety. There was no uncertainty of the unknown or what may lay ahead in the future.

But soon, all of that would change. Calida's entire world would be turned on its head and she would have to adapt. She hadn't felt this way since she had been first brought to the monastery and left her old life behind. It was a big change and now everything would change again.

How had it come to this so soon? This day that had seemed so very far away suddenly loomed on their doorstep. The thing Calida had so yearned for was finally upon her and now she wasn't sure she wanted it.

Lorelei would also graduate with her this year. Her choice to study midwifery had been a success. Thalia had qualified for early graduation and Calida was relieved her younger sister would not be left behind when she herself graduated.

Mordred was the only one out of their small group that wouldn't be graduating that year. He hadn't done well enough to qualify for early graduation, though Calida had thought they might push him through anyway. If he'd been a sky witch, they probably would have, but an earth witch was useless in the fight against piracy.

As the fateful day neared, Calida imagined what her new future would look like. It was so far away from what she had pictured all those years ago, when she had wanted to be a soldier. She had been thirteen then, but she was nineteen now. Nearly a grown woman. Decisions would have to be made soon, about marriage and a family.

But that could wait for another time.

* * *

The night before the graduation ceremony, Mordred sought Thalia out as she had expected he would. They had kept up their secret training sessions all the way up until earlier that very day. His improvement was marked, so much so that Thalia had been surprised he hadn't been chosen to graduate early with her.

Gone was the small, sallow boy she had first met. He was taller than her, broad in the shoulder, though still lacking a certain confidence, a vulnerability he shared only with her.

Perhaps that was why he hadn't been chosen. With her gone, he would have to learn to be on his own for another year. Maybe that was the thing he needed most, to bring him the rest of the way out of his shell.

"You're leaving tomorrow," he said softly, his voice so deep now she could barely hear him.

"Yes."

"I'll miss training with you," he said, then added, "I'll miss you. I didn't have many friends here, even with the others. You didn't have to take the time to bother with someone like me, but you did." He looked down, scuffing the ground with his boot. "I suppose what I'm trying to say is thank you, for everything you've done for me." He raised his eyes. "I won't forget it."

Neither will I. Thalia inclined her head slightly. "You've done well. You'll be off to your own placement before you know it. Whatever you do, I trust you'll go far."

He glanced away again, flushing slightly. "That's high praise. I wish you luck."

Mordred turned and walked away.

Thalia inhaled deeply. By tomorrow, she would have left the monastery behind forever. All of her patience will have finally paid off.

* * *

The morning of the ceremony, all of the graduating witches were given ceremonial robes to wear, each one still designating the type of witch, but with a sash of a different color that represented which placement they were best suited for. Calida's sash was white for healing, Lorelei's striped white and gray for midwifery. Thalia's was blue and red, signaling that she would be bound for a naval ship, both for the purpose of protecting it as well as ensuring favorable weather. Arin's sash, annoyingly, was pure red for the military.

Each of the instructors that were gathered also wore ceremonial dress. They organized the students into neat rows in the keep courtyard.

"Now remember," headmistress Anise called out, "when His Majesty arrives, make sure to stand at attention. If he asks you a question, answer respectfully and don't look him in the eye. Is that understood?"

As one voice, they answered in the affirmative.

"Good. The royal procession should arrive at any moment."

It took longer than a moment for the king to arrive and Calida shifted her weight uncomfortably. She was hot standing in the direct sunlight in her stupid woolen robe. There was not the slightest shred of a breeze and her feet

156

hurt. How very like royalty to inconvenience everyone else by making them wait.

Her irritation evaporated at the sound of hooves thundering over the ground. She had never seen the king before and wondered what he looked like. What would he think of them? Of her? What if she managed to displease him somehow with her mere existence?

Don't be stupid, she chided herself, inhaling deeply. *He needs us. His kingdom would be nothing without us.*

The thought made her stand up a little taller, but she knew, deep down, that the king was a man who essentially owned her. He controlled her destiny, not her. Her very life rested in his hands. If he wanted, he could take everything from her.

There was a reason witches both feared and hated him.

Four black horses pulled an elaborate carriage beneath the entrance arch, the carriage doors embossed with a regal griffin, Alara's symbol. Calida glanced at it and remembered reading something in history class, back at her old school, about how the griffin and other mythical symbols had been beliefs of the kingdom that used to rule this land, before Alara conquered it. The new kingdom had chosen to adopt the symbols they liked as their own, but no Alaran believed in such creatures.

The memory felt like a lifetime ago. No, like someone else's life entirely.

Behind the carriage came mounted soldiers, wearing the red and gold uniforms of the royal guard. No doubt there were a few witches among them, ready to interrupt and neutralize any threat that may present itself.

The driver of the coach dismounted and came around to open the door. A middle-aged man stepped out, wearing ceremonial dress. His scarlet coat was made of velvet and the golden epaulettes on his shoulders gleamed in the sun. A cluster of medals were pinned to his breast. There wasn't a visible wrinkle to be found on his white trousers and his polished black boots shone. A sheathed sword hung at his hip and he rested one gloved hand atop it.

His deep chestnut hair was swept back from his face, a touch of silver at his temples. His beard was short, precisely trimmed, not a hair out of place.

As if there was any doubt as to who he was, a golden crown perched atop his head. And yet, for all his grandeur, the king's jacket hung oddly on his frame, as though it had been tailored for a larger man. The skin beneath his eyes was sunken and thin, the lines of age etched deeply.

Behind him, a younger man stepped out, also in ceremonial dress, but he wore no crown or sword. There was only one medal pinned to his chest. His hair was blond, not quite golden, as if he didn't spend enough time in the sun. But the jawline and cheekbones were the same as the man beside him.

The prince, Calida realized. She hadn't known he would also come to survey the newest batch of graduates.

She had heard things about the prince before, but had never laid eyes on him. She had hoped Horus would catch a glimpse of the monarchs whenever she sent him up to the palace, but she hadn't been so lucky. He appeared to be about her own age, undeniably handsome, standing with the regal, confident air of one born to privilege—and aware of it.

Headmistress Anise bowed before the two men. "Your Majesty, Your Royal Highness, may I present the Erlohn monastery's newest graduates."

King Wilhelm strode toward them, one hand remaining on the hilt of his sword. His eyes traveled over each of them in turn and it was hard to remember that she should keep her head down, never returning his gaze. How desperately Calida wanted to stare him down, to let him know that she would never allow him to own her.

Horus shifted on her shoulder, sensing her emotions. Each witch had stood with their familiars. All except one…

The king paused before Lorelei. "Where is your familiar, girl?"

She visibly trembled before him. "S—she died, Your Majesty."

He frowned. "Odd for a witch to lose their familiar so soon." He glanced at her sash. "What is your placement?"

"Midwifery, Your Majesty."

So the king hadn't even bothered to learn what the different sash colors meant. Calida could have snorted in disgust.

He grunted. "Well I suppose a familiar is hardly necessary for that." He turned back to the headmistress. "This class is even smaller than last year."

She bowed her head. "Apologies, Your Majesty. We've had fewer students coming in every year—"

"It's not good enough. We need more."

"W—we've tried to push through those that were deemed good enough. We have a few early graduates this year, Your Majesty." The headmistress walked over to where Thalia stood, tall and proud. "Thalia was the best student in her class and shows remarkable promise."

Calida stiffened as the king made his way over to her sister.

"Sky witch," he murmured. "I see you are to serve in my navy."

So he did know what the sashes meant! Or at least, those he deemed most important. No doubt midwifery wasn't something he concerned himself with.

"Yes, Your Majesty," Thalia answered, her voice clear and confident.

The king nodded. "Good. You will be a valuable asset in the fight against piracy."

A valuable asset. That was all her sister was to the king. All any of them were, only some were more valuable than others.

He stepped back. "The headmistress will send for you when she has word of your placements. For some of you, it will take longer than others. In the meantime, you will remain here at the monastery until such placements can be found. Some of you will leave as early as tomorrow morning. Alara is proud to have such selfless servants as you and thanks you for your service."

Selfless! As if they had a choice.

Calida felt her hands form into fists. She hadn't realized that she might be forced to stay at the monastery for a little while longer, if a placement for her couldn't immediately be found. Daniel had left almost at once. She supposed there was no shortage when it came to the need for farmers.

There was a moment of silence following the king's pronouncement and then he turned away quickly, a cough bursting from his lips. The prince's brow furrowed and he stepped closer to his father, reaching out to lay a hand on his arm. The king shook him off brusquely, pressing a handkerchief to his mouth. It disappeared as quickly as it had emerged—but not before Calida caught a glimpse of red staining the previously pristine fabric.

The king turned and walked back to his coach. The prince lingered for a moment, his eyes roaming over the assembled witches. He hadn't said a word the entire time. Calida wondered what it must be like, living in the shadow of such a domineering father. The king wasn't likely easy to please, if he was ever truly pleased with anything.

As if sensing her thoughts, the prince's gaze met hers for a brief moment and then he was gone, following after his father. Only when the carriage had rolled out of sight did they allow themselves to relax.

Headmistress Anise nodded curtly to them. "About your business."

Calida made her way over to Lorelei. Sweat dripped down the back of her neck, but the other girl looked far more uncomfortable, so pale Calida feared she might faint.

"Oh, skies, did you see the way he looked at me?" Lorelei gasped. "My heart was hammering so fast I thought it would explode."

"You did fine," Calida assured her.

"I was so frightened. He wasn't the least bit pleased that I didn't have a familiar. I think it's just as well I chose to be a midwife. If I had been anything else, I don't know what he would have done."

"It's not your fault." Calida had been about to say something disparaging about the king, but swiftly thought better of it as Master Kallias approached. She avoided looking at him, reminded of her shameful failure in his class.

"Lorelei," he barked.

She paled even further. "Yes?"

"The headmistress wants to see you."

With a fearful glance at Calida, Lorelei left for the headmistress's quarters. Calida watched her progress as she approached one of the towers along the wall.

She waited for her friend to return, but she didn't. Nor was she present that evening at dinner. Calida found Lorelei in the dormitory, packing her few belongings.

"I've got my placement!" Lorelei explained. "I'll be off tomorrow morning."

Calida hugged her, trying to ignore the pang in her chest. "I'm happy for you. Really. I hope it's everything you hoped for."

It was already happening. They were being split up, sent down diverging paths, away from each other.

Lorelei nodded. "It may not be glamorous, but it's important work. Any word on your placement yet?"

"No. It may take a while."

"I wouldn't think so. People always need healers."

Calida wouldn't have thought that it would take too much time either, but perhaps she wasn't as good as she thought she was. Maybe there was no place that had an opening at the moment. Whatever the reason, she kept hoping to be told that the headmistress wanted to see her, and that it wouldn't take too long, before everyone else she knew moved on without her.

* * *

Half an hour before dinner, Thalia received the news that the headmistress wanted to speak with her. She made her way up the winding stairs to the top of the tower, the first time she'd done so since initially arriving at the monastery at the age of twelve, six years ago. She knocked and was told to enter.

The headmistress stood behind her desk, sorting through sheafs of paper. She looked up briefly. "Ah, Thalia. Please, come in."

"You wanted to see me, headmistress?"

"I took the liberty of finding some placements ahead of time for the students that showed the most promise. Serving in the navy is one of the most prestigious placements and I had no trouble obtaining a position for you."

Thalia bowed her head. "Thank you, headmistress."

"You'll leave tomorrow morning with the rest of the graduates who have already been assigned. Pack whatever you need and say your goodbyes. The ship you'll be serving on is—" She broke off, consulting her notes. "—The HMS *Hunter*. I'm told she's a frigate, modest compared to a man o' war, but good for a first assignment."

"I look forward to it."

The headmistress nodded. "That was all. Dismissed."

* * *

Thalia stepped into the dormitory as Lorelei was still packing and Calida glanced up.

162

"I've been given a placement. I thought you should know."

Calida summoned a small smile. "Congratulations."

"Have you gotten anything yet?"

"No." Calida didn't really want to talk about it.

By the next sunrise, both Lorelei and Thalia would leave her. She would have no one left at the monastery other than Mordred and she had never been as close to him as Thalia had.

"It'll come through. Any day now."

Calida wished she could share her sister's confidence. But how soon she received her placement didn't really matter on the one hand. She and her sister would be separating in a way they hadn't since Calida had left to join the monastery. And even then, she'd known Thalia would follow after her in a year's time.

They were graduating at the same time, but that was where it ended. She remembered how they had planned to both become soldiers so they could serve together and how that plan had fallen apart in spectacular fashion. It seemed so naïve now, the dream of a little girl who didn't know how the real world worked.

Still, it made her sad that her sister would be going off into the world without her, a path she couldn't follow. Earth witches had no business or use being on a ship and Thalia wasn't a healer.

Suddenly, the air in the dormitory seemed stifling and Calida had to get out. Excusing herself, she ducked outside, breathing deeply, trying to force down the wave of emotion that threatened to overwhelm her. Everything was changing too fast and there was nothing she could do to stop it.

Life at the monastery had been boring, to be sure, but why had she ever wished that things would change? She hadn't truly known what it was that she was wishing for. And now that she had it, she didn't want it.

She blinked back tears, feeling ridiculous. She was far too old for that.

Calida looked up, freezing, as a familiar figure rode through the stone archway. It was the prince from earlier that morning, astride a magnificent chestnut horse. He was dressed more casually now, his ceremonial dress gone, but there was no doubt it was him.

What was he doing back here—and alone?

He dismounted and began leading his horse toward her. Calida looked around but there was no one else nearby. The courtyard was all but deserted, the others busy preparing to head off to their placements in the morning.

"Hello," the prince called, smiling at her. "Is there a stable here where I can leave my horse?"

"Um," Calida stammered, trying to recall the proper way to address him. What had the headmistress called him earlier? "Y—yes, Your Royal Highness." Had she gotten it right?

He was still smiling at her. His teeth were bright and *almost* perfectly straight. Calida stared at that small flaw, fascinated. It made him seem somehow more human. Approachable.

"I don't suppose you could show me the way?"

"Oh!" What an idiot she was. "Of course. It's this way."

The stables were empty of people at that time of day as Calida slid the door open. The horses turned in their stalls to stare at them, ears flicking casually. She stopped at the first empty stall they came to, realizing there were no attendants.

The prince would have had grooms at the palace to look after his horses. He couldn't be expected to do it himself.

Calida reached up to take the horse's bridle. "Here, allow me."

"Thank you." He stepped back and she set about her task.

She expected him to head to the headmistress's quarters or attend to whatever it was that had brought him here, but instead he lingered, standing there, watching her.

Calida glanced at him. "You're making me nervous," she said, wondering if she was being too familiar with her speech.

"Sorry," he said sheepishly. "But you look like you have things well in hand. You have a way with animals. Is that your placement?"

Calida stroked the horse. "I don't have a placement yet, but when I do, it will be healing, not caring for animals."

"If you're even better with people than you are with animals, you must be a very fine healer."

"I'm all right." *I can't be much of one if no one's shown any interest in me yet.*

"You're too modest, surely."

She desperately wanted to ask him why he had come back, but that seemed too forward.

The prince considered her. "Is healing the placement that you want?"

Calida let out a humorless laugh. Part of her knew she should keep her mouth shut, hide how she really felt, but after the day she'd had, disappointing in every way, her restraint had worn thin.

"It's what I'm good at. What I'm made for."

"That's not the same thing."

"What we want doesn't matter. We don't get to choose, Your Highness. That's the way it's always been."

"It doesn't always have to be that way," he murmured.

Calida paused and looked up at him. It sounded like something Thalia had once said. "What do you mean?"

He regarded the tops of his polished boots. "My father has set ways of thinking about things and how they should be done, but maybe those things should be changed. I think people would actually be more effective workers if they were allowed to do the jobs they wanted, rather than the jobs they're forced to do simply because that's what they're good at. Just because you're good at something doesn't necessarily mean you enjoy it."

Calida stared at him, stunned, unsure what to say. Whatever she had expected from him, it was not this.

He caught her gaze and then looked away again, his cheeks coloring. "I don't know. Maybe I'm completely wrong about the way things should be done." He sighed and then added, so softly Calida wasn't sure he was even talking to her, "I just want to be a good king."

"But surely you've a long way to go until you have to worry about that."

"Not as long as I'd like."

She stayed silent, waiting to see if he would elaborate.

"I don't know if you noticed earlier, but my father isn't well."

"I did," she admitted.

The prince's lips twisted into a frown and he nodded. "He has his good days and bad days. Today was one of the better ones. At least he felt like going out. He's kept his condition a secret from the public, afraid of the uncertainty or unrest such knowledge might cause. The idea of a young, inexperienced prince having to ascend the throne so soon…he didn't think the news would be well received."

"What's wrong with him?" The conversation was taking a decidedly more familiar turn than she would have anticipated. "And if it's a secret, why tell me?"

That earned her another of his smiles. "Truly? I don't know. I suppose I feel the need to tell someone. Someone outside of it all. Someone impartial."

Calida thought she was hardly that.

"As for what's wrong with him, no one knows. He's lethargic. On the really bad days, he lacks the strength to get out of bed. He's lost a lot of weight. He has no appetite. Some of the doctors have suggested that it's melancholy, brought on by my mother's death, but that happened years ago. We've brought in healers from all corners of Alara, witch and ordinary alike. None have been able to find a cure."

"I'm sorry," Calida said and surprised herself by how much she meant it. She didn't like the king and the way things were under his rule, but no one deserved to face down the possible death of a parent at the hands of an illness, mysterious or otherwise.

The prince shook himself suddenly as if he had been daydreaming. "How terribly rude of me. I just realized I haven't introduced myself. I apologize; I have a lot on my mind or else I wouldn't normally be so discourteous."

Calida smiled. "I know who you are. You're the prince."

"Please, call me Niklaus. I get enough of that Royal Highness drivel up at the palace. What do they call you?"

For some reason, Jeremy's voice leapt into her mind, whispering *firebrand*.

She shook her head. "Calida."

"That's a lovely name. Much better than Niklaus, at any rate."

She smiled at him and stepped out of the stall, her task finished.

He surveyed her work. "You've done a magnificent job. I'd love to talk more—truly, I would—but unfortunately, I must speak with the headmistress. It's been a pleasure meeting you, Calida."

He turned and exited the stables, his boots echoing on the floor. Calida watched him go, thinking back over their conversation. She had been prepared to hate him for his connection to the king. He was royalty, after all, spoiled and privileged and the reason for all her misery.

And yet, he wasn't anything at all like what she had expected. Despite her previous intentions, she could not bring herself to hate him.

She returned to the dormitory, watching the door to the headmistress's quarters, waiting to see when he would reappear. He left only minutes later, heading back to the stables. He led his horse outside, fully saddled and ready to ride, swinging up onto its back.

So he did know how to see to his own horse. Another surprise. It seemed Prince Niklaus was full of them.

Calida watched him ride away, wondering what it was that had brought him back to the monastery.

CHAPTER 12

By the next morning, a third of the graduating students were gone.

Calida had bid Thalia and Lorelei farewell, hugging each of them in turn and forcing herself to watch as they left the monastery for good, leaving her behind.

The younger students went about their business, but the monastery grounds felt strangely empty to Calida. She helped out with tasks that needed to be done, seeing to the animals, picking fruit from the orchards, and even tending to some of the beehives outside of the keep walls, but she had no more classes to go to and she spent most of the day feeling listless.

If she had thought life at the monastery boring before, it was downright torturous now. Any moment, she expected to be summoned to see the headmistress and be informed of her new placement, but it never came. How long would she be forced to wait?

* * *

Thalia arrived at the Brisban harbor where the royal navy lay anchored. It was a breathtaking arsenal of ships, ranging from frigates to massive galleons, masts studding the sky, white canvas furled.

She'd been instructed to report by ten that morning and time was quickly running out. The coach that had come to fetch her at the monastery hadn't been as quick as she would have liked. It wouldn't do to be seen arriving late.

Walking briskly, she searched for the HMS *Hunter*. Headmistress Anise had said that it was a smaller ship and Thalia knew the various types of ships from her classes.

As she walked, she glanced at the names on the ships, written across the back of the stern, until she came to the one she wanted. The *Hunter* was a three-masted, square-rigged vessel. Thalia wouldn't know how many guns she possessed until she was on board.

She took a deep breath. This was to be her new home. Before long, she would have the ins and outs of this ship memorized, as familiar to her as the back of her own hand.

A burly man stood on the dock, guarding the gangplank, a roster in hand. "Name?" he barked as Thalia approached, Jade trailing behind her.

Her blue tunic should have identified her as a witch, but she answered anyway.

"Thalia, sky witch assigned to the HMS *Hunter*, reporting for duty."

The man jerked his head toward the ship behind him. "On you get."

She strode past him, head held high. Whatever happened and regardless of this man's opinion of witches, she refused to be intimidated. She held all the power on this ship, after all, and they would do well to remember it.

The crew was assembled on the main deck, staring up at the quarterdeck, where the captain stood at the helm, waiting to address them. Now that Thalia had arrived, he gave the normal crew their instructions before privately pulling her aside.

He grimaced as he took in her appearance from head to toe. "I've been told you're one of the best there is and I hope that means you won't be with us long before being transferred to a larger ship. I mean no offense, mind, and I'll be glad of your presence should we encounter any trouble, but I wish they wouldn't send female witches. It makes things difficult with the men."

"I know my responsibilities, Captain," Thalia replied. "I'll do my job. See that your men do theirs."

In a way, it felt strange speaking to him in such a manner. She was only eighteen and he was her commanding officer and elder by several decades. But she was a soldier, of sorts. She had worked hard to get here and knew what she was capable of.

She wasn't worried about being surrounded by men. No doubt they would find her presence something of a distraction and a temptation. She was aware that she was beautiful, with her flaming hair and dark blue eyes. Tall and lean, yet curved in all the places a woman should be. What man wouldn't be tempted?

But she'd had no trouble dealing with the pirates on the beach and if any of these men got any ideas, she'd make sure they had cause to regret it.

No, she wasn't afraid of men.

The captain nodded. "Very well, then. You'll find your uniform and everything you need below decks. Welcome to the *Hunter*."

* * *

By the third day, over half of the students from her year were gone and still no word had come for Calida. Perhaps her destiny would be to remain at the monastery forever, taking over for Irjah upon her retirement as the healing instructor.

She was laying beneath an apple tree, staring up at the dappled branches and wishing she were someplace else, wondering how Thalia was faring, when a voice spoke above her.

"You look like you're in desperate need of a diversion."

Calida sat up and spun around to see Niklaus standing over her. He'd returned.

She stood, brushing grass off her tunic. "More business with the headmistress?"

"Not this time. No word on a placement yet?"

She sighed. "No. Almost everyone else has left. I'm worried I'll still be stuck here when the next batch of first years arrives."

"Well you must have plenty of time on your hands. What do you do for fun?"

"Climb trees. I like to go down to the river, but nothing is much fun now that my sister and best friend are gone." In fact, she'd been talking to Horus now more than ever. He was the only company she had.

She had sent the hawk out to check on Thalia, searching for a ship called the *Hunter*. He had found it as it pulled out of the harbor. Thalia had been on deck, at the helm behind the captain, the white sails billowing as they filled with wind, aided by her magic. She looked resplendent in her uniform, with the gold embroidery and epaulettes. The fabric was a vibrant royal blue instead of the typical red, signifying her status as a sky witch.

Calida's heart had swelled with pride as she watched her sister, standing tall and proud. She had certainly achieved a good placement and even though it meant they were now apart—Calida stuck on land and Thalia sailing the seas where Calida could not follow—she was still happy for her.

"What about riding?" Niklaus asked, breaking into her thoughts. It took her a moment to understand what he was saying.

"I haven't ridden in years." *Not since I was removed from the combat class.* Only soldiers would need to know how to ride, after all.

"Would you like to go for a ride now? My horse is waiting just outside."

"I don't have a horse." She didn't presume to think he was suggesting they both ride on the same one.

"There are plenty of horses in the stable. I'm sure no one would mind if you borrowed one."

Calida thought they very much would mind. It wasn't allowed. She wasn't a soldier and the horses were off-limits to her, other than caring for them.

"You can do that?" she asked without thinking.

Niklaus gave her a bemused look. "Of course."

Stupid. He's the prince. He can do whatever he likes.

"Well…all right then." Surely if she were with the prince, no one would dare object to what she was doing.

"Wonderful. I'll meet you outside."

Hoping that this wasn't, absurdly, a trap of some sort, Calida ducked into the stable. She quickly found the horse that she'd ridden all those years ago during her training. He looked up as she approached and nickered softly to her.

Calida wasted no time slipping the tack on. She led the horse outside and climbed up into the saddle, meeting the prince beyond the keep walls. She was a bit out of practice, but she remembered well enough. Perhaps riding was something you never truly forgot.

If only Arin could see her now. The prince had asked her to ride with him. She wouldn't go so far as to say the two of them were friends—it was far too soon for that, though they certainly weren't unfriendly with each other—but there had to be a reason he had suggested such an excursion to her.

"Where are we going?" she asked.

She noticed a few mounted guards standing just outside the archway. A quick glance over her shoulder as they set off revealed that the guards were following behind them at a discreet distance. Of course the prince would never travel anywhere completely alone.

"I thought we could just ride around," Niklaus replied. "I imagine you don't get to leave very often."

You have no idea. Calida thought of her trips into town to see Jeremy. She likely got to leave more often than the prince realized.

They moved through the forest at a brisk trot, the trees too dense to risk going much faster. They said nothing on the ride, Calida focusing on the task at hand. It felt good to finally be on horseback again, the wind flowing through her hair. It was something she'd never expected to feel again.

Niklaus looked at ease on the back of his horse, handling the animal with a confidence that spoke of years of experience. He'd probably been taught to ride from the moment it was physically possible for him to do so. The chestnut coat of his steed shone in the sunlight, muscles rippling.

The horses at the monastery were by no means shabby, but neither were they the best breeding had to offer, and they were intended for training purposes only. They would never see actual battle. Calida thought her horse seemed tawdry in comparison to his.

They broke free of the trees and Calida found herself back on the beach that she, Lorelei, and Thalia had snuck down to on that fateful night. She shuddered slightly, remembering the look on her sister's face as she choked the life out of a man, how frightened she herself had been, and how close they had all come to dying.

But the sun was out this time, clouds scudding across a blue sky. It wasn't dark and there were no pirates to ambush them. Besides, even if there were, Niklaus's guards weren't far behind. She was safe here.

They slowed the horses to a walk along the shore where the sea met the sand, a trail of hoofprints stretching out behind them.

Calida broke the silence. "So what brought you back to the monastery, Your Highness? Surely you didn't come just to ride with me." She kept her tone light, teasing.

"Call me Niklaus," he reminded her.

Calida thought about saying it, but the name still sounded too familiar to use.

"Truthfully?" he asked, twisting in the saddle to face her. "I came back to see you."

"Me?" Calida said in some surprise. Why on earth would the prince bother to come back to see her? She had enjoyed their last conversation, but whether or not he felt the same, that was no reason for him to come all the way back just for her.

His eyes were looking forward, but she didn't think he was really seeing the beach stretched out before them. "I have a placement for you, if you want it."

Her pulse spiked. She had been eagerly awaiting news of a placement every moment she wasn't busy helping out around the monastery. She tried to stay busy because it was the only way, other than sleeping, to keep her mind off of it, but there simply wasn't much for her to do now that she had no classes.

"What is it?" she asked, trying not to sound too eager.

"I want you to come to the palace and attend to my father."

"Me?" Calida repeated, even more incredulous than before.

Niklaus shrugged, but she could see the lines of tension in him. "You are a healer, are you not?"

"Well, yes, but…what could I possibly do that the best healers in the kingdom couldn't?"

"I don't know," he sighed, sounding so defeated. "At this point, I'm willing to try anything. My father is a hard man, but he's still my father and in my own way, I love him. I'm not ready to say goodbye."

No one ever is.

It was on the tip of Calida's tongue to refuse, to say that it was impossible. She was an inexperienced healer, after all, who had yet to receive an official placement. She'd never gone out into the real world and practiced her craft. Who was she to heal the king, who suffered from an illness even the best healers could not identify?

But then a different thought came to her. What if she *could* somehow heal him? If she could save the life of the king, she was willing to bet that he would give her whatever she wanted. She would never have to worry about getting a good placement again. Her purpose as a witch was to serve the kingdom, after all, and what better way to do that than save the life of its monarch?

She could have whatever life she wanted, if she were successful. She would be free.

And Thalia. Thalia could be part of that deal. Her sister could be free, too.

Calida closed her eyes. Who did she think she was? It was an impossible dream. She was nothing compared to the best healers the kingdom had to offer. How could she succeed where they had failed?

But still…it was an opportunity that she couldn't afford to pass up. She had to at least try. If she didn't, there was no chance at all that she could heal the king and her dreams would remain just that and nothing more.

If she had even a chance, no matter how small, at a better life, a chance to escape the expectations that had dogged her since birth, she had to take it.

She looked up at Niklaus. "I'll do it."

He looked slightly startled by the intensity in her voice, but the surprise quickly gave way to relief. "Thank you, Calida."

"Don't thank me yet," she warned. "I may not be able to cure him." *In fact, I probably* won't *be able to.*

But surely he had to know that. She was inexperienced and so young and yet he was putting his faith in her. He must have been truly desperate.

"All we can do is try," he murmured. "I won't give up on him."

"How long will I be staying at the palace?" *Until you realize there's nothing I can do and kick me out?*

"As long as it takes."

It wasn't a very specific answer but they were both dealing in uncertainties.

"I have one request, then," Calida ventured, knowing she should merely be grateful to receive such a placement—she was going to the palace!—and she was grateful. She was in no position to make requests or demands. It wasn't as though she were the best, most renowned healer in the kingdom. But in this, too, she must try.

"Anything."

"I want my sister to stay at the palace with me. She's a sky witch, assigned to the ship HMS *Hunter*. Her name is Thalia."

"I'll arrange it," he promised. "But if they've already set sail, it may take some time."

"I understand." Calida could wait, as long as she knew Thalia was on her way back to her.

They would both be staying at the palace! It was grander than any dream she could have envisioned for herself. But they wouldn't stay forever. She needed to find a way to cure the king in order to earn her place there and by extension, Thalia's as well.

If she couldn't, there was no need for them to remain. She would have to try her best, putting all she had learned during her time at the monastery to the test. She wished she had paid more attention during the lessons about various diseases and their cures.

"When do we leave? I may have to borrow a few things from Irjah…" Calida had no idea what she would even need.

"You'll have access to the infirmary at the palace," Niklaus assured her. "Any medical supplies you may need will be there. As for when we leave, we can go at any time."

Calida felt a lurch in her chest as her heart missed a beat. She could leave now if she wanted. *So soon.*

"I can go whenever you're ready," she replied. She had next to no belongings to call her own and nothing to pack. "I would just need to get my familiar. I'm afraid I don't…have much to bring with me."

"That's fine." Niklaus turned his horse back toward the monastery. "Everything the palace has to offer will be at your disposal."

"I suppose I'll have to inform the headmistress," Calida said, following after him.

"She already knows."

* * *

There was no coach to collect her and so, after fetching Horus, they made the journey to the palace on horseback, taking the horse from the monastery with them. Niklaus assured her that he would see it safely returned once they were done.

Calida had made the journey to the palace many times in her mind, linking her vision with Horus, and knew it was a good distance away. But she didn't appreciate how truly far it was until she had to traverse the distance on horseback. Horus could fly directly there without being limited to the roads.

By the time they arrived, it was late afternoon and Calida ached from being in the saddle so long. She was dusty, hungry, and in need of a good nap, but she didn't complain, knowing how lucky she was. She wouldn't do anything to put her position here at risk.

They were met at the front gate by servants who took their horses. Niklaus led her up the stairs into the palace itself and Calida followed, every step painful. She was almost too exhausted to appreciate the finery of the palace itself, but one look nearly took her breath away and she momentarily forgot to be tired.

Their footsteps echoed off white marble floors, polished to a sheen, and the high vaulted ceilings with their crystal chandeliers. Everywhere she looked, servants in red and gold livery bustled about. She had never seen so many people on any of the occasions she had sent Horus, but the palace didn't have many windows.

Instead, the palace was a place of marble and stone, ivory and gold, lit by a million candles, the flames reflecting off every gilded surface and facet of crystal.

Calida glanced down at her reflection on the floor. She felt frumpy in her plain monastery tunic, her red hair wild and untamed. She looked like what she was—a peasant. A nobody. She didn't belong in this world and she never would.

She reminded herself to keep her head high. She was the witch who was here to save the king, after all. Why shouldn't she belong here or deserve respect? Niklaus respected her; she was here at his request.

"Coming?" he asked, a hint of amusement in his voice.

Calida looked up. He'd walked on without her before realizing she had stopped. Blushing at being caught gawking, she hurried after him, Horus perched on her shoulder. He led her down winding halls and more rooms than she'd know what to do with, before halting in front of a plain wooden door.

"This will be your quarters," he explained. "I'll leave you to get settled in. Later, I'll fetch you and take you to see my father. If you need anything, just ask one of the servants. They'll be more than happy to help. I know this place can be a bit of a maze at first."

Calida's head spun. So much had changed in so little time.

She smiled gratefully. "Thank you."

He nodded to her and left, no doubt seeing to his other duties, whatever those might be. What did a prince do all day? She shook her head. She had her own duties to focus on now.

Calida pushed open the door, took one look at the bed and nearly wilted. It was the largest bed she'd ever seen, canopied, the sheets red silk. What a far cry from the bunk she'd had at the monastery.

She crossed the room and sank down onto it. It was the softest thing she'd ever laid on, like how she imagined being enfolded by a cloud must feel. What must it be like to live this way all the time?

She fell asleep faster than she ever had before.

* * *

Upon waking, she was briefly disoriented as to where she was. The dying light of the sun streamed through the window as it sank below the horizon. Calida sat up, gazing at the room around her. She was at the palace. It wasn't all a dream; it had really happened.

Niklaus had yet to come for her. She stood, crossing over to the wardrobe and pulling the doors open. He'd said he would take her to the king and she didn't want to appear before him dressed in her plain tunic. And she was sick of wearing nothing but green, nearly every day, since she turned twelve.

The only exception had been whenever she'd snuck into town, wearing someone else's stolen clothes. She never wanted to wear the color again. She thought of the sea, its rich blue color and all the places it could take her.

The color of Niklaus's eyes, she thought briefly before blushing in embarrassment and pushing the thought away.

It was blue she wanted to wear, even though she wasn't a sky witch. She had always wished that she had been one, but a sky witch could do nothing for the king.

Calida found a blue dress in the wardrobe, made of light cotton, and slipped it on. She would have loved to wear silk, but given her precarious position, humility would likely serve her better.

The dress was slightly too large, brushing the floor, but it would have to do.

The quarters she had been given consisted of three rooms: the bedroom, a sitting room, and an attached bathroom with room dividers and a porcelain bathtub. She debated having a bath, glancing at the lotions, soaps and salts that had been laid out. She was still dusty from the long ride, but there was no water and she wasn't sure she had time.

Calida crossed to the dressing table and peered at her reflection in the mirror. She ran her fingers through her hair, trying to bring some order to the disarray. She frowned at the freckles across her cheeks, at her gray eyes, so dull compared to Thalia's. She looked like what she was: a mere girl, her features still clinging to youth, making her look younger than she'd like.

Did she really think she could cure the king?

A knock on the door startled her and she turned away quickly. "Come in."

The door opened and Niklaus stepped inside, taking in her appearance.

She tried not to fidget, feeling defensive beneath his gaze. What did he see when he looked at her?

"It was all I could find," she said, gesturing to the dress, "that would fit."

"We can have some dresses made later," he said. "Don't worry. Are you ready?"

She nodded, unsure of what she would find or what she had quite gotten herself into.

"This way." He jerked his head, indicating she should follow.

This far into the palace, it was much quieter and less hectic than it had been when she'd first arrived. Perhaps things were finally beginning to settle for the evening. Or maybe the servants were needed elsewhere. As she stepped out into the hallway, Calida caught a whiff of something cooking and it smelled delicious.

Her stomach growled as if on cue, but to her immense relief, Niklaus made no comment. She trailed behind him as he led her to the king's quarters.

He paused outside the door. "He's in a bad way at the moment, so I doubt he'll even realize you're there. Make your examination and then we'll discuss your findings elsewhere. I want him disturbed as little as possible."

Calida nodded to show she understood. She needed to push aside her dislike of the king and not let it cloud her judgement. The man was ill and she was a healer. She needed to be professional.

Niklaus pushed the door open and they walked in. The room was stifling; a fire had been lit in the hearth, which shouldn't have been needed in this tropical climate. Within moments, Calida was sweating and she was glad she hadn't chosen to wear anything heavier.

With a glance at Niklaus, she crossed over to the canopied bed. The king lay back, propped up against the pillows, wearing a loose white shirt. His eyes were closed, his skin covered in a sheen of sweat.

In that moment, he didn't look much like a king. Gone was the confident, powerful man who had come to the monastery. Still, she hesitated before reaching out to him. He was still the king, the most powerful man in Alara, even without any magic of his own.

Niklaus came to stand unobtrusively beside the bed, hands clasped behind his back.

Calida reached out, touching the king's forehead. *Fever.*

Gently, she rolled his sleeves back, exposing a collection of ugly bruises on his forearms. Calida looked up at Niklaus and his lips thinned. How had his father come by so many bruises?

She could hear his labored breathing as he struggled in the grip of the fever. His frame seemed too thin and she remembered what Niklaus had said about the king having lost weight and having no appetite.

There was little more a physical examination could tell her in this state. She stepped back from the bed, signaling to Niklaus that she was done. He left and she followed, ducking into a separate room.

"Well?" he asked.

"The bruises—"

"There are more," Niklaus said quietly, "on his back and legs. We don't know what's causing them. He hasn't fallen or bumped into anything." He tried to hide it, but she heard the frustration in his voice. "Do you know what's wrong with him?"

Calida hesitated. "I…read about the symptoms of this condition at the monastery while I was training with Irjah."

"So you know what it is?" Hope flared like a candle in his eyes and Calida hated that she had to put it out.

"No one really knows what the cause is or how to cure it. But it has been observed before and in every instance thus far, it's been fatal."

His face fell. It was not the news he had been hoping for.

"That's what some of the others said," he murmured. "I didn't want to believe it. I had hoped that at least one of you might be able to find a cure…"

So he had known and hadn't wanted to accept it. Desperate to avoid a certain death sentence, he had been frantic enough to seek out an untested witch, in the hope that she might be the one.

Panic seized Calida. She hadn't expected to be foiled so soon. She'd only just arrived; she couldn't be sent back to the monastery now! If she wanted to keep her position here, she would have to try something no one else had.

"Is he in any pain?" she pressed on. "Are there any other symptoms I should know about?"

Niklaus nodded. "Some days he seems fine, but the pain keeps him in bed, even without all the rest of it."

"I could get some opium for the pain and—"

She trailed off, looking at his expression. She wasn't telling him anything the other healers hadn't already. This, too, had been suggested.

Calida felt frustration well up inside of her. She'd known it wouldn't be easy, but perhaps she underestimated how hard it would be. She had to try something. She had to succeed or her dreams would never become reality.

But asking her to discover a cure to a disease no one had been able to cure in skies only knew how long…

Think! There must be something.

She mentally ran through the list of herbs she had learned, searching for one that might prove useful.

"Do you…have any rainleaf?" The herb could be used to reduce fevers. If nothing else, it might make the king more comfortable. She didn't know what else it might do or if it might cure his mysterious illness, but it was worth a try.

"Rainleaf?" Niklaus shook his head. "It only grows on Amberleigh."

The pirate haven.

"There's no way we can get it," he added. "You know, we tried to conquer that island once. Those pirates are barbarians. They don't like each other, but they hate us even more and that was enough for them to rally against us. Greedy as they are, I doubt they'd even try to sell any to us."

Calida chewed her lip. "I can get some."

If she asked him to, Jeremy could get her some. She was sure of it.

Niklaus eyed her. "Do I want to know how?"

"Possibly not," Calida admitted, doubting he would be too pleased to know she associated with one of those pirates. "But I *can* get some."

"Do what you have to. It's one of the few things we haven't tried yet." He sighed. "Dinner is in half an hour. I'll show you the infirmary while we wait and you can get the opium."

She followed him down the twisting, winding corridors. Wall sconces had been lit at regular intervals along the halls, their flickering flames casting strange shadows. It was still oddly quiet. *I suppose with a building this large, even full of servants, you can still feel strangely alone.*

"Has my sister left yet?" she asked as they walked.

He nodded. "It will take some time for a message to reach the *Hunter.*"

"You can give your message to my hawk. He can carry it."

He looked at her, considering. "Unusual. But effective."

* * *

Niklaus took her to the infirmary, where she retrieved the opium and carefully administered it to the king. She realized this was the first official thing she had done outside of training and the thought filled her with anxiety. She would have to trust that the training she had received would be enough to see her through.

Afterwards, Niklaus invited her to dine with him, explaining that he disliked eating alone and that he found himself doing so more and more often since his father's illness.

Feeling a bit sorry for him and very hungry, Calida accepted. There followed the most glorious meal that she could have imagined, which made the food at the tavern seem bland and that served at the monastery utterly unpalatable.

Each course seemed more delicious than the last. There were soups and fresh fish, breads that were sweet and soft, roasted fowl smothered in tangy sauce, fresh fruit—of every kind the island seemed to offer. And then there was the dessert. Calida was stuffed from all of the other courses, but she couldn't pass up the chance to try a little bit of each of the decadent cakes and puddings.

At last, she fell back in her chair, knowing it had all been a mistake and that she was likely to be sick later. She had planned to leave after dinner and see if Jeremy was in town, but the idea of riding a horse all the way there was in no way appealing.

"I've never eaten so much in my life," she groaned.

Niklaus laughed. "It's the least I can do since you agreed to help. I don't suppose I can tempt you with any more wine?"

Oh, the wine. Calida felt a little bit sick *and* drunk, but the wine had been so good she hadn't been able to refuse when offered more.

She just hoped she managed not to make a fool of herself.

"I think I've had enough, Your Highness." She felt a belch coming on and unsuccessfully tried to stifle it. Heat rushed over her skin, from the roots of her hair to the middle of her chest.

Calida expected the prince to be horrified by such uncouth behavior. Was there any further proof that she didn't belong in the palace? She was just some peasant from nowhere who couldn't even manage proper manners.

But instead, he was roaring with laughter, his chair tipped back on two legs. No doubt brought on by his contagious laughter and her tipsy state, Calida found herself howling along.

He leaned forward, his chair returning to earth with a thud. "I like you."

Calida smiled stupidly. "I like me, too."

Her mirth faded by the time dinner ended and she was alone again. The time had come to try and find Jeremy. The grave reason behind the task sobered her. She only hoped he was there. If not, there was no telling how long they would have to wait for the rainleaf and by then, it could be too late.

Waiting for her stomach to settle a little before she set out, Calida sat at the desk in her room, sketching the rainleaf plant so that Jeremy would know what to look for if he didn't already. Horus perched on her desk, watching her quill scratch over the parchment. It had been part of her job while training under Irjah to not only be able to identify the different types of plants on sight, but also draw them. She had no way to color the image; black and white would have to do.

She sighed, sitting back and surveying her work. It wouldn't have passed muster with Irjah; she hadn't taken her time. But she needed to be quick and it would suffice.

Calida looked up at the sound of a knock, recognizing it from before. "Come in."

Niklaus stepped inside, holding a rolled scroll in one hand. It had been sealed with red wax, bearing the royal seal. "I have the message for the *Hunter.*"

"Thank you." She reached out and took it from him, handing it to Horus. The hawk gripped it in one foot. Calida stood, folding the drawing of the rainleaf and slipping it into the pocket of her dress. "I'm going out to meet a contact who can help us get some rainleaf. I'll send Horus with the message on my way."

He nodded. "Good luck."

As she left, with the help of some of the servants guiding her down to the stables, Calida realized just how much trust Niklaus was putting in her. The best healers in the kingdom had failed to find a way to heal his father. It was up to her now.

But if Jeremy wasn't at the tavern, their chance would be over before it could really begin.

As soon as she stepped out into the warm night air, Horus launched himself from where he'd been perched on her shoulder. Calida watched her familiar disappear into the dark sky, bearing a message from the prince. Somewhere out there, Thalia was on the open sea, waiting for him.

Calida turned to the stables and quickly set about harnessing a horse. The trip into the town where she had always met Jeremy was much faster on horseback, though painful every step of the way. She was still sore from her long ride earlier that day, feeling every jostle along the path. She would definitely need a long, hot soak in the tub later.

It would be her reward—if she succeeded.

She tethered the horse outside the tavern and stepped in, searching for Jeremy. This would be the first time she had seen him since informing him that graduation wasn't far off and warning him that she might not be able to see him again. She'd had no idea at the time that he would be so vital to her new placement.

They spotted each other almost at the same time and Jeremy crossed over to meet her. "Almost didn't recognize you, dressed like that." He grinned. "You've clearly gone up in the world."

Even though her new dress was cotton instead of silk, it was visibly of higher quality than the tunics she had worn at the monastery.

"You have no idea," Calida replied, sitting down at a table across from him. She kept her voice pitched low as she filled him in. "The king is ill. You're to keep that information to yourself. Very few people know and the crown wants to keep it that way."

"My lips are sealed, firebrand."

She trusted him. He'd kept the secret that she was a witch, after all, though now that she had moved on from the monastery and was out among the general public, it didn't matter so much. There was no need to sneak out anymore and no danger from being caught.

Likewise, she had kept his secret, but still a frisson of worry went through her. What might one let slip under the inebriating effects of alcohol? Calida knew the crown wanted such information kept quiet for several reasons, not least of which being that it might weaken the kingdom. Someone might take advantage of such information and strike while Alara's leadership was vulnerable.

Someone like the pirates of Amberleigh.

Calida pressed on. "The prince has asked me to try and heal him. That's my new placement, up at the palace."

Jeremy let out a low whistle, mostly drowned out by the other conversations taking place around them. "Look at you. If I didn't love the sea so much, I'd be jealous."

"I need your help, though. The best healers in all of Alara haven't been able to heal the king and the prince is desperate enough to let me try. I want to give him some rainleaf, but it only grows on Amberleigh and I need you to get some for me."

"Anything for you, firebrand, but I don't know how long it'll take me."

"Just get it as quickly as you can." She could send Horus down to the tavern each night, looking for the *Sea Witch* to see if Jeremy was there or not, saving her a ride down every time.

Calida fished the sketch out of her pocket and handed it to him. "This is what it looks like. The leaves are bright blue. You can't miss them. Get as much of it as you can find."

He stared at the drawing and then tucked it away. "You can count on me."

She smiled, relieved. "I knew I could. Thank you."

Calida found Niklaus still awake when she returned, despite the late hour. "Were you successful?"

"I don't know how soon I can get the rainleaf, but I *will* get it." Of that, she was certain. How effective the herb would be, she was less sure.

He nodded, expression inscrutable. "I'll bid you a good night, then."

She watched him leave. "Good night."

She wanted nothing more than to fall into bed herself.

But first, a bath.

CHAPTER 13

The first pirate ship was spotted off the coast of Indris. She flew no colors, as pirate vessels were wont to do. When signaled, she refused to display any. Squinting against the harsh glare of the sun, Thalia could see the changes being made to the sails as the ship slowly turned away from them. They were going to try and make a run for it.

It was a schooner, a smaller ship than the frigate Thalia sailed on and under normal circumstances, the pirates would have been able to outrun them, their ship lighter and quicker. But these circumstances were anything but ordinary.

At the helm, the captain turned to her. "Get us in range."

Thalia nodded and the sails above billowed, snapping taut, as she filled them with a stronger gust of wind. She'd been letting the wind move them along without her assistance, but now that a target had been spotted, she stepped in once more.

She reached out, feeling the sea beneath them, commanding the waves to push against their hull, urging them on faster. Her blood thrummed, muscles singing as she called upon her power. This was what she was meant for. There would be no holding back here.

In less than half an hour, they had closed in on their prey. Thalia could see the men scurrying about on the deck of the enemy ship, the gun ports opening up. The stern chasers fired a warning shot which fell short, splashing harmlessly into the water. Neither ships' guns were yet in range.

Thalia smiled to herself. The *Hunter* had guns of her own, more than the pirates likely carried, but there would be no need for them. Perhaps the best part of employing sky witches in the navy was the assurance that no Alaran need be harmed in the engagement.

The only people sent to a watery grave would be the criminals who preyed upon innocent merchant vessels.

"Whenever you're ready," the captain murmured.

Facing the pirate ship, Thalia squared her shoulders and lifted her arms. The sea around the ship began heaving, rising up as she compelled it until a massive wave towered over the pirates, hanging suspended for a moment.

Thalia closed her hands into fists and the wave crashed down upon them. An earsplitting crack rang out as the wooden ship cleaved in two. She lowered her hands. The remains would slowly sink down to the bottom and the crew would drown. They were too far away from Indris's shore to make a swim for it, but just to be sure…

The water swirled around the men, pulling them down into the depths.

Thalia placed her hands behind her back and the captain nodded to her. "Well done."

A screech sounded above them and Thalia looked up, shading her eyes with one hand. She could just make out the silhouette of a bird as it drew nearer. What was a bird doing out here? Had it come from Indris?

The bird swooped down, crossing the deck, and landed on her shoulder. Thalia recognized it now. Her sister's hawk.

"What is it?" she demanded, knowing the familiar couldn't speak to her. "Is Calida in trouble?"

Only then did she notice the scroll the bird proffered to her. She took it, breaking the wax seal and quickly scanned the letter.

"What is it?" the captain barked.

She handed him the prince's message. "I'm to report to the palace at once."

He scowled. "Damned nuisance, having to go all the way back. But orders are orders."

The hawk lifted off, going ahead of them, as the captain shouted out orders to the rest of the crew, informing them of the change in plans.

Thalia felt a slight prickle of irritation at being called away from her placement when she'd only just arrived. But her curiosity was stronger still.

What did the prince want with her? There was only one way to find out and the faster they returned, the sooner she'd get answers. Thalia lifted her arms and thrust them forward. The ship lurched beneath her from the force of the gale.

* * *

They returned to the Brisban harbor in record time, Thalia having urged the ship on, straining her power to the limit.

"We'll wait here for you," the captain informed her before she departed. "If you can't return, send word."

Thalia nodded and set off for the palace at once, the prince's message clutched in her hand. She presented it to the guards at the gate and was admitted into a world of gleaming marble, tapestries, stone statues, and decorative plants in urns. There were almost no windows and the vast majority of light came from candles and torches.

She hated it almost at once. Where was the sky? Being able to see it, knowing her power was easily accessible, right at hand, made her feel in control, less uncertain of what was to come. The first thing she'd change, if it were up to her, would be to open the place up. To make it a palace of glass and marble rather than cold, unfeeling stone.

"Thalia!"

She looked up to see—impossibly—Calida hurrying toward her, dressed in what looked to be royal blue silk. The gown fit her incredibly well, as though tailor-made for her.

But that made no sense. Why was her sister wearing silk? Why was she here? And why was she wearing a sky witch's colors?

Her sister embraced her and Thalia was almost too shocked to return the gesture.

"What are you doing here?" Thalia demanded once she'd been released.

Calida beamed at her. "This is my placement." Briefly, she told Thalia about the king's illness and the prince seeking out her help. She took Thalia's hands in her own. "I asked him to invite you. Isn't it wonderful? I'm so glad you're here."

Thalia withdrew her hands. "Calida, why am I here?"

Her sister frowned. "I should think it's obvious."

"Well it isn't." She wasn't a healer. Why was she needed? Why had she been called away from her own placement to a place where she was essentially useless? There was nothing she could do for the king. "Care to enlighten me?"

"I just thought you'd like to stay here, at the palace."

Thalia glanced around. Certainly, she'd never expected to set foot here. Perhaps if she'd been given a medal, one day, for her service in the navy, but not now. Not for no reason other than her sister had a connection.

It wasn't where she belonged. But then, Calida had given her an opportunity. She could see her sister's expression wavering, bordering on disappointment with the way Thalia had reacted.

She could make this work. She could belong anywhere she wished.

She summoned a smile. "I suppose it's infinitely preferable to staying on a ship surrounded by a bunch of smelly men."

Calida grinned. "I knew you'd like it." She took Thalia by the arm. "Come on, I'll show you to your room."

"There's just one thing," Thalia said as they began walking. "How long do you expect this to last?"

"What do you mean?"

Thalia was tempted to stop walking and force Calida to look at her, she was so incredulous. "You can't possibly expect to heal the king, Calida. You said it yourself just now, the best healers in the entire kingdom have tried and failed. What are you compared to them?"

Her sister did stop walking then and turned to look at her. "You could at least try to believe in me."

Thalia scowled. She hadn't said anything that was untrue, and yet it had been the wrong thing to say.

"I am not going to lie to you."

"You don't think I can do it," Calida said flatly.

"It was thoughtful of you to invite me here. I think we should enjoy this while it lasts, but don't get used to it."

If she played her cards right, she could find a way to make this last. But even if not, at least she had a placement to go back to. The navy would always welcome her back. But Calida had nowhere else to go.

Calida released her arm. "I'll find a servant. They can escort you the rest of the way. I have a patient to see to."

She turned and walked away, footsteps ringing on the marble floor, leaving Thalia alone.

* * *

Thalia's reaction stung, more than Calida cared to admit. To have her own sister, the person whose opinion she valued most, not believe in her struck a blow to her confidence.

Maybe Thalia was right. Maybe she couldn't do this. Who did she think she was? She was a fraud, playing at being a healer, and once Niklaus discovered how much of a fraud she was, she'd be out on her ear. No placement, no future.

Furious, Calida shoved the thoughts away. She didn't need them. She needed to believe in herself, if no one else would. That belief was the only one that mattered.

Fortunately, within the week, Horus reported from the tavern with news that Jeremy had returned. Flying down the steps to the palace, a satchel draped across her shoulder, Calida borrowed a horse from the stables and rode into town bareback, without even bothering to saddle the horse first, she was in such a rush.

She burst into the tavern and met him halfway across the room. "Do you have it?" she asked eagerly.

She had continued to check on the king every day and his condition had not improved. This experiment of hers might be the only way to save him and time was running out. He didn't say as much to her, but she knew Niklaus was growing impatient.

"I do," Jeremy replied. "It's still on the *Sea Witch*."

He led her outside, along to where his ship waited. Calida remained on the dock, by the gangplank as he climbed up and disappeared below. He returned with a bundle, wrapped in oil cloth. Hurriedly, Calida unwrapped it and found herself staring down at a collection of bright blue leaves.

She smiled. "You did it." She retied the bundle and placed it safely in her satchel, then rose on her tiptoes to kiss his cheek. "Thank you."

Jeremy grinned. "I hope they do the trick, firebrand. Let me know if you need any more."

"I will. I'm sorry I can't stay, but I need to get these to the king as fast as possible."

"I know. Go on. And if this plan of yours works, come back and buy *me* an ale sometime."

"I will," Calida promised. "We'll empty out the royal coffers and buy drinks for the whole town."

"Now *that* I like the sound of."

With a parting reminder to be careful, Calida left him there and fetched her horse, flying back to the palace at a gallop. It was all she could do to hold on, but she didn't dare slow. Every moment mattered.

Returning to the king's room, Calida instructed a servant to brew some tea and then waited for it to arrive, tapping her fingers on her knee impatiently. She took the tray from the servant when it arrived and set it on a side table, glancing at the king. The room was blessedly cooler this time, but he still lay back against the pillows, looking drawn and pale.

Taking a deep breath, inhaling the aroma of the tea, Calida withdrew the package of rainleaf and opened it. She selected a single leaf, about as long as her hand, and crumbled it into the tea. She gave it a vigorous stir for good measure and then helped the king drink it. He let out a sound of displeasure at the taste and tried to refuse any more, but Calida persisted, staying with him until there was nothing left but dregs.

She stood back. It was all she could do. Only time would tell if it made any difference. And if it didn't…she didn't know what she would do then.

* * *

Calida awoke to pounding on her bedroom door. She groaned and sat up. Sunlight poured through the windows, but from the angle, she knew it was earlier than she would have preferred.

The hammering continued, urgent, not to be ignored. "I'm coming," she called, fumbling for her robe.

What could be so urgent so early in the morning? A sudden, terrible thought struck her, shaking off any remaining sluggishness. She had given the king the rainleaf only the night before. What if he was now dead? What if she had killed him?

Rainleaf wasn't deadly, or at least she'd heard of no such cases, but then again, he was suffering from a mysterious illness. There was no telling what effect it might have had.

Oh, skies, what if I killed the king? Would they execute her for regicide? And what would they do to Thalia? She should have never asked for her to be brought to the palace.

Calida had just managed to slip her robe over her lacy nightgown when the door opened and Niklaus strode in. She stared at him with frightened eyes, but his expression was jubilant.

"What did you give him?" he demanded. "Was it the rainleaf?"

"Y—yes, I got some, just like I said."

"Whatever you did, it worked. It's the most improvement we've seen in weeks. The fever's broken and he's alert now. He's even asked for breakfast to be sent up." Niklaus grabbed her wrist. "Come on."

"Where are we going?" Calida yelped as he pulled her toward the door. She was so limp with relief that she *hadn't* killed the king that she wasn't even resisting.

"I want him to know that you're the one responsible."

"But I'm not even dressed!" If she'd been horrified by the idea of the king seeing her in monastery dress, the idea of being seen in her nightgown was even worse.

No doubt her eyes were puffy and her hair a rat's nest.

But Niklaus didn't slow down. She could feel the excitement practically radiating off of him. No doubt he wasn't even listening, he was so thrilled.

He pulled her into the king's room and sure enough, Wilhelm was sitting up in bed, a tray of food resting before him. His cheeks looked just as sunken as before, but the pallor was gone. His eyes, when they turned to her, were still too bright, the look of one recovering from a fever, but she had to admit, it was a marked improvement over last night.

"Father," Niklaus said breathlessly. "This is the witch from the monastery that I brought in. She's the one who cured you."

"I'm not cured yet, boy," the king barked, his voice still slightly rasping. He gestured to Calida. "Come here. Let me take a look at you."

Swallowing, Calida stepped forward, feeling ridiculous.

"I remember you from the monastery. Healer, are you?"

Mutely, she nodded and then remembered herself. "Yes, Your Majesty."

"You're very young."

Calida lowered her gaze.

"I don't know if this treatment you've proposed will be successful in the long run. Time will tell. Nevertheless, you've given us some hope, and for that I'm grateful. You've done your kingdom a great service."

Calida let out a shaky breath. "Thank you, Your Majesty." She was afraid to look up, afraid that her triumph would be written too plainly across her face. The king was grateful to *her!*

He looked back up at his son. "Leave me."

Niklaus bowed and Calida took that as her cue to do the same. As she backed out of the room, she no longer cared that she was wearing a nightgown. The rainleaf had worked! Or at least, it had done something. For the first time, she allowed herself to believe that she could truly do this.

She stopped as Niklaus reached out and took her hand. His voice was very quiet when he spoke. "I know we're not out of the woods yet, but you've given us more than anyone else has thus far. Thank you."

Calida looked up at him, into those clear blue eyes. There was something about the way he was looking at her, a sort of tenderness that hadn't been there before.

She sucked in a breath. "Thank you for giving me the opportunity. I hope I don't let you down."

Impulsively, he lifted her hand, pressing it to his lips, before releasing her and striding off down the corridor. Calida stood there, peering after him, until his form had disappeared around the corner.

* * *

Calida used her supply of rainleaf sparingly, but she knew she would have to ask Jeremy to get some more, sooner or later. She didn't know if she was merely prolonging the king's life and would need to keep giving him rainleaf until the end, or if she was actually curing whatever ailed him—but it didn't really matter either way.

By the third day, the king was able to get out of bed. By the end of the week, he seemed restored to his former self, though the bruises had yet to fade from his skin. Niklaus was more cheerful than she had yet seen him. The dark circles beneath his eyes were gone. Calida had done it, or at least, she'd done something. Every day that went by brought her closer to her goal. It felt real now, no longer impossible, but something tangible, that could be achieved.

Niklaus invited her and Thalia to go riding with him on the palace grounds, through the extensive forest gardens. Calida eagerly accepted. She hadn't seen Thalia much since her sister had arrived at the palace and they had exchanged words. Calida felt a bit bad for the way that had gone, but she hoped that Thalia would have some faith in her now that the king had shown such signs of improvement.

The two sisters rode side by side along the rocked pathway, two rows of trees on either side of them, stretching out for miles. Niklaus rode slightly ahead of them, on his magnificent chestnut horse. The guards trailed behind, never absent, but as unobtrusive as possible.

"It's funny," Thalia murmured, breaking the silence. The horses were moving at a walk and so far, the only sound had been their hooves crunching against the gravel.

"What is?" Calida asked, glancing at her.

200

Her sister wore a high-necked royal blue gown with long, flowing sleeves. Part of her bright red hair had been swept back from her temples and pinned behind her head, the rest of it hanging free. It seemed that palace life suited her just fine. Calida frowned slightly as she took in her sister's dress.

She wore silk herself, something she allowed now that she felt she had earned her place at the palace, but she had taken to wearing blue. It was her favorite color and she thought it suited her much better than green.

Her gown was more of a misty blue compared to the rich tones of Thalia's. But blue suited Thalia more, with her dark blue eyes, and it was a sky witch's color. Much as she loved it, Calida didn't want to wear blue if it meant paling in comparison to her sister.

She didn't want to be in anyone's shadow. She wanted to stand out.

Thalia glanced at Niklaus and lowered her voice slightly. "You were the one who always hated the king and the system he put in place for us. You were the one who always raged against the fate that was decided for us. And yet you saved his life."

"I haven't saved him yet."

"You're well on your way, from what I hear."

"What you hear is exaggerated."

Calida had heard the talk making its rounds in the palace. Those who knew of the king's illness were flush with hope that he had been saved and that they wouldn't have to fear the uncertainty that came with a change of power.

She saw the way that people looked at her, the way they spoke of her, and always felt a moment of pride. She had done this. But she wasn't foolish enough to think that the king was out of danger yet. He seemed much improved, but that didn't mean he was cured.

Thalia adjusted the reins in her hand. "Calida…I appreciate you bringing me here and I'm sorry I didn't believe in you. Your power…is different than mine, but that doesn't mean it's not useful or important. I see that now. But there's nothing here for me. I'm not useful here like you are. There's…nothing for me to do, no purpose for me."

The words meant a lot coming from her. *She believes in me now.* But she was also right. Thalia's placement had been in the navy, on board a ship, protecting it and hunting down threats to the kingdom. Her power was of little use here and for a moment, Calida felt guilty for taking her sister away from where she was meant to be.

"Do you want to go back?"'"

Thalia shook her head. "I thought I knew what I wanted. Now I'm not so sure."

"I thought you'd like it here."

"I do. It's just that you have your place here and now I need to find mine." She leaned closer. "But one thing I do know is—I'm glad we're together again."

Niklaus turned around to face them. "What are you girls talking about back there?"

"Nothing," Calida called, sending her horse into a trot to catch up to him. "Just sister stuff."

"Well I wouldn't know anything about that." He glanced at the sky. "Looks like it might rain. Race you back to the palace?"

Calida was tempted to ask Thalia to forestall the rain so they could keep riding, but it seemed ill-advised after their conversation. Thalia had said that she needed to find her own place at the palace and she wouldn't thank Calida for using her as a means to manipulate the weather in her favor.

She smiled. "You're on." She called to Thalia, "Race you back to the palace!"

In that brief moment, Niklaus spurred his horse onward and Calida hurried to catch up, but Thalia didn't bother chasing after them and soon, she was left behind.

* * *

Niklaus stepped into his father's study. The king had been spending more time here since he had recovered his strength, just like he always used to. Niklaus had always been fond of the room. It was small for a room in the palace, but that gave it a more intimate feel that was missing from the more formal rooms.

Surrounded by the smells of old books and leather, Niklaus remembered spending many evenings here as a child, playing quietly by the hearth while his father looked over papers at his desk.

"You wanted to see me, Father?" he asked, closing the door behind him.

His father rose from behind the desk. It had only been a little over a week and already his skin had regained a healthy color. Now that he was eating regular meals, he no longer had the thin, skeletal look of a bird, small and frail.

"I have spoken with my advisors and we are in agreement. In two weeks' time, a ball will be held here at the palace. It will be a good opportunity for me to be seen and assure those present that all is well."

"Are you sure you're up to it?" Niklaus asked. "It hasn't been that long and you don't want to push yourself too soon—"

The king glared at him and he fell silent, feeling at once like a small boy again, being chastised. He needed to point out such things, but he should have known that his father wouldn't thank him for it, especially once his mind had already been made.

Still, if Niklaus thought this ill-advised, he might speak with Calida. As the king's healer, she had some authority when it came to his health and what he should or should not be doing at this point.

"The invitations have already been sent out. The lords will be present, along with their wives and any daughters they may have."

Niklaus looked sharply at his father. "Daughters?"

"I know we've had this conversation before and I like it as little as you, but we'll keep having it until something is done. It's time for you to find a wife, Niklaus. I know you've been busy dealing with things during my illness, and you've done admirably, but that only reinforces my point. I don't know how much longer I have left, but when my time comes, I will be able to die peacefully knowing that I leave the kingdom in good hands and that you won't have to rule on your own." The king's face shadowed. "No one should have to bear that burden alone."

Niklaus knew his father was thinking of the queen, dead now for several years. It hadn't been easy on his father and he had seen the way he suffered without her by his side.

He swallowed. "You shouldn't have to worry about that. You're cured. Calida's done a magnificent job—"

"I have no complaints about her care," the king interrupted. "But you and I both know I'm not cured. Not yet, anyway." He rolled up one sleeve, exposing fresh bruises beneath. "In however much time that is left to me, I want to see you settled. It would ease my mind greatly and I know those of the people as well."

Niklaus sighed. There was no point in arguing—there never had been—and deep down, he knew his father was right. At the very least, they had been given a reprieve and even if the king was healed, he still would not live forever. Eventually, Niklaus would have to find a partner to rule beside him.

"Very well, Father. I can't promise that I will find a wife at this ball of yours, but I will keep an open mind."

The king nodded and laid a hand on his arm briefly. "Good man."

"There's just one thing."

"What is it?"

"May I invite someone?"

* * *

"A party?" Thalia asked, coming further into Calida's room.

Calida sat on the edge of her bed, stroking Horus's feathers where he perched on the bedpost. "Niklaus just told me. All the nobility will be there."

Thalia inhaled deeply. "Well, we have to go, obviously. We can't refuse the invitation."

"Why do we even have to be there?" Calida flopped back onto the bed. "What do we want with nobility?"

"You mean you're not simply thrilled to get all dressed up and hobnob with the rich and famous? Isn't that every girl's dream?"

Calida snorted. "Not mine."

The whole idea of the ball seemed incredibly dull to her. She'd much rather go out riding than spend the whole evening surrounded by a bunch of stuffy nobles who possessed an overinflated sense of self-importance. But if Niklaus wanted her to be there, then she would go.

"Well, you'll have to be there," Thalia replied. "Everyone will want to catch a glimpse of the witch who saved the king."

* * *

When the night of the ball arrived, Calida resigned herself to a long, boring evening. She dressed simply in a green silk dress, fashionable enough for the occasion, but not so that there was any risk she might outshine any of the nobility.

As much as she despised wearing green and had sworn it off, she thought it a wise decision to wear the color of an earth witch. It was what would be expected of her. She left her hair down in its natural waves. With Horus perched on her shoulder, she followed the servant that had been sent to escort her.

Thalia joined her in the hall, escorted by a servant of her own. She wore a stunning gown of blue silk that flowed over her like water. It seemed to shimmer and change shades slightly beneath the lights as she moved, one moment a light blue and the next, dark like the sun rolling over the sea. Her own familiar was not with her, but Calida had thought it best to bring hers. She was, after all, a witch and a healer, and that was why she had been invited. There was no ignoring the fact.

"What did you do to your hair?" Calida hissed at Thalia. It had been pinned up in an intricate style, exposing her sister's slender neck and shoulders.

"I had one of the servants arrange it for me," Thalia replied and Calida immediately wished she had thought of that.

If her plan had been to blend in, Thalia's had been to stand out. No one would look at her and assume she was a witch. They would mistake her for one of their own.

One of their own…who never had to be separated from their families and sent to live at a remote monastery for years.

Refusing to be intimidated—the nobility were still just people, after all—Calida stood straighter with her head high, though Thalia was taller than her. Together, they strode into the crowded ballroom. Every inch was nearly filled with people pressing closely together. There was no furniture in the room, aside from a few chairs against the walls, where people could sit and relieve their aching feet.

Servants moved deftly through the crowd, bearing trays of canapes and fluted glasses of a bright liquid Calida couldn't readily identify. The lords were all dressed entirely in black—or military-style uniforms—their shoes polished, hair gleaming with pomade. The women moved about in large frilly dresses that were far too wide to be practical. Calida wondered how many more people could have been fit into the room if not for such wide skirts.

In contrast, Thalia's gown hugged her waist and hips before flaring out at the knee. Calida noticed her sister drew several stares as she moved into the room. She herself did not go unnoticed either, though not for the same reason.

At the monastery, Thalia had never tried to stand out, but here, she drew a crowd.

Stomach twisting, Calida turned away. The air was warm from the press of so many bodies in the enclosed space and she instantly felt a bit claustrophobic. With her sister sailing off into the crowd as if she belonged there, Calida remained where she was, hoping to be left alone.

She could see the king standing at the other end of the room, in the same ceremonial dress he had worn to the monastery the day she had graduated. He was deep in conversation with yet another noble Calida didn't recognize.

Niklaus stood beside him, also in ceremonial dress, and as Calida watched, more than one woman came up to him, dragging a much younger woman along with her that could only be her daughter. The daughter simpered and made eyes at the prince, but Calida could tell Niklaus wasn't really interested. He replied to whatever she said briefly, the picture of utmost politeness, but refusing to be drawn out.

He's just as miserable as I am.

Suddenly, she became uncomfortably aware that she was being stared at. Calida looked up and saw a cluster of women watching her, whispering to each other behind their feathered fans. She felt her cheeks flush and looked away, wondering what they were saying.

Sensing her discomfort, Horus shifted slightly on her shoulder. Her gown had sleeves, unlike Thalia's, but the silk was thin and she knew the hawk was being very careful not to accidentally hurt her with his talons.

Perhaps bringing him along had been a mistake. He was attracting a lot of unwanted attention, but she should have expected that. No one else in the room had a hawk perched on their shoulder.

"I can leave if you'd like," he murmured softly, gazing around at the crowd. He fixed the gossiping group of women with a hard, unblinking stare, and Calida was amused to see a few of them squirm.

"No," she replied. "It's all right."

Though she tried not to, she couldn't help but catch a few snatches of conversation.

"I heard she's from the Erlohn monastery."

"Well of course she is. She's a witch."

"Shouldn't she be dressed like the other servants, then?"

"She does clean up rather well. For a witch, I mean. Do you think she has all of her teeth?"

Calida ground the teeth in question together. They spoke of her as if discussing a prize brood mare! *Come over here and you'll find out exactly how many teeth I have.*

One of them sniffed. "She's younger than I thought she'd be."

"I wonder where her witch-mark is. You know I heard…"

Calida tried not to listen to the rest of it, but there was no ignoring the vulgar insinuations. She refused to look at them. If they thought her little better than a servant, they would expect her not to make eye contact. Her hands were clenched into fists and she practically shook from anger.

To them, she was nothing more than a novelty. Something to be gawked at.

"They've probably never met a witch before," Horus suggested and he was likely right. When or why would nobles ever cross paths with a witch? They were a lower order.

"So what is it that you do?" There was a pause and then the same voice added, "Do you suppose she's deaf?"

Calida hadn't realized that one of the women had stepped closer and was now addressing her directly.

She looked up sharply. "I can hear you." The words came out more forcefully than she'd intended, but it was so hard to remain polite.

The woman took a half step back and adopted an affronted expression, one hand going to her bosom. Her silver hair was piled high atop her head, far too high to be natural. A large white feather was attached to her headband and she wore too much rouge. Calida thought she looked ridiculous and longed to tell her so, but she mastered her temper and schooled her features.

"I asked what it was you do here at the palace." The woman still spoke too loud, as though not convinced Calida could hear. Or perhaps she merely thought her stupid.

"I'm a healer," Calida answered. That should have been obvious by now. They should have already known.

"You are the one who healed the king?"

"That's right."

The woman looked her up and down. "To think that you managed to do what every other healer could not." Her voice was heavy, laced with doubt.

Calida gave a tight smile. "I was trained well."

"I think it's marvelous that the king's finally found a replacement for his personal physician," one of the women remarked. "Must be nice having your own private healer."

A young woman came to stand at the elbow of the woman who had first spoken. "Can we get one, Mother?"

Calida could no longer make out the conversation over the rushing of the blood in her ears. Though no one else approached her, she could still see eyes flicking in her direction, lips moving in whispered conversation.

She wondered what else they said about her, her imagination filling in the gaps. How she was too thin, her hair looked like a rat's nest, how she didn't even know how to dress properly and it was an embarrassment for the king to display her, no matter how good of a healer she was.

She clenched her jaw so hard her temples ached. She hadn't come to be made fun of and she wasn't going to stand there to be stared at and gossiped about. She didn't know why Niklaus had invited her, but she wasn't staying a moment longer.

They already thought her uncouth, some wild thing less than fully human. The fact that she left early, without speaking to the royals first, should come as no surprise to them.

Calida strode out of the ballroom and into the hallway without looking back.

* * *

Thalia watched her sister leave out of the corner of her eye and felt a flicker of disappointment, but not surprise. She made no move to go after her.

Calida could be unreasonably stubborn; there was no point in trying to convince her to stay. She would only be wasting both of their time. If there was anything to be gained by staying, Thalia would stay. They had been offered an opportunity afforded to no other witches and Calida was a fool not to take full advantage.

Thalia could never change the way the nobles saw witches, but for just one evening, she could become what they wanted to see when they looked at her. It was nothing more than a game, each person present playing their own role.

"Your gown is very beautiful."

Thalia turned to face a young woman that had been talking with the prince only a few moments ago. Her hair was dark, thick, and curled slightly.

"Thank you," Thalia said simply. It was always best to compliment someone else. It pleased them to know that you'd noticed something about them and approved. "I adore your hair. Such a lovely color."

The girl smiled appreciatively as Thalia knew she would. "I don't remember seeing you here before and I'm sure I would have. Which house do you belong to?"

"Oh, I don't." Thalia smiled and lowered her gaze humbly. "I'm just a witch. The sister to the one who healed the king."

The other girl's eyes widened. "I mistook you for a noble." She looked at Thalia's dress. "A sky witch?"

"That's right."

"I've never met a witch before. What's it like?"

"Oh, it's…nothing special, really. What's it like being a member of the nobility?"

"Nothing special," the girl answered and they shared a laugh. "Where's your familiar? You do have one, right?"

"I left her in my room. It's so crowded, I thought it best not to bring her."

"What do you make of staying at the palace?"

Thalia hadn't expected so many personal questions. She would have much rather asked the girl about herself, but she would answer.

She laughed softly, looking around the room. "I'm grateful to be here, but I confess, I find it all a bit overwhelming."

"You get used to it." The other girl nodded to her and moved on. She hadn't even asked Thalia her name.

Thalia sighed, grabbing a glass as a servant passed by, bearing a tray. She hadn't asked for the girl's name either, but she didn't care. Their conversation was of no importance and they wouldn't likely remember each other. She let the smile fade from her face.

Such people were exhausting to talk to, interested only in themselves and what they had to say. Never truly listening, always with their next response ready at hand, saying nothing much of anything.

"Excuse me, I don't believe we've met."

Pasting the smile back on her face, she turned to see a young man. His suit fit him exceptionally well. He was a few inches taller than her, but not so tall that he towered over her, making her feel small. He had a thick head of dark hair and eyes so dark they were nearly black. There were faint pockmarks across his cheeks, but his jaw was nice and strong. Overall, pleasant to look at.

"No, I don't believe I've had the pleasure. I'm Thalia," she said, extending one hand. "My sister is the witch responsible for healing the king."

He took her hand and kissed it as he would for any noble. When he introduced himself, she filed the name away, should it prove useful later on.

"I've never met a witch before," he confessed. His eyes roamed over her and she wondered if he was searching for her witch-mark or merely enjoying the view. His gaze lingered on her cleavage and she thought it must be the latter. *Skies, men were too easy.* "Is possessing unnatural beauty part of it or are you the exception?"

Thalia summoned a laugh, lowering her gaze demurely. Let him think she found him charming. "There's nothing special about us, I'm afraid. We're dreadfully dull."

"I'll be the judge of that."

Ignoring the party around her, Thalia listened to the young lord talk about himself, giving him her undivided attention. People liked when she did that, as they so little found it from anyone else. She laughed at his jokes, which were in no way amusing.

She was the very image of what he expected to see, a humble girl, a bit naïve, simply grateful to be at the palace, and a little overwhelmed by it all. A charming girl from the country, yet perfectly polite and proper.

When he extended his hand and asked if she would like to dance, there was only one answer she could give.

She acquiesced, allowing him to lead, aware of the stares. The women looked at her with envy, the men with want.

It was nothing more than a game, far from the most enjoyable, perhaps, but easily played.

* * *

As soon as the latest young woman excused herself—Niklaus had already forgotten her name—he scanned the crowd, looking for Calida. Her red hair should have made her easy to spot, but he saw only Thalia, twirling in the arms of some young lord.

The younger sister looked regal in her blue gown. She could have easily been mistaken for one of the nobility and with her sharp cheekbones and dark blue eyes, she was easily more beautiful than most of the young women that had been presented to him that night.

Niklaus made his way over to her, addressing her dance partner. "Excuse me, would you mind if I borrowed the lady for a moment?"

How ridiculous to pose such a question, the answer taken for granted. No one would dare refuse him anything.

With a flicker of a frown, quickly masked, the young lord surrendered Thalia. She turned to Niklaus. "You wanted to dance, Your Highness?"

He smiled. "No, though I'm sure you're very good at it. I thought you might appreciate being rescued."

She smiled in return, and the gesture struck him as genuine in a sea of affectations. "The thought is indeed much appreciated, Your Highness."

"Have you seen Calida?"

She blinked at him, nearly as tall as he was. "She left a few moments ago."

He thanked her and began making his way through the crowd, toward the doors that led out of the ballroom, ignoring any attempts to draw him into conversation. Niklaus stepped out into the hall and glancing right, saw Calida striding away with purpose, her hawk still perched on her shoulder.

* * *

"Calida!"

She spun around to see Niklaus at the other end of the corridor, where she'd just come from, outside the ballroom. He jogged to catch up with her, boots echoing on the marble floor.

"What are you doing here?" she asked, glancing over his shoulder as he reached her. "Won't you be missed?"

"Thalia told me you'd left. The party's not over yet. Is something wrong?"

She frowned. "I didn't want to stay for the rest of it. I didn't come to be mocked, to be laughed at."

"What do you mean?"

"You should have seen the way they looked at me. The things they said. Why did you invite me?"

He grimaced. "I thought you might enjoy it. Forgive me, I should have anticipated this." He ran a hand through his hair. "Truth be told, I don't enjoy such events myself." He half smiled. "I wish I could leave as well, but your absence will not be nearly as conspicuous as mine."

Calida tilted her head. "You don't have to go back, you know. You could just…walk away."

He laughed. "And go where?"

"Come with me." She turned and kept walking down the hall.

"You're going to get me into trouble, Calida." But he didn't sound overly troubled and she could hear his footsteps following.

Moving quickly, she led him through the passageways that she had rapidly grown familiar with. Nearly every spare moment had been devoted to learning the ins and outs of her new home. He was still with her when she stepped out a side door and into the night air, cool and refreshing after the stifling ballroom.

Niklaus stopped, looking up at the palace behind him, the windows lit golden from within.

"Still tempted to go back?" she asked.

He turned back to her, the moonlight reflecting on his golden hair. "Not in the least." He fell into step beside her. "I suppose I should feel bad, but if I have to sit through one more conversation with the daughter of lord so-and-so, I think I'll go mad. My father won't be pleased to learn I've run off. That's why he arranged this party in the first place."

"I thought the purpose was to reassure everyone that he was well again."

"Partly that," Niklaus nodded. "But he also intends for me to find a wife. He said he doesn't know how many more days he has left and wants to know the kingdom is secure and that I won't have to lead on my own."

"Oh," Calida said softly.

"Some days I do wish I could just run away, but I can't. This isn't just about me. I have to do what's best for my kingdom. I can…escape for a little while, like right now, but sooner or later, I have to face the truth."

Calida stopped and looked at him. She had never considered that he might be even more trapped than she was. His fate, much like hers, had been decided for him, from the moment of his birth.

"I never wanted to be a witch, to be sent to a monastery, away from everyone I knew so that I could learn how I might best serve the kingdom. To have my destiny decided for me. I wanted to travel, to see the world. I still do. I know what it is to feel trapped."

Perhaps they understood each other more than she thought.

"Those people back there," she continued, nodding her head toward the palace. "When they look at you, all they see is the prince, the future ruler of Alara. When they look at me, they see just another witch. As if we can't be anything more than that." *I want to be more than that.*

Niklaus stepped closer. "The day we met, in the stables, you spoke to me in a way no one ever has. You treated me as if I were just an ordinary person and not the prince. As if I were your equal. I want to believe that you see something more than my title when you look at me. You're not just a witch, Calida. Not to me."

She sucked in a breath, aware of how close he was. She could feel the heat of him. "I do see you. When we first met, I was prepared to dislike you on principle. You were the prince. I thought you couldn't possibly understand what it was like to have your whole life planned out without your approval. I guess I thought you could do whatever you liked. Now I see how wrong I was."

"You've done something that most people are too scared to do. You've let yourself be honest. Real. Without pretention. I know you'll be honest with me and not simply tell me what you think I want to hear. You'd be surprised how rare that is at court."

"I'm not one of them," Calida said, thinking of the simpering girls she had seen earlier. "And I never will be."

For the first time, she felt proud of the acknowledgement instead of ashamed. She didn't want to be like them. She wondered deep down what any of those girls were really like when they dropped the act, stripped of all the layers of artifice they cloaked themselves in.

But the thought didn't last long.

"Good," Niklaus whispered.

And then he closed the distance between them and kissed her in the dark.

CHAPTER 14

As Niklaus had predicted, his father was not pleased with him when he summoned him to his study the following morning. The king was still in his robe and looked slightly tired after such a long night. Niklaus knew he'd been right and that his father was pushing himself too soon, but he knew better than to say it. Dealing with all those nobles would be tiring enough for anyone.

"You and a certain healer were conspicuously absent for much of the party last night."

"I'm sorry, Father." Niklaus did not offer an excuse. There was none that would satisfy the king.

"Perhaps it was a mistake to invite her," the king went on. "Such behavior was inappropriate. I suppose she can't be expected to know much about decorum or the ways of court."

"No, sir," Niklaus said automatically, thinking that if his father knew about the kiss, he would have sent Calida packing no matter how good of a healer she was.

"Still, her sister proved surprisingly popular. Many of the people I spoke with had nothing but praise for her. What was her name again?"

"Thalia."

"Ah, yes, Thalia." The king sank heavily into the chair behind his desk. "I hardly think I need ask, but have you decided on a suitable wife?"

Niklaus sighed. "No, Father."

"No, how could you have, when you rudely left your guests and refused to give any of the girls presented to you the time of day? I expected better of you, boy. I suggest you don't delay any further or I'll be forced to choose a bride for you."

But Niklaus knew it was an empty threat. He knew Alaran law and more importantly, so did his father.

* * *

Calida awoke feeling more tired than she had when she'd finally crawled into bed late last night—or perhaps it had been early morning by then. She didn't know how long she and Niklaus had stayed out, walking the palace grounds together, beneath the moonlight, talking or simply enjoying each other's company. They had watched from the shadows as, one by one, the nobles returned to their carriages and finally departed.

Only when they were sure that the party had come to an end did they sneak back into the palace and head for their own rooms. Calida had been unable to fall asleep for some time, too excited and busy thinking over everything that had happened. If she'd gotten even a couple hours of sleep, she would have been surprised.

She lay in bed still, muted light streaming through the windows. It wasn't the bright intensity of sunlight; it was too dull for that. Calida could see gray clouds through the window, storm clouds, and she could hear rain thrumming on the roof above her.

She knew she should get up and face the day ahead, but she wanted to remain in bed a moment longer, savoring the events of last night. They seemed like a dream when reviewed in the light of morning, as though they might evaporate like mist before the sun.

Had it all been real? She wanted it to be real.

Calida flinched as her bedroom door opened and Thalia, already dressed, crossed the room, throwing the curtains even wider.

"Still in bed, I see. You'd better get a move on. The king will be wanting his morning dose of rainleaf."

Calida sighed and tossed the covers back, knowing her sister was right. She crossed to the wardrobe and began rifling through it, searching for something to wear.

Thalia sat down on the stool at her dressing table. "I saw you leave last night. You didn't come back."

"And why would I?" Calida asked, holding up a dress of dove gray. It wasn't her favorite color, but maybe it would complement her eyes the way blue seemed to for Thalia.

"You should have heard the way they were talking about me," she added, moving behind the room dividers to change. "You would have left, too."

"Maybe, but no one said anything rude about me. And even if they did, what do you really expect? We don't belong here, they know it, and they want to make sure we know it, too."

"Well they did a fine job."

"You can't run off every time someone says something you don't like," Thalia pointed out. "Especially now. These are powerful, important people. We need their approval. If they think you're rude, they might demand to have you removed from your position. Besides, by storming off, all you did was let them know how much they got to you."

Calida slipped the dress over her head, pulling her hair out from under the collar. She knew Thalia was right, as usual, and she'd behaved foolishly. She hadn't even stopped to consider that her actions might reflect poorly on the king—

or worse, on Niklaus, since he had been the one to bring her to the palace in the first place.

But neither could she bring herself to regret her actions.

"The prince asked after you," Thalia said casually. "I told him you'd left and he followed after you. *He* didn't return either and unlike with you, people noticed."

"He said he didn't want to go back," Calida replied, stepping back out from behind the room divider. "I told him if he didn't want to go, then he shouldn't, and so he decided to stay with me."

Thalia raised a perfectly arched eyebrow. "All night?"

Calida ignored the implication. "Yes. We talked about things, about how he actually has more in common with someone like me than with any of the nobility." She took a deep breath and spun around to face her sister, her secret bursting at the seams, eager to be told. "He kissed me."

Neither Thalia's tone or expression changed. "Did he?"

"That's all you have to say?" Calida asked, moving over to the dressing table and booting her sister off the stool. She needed to fix her hair.

"What do you expect me to say?"

"I thought you'd be happy for me."

"Why would I?" Thalia seemed genuinely confused. "The kiss doesn't mean anything."

"How can you say that?" Calida demanded, tugging the brush through her hair. "He wouldn't have done it for no reason."

Thalia let out a sigh. "You don't get it, do you?"

Calida twisted on the stool, glaring at her. "Well are you going to tell me or keep all the answers to yourself?"

"All I'm saying is that you should be careful. The prince can't possibly harbor any feelings for you. He's just doing it to manipulate you."

Calida scoffed. "Like you know anything about that."

"He won't marry you, Calida," Thalia said, speaking slowly as if to a simple child. "What do you think the party last night was for? The whole purpose was so he could find a wife."

"I know that already. He told me."

"Then you know it's true. He wouldn't choose to marry you. You're nothing compared to a nobleman's daughter and that's who he's expected to choose. So if he can't marry you, perhaps he hopes you'll consent to be his mistress."

"That's a horribly cynical thing to say."

"Why shouldn't it be true?" Thalia challenged, crossing her arms. "You have no prospects outside of the palace and your place here isn't certain. It will only last as long as you can keep the king alive. Whether you like it or not, you're dependent upon the good graces of the crown. The prince probably feels you'll do whatever it takes to keep your place here and if that means sleeping with him, why not?"

"Clearly, you don't know him very well," Calida said, putting the brush down and surveying her reflection. "Why do you think men always want something from me?"

"Because they usually do. It's the way the world works. And when you're as powerful as the prince, you feel there's nothing you're not entitled to."

Calida stood and brushed past her sister. "Well thank you for the warning, but I'll take my chances."

She didn't believe Thalia for one moment, though she didn't doubt her sister's intentions were sincere enough. She and Niklaus had something in common that Thalia didn't understand, something that Calida herself had only come to realize last night as they spoke.

Neither one of them were free to choose their own destiny and it was a rare occurrence for someone to look past their titles. To most people, they would only ever be the prince and a witch.

She was someone who could look past that and see the real person beneath. That was who she was to Niklaus and who he was to her.

Thalia had been wrong about Jeremy. Why shouldn't she be wrong about Niklaus?

* * *

To Calida's dismay, she didn't see Niklaus that morning. He wasn't with the king when she went to see him and she wondered if he were somehow being punished for leaving the party. If so, she felt a pang of guilt. It was her fault; she'd encouraged him.

She wondered also if the king would mention her own flight from the party, but he didn't. He said nothing as she crumbled the dried rainleaf into the strong black tea, giving it a thorough stir. She was running dangerously low on the herb now and would need to get some more soon.

Niklaus remained conspicuously absent the rest of the day. Calida tried to distract herself from thinking about him—and subsequently missing him and wondering where he'd gone—by counting and sorting the herbs in the royal infirmary, taking stock of what she had to work with. But such tasks could only keep the thoughts at bay for so long.

After that, she made her way to the conservatory. The air in this room was always humid and uncomfortably warm, best suited to the many colorful plants that grew within. But it was the best source of natural light in the whole palace, the circular room enclosed on all sides by windows.

She'd already been there a couple of times before and it was one of her favorite places in the palace. Quiet, secluded, no one ever seemed to venture inside while she was there, leaving her in peace.

Unfortunately, that also left her with her own thoughts, something she didn't much want at the moment. She thought back to Thalia's warning and the fact that Niklaus had yet to appear. Surely he'd want to see her after the intimate moment they'd shared last night. Did it mean anything to him or had her sister been right?

She thought about the way she'd felt when Jeremy had failed to appear as quickly as she would have liked, how ridiculous she'd been, letting her irrational fears run away with her. She was being no different now, when she was older and should have known better.

Niklaus was the prince. No doubt he had many duties to attend to, that she couldn't even begin to guess at, and couldn't devote every waking moment to spending time with her. It was selfish and unreasonable for her to expect him to drop whatever he was doing and rush to her side.

She still didn't think Thalia was right, but there was no denying the possibility that she might have made more out of the kiss than Niklaus had intended. She really didn't have much experience when it came to such things, but it didn't seem like the type of thing one did lightly.

As evening fell, Calida sent Horus out into town to check the ships along the dock as she always did. He returned within the hour, bearing news that the *Sea Witch* was in port and that Jeremy had returned. Her heart leapt at the news, looking forward to seeing her friend again and replenishing her dwindling supply of rainleaf.

But then Horus added something that made her hopes plummet. "*The* Sea Witch *looks like she's taken some heavy damage.*"

Her mind instantly went to the worst possible outcomes. What if Jeremy had been hurt in the engagement or worse, killed? Suddenly, she didn't care about the rainleaf any longer. She needed to know he was all right.

Running down the palace steps, Calida rushed to the stables, borrowed a horse and set out for the tavern. The building was less full than usual and not as boisterous. It seemed quieter when Calida stepped inside. She hadn't bothered to change out of her gray dress, but the cloak she'd thrown over it helped conceal that she was dressed more like a noblewoman than the class of people who usually frequented such establishments.

She spied Jeremy almost at once and felt a surge of relief as she waited for him to make his way over to her. Calida frowned as she took in the sight of him. His white shirt was torn, a bloodied bandage visible, wrapped around his upper arm. He'd been hurt, just as she feared.

She ignored the wrapped parcel he held out to her. "What happened?"

His mouth twisted. "Had an engagement with a naval ship. Good thing there was no sky witch on board, or we'd have been sunk before we could even roll out the guns. I was one of the lucky ones, but we lost a few men."

Calida lowered her voice. "Horus saw your ship. Are you sure it's safe, bringing such a damaged vessel here?"

She knew it was dangerous for him to come at the best of times, but anyone could tell just by looking that the *Sea Witch* had been in an engagement and come out the worse for wear. It drew attention and even worse, someone might recognize it.

"No, it isn't safe, but I made the call to come anyway. I had to give you this." Jeremy nodded down to the parcel he still offered her.

Calida reached out and took it. "*You* made the call?"

Before, he'd always made it sound like it wasn't up to him when the *Sea Witch* came into harbor and he could see her again. The decision wasn't his to make and so he had to wait. But now…

The face he made was part grimace, part smile, but there was something strangely proud in it. "I said we lost a few men. One of them was the captain. I'm captain now."

"Congratulations," Calida said, not knowing if it was at all the right thing to say.

He had been promoted. He was commander of his own ship—it really was *his* ship now. But it had come at a high price. For all she knew, he might have been close to the man he now replaced and mourned the loss as much as celebrated the promotion.

"Thanks. I'll try my best to be a good captain, but I'm off to a rocky start. The other men didn't want to risk coming here tonight, but as I said, I needed to give you the rainleaf. I know how important it is to you, firebrand, but I can't stay. Walk with me and we'll talk on the way back to the ship."

He moved past her and out the door. Calida followed, clutching the packet of rainleaf.

"Now that I've passed that on to you, my crew and I need to leave. We can make repairs to the *Sea Witch* at Amberleigh. If we manage to make it there without being spotted or killed by the navy first, I might stand a chance at keeping my new position."

"Is it that precarious?"

Jeremy shrugged. "Mutinies do happen, especially when crews become dissatisfied with their captain's leadership. I've already taken a risk coming here tonight, a risk they didn't want me to take. Until we weigh anchor, we're not out of danger and even then, we're not safe. So it's yet to be seen whether my risk pays off or blows up in our faces." He grinned suddenly. "I must say, though, I never expected my death could come about as a result of a mutiny."

"You shouldn't joke about such things," Calida scolded gently, hugging the packet of rainleaf to her chest. "You're too young to think about dying."

She knew that wasn't true. Being a pirate was a dangerous life to lead, full of risks at every turn. And yet here he was, risking his new position and his very life by coming to see her, to give her the herb that kept her position at the palace secure.

"Pirates typically don't live very long."

Calida nearly stopped walking, but if she did, so would he and he needed to get back to his ship and be off as soon as possible. So she forced herself to keep walking.

"I'm sorry. You're putting yourself in so much danger all because I asked you to bring me herbs."

"No one else can do it for you," Jeremy pointed out. "I said I would do it. It's a pleasure to help out a friend. I'm no stranger to risk."

"Still…I wish I could pay you for them somehow, but they don't see fit to pay me up at the palace. I suppose I do get to live there and enjoy everything it has to offer for free, but you could have used the money to repair your ship."

"Don't worry about it. Though I have to warn you, I don't know how much longer I'll be able to get you the rainleaf."

"Just do what you can."

Mentally, Calida made a note to bring something of value next time, something she could give him to sell, as a way of saying thanks. He deserved something more than just her gratitude for risking so much.

"You know," she added, "you may be a pirate, but by giving me these herbs, you're doing the crown more of a service than anyone realizes."

Jeremy laughed and came to a stop. They had reached the *Sea Witch* and Calida could now see the ship's sorry state for herself. Jagged holes had been blown in the hull, thankfully just above the waterline. The railing had been splintered and broken in places and the foremast—the mast that had once been Jeremy's responsibility—had snapped in half, leaving the rigging and sails ragged and limp.

"It's bad," Jeremy acknowledged. "But she's come through worse."

I hope you're right.

He turned to her. "I must be off."

"Be careful. Don't take any unnecessary risks."

He grinned, climbing up the gangplank. "I never take unnecessary risks, firebrand. Only the necessary ones."

She shook her head, watching him go. If he died out at sea, there would be no one left to bring her rainleaf. And the king would be doomed.

Funny how her fate, and that of the king, were now directly tied to Jeremy's own.

She tried to push the thought away, but she couldn't help but fear that this might be the last time she ever saw him.

CHAPTER 15

She saw Niklaus the next day at breakfast, having returned from wherever it was he'd been hiding. The rain the previous day had moved on, quick as it had come, and Calida looked forward to an afternoon of riding. Niklaus asked what her plans were for the day and she told him.

He laughed. "Won't you get tired of it?"

Calida shrugged. She hadn't really thought that much about it. "After I was expelled from Master Kallias's class, I didn't think I'd ever get the chance to ride again. I still don't know how long it will last. I intend to take every advantage."

Would she ever get tired of the feel of the wind in her hair, the powerful movement of the horse beneath her, muscles rippling, the two of them sharing a connection as if they were one? No, she didn't think so. It was as close to pure freedom as she had ever felt, that first day on horseback. She wondered if Jeremy felt the same way about the *Sea Witch*.

Niklaus frowned and reached for another piece of toast. "I don't know much about the way things are done up at the monastery. Why couldn't you go on riding? I'd think that a useful skill everyone should know."

"You'd think so, wouldn't you? But only soldiers learn to ride at the monastery."

"You trained to be a soldier, then?"

Calida sighed softly. It wasn't something she liked thinking about—that horrible night when Arin had killed both of the prisoners and she'd been too weak, too afraid, to do it. She wondered where Arin was now.

"I did. I thought it was what I wanted, but my placement was healing. Thalia was the soldier, not me." Even though Thalia had been removed from her own class, it had been for a completely different reason.

"Well, for what it's worth, I'm glad. If you hadn't become a healer…I might have become king already."

She was tempted to ask him if he had gotten into trouble over leaving the party early, but it didn't seem like the right time.

After breakfast, they both returned to their rooms to change into something more suitable for riding and then reconvened at the stables.

Niklaus took her on a different route this time and Calida was content to go along, keeping her horse beside his. They had gone down to the beach and in the distance, she could see a tower, slowly growing larger and more defined as they approached. It sat along the western coast, on a strip of land that stretched out into the water.

"Is it a lighthouse?" Calida asked, leaning forward in the saddle. She had never seen a lighthouse before.

"No," Niklaus replied. "It's a watch tower, of sorts."

As they drew near, she could see that it was very tall, composed of gray brick, and there were glass windows at the very top, reflecting the sun. Cannons bristled menacingly from the battlements, for the purpose of defending the shore from invaders.

"Have you ever had to use it?" she asked.

Niklaus craned his head to look up at the tower. "Not in my lifetime. It's only really useful against invasion from the sea and where would such a threat come from? The pirates aren't foolish or organized enough to attempt such a thing. Indris is a protectorate of ours and we currently have no hostilities with Daera."

"Let's hope it stays that way," Calida murmured. She didn't like the thought of war.

"Agreed. If war does come one day, I want to be long dead by then."

Calida looked up at the tower, feeling a sudden sense of sorrow rush over her despite the fine weather and the breeze coming off the sea. Things were peaceful now, but nothing ever stayed the same.

She hoped Jeremy had made it safely to Amberleigh.

Niklaus shifted in his saddle. "How was my father this morning?"

Calida returned her thoughts to the present. "The same. The bruises still aren't fading. I'm not sure they ever will."

He nodded. "Well, he's grateful for every moment you can give him. And so am I."

"How did he react to you leaving the party?"

"Not well," Niklaus said with a small smile. "But that's to be expected. He's disappointed that I didn't find a wife."

"Do you even want one?"

"What I want doesn't matter," he said simply. The familiar, rehearsed answer.

Calida nodded. There was no point imagining or wishing otherwise because nothing else could be so. He was a prince and she a witch, but they both still served the kingdom to the best of their own unique ability.

The life of royalty had seemed one of privilege to her, before she'd come to stay at the palace. And in a way, it still was. Niklaus would never have to want for food or clothing or shelter. In that regard, he would have the best of everything. But luxurious as it was, the palace was just another cage.

A gilded one, perhaps, but a cage all the same.

He had no more control over his own fate than she did. He could always choose to be a poor king, she supposed, and do whatever he fancied, at the expense of others, but that wouldn't set him free.

She wondered if he would have been willing to trade positions with her. Would he rather have lived the life of a peasant instead? Perhaps having less responsibility on one's shoulders was preferable, even if you could never truly be free.

But she didn't ask him such a thing. There was no point.

* * *

As life at the palace settled into a routine, Calida's fears began to lessen. She had her fresh supply of rainleaf and so there was nothing for her to worry about. She still sent Horus down to the docks each evening, even though she knew it was far too soon for Jeremy to have returned. The king's condition neither improved nor worsened noticeably.

Despite the luxury surrounding her at every turn, Calida soon began to feel listless and bored, much the same way she had at the monastery. This life was undeniably better, but the monotony wore at her. She felt guilty for it, knowing she should simply appreciate what she had been given, the sheer good fortune and luck that had landed her here.

She wondered if she would always feel this way, sooner or later. Was she doomed to eventually tire of everything? Was there nothing and no place that would satisfy her? It was a thought she didn't like to dwell on.

Still, the king wasn't the only one who needed her services as healer. The servants in the kitchen often suffered burns or accidentally cut themselves while preparing massive meals each day. Those were simply injuries, most of the time, and easy to treat. Illnesses took longer, but it was never anything serious.

Never a challenge like the king's mysterious malady.

Each day, Calida took stock of the supplies in the royal infirmary. If she didn't keep a close eye on such things, she could burn through them before she knew it and not have what she needed when the time came.

She was busy rolling bandages when she heard footsteps hurrying down the corridor and Niklaus called her name. Calida turned to face the door as he staggered inside, carrying a small child in his arms.

He hurried over to her. "He's one of the servant's sons. Fell out of a tree and hurt his leg."

Calida gestured to one of the empty cots. "Put him there."

The boy couldn't have been older than eight. He was trying to put on a brave face, but she could tell he was in obvious pain, eyes glistening with tears. Niklaus remained beside him, holding the boy's hand as Calida made her examination.

She knew which leg had been injured simply by looking at it and she gently ran her hands down the limb, feeling the bone and tissue beneath. The boy whimpered and turned his head away.

"It's broken," Calida announced. "But not too badly. I'll need to set the bone and fetch some opium for the pain."

Her supplies kept neat and labeled, it took only a few seconds to locate what she searched for. She gave the opium to the boy and waited for it to take effect. Still, the procedure would be far from painless.

She looked up at Niklaus. "Keep him still."

Calida took a deep breath and set to work. She had never done this before on a real person, on her own, but she knew how important it was to keep calm and not let her nerves show. The child was already frightened, but if she projected calm confidence, he would feel better, knowing she knew what she was doing.

Irjah had taught her well and it was over within minutes. She attached a splint to keep the bones in the proper position while they healed and stood back. The boy had gripped Niklaus's hand so hard, it was blanched white, but he had made no complaint.

"He'll have to stay off it," she warned. "If he doesn't, the bones won't heal properly and he may have a limp for the rest of his life. No more climbing trees for a while."

Niklaus nodded, helping the boy up. "I'll take him to his mother and let her know."

She waited until he returned, this time alone. "That was a good thing you did, bringing him here," she said softly. He could have ordered another servant to do it, but he'd gone out of his way to bring the child to her himself.

Niklaus looked slightly embarrassed. "Anyone would have done the same."

"No, they wouldn't. You have a way with children."

"You're the healer, not me. I didn't do anything."

"You could have left him there, but you didn't. You're not that kind of person and sometimes, that's just as important as any healer's skill."

He smiled at her and she felt that familiar fluttering in the pit of her stomach. She thought back to the night of the party, when he had kissed her. They hadn't spoken of it and there had been no repeat of the incident.

Maybe he had acted out of impulse more than anything, but Calida still didn't think Thalia was right. There had been no malice behind it. There was no malice in the young man standing before her, who had dropped everything to carry an injured child to her door. She couldn't believe it of him.

There was no guile there.

* * *

At last, with the slow, agonizing dread of the inevitable, Calida's supply of rainleaf had nearly run out. She had only two leaves left, one for tomorrow morning and the evening after that. In twenty-four hours, she would have no more remaining and would need to find some way of getting it—and fast. The thought made her feel sick with worry.

She knew she should probably tell Niklaus of her predicament, but she didn't want to worry him or admit that her supply, and thus her position, were so vulnerable.

So far, Jeremy had managed to come through for her, but that couldn't last forever. Sooner or later, time, much like her supply of rainleaf, would run out and then what would she do?

She had spent the better part of an hour fretting over the situation when Horus returned, announcing that the *Sea Witch* was once again anchored in the harbor.

"Oh, thank the skies." Calida leapt up from where she'd been sitting and raced for the door.

She tried to brace herself for potential disappointment. Just because Jeremy had returned did not mean he'd managed to get any rainleaf. He'd probably been busy with the many repairs to his ship and his new responsibilities as captain, the herb the furthest thing from his mind.

On the way to the tavern, Calida paused, taking in the *Sea Witch*'s appearance. There was no sign of the damage she'd sustained the last time Calida laid eyes on her and she felt a rush of relief. If the ship was here, that must mean Jeremy was, too. The rest of the crew wouldn't have risked coming here; there would have been no reason to.

And that meant he must not only still be alive, but still be captain in order to make the call to come into town.

She stepped into the tavern and spotted Jeremy sitting at the table in the corner where she had always sat when coming into town with Daniel. There was a tankard of ale on the table and a plate with the remains of a meal, indicating he'd been there for some time.

He looked up as she entered and got to his feet.

Calida summoned a grin. "I see you're still in one piece." She wanted to ask him if he'd managed to get any more rainleaf—the panic was nearly choking her—but she knew how rude that would seem and his life mattered far more than any herb.

Jeremy nodded. "The crew still tolerate me for the moment." His tone was light and she could tell he was joking.

"I saw the *Sea Witch* as I came in. She looks good as new."

"The repairs took longer than I thought they would. We lost a lot of time that should have been devoted to hunting down merchant vessels and refilling the coffers. But it also meant that I had plenty of time to get what you wanted."

Calida stood up straighter. "You have some?"

"Not here. It's still on board the *Witch*." He gestured for her to follow him and they began making their way back toward the docks.

Calida trailed after him, heart still thudding painfully fast. She didn't want to tell Jeremy how close her supply had come to running out. She waited at the foot of the gangplank as he climbed aboard to fetch the rainleaf, but instead of the wrapped bundle she expected, he returned with a small pot containing a live rainleaf plant.

"I didn't know how much longer I'd be able to do this for you," he explained. "It seemed like a risk that wasn't sustainable, so I got you this instead. I thought you could maybe plant it at the palace, take what leaves you needed from it, and then perhaps grow a second plant from it."

Reverently, Calida reached out and took the pot. It was heavier than she expected. The rainleaf plant was short and squat, the thick trunk a light tan color. Bright blue leaves drooped from the branches.

"Thank you," she murmured, then smiled up at him. "This is probably the only live rainleaf plant to be smuggled out of Amberleigh. Do you know how much this is worth?"

Jeremy shrugged. "No idea. Admittedly, it doesn't look like much."

But to her, it was priceless. If she managed to grow the plant in the conservatory and get more plants from it—and there was no reason why she shouldn't, having learned such things at the monastery—then she would be set permanently. There would be no more fear of running out. However much rainleaf the king needed, he would have.

"I don't have any money to give you, but I do have this." Calida carefully set the pot on the ground and reached up to unhook the necklace she had brought with her.

It was a small silver piece she had found in one of the drawers in her room. She had no idea who it belonged to. Perhaps it had been unintentionally left behind by one of the room's former occupants—a careless noble, perhaps.

Regardless, Calida knew that it hadn't been placed there for her and taking it felt a bit like stealing. But Jeremy deserved something for everything he'd done for her and this was all she had to give him.

Besides, she told herself, if it did belong to some noble, they had so many jewels they'd hardly miss this one.

She held it out to him. "It's not much, but it might fetch a decent price."

"You didn't have to, you know that."

"I wanted to. Besides, the repairs to your ship had to cost something and you said it yourself, you lost the chance to make up the cost because the repairs took so long. You could be out there looking for prey right now, but you're here, to see me." She gestured to the hanging necklace. "I certainly don't need it. I have everything I could ever want up at the palace now, thanks to you."

He took it then. "Thank you."

Calida picked the pot back up. "With any luck, and if I'm a decent earth witch, I won't need to come to you for any more rainleaf. But if you're here, I'll always stop by."

"If it's not too much of a risk, I'll be here. We'll see."

"I'd better get this back to the palace before my arms fall off."

With the usual warnings to be careful, Calida left him there, standing before his ship, and made her way back. The return ride was much slower, Calida carefully cradling the pot of rainleaf. She didn't want to risk dropping and damaging it.

It was late by the time she returned. Other than the pot in her arms, she had no more rainleaf left, having given the last dose to the king earlier that evening.

She headed straight for the conservatory, set the pot on a side table, picked up a spade, and began hunting for a place to put her new plant. It would need to be fairly open; she didn't want the rainleaf crowded by any of the other foliage.

In the end, she found an open space beside a *bellavexis* plant, more commonly known as silk snare. What the plant was doing here, Calida didn't know. It had no harmless medicinal uses, but its fragrance was quite pleasant. Perhaps that was explanation enough. She shook her head. Royals did not need reasons for the things they did.

She got to work, carving out a hole in the soil that would be big enough. When that was done, she retrieved the pot and carefully emptied it, placing the rainleaf plant in its new home, smoothing the dirt with her hands.

"Is that what I think it is?" a voice asked softly from the doorway.

Calida turned to see Niklaus standing there. "A live rainleaf plant, straight from Amberleigh." She finished smoothing the soil and stood, brushing her hands off as best she could. "I need to find some water," she added, almost to herself. She didn't know how long the plant had been on board the *Sea Witch*, but the soil had felt quite dry to the touch.

"Allow me." She watched as Niklaus fetched a watering can and filled it from a faucet nearby. He carried it back over and handed it to her. "You'd know better than I how much water they need."

Calida took the can and began sprinkling water over the plant, watching as the dry soil soaked it up, droplets landing on the brightly colored leaves.

"I don't know how you managed it," Niklaus remarked. "And I won't ask. But I'm grateful."

For a moment, Calida was tempted to tell him exactly how she had come by the rainleaf, to explain that at least one pirate on the Atlas Sea was a good man and didn't deserve to be hunted down by the Alaran navy. But she didn't think Jeremy would thank her for it and so she said nothing.

She set the watering can back down.

"The fever's come back," Niklaus said quietly.

Calida turned to him in alarm. "When did this happen?"

"After you left."

She would have already administered the last dose of rainleaf by then. "But I'd already given him rainleaf for the night," she protested. "Maybe it was too old and I needed something fresher." She glanced at the plant before her, still glistening with moisture. "Maybe I should give him some more."

"It's fine." Niklaus gripped her shoulders to keep her from rushing off and undoubtedly doing something rash. "Give it time to work. He's still lucid, unlike last time."

Well, that's something at least. Still, the king had been doing so well. The bruises had stubbornly refused to disappear, but he'd shown no sign of a relapse. This newest development only confirmed Calida's worst fear and something she'd likely known all along, refusing to admit to herself.

She hadn't cured the king.

She sank down onto one of the benches. "I didn't cure him. I only alleviated the symptoms and made him feel better." He might have felt better, but the illness still lurked inside, biding its time, waiting.

And eventually, it would return and it would be over. There would be no more delaying the inevitable.

Calida couldn't bring herself to look at the prince, afraid he would see the knowledge of her own failure in her eyes. "I'm sorry. I haven't done what you asked me to."

"All I asked was that you try. And you exceeded all expectations. No one can ask more than that."

"But I haven't cured him!"

"Neither had any of the other healers and you've done a damn sight more than they have!" Niklaus said, taking her hands in his. "You've given us hope. Time. If you had never come here, my father might well have died by now. Anything you can give is a blessing."

Calida stared down at her hands in his, the dirt beneath her nails, and felt unworthy.

He released her and sat beside her with a sigh. "Whatever is wrong with my father can't be cured. I can accept that. But I want as much time with him as I can get. You've given me that chance, Calida, and I haven't properly expressed my gratitude."

"I'm just doing my job. It is, after all, the best way I can serve the kingdom." Calida let out a little snort at the irony of that. But really, he'd given her more than her sort ever had a right to hope for.

A witch enjoying a life of freedom and luxury at the palace was unheard of.

Niklaus frowned. "That's just it. It shouldn't have to be this way. I don't think I could convince my father that things need to change, but…I could make them change, when the time comes. If I had never met you, I wouldn't have known what things were like at the monastery. You shouldn't be robbed of your freedom simply because you're born a witch."

A sudden thought struck her. "What would happen if a royal were born a witch? Would they be sent to the monastery, too?" Somehow, she doubted it.

He shook his head. "Wouldn't happen. Or I should say, it hasn't happened. The nobility keeps their bloodlines free of any witches for that very reason, though that's no guarantee. Anyone can be born a witch, whether it runs in the family or not. But no, I doubt a royal would be sent to the monastery." He looked at her. "But you know, that would be the perfect way to show how things are changing. To show that witches are people, too, and should be treated as such instead of viewed as nothing more than servants."

"What do you mean?"

Niklaus reached out, taking her hands again. "You've seen me in a way no one else ever has, in a way no noble certainly would. We have more in common than we do differences and I think, because of that, we also understand each other in a way no one else could. I must confess, the day I came to the monastery, I had an ulterior motive other than just needing to see the headmistress. I came to see you."

"Oh?" Calida felt herself flush and could only imagine how red she must look in the moonlight streaming through the many conservatory windows.

"I noticed you, during the presentation of the graduates. I thought you were the most beautiful girl I'd ever seen and I wanted to see you again." Now it was his turn to blush. "I suppose that's a bit shallow. But then I spoke to you and you treated me the same way you would treat anyone else. You didn't act like I was someone special. You made me feel ordinary, something I've never felt before, but more than that, you made me feel as though you really saw me. You weren't blinded by my titles or the crown. I think that's a good thing for a ruler, even a future one, to be reminded of.

Strip away all the finery and what am I? What do I have left? I'm no different than you and I shouldn't forget that."

He cleared his throat. "All of that to say, Calida, I think you make me a better man. My father's relapse this evening only heightened the fact that none of us knows how much time we have left and I still don't have a wife. I want a queen who would rule beside me, keep me accountable, and understand me. I don't think I will find that among the nobility that was presented to me the night of the ball. I have found it in you. The decision is entirely yours, of course, but I must ask. Will you be my wife?"

Calida stared at him, dumbstruck. She tried to form the words to say, but there were too many in her mind, clambering to be first, that in the end, nothing came out at all.

"You don't have to answer me right away," he said hastily. "I realize it's a lot to take in all at once and I shouldn't have imposed it all upon you so late."

"B—but I'm not royalty," she blurted. She wasn't sure that was what she meant to say, but it was probably the biggest obstacle. There was no getting around it.

Niklaus smiled. "You don't have to be. Alaran law states that royals can marry whomever they wish, as long as they have the approval of the reigning monarch. Given all you've done for my father, I can't imagine he wouldn't agree to it."

And just like that, the greatest obstacle fell away. *The only obstacle, really.* The only one standing in her way now was herself.

She had barely allowed herself to dream of staying at the palace, of healing the king and him being so grateful that he would grant her anything she wished. The idea that she could ever become queen had never crossed her mind, yet here it was before her, a possibility hinging on her decision.

She thought of the night of the ball, when Niklaus had kissed her, the way he made her feel, the fluttering sensation in her stomach when he smiled at her. He was right—they did understand each other in a way others didn't. They were both trapped, bound by a fate neither of them chose.

But perhaps they could free each other.

Being queen was Calida's decision to make. She could choose it for herself if she wanted. Niklaus had opened the door for her. All she had to do was walk through. She could change her fate in a way she had never imagined and in doing so, maybe change his as well.

Think of all the good we could do together. All of the changes that could be made when he was king and she queen. Witches could have entirely different lives. The tradition of the Erlohn monastery that had endured for generations could finally come to an end.

A lifetime spent in comfort, luxury, and power, with a man who loved and valued her. It was a dream too good to be true and all she had to say was *yes* and it would be hers.

Calida looked at Niklaus. His eyes were both hopeful and anxious. She knew this was one of the rare crossroads of life, where everything was about to change and nothing would ever be the same.

She decided to charge into the unknown, head-on. "Yes," she said, her voice coming out breathier than she'd intended. "I will."

CHAPTER 16

Niklaus knew better than to break the news to his father that same night. It was far too late as it was and in his current fragile state, he didn't want to do anything that might upset him.

In the morning, he accompanied Calida as she administered the rainleaf. The king looked better than he had the previous evening, alert and sitting up in bed. The fever seemed to have dissipated. Niklaus stood there patiently, observing the proceedings, waiting for Calida to leave before speaking to his father.

On her way out, she glanced at him nervously. Niklaus gave her what he hoped was a confident nod and then she was gone, closing the door behind her.

He took a deep breath. "How are you feeling, Father?"

"Fine," came the reply. "Though I warned you that I wasn't cured. I don't think I ever will be. Last night's episode was a reminder that I don't know how much time I have left and you still need to find a wife."

Niklaus was relieved that his father had given him an opening. The task ahead of him was difficult enough as it was; he was grateful for any help he could get.

"Actually, I have found a wife."

The king turned from where he had been staring out the window at the city below. "You have? Who?"

"Calida has accepted my proposal."

It took a moment for the name to register. "The healer?"

Niklaus nodded. "We need only your permission."

"No," the king said emphatically. "I will not give it."

Niklaus was taken aback by his father's passionate refusal. He had expected approval, perhaps not enthusiastic approval, but surely not such staunch opposition.

Well, if he had to plead his case, he would. "Father, she saved your life."

"As I said just a moment ago, she did not cure me. You and I both know it. She may have bought me more time than I otherwise would have had, and for that, I'm grateful, but that does not extend to putting half of the responsibilities for the future of this kingdom in her hands. She is inexperienced. She has no idea what will be expected of her."

"I could teach her—"

"I don't know how much time I have left," the king cut across him. "It might be another year, if I'm lucky, but let's say it's a few years. Even in that amount of time, you couldn't possibly prepare her for everything she needs to know. Why couldn't you have chosen from amongst the nobility? Those girls have been preparing for this sort of thing their entire lives. They know the history of our kingdom and that of Daera as well. They know customs and policies."

"They don't understand me the way she does, sir," Niklaus said quietly, aware of how insipid the argument must sound to his father's cynical ears.

"She's a witch!"

"She's more than just a witch to me. I want a wife who will love and understand me, not just go about her duties."

The king leaned forward in bed. "This isn't about what you want, boy. It's about what's best for the kingdom."

Niklaus nearly flinched but he managed to keep his expression neutral. Where had he heard that before? "So you won't give your permission, then?"

"No, I won't."

"I had hoped you wouldn't say that. Is there nothing that might convince you to reconsider?"

The king was silent for a few moments, fingers restlessly picking at the bed covers. "If you can prove to me that she's capable of doing what will be expected of her with both grace and efficiency, then maybe I will reconsider your request."

Niklaus knew it was the best he could hope for and so he took it.

He bowed his head. "Thank you, Father."

He took his leave and found Calida in the conservatory, tending to the rainleaf plant. She stood before it, hands raised, and seemed to be concentrating very hard. Niklaus had no idea how her strange magic worked, but at the moment, he could detect no difference in the plant from the way it had looked last night.

She started and whirled as he approached. "What did he say?"

Niklaus pursed his lips. "He's refused to give his permission." Her face fell and he quickly added, "Don't worry. We're still engaged. Nothing can change that."

"But we can't get married."

"He said he's willing to reconsider if you can prove that you're capable of carrying out the duties that will be expected of you." He reached out, taking her hands. "It doesn't matter. He'll come around and even if he doesn't...I'm willing to wait. I don't like going against his wishes, but he doesn't know you like I do. He doesn't see what I see. And that's why all of this needs to change."

She took a deep breath. "What do I need to do to prove myself?"

"You'll be responsible for managing the household, mainly. Managing servants, planning menus, ordering supplies, managing the budget, hosting feasts and parties—that sort of thing."

"None of my training at Erlohn prepared me for any of that," she murmured.

"Why would they? None of them ever expected to one day see a witch on the throne. It's not as difficult as it sounds. I'm sure you'll prove more than capable."

"Surely it can't be as hard as learning how to fight or heal wounds."

Niklaus smiled. "That's the spirit. Now I must go. I'll speak to the cooks and see if it's not too late to change tonight's menu. If not, you can start there." He nodded to the rainleaf plant. "I'll leave you to your work." Briefly, he kissed her hands and left.

* * *

Calida thought about what he had said long after he'd left.

Her heart had sunk at his words and she'd struggled not to let it show. Niklaus had spoken as though it were all nothing, really, but it sounded tiresome and pointless to her. She was no hostess. She didn't even like most people, preferring the company of animals.

People inevitably disappointed you, in one way or another. The few people she knew and kept close were rare exceptions and they were enough for her.

But then, the more she considered it, some of her doubt began to fade. His belief in her bolstered her spirits. He cared for her so much that he was willing to defy his father. She felt a rush of warmth—and no small amount of pride. It was a heady feeling.

She could manage. She would. If there was something she wanted badly enough, there would be no standing in her way. Wasn't the fact that she was standing in the palace at that very moment, when so many others had failed, proof enough of that?

She had learned how to do simple mathematics at her ordinary school, before leaving for the monastery. Surely that should be enough for managing a budget. Only now she had nearly unlimited wealth at her disposal, far more money than she ever would have imagined having to manage.

None of the rest of it sounded too hard or onerous—aside from the hosting of events. If that meant having to mingle and be polite to the same type of people she had encountered the night of the previous party, Calida wasn't looking forward to that in the slightest.

But she supposed she could pretend to be friendly for a few hours at a time, if it meant her and Niklaus getting what they wanted. It seemed a small price to pay.

One way or another, they would get what they wanted. Either she would manage to convince the king to change his mind or they would simply have to wait until he had died and Niklaus ascended to the throne, leaving them free to marry as they pleased. The latter would be a more regrettable outcome—of course it was better to have the king's approval—but she supposed it was really only a matter of time.

If she failed at the task the king had set before her, no matter. She would get what she wanted in the end. That assurance relieved some of the weight that had descended upon her shoulders. She didn't have to be perfect or even good enough. She just had to be patient.

No doubt by the end of the day, the palace would be humming with news of the engagement, but Calida wanted to tell her sister first, before the gossip mills started churning. She deserved to be told the good news personally rather than hear it second-hand.

As soon as she finished with the rainleaf plant, she would go.

* * *

Thalia turned from the window as Calida burst into her room, practically hopping with excitement. She hadn't seen her sister so eager since the day she had arrived at the palace—and perhaps not even then.

"What is it? What's happened? Have you cured the king?"

"No," Calida replied. "It's something even better than that."

Better than curing the king? Thalia couldn't imagine what that could be. "Well, are you going to tell me or leave me standing here in suspense?"

"Niklaus asked me to marry him," Calida announced. "And I said yes." She raced across the room, embracing Thalia with more enthusiasm than grace. "I'm going to be queen!"

Thalia stared at her sister, wide-eyed, after she had been released. It wasn't often that she found herself truly surprised, at a loss for words, but she could think of nothing to say. What would Calida want her to say? Judging by how excited she was, she would undoubtedly expect Thalia to react with excitement of her own and express her happiness for her.

She shook herself out of her shock and summoned a smile. "That's wonderful news!" Privately, she wanted to ask, *how on earth did you manage* that? But she kept such thoughts to herself.

Calida nodded. "I told you that kiss meant something." Her tone was a little smug for Thalia's liking.

"So, when's the wedding?"

Some of her sister's enthusiasm faded. "I don't know. By Alaran law, Niklaus can marry whomever he chooses, but we can't marry without the approval of the reigning monarch and the king refuses to give it. Unless he changes his mind, we'll have to wait until he dies and Niklaus takes the throne."

"Well is there anything you can do to help change his mind?"

Calida nodded again and outlined the things Niklaus had told her, the responsibilities that she would be expected to perform as his wife.

"I'm sure you'll handle them just fine," Thalia said encouragingly. "Nothing can stop you when you decide you really want something."

"I knew you'd understand. I wanted to tell you before it becomes common knowledge." Calida hugged her again, briefly. "I need to go. There's so much I need to learn."

Thalia returned the embrace, keeping her smile in place until Calida had left, closing the door behind her. Only then did she allow herself to frown. Her sister, the future queen of Alara? The idea was so absurd as to be laughable.

What did Niklaus see in her? She was opinionated and stubborn, irresponsible and easily dissatisfied with things. If it wasn't her personality, then what? It couldn't be her looks. The boy had eyes, after all. That wasn't to say that Calida was unattractive. Quite the opposite, in fact, but...

Thalia turned to the mirror above her dressing table and surveyed her own reflection. Her hair was a darker red than Calida's and straighter where her sister's was curly. Thalia's face was less round, her cheekbones sharper. Her lips were not quite as full, perhaps, but her eyes were a dark blue where Calida's were the gray of storm clouds. And Thalia had none of those freckles that her sister had. She was taller, her figure fuller. What wasn't there to like?

Being the sister of the queen wouldn't be a bad thing, Thalia supposed, but even so, she had never exactly been wholly in her sister's shadow, despite being younger. She had been born a sky witch, the favored and more powerful of the two, while her sister had been only an earth witch.

She had been the one to have a plan for her future while Calida moaned about how unfair the world was. Thalia had been the one so dedicated to her goal that she had kept the extent of her power hidden from the other students and endured bullying for it.

And all for what? What had it gained her?

Calida had never had a plan. The best she could have hoped for, like most of the subpar students, was to achieve a good placement. Even if it wasn't all she wanted out of life, it was the best she could hope for. And yet, she had somehow managed to snare herself a prince. The irony wasn't lost on Thalia.

She was the one now who had no purpose, who was a mere accessory. She would be allowed to stay at the palace because of Calida, but it wasn't because she had done anything herself to deserve it. She hadn't earned her place here.

Thalia clenched her hands into fists, glancing out the window at the gray sky beyond. It looked as though a storm brewed outside, a particularly nasty one. The sight was all she needed to be able to summon her power and briefly, a sharp wind rose up within the bedroom, stirring the curtains and bedsheets.

It wasn't good enough, but there was nothing Thalia could do about any of it.

After all, who could come between true love?

* * *

Niklaus returned to Calida later that same morning. "I can't stay," he said hurriedly. "But I wanted to tell you that I've spoken to the cooks. They haven't yet begun preparations for dinner this evening so you can go down to the kitchens and decide what you'd like the meal to be."

And then he was gone again. Swallowing down her nerves, Calida made her way deeper into the palace, descending the stairs to the massive kitchen. It was a large open room, with several stoves going, servants bustling about from the back pantries, carrying or replacing items they'd been ordered to retrieve. Some of them were hard at work at several sinks, washing various vegetables or cuts of meat. Onions hung from the ceiling above her head, along with dried herbs.

A large, harassed-looking woman pointed at Calida with the tip of the knife she'd been using to trim another cut of meat. "Oi, girl! Stop gawping and put on an apron!"

Calida reddened, realizing the cook thought she was one of the help. "Um…" She was so nervous; how could she be expected to do this and what exactly was she supposed to do? "Niklaus sent me to look over the menu with you."

The woman's demeanor changed at once. "You must be the girl he mentioned. The future queen, I hear."

She gave Calida an appraising glance, one eyebrow raised, and Calida couldn't tell whether she approved or not, but doubted the woman was impressed. She didn't seem the type of woman to be impressed by much of anything.

Calida nodded. "That's right."

The woman grunted. "Apologies, then, miss." Approving or not, she knew better than to treat Calida with anything other than the respect her position warranted. "Come here and I'll show you what options we've got for tonight and you can pick whichever you think appropriate."

Calida followed her deeper into the kitchen and glanced at the menu that had been prepared. She didn't know what half of the meals even meant, so unused was she to such rich variety. She bit her lip, wondering if she should ask the gruff cook for help, but she didn't think that would be looked upon favorably.

The other girls—that Niklaus had been expected to choose from—would have already known what to do and so she would have to appear confident and learn fast.

For the first course, she chose a type of soup. The entrée would be fillets of rabbit, which sounded interesting. There would be boiled ham for the second course, preserved fruit and grilled mushrooms for the third, followed by dessert.

The cook's impassive face revealed nothing about the nature of her selections. Calida left the kitchen not knowing if she had chosen properly or committed a grave error, but she supposed she would find out come dinnertime.

* * *

Dinner was a small affair, as usual, with the addition of two guests that Calida had not foreseen. Thalia, who had taken to having meals sent up to her room, was present, perhaps eager to see how well Calida fared in her new role and offer support if needed. Her sister's presence didn't cause Calida any further anxiety, but the second guest did.

The king had also deigned to be present. Calida didn't know why she should have anticipated anything different. His brief relapse seemed to have been just that—brief—and he had recovered nicely, returning to the previous good health he had demonstrated over the past few weeks.

Still, she couldn't shake the feeling that he was there to survey her work and satisfy himself as to her suitability or not. After all, it was him that she needed to convince.

The courses went by much faster than she remembered from the night she had eaten dinner with Niklaus. The food that had been laid out on the table before them had been cooked to perfection and looked appealing. Calida could find no faults with what she had chosen, savoring each bite. Surely there were no complaints to be found.

No one spoke much as the dinner progressed and when they did, it was certainly not about the food. Calida couldn't see that she had done anything wrong, but a pervading sense of wrongness hung over the room. She knew she had committed her first mistake, but couldn't figure out what she had done.

There was no mistaking the king's dark expression, the way his lips thinned as he surveyed the meal set before him.

If she expected him to tell her what she should have done and how she could improve, she was sadly mistaken.

She was on her own.

No doubt because he didn't want to change his mind, he preferred to see her flounder. The thought angered her and she spent the rest of the dinner quietly contemplating uncharitable thoughts toward the current monarch.

When the meal had concluded and the king retired to his own quarters, Calida hurried over to Niklaus, grabbing his arm. "What did I do? Was the food not prepared properly?"

If that were the case, she would have to give the cooks an earful. As servants, she was now in charge of managing them. Perhaps they resented that, viewing her as little more than an upstart and certainly no better than themselves. She'd have to put a stop to that and quickly.

"It's not that," Niklaus said quietly, as servants bustled into the room to clear the empty dishes away. They had eaten all the food so that must be a good sign. "There was nothing wrong with the food, but you picked too conservatively."

"What do you mean?"

"I mean, you didn't choose enough dishes for each course."

Calida had thought it plenty of food. Was the fact that it had all been eaten at the end a sign she hadn't, in fact, chosen enough?

"But…" she protested weakly, "there was only the four of us. I didn't think I was planning a feast."

"Be glad you weren't. A feast would have required far more."

Calida looked away, trying to blink back the sudden threat of tears. She had failed the first challenge set before her. It was not an auspicious start.

But was that really surprising? Had she, or anyone else, any right to expect any other outcome, when she had no knowledge, no training, and, it seemed, no support? Why hadn't anyone offered to help her or give her some sort of advice before she made a fool of herself in front of everyone?

In front of the king.

"No doubt the king only feels his opinion of me is justified now."

"Everyone makes mistakes," Niklaus said gently, turning her to face him again. "You've only just begun. Even he can't be too hard on you. You'll get it right next time."

She nodded, squaring her shoulders. She had only just begun and should set more realistic expectations for herself. She couldn't allow herself to give up so early in the game. It was precisely what the king wanted and more than that, expected.

As he made his way out of the dining hall, Niklaus imparted one last piece of advice, "Just remember, what may seem like a lot of food to you may not really be all that much."

A part of Calida resented the remark. What was he saying, that because she was a peasant and wasn't used to such luxury, she didn't know what was considered an appropriate amount of food? She would have thought the amount she'd chosen for tonight was more than enough. It had all been eaten, without any waste, and everyone had left the table feeling satisfied, hadn't they?

But fine, if that was the way things were, she'd be sure to pick enough food for dinner tomorrow. She'd go see to the menu right now, while it was fresh in her mind.

In the kitchens, she found the servants gathered around a long table, eating their own dinner. The cook Calida had encountered earlier glared at her as she entered and rose.

"Can I help you?"

"I—" Skies, what was it about this woman that made her feel so inadequate? "I wanted to go over tomorrow's menu."

The cook jerked her head back toward the room where they had reviewed the menu earlier and Calida studied it again, trying to take her time, painfully aware of the other woman's gaze boring into her.

But she refused to be rushed and made her decision, careful to choose more than she had before. The first course for tomorrow's dinner would feature carrot soup, fried fish, stewed eels, and pea soup, followed by lobster, sweetbreads, and oyster patties. For the second course, she chose roast turkey, boiled ham, and roasted pork with apple sauce. The third course would be minced pies, plum pudding, and roasted pheasants, followed by cheesecake and apple tarts for dessert.

It seemed like a menu worthy of a feast, but these were royal appetites she was catering to now. None of them could accuse her of choosing too conservatively now and there ought to be enough for everyone to pick what they wanted.

As she left the kitchens, she caught a glimpse of some of the servants' stony expressions as they watched her go and Calida wondered what she had done to upset them. She supposed she could always ask, since the servants were now her responsibility, and so she waited until their dinner had broken up and then snagged one of the maids as she left the kitchen to resume her duties.

"Miss?" the maid asked, regarding her with wide eyes. "Am I in trouble?" Already she knew that Calida was now the one she had to answer to.

"No, you're not in any trouble," Calida replied. "I just couldn't help but notice a rather tense atmosphere at dinner and I wondered what that was all about."

The girl visibly relaxed. "The cooks make a separate meal for the servants, but we also get to enjoy anything that's left over from dinner upstairs. Tonight, there was nothing left over."

So that was it. By her choosing not enough food, she had deprived the staff of something they usually got to enjoy as well. In her first night, she had managed not only to disappoint the king but upset the staff as well. *Great.* At least the young maid didn't seem to hold it against her.

Perhaps she saw how much Calida was out of her depth and pitied her.

"Right," Calida murmured. "I'll do better next time."

The maid smiled. "I'm sure you will, miss."

She didn't.

The next dinner was another disaster, for the complete opposite reason. There was so much food left over that Calida doubted the servants would be able to eat it all, but perhaps they would be grateful to have so much good food.

If anything, the king left dinner that evening looking even more displeased than before. Still, he said nothing to her. But before he left, she overheard him muttering to Niklaus. She couldn't hear every word, but she caught enough— something about spending and being wasteful. The meaning was clear and her cheeks heated with shame.

He could have called Niklaus in to speak with him privately after the fact, but instead he'd chosen to do it where he knew she would overhear, humiliating her further.

Niklaus sent her a sympathetic look across the room.

"So I picked too much this time," she vented to him once they were alone. "What's the happy medium here? I could find out by trial and error but I'd rather not have to do it this way."

He threw her a line and told her what to look out for on each of the meals. He even went so far as to tell her certain dishes that his father couldn't stand and to avoid at all costs. Dinners went more smoothly after that. Occasionally, she still chose something that wasn't to everyone's liking, but she had also provided alternatives for that very reason.

She moved on to planning the noon meals as well. Breakfast was, thankfully, not something she had to worry about since everyone rose at different times. She was also thankful that she hadn't been asked to plan the menu for a party, but she knew it was only a matter of time.

With the planning of meals no longer the challenge it once was, Calida moved on to tackling her other responsibilities. She learned what the appropriate costs of food and other supplies were and allocated the proper amount of money to the servants when they went out shopping, instructing them to buy only the best quality.

She had a private tutor who attempted to teach her the history of the kingdom she would one day help rule, but Calida found such things boring and incapable of holding her interest. Sitting in a stuffy classroom, listening to the tutor prattle on in his monotone drawl, lecturing on things no one cared about reminded her too much of the monastery—something she'd thought she left behind and possessed no desire to return to.

But worst still, she found she could no longer leave the palace grounds unaccompanied. The royal guards would follow her wherever she went, as they had Niklaus whenever he left the palace. And that meant she couldn't go see Jeremy when he returned to the harbor. Calida couldn't very well stroll into town with an escort of guards behind her. It would draw entirely too much attention and she didn't want them to know about Jeremy. They wouldn't take too kindly to a pirate visiting the mainland.

And so she found herself stuck inside most evenings, staring out the window at the cities and towns that lay below the hill that the palace stood on. At first, Calida had still sent Horus out to see if the *Sea Witch* was in the harbor, but she had stopped. The knowledge that Jeremy was there, waiting for her, and she wouldn't be able to come, tore at her heart.

He knew about Horus and that she sent him to scout for her. He knew that she would know if he was there or not and would wait for her. She wondered what he must think when she failed to arrive. Did he think she had become too snobbish, living a life of luxury up at the palace? Did he think she now thought herself above him and since he had given her what she needed in the form of a live rainleaf plant, did he think she no longer needed him?

Calida knew how hurt she would have been if the roles had been reversed. She hadn't even had the chance to tell him how much her life had changed. If he'd known about the proposal and engagement, he'd have understood. She had too many duties thrust upon her now and couldn't get away even if she wanted to.

She supposed she might be able to ditch the guards, but if the king found out, and he surely would, he wouldn't be the least bit pleased. She was already on thin ice with him and there wasn't room for the slightest mistake.

In the end, Calida compromised. She wrote a simple message, saying that she was unable to leave the palace, gave it to Horus and instructed him to pass it along to Jeremy.

Horus returned empty-handed and confirmed that he had delivered the message and that Jeremy had given him a verbal reply, saying that he understood and for her to come when she could.

But I can't, Calida thought miserably. She couldn't even tell him the real reason why she couldn't leave, not wanting to put such a thing in writing. The king hadn't wanted any of the commoners to know that the future queen was a witch and she couldn't risk the note falling into the wrong hands or being seen by the wrong set of eyes. Even if she instructed Jeremy to destroy the letter, it was a risk she simply could not take.

At least, she wasn't desperate enough to take the risk yet. If she wanted the king's approval, if she wanted to keep her place at the palace, she couldn't do anything to risk it.

CHAPTER 17

Slowly, Calida adjusted to her new role. It was harder than she'd thought it would be, but she was a fast learner. And though it became less challenging, it was no less tedious.

On top of her new duties, she still had to care for the king, whose health remained much the same, with the occasional relapse, but nothing serious.

At the end of the day, she was exhausted by the sheer amount of work that was expected of her and she wondered if Niklaus often felt the same way. She rose early and retired late, kept busy the whole day with one task or another. Something unexpected almost always seemed to come up. She barely had any time for herself—or Niklaus—and she suspected the king's hand was behind that as well, hoping to wear her down and break her resolve.

She stubbornly vowed that would not happen. Kings did not live forever. This was her destiny and she loved Niklaus. The hardship and tedium would all be worth it…one day.

Despite that, doubts, like vultures, were never far away. Circling. Waiting. The challenge gone and the tasks set before her more drudgery than anything else, Calida began to wonder if anything would ever change. If this was all there was to her life now.

One night, long after she should have been in bed, Calida sat in a corner, pouring over a budget that refused to be balanced. Never the best with numbers, the task was exacerbated by the late hour, the figures seeming to swim before her eyes, melding into one another.

Calida blinked furiously, trying to clear her blurring vision. Her temples throbbed, her eyes strained from both the long day and the darkness, her only source of light a single candle.

Sighing, she sat back, turning to look out the window. The sky was overcast, the moon hidden, but the towns below were lit invitingly. What were the people down there doing? Not struggling over a budget that should have been the responsibility of more than just one person, surely.

A wave of unhappiness washed over her. She had been feeling that way more and more lately. Listless, unmotivated, unhappy. She couldn't seem to shake the sense that this was not what she was meant to be doing. She didn't *want* this.

What she wanted was to leave all of this behind, even if only for a few hours, and go out riding. To feel the wind in her hair, the sand on her bare feet, the air on her face. She wanted to recapture that feeling of freedom.

But how free could one feel when constantly shadowed by a posse of guards, whose presence constantly made her feel as though she needed a babysitter.

Calida scowled and, rubbing her brow, turned back to the budget. By the time she finished, there wasn't much of the night left and when she laid down, hoping to snatch a few paltry hours of sleep, her throbbing headache robbed her of even that.

She was in a fine mood the next morning, her frustration loosening her tongue. But she felt the need to vent to someone before she exploded. Thankfully, there was one person in the palace who could be counted on to understand.

Thalia wasn't of this world either and Calida knew anything she told her sister wouldn't make its way back to the king.

She wasn't so open with anyone else, not even Niklaus. The king was still his father and he, unlike her, had been very much born to this type of life. In that regard, he might not understand what it was like for her, since he had never had to struggle in the way she did.

"Why does any of this matter?" Calida demanded one evening. She was in Thalia's room, sitting on the edge of the bed while her sister leaned against one wall, arms crossed, listening.

"I suppose you can't be expected to rule a kingdom efficiently if you can't even manage servants," Thalia said pragmatically.

"Yes, but why do *I* have to be the one to do it? Why can't they leave it to someone else, someone more experienced?"

"I think you're doing a fine job. You've got the hang of it, at least."

"That's my point!" Calida exclaimed. "Now that I've proven I know what I'm doing, why do I have to keep doing it? Why can't I delegate the task since I'm going to be queen one day? Isn't that what queens do—delegate?"

"I suppose you do have a point there," Thalia agreed.

"But I'd need someone I could trust not to mess things up and I don't know who would honestly want to do such a thing."

"I'll do it for you," Thalia offered.

Calida looked at her in some surprise. "Are you sure? It's incredibly boring."

Thalia shrugged. "So is moping around the palace with little to do. Besides, you've got enough on your plate with the king, keeping him alive and all."

It really wasn't all that hard anymore. Calida's rainleaf plant had grown remarkably well under her careful watch. It had produced seeds and she had even gotten another rainleaf plant to grow so that she now had two. The chances that she would run out of the precious herb were slim to none.

"I'm already bored," Thalia added, pushing off the wall. "At least this way, I'll have something to do. And you won't have to worry about continuing to slave away in the hope of impressing a king who's not even paying attention."

"You really think he hasn't noticed my improvement?" Calida asked, her hopes plummeting.

Thalia shook her head. "Oh, he might have noticed; he just doesn't care. He's already made up his mind against you and he doesn't want to be proven wrong, much less change his mind. I hate to say it, Calida, but you and the prince will just have to wait until he's dead."

Anger speared through Calida. Thalia was right. The king didn't like her, didn't think her a suitable partner for his son and certainly not fit to rule as queen one day. In that case, then what was she doing all these pointless, menial tasks for? Who was she trying to please? She didn't need the king's approval. She just needed to be patient and wait for him to die, then she and Niklaus could be married without opposition.

"You're right," she sighed. "Are you sure you don't mind, taking on the extra work?"

"I don't mind."

"Thank you." Calida crossed the room and embraced her sister. It was a generous offer on Thalia's part and Calida couldn't even begin to express her relief. "I won't forget what you're doing for me."

"Don't worry about it." Thalia smiled. "Just focus on what's really important and enjoy yourself."

Calida did, focusing on the more enjoyable aspects of her new position, such as attending horse races or watching fencing matches. She even had the time now for Niklaus to teach her a few fencing moves, though she wasn't nearly as good as he was and despaired of ever becoming so.

She heard no complaints when it came to her other, former duties and so she assumed that Thalia must have everything well in hand, executing each task with the usual brisk efficiency that marked her approach to all life's challenges.

Calida smiled to herself. She had been right to leave such things to her sister.

All she had to do now was wait.

* * *

Thalia went to work at once, taking careful stock of what was in the kitchens and then planning out the menu days in advance so she wouldn't have to come back every time. She left instructions for the cooks to inform her if some issue should arise, but she felt confident in her ability.

She had listened to Calida complain about the duties that were required of her enough to be quite familiar with them. She'd paid careful attention at each dinner she'd attended, taking note of what had been served and what hadn't—and how each dish had been received.

She knew the king's little idiosyncrasies; knew that he liked onions raw but not cooked, and that he couldn't abide the green herbs that were sometimes used as garnish on a dish. He thought they had absolutely no value and their inclusion hadn't earned Calida any points in her favor.

Her sister had been right about one thing—it was mind-numbingly dull work, repetitive from one day to the next, but it wasn't difficult.

The task that Thalia found to be the easiest and most interesting was the managing of the servants. The maids had many tasks to keep them occupied, from the opening of windows and shutters in the morning to cleaning furniture, making beds, and assisting with the laundry. They were on their feet all day and it wasn't surprising if they forgot something on their long list of things to be done.

Others occasionally tried to shirk their duties and took more breaks than was strictly necessary. Thalia kept an eye on them in her spare time, surreptitiously watching and assessing what kind of worker they would be. From Calida, she had learned which were the best workers and could be relied upon.

She pulled one such maid aside, the same one that Calida had asked for help the night her first dinner had gone wrong, and instructed the girl to keep an eye on the other members of staff, reporting back to her. Thalia slipped the girl an extra coin or two for her efforts, knowing how much money meant to her. She had learned the maid was an orphan and the only relative she had left was an elderly grandfather who was not in the best of health. With the extra money, she could afford better care for him and her dependence on such a thing also made her unlikely to refuse to spy on her fellow servants. She would do whatever Thalia asked of her, to the best of her ability.

Thalia noticed that another maid worked very hard, but seemed to perk up and do even better when told that her work was appreciated. Thalia gave her a flower during the first week she had taken over for Calida. She had taken it from the conservatory and it was a lovely green, complementing the girl's eyes.

"For your hair," Thalia explained, tucking it behind the maid's ear. "Best not wear it while you're on duty, though."

It might attract unwanted attention from the male servants and provoke jealousy in the other female staff. The maid grinned and nodded enthusiastically to show she understood. Thalia never caught her wearing the flower when she shouldn't and when it wilted and died, she carefully placed another new flower in the rooms Maisie was responsible for cleaning, where she would be sure to find it.

Simple gifts such as those made Thalia more popular among the servants than she thought Calida had ever been, but she was careful not to appear too approachable overall, lest they think she was soft and begin to take advantage.

The male servants gave her the most trouble. Footmen were responsible for cleaning leather, polishing glass, and preparing the carriages, among other things. One of them, she had been warned, was fond of sleeping in and had decided to test his luck when he heard there was new management. Thalia saw to it that he regretted the decision.

She marched into the servants' quarters, the ring of keys—which would be given to a housekeeper in a lesser household—jangling at her hip. She strode into the footman's room, finding him still in bed, snoring.

Wind howled as the room suddenly filled with a gale, stripping the blankets off the sleeping form and hurling the footman out of bed. He let out a startled cry and landed on the floor amidst a tangle of covers. He turned toward the open doorway, eyes wide with terror.

Thalia stood, hands on hips. "I believe you have somewhere to be," she said softly, her voice at odds with the shrieking wind that had died almost as quickly as it had come.

Scrambling to his feet, the footman hastily dressed and went about his duties. Calida, being unable, had never summoned a storm in his room before. Thalia had no more trouble from him.

She ensured that those servants that required a kind word or a small token of appreciation got them and the ones that needed a harsh word or swift punishment were thus managed. It was all very individualistic and whatever worked best for any given person was what they received. A blanket approach, she knew, would not work.

She didn't care if the servants liked, feared, or even respected her as long as they obeyed and did what they were supposed to do.

One of the most egregious offenses she had to deal with occurred when she caught one of the maids stealing.

The queen's room had been kept exactly the way the woman had left it on the day she'd died. No one was to enter except to clean and nothing was to be moved, per the king's wishes. It was a stuffy, oppressive room, a shrine to the dead. But it must be cleaned, dust and other signs of disuse swept away, maintaining the illusion that the dead woman could waltz in at any moment and pick up the pieces of her old life.

Thalia paused in the doorway, watching the maid go about her work, and saw the exact moment she slipped the necklace into her pocket. *As if no one would notice!*

She marched up to the girl, footsteps echoing on the hard marble floor. The maid quickly plunged a hand into her pocket, as though to conceal what she'd taken or hastily put it back, and then hesitated, caught between the two.

Thalia snatched her right hand and with a sharp twist, broke a few of her fingers. The girl gasped, staring at her in a mix of hurt and shock.

Thalia glared at her without a shred of sympathy. "Go see the healer and then get back to work. I still expect all of your duties completed by the end of the day in spite of this little detour or I'll know the reason why. Now go." She gave the maid a little shove and then called to her, "And if I ever catch you stealing again, you'll be out on your ear. Is that understood?"

The maid nodded and hurried away, clutching her injured hand. Gingerly, Thalia replaced the necklace precisely where it had rested on the dresser before, the dark sapphires winking up at her.

Calida had confessed to Thalia once that she felt like an imposter, bossing around servants that were barely younger than her—and sometimes quite older.

But Thalia had served on a naval ship surrounded by men, however briefly. Most of them had been older than her and didn't believe a woman should be on board, witch or not.

Though it had only been for a short time, the experience ensured she was comfortable in her new role.

Ordering around a few servants was nothing compared to being in the navy.

CHAPTER 18

The days slipped by and soon, half a year had passed since Niklaus had asked Calida to marry him. She was able to breathe more freely now that she had entrusted the more mundane aspects of her new role to her sister. Thalia must have been doing just fine, because Calida hadn't heard even a rumor of complaint.

Still, very little had changed. The king's health was the same as it had always been, suffering the occasional relapse, but otherwise holding steady. He had lived longer than even he had thought and it seemed he might yet live a long time still. Despite the gift that Calida had given him and continued to give him every day, he showed no sign of changing his mind regarding the marriage.

Privately, Calida was starting to resent the whole thing. Here she was, helping to keep him alive, the very man who stood between her and Niklaus's happiness. It would have been one thing if he had relented and changed his mind, but Calida now believed that Thalia had been right once again. The king had no intention of ever granting his permission.

And he never had. Nothing Calida had done or could ever do would be good enough. He'd merely said he would reconsider, giving her false hope, and all for what? So he could amuse himself, watching her trot about like some trick pony, making a fool of herself? Well, no more.

When she tried to talk to Niklaus about it, he merely said that they would have to wait and reiterated his willingness to wait as long as it took.

"You're his son," she told Niklaus one day. "Can't you ask him to reconsider? Beg, if you have to?" She knew how degrading having to beg would be and how much she would have hated it had the positions been switched, but she was feeling desperate.

Niklaus shook his head. "It doesn't work that way. He's...stubborn." He smiled at her. "But luckily, so am I and I'm willing to wait him out." He frowned suddenly, taking in her expression. "Here, you're not having second thoughts, are you?"

"Of course not!" Calida moved toward him, pressing her cheek against his chest. "I just hate that we have to wait and not knowing how long it will take."

"I know." She felt him press his lips to her hair. "The day we can finally be together will be one of both joy and sorrow for me. I want us to be married, but I also know that will mean losing my father."

The only family he had left. *And after he fought so hard to save him.* Calida felt a sudden surge of guilt for her earlier uncharitable thoughts toward the king. The man was still Niklaus's father, the father of the man she loved, and she wondered what Niklaus would have thought of her, how he would have reacted, had he known how she felt in her heart.

"It's just sad all around," she murmured.

"It is. I thought he'd come around and he might still, but I don't see what more you could have done to convince him." Niklaus smiled sadly. "We'll just have to be patient a while longer."

Calida appreciated his patience, but the more time wore on, the harder she found it. They had to wait until the king was dead and she was the one prolonging his life, at this point against her own best interests.

Even though he remained unwilling to grant permission for them to marry, the king must have accepted that his son had no intention of breaking off the engagement and that Calida would one day become queen. He announced a feast would be held at the palace, at which Calida would be introduced in her new role to some of the nobility.

It was an event Calida dreaded. Everything would have to go perfectly at this feast and she found herself racing into the servants' quarters to find Thalia. She needed to go over the menu with her and reassure herself that all was well.

She nearly collided with her sister in one of the hallways. "Thalia," she panted. "The feast…the menu…"

"It's already been taken care of," Thalia replied, her quiet confidence immediately easing some of Calida's fear. "You're welcome to check the menu yourself, but I think you'll find everything satisfactory."

Calida *did* want to see the menu for herself, but she wondered if asking such a thing would be insulting. Was she demonstrating, somehow, that she did not fully trust Thalia to handle such things by asking to double-check her work?

She took a deep breath. "I trust you. I'm sure it's all well in hand."

"Wonderful," Thalia agreed. "Now you need to decide what you're going to wear to this dinner. You'll be presented as the prince's fiancée, after all, so you'll want to make a good impression."

Calida followed her sister up the stairs. "None of them like me. They may not say so to my face, but none of them believe I'm worthy of such an honor and they'll undoubtedly resent the fact that the prince chose me instead of one of them. They might think I bewitched him or something, since none of them seem to know what witches *really* do."

"It doesn't matter whether or not they like you," Thalia replied, "though you should make an effort. What matters is whether or not you can convince them that you *deserve* to be here. Do you think you can do that?"

"I suppose I'll have to."

"You'll be fine. Remember, you're the future queen. Act like it and don't let them forget it for a second. You may be only a witch in their eyes now, but one day they'll have to answer to you. Each and every one."

Calida smiled at the image her sister's words conjured. "I wish I had your effortless confidence."

Thalia snorted. "Effortless? Hardly. The trick is to appear confident, even if you don't feel it. Especially if you don't feel it. If you can convince everyone else that you are, then you'll start to believe it too."

They had reached Calida's room and Thalia helped her select a dress, holding up one of scarlet silk. "What about this one? It's Alara's color."

"It'll clash horribly with my hair," Calida protested.

"All right, how about this one?" It was a gown of gold. "They often pair it with their official color. Niklaus will be in ceremonial dress so he'll be wearing scarlet. You'll compliment him perfectly."

Calida still had reservations, but she had to admit that Thalia was right about needing to match her fiancé. They must present a united front. "The gold it is, then."

The night of the feast, Calida even had Thalia fix her hair, braiding and pinning it elaborately. Her hair was thick so the end result had plenty of volume and, when paired with the gold gown, was visibly stunning.

"You've outdone yourself," she told her sister.

Thalia wore her signature sky witch blue, which set off her red hair and dark blue eyes. She gave Calida a playful shove. "Stop gawking at yourself in the mirror before you make us both late."

The two of them were escorted into dinner, as was customary for such a formal event. Calida was seated beside Niklaus, Thalia across from her, and she felt him squeeze her hand briefly beneath the table. She recognized some of the nobles present from the previous party she had attended, but couldn't remember any of their names.

She glanced down at the array of silverware arranged before her. By now, she knew which fork and knife were to be used on what dishes and if any of the nobles present expected her to make a mistake and show herself to be the peasant they believed she was, she intended to give them no such satisfaction.

The many courses rolled out, a variety of dishes included in each one, containing something for everyone. Calida sampled what she liked and silently marveled at Thalia's skill. She had been right to trust her; she couldn't have done better herself.

Inevitably, conversation ensued, the topic of choice being Calida herself. Per Thalia's advice, Calida smiled at their inane questions and kept her answers simple, never revealing too much.

"You want them to think you're mysterious," Thalia had said. "Mysterious people are naturally interesting as long as the mystery remains. If they end up thinking you slightly simple, that's still better than coming across as arrogant."

Calida wasn't convinced she had mastered the art of being mysterious. She thought she sounded vapid instead, her answers short and simple because she couldn't carry a decent thought in her head, but at least she didn't see how they could think her arrogant.

She didn't care what they thought, really, so long as the king was satisfied with her performance. *Performance…as if I'm a trained monkey.* She wished Horus could be there with her. He would have made some clever remark about one of the nobleman's facial features or a noblewoman's hairstyle and relieved some of the tension she felt.

But he was waiting for her in her room, eager to hear all about it; she hadn't been allowed to bring him. No 'filthy' animals were allowed at the table.

Still, if she could, she had promised to bring him a piece of one of the meat dishes. Smuggling it out would be the tricky part.

Horus may not have been able to rescue her, but Thalia could. In any of the tense, awkward moments, she seemed to know exactly what to say, coming off as witty and not at all forced. She even made a few of the nobles laugh, complimenting them in a seemingly genuine way that Calida could never have managed, and taking the attention completely away from Calida, for which she was grateful.

As for specifics as to what was said or even eaten, Calida could not have said afterward, aside from the piece of fish she had managed to conceal, wrapped in a napkin for Horus.

Niklaus murmured briefly to her once it was over and they went their own ways, "You were great."

She felt as though she'd been holding her breath the whole time, trying to keep her true feelings from bleeding through and focusing so hard on saying the right thing that she'd occasionally stammered instead. But overall, she thought the evening had been a great success. No one could have expected anything better from someone who had not been born to such a world and had, really, only a short time to adapt.

Pleased, she hurried back to her room to change and then she needed to prepare the king's rainleaf. Calida tried not to think about Jeremy as she made her way to the conservatory, selecting a dried leaf from her supplies. It had been so long since she'd seen him, the longest she'd gone between visits since the first time she'd seen him and then had to wait for him to return. Now he was the one waiting for her.

She heard the door as it opened, footsteps trailing light over the floor, and looked up as Thalia came into view.

"Thought you might want this." She held out a steaming cup of tea.

"Thank you." Calida took it, setting it on the table beside the waiting rainleaf. She would have summoned a servant to make the tea for her and bring it up but Thalia's gesture saved her the trouble.

Thalia wrung her hands, as though nervous. "So, how do you feel about tonight? Do you think it went all right?"

Calida sighed, her previous elation vanishing. "I think so, but I also know it's not good enough. Even if every single aspect of tonight went perfectly, the king would still find something to nitpick. You were right; he's never going to change his mind about me and part of me doesn't see the point in trying to please him anymore. And here I am." She glared down at the leaf as she viciously crumbled it into the cup of tea. "With every dose of rainleaf I give him, I'm only prolonging the inevitable and denying myself what I really want."

There was a part of her that wished she'd never thought to try rainleaf or that it hadn't been as successful as she'd then hoped. But then, she never would have stayed at the palace and ended up in her current position.

"No man can live forever," Thalia murmured. "Not even him."

Calida took a deep breath, drawing some consolation from the fact that not even kings, with all their wealth and power, were immortal. All the power in the world would not grant them immunity from death.

"What plant is that?" Thalia asked, pointing.

Calida glanced over her shoulder at the plant nestled beside the first of her rainleaf plants, the one Jeremy had given her. "*Bellavexis*. Devil's blood. Silk snare. I learned about it at the monastery. Nasty stuff. Stay away from it."

"Why, what does it do? Aside from smell lovely."

"It makes people docile, compliant, at the expense of their memory, if they take it long enough."

"Hm." Thalia's eyebrows rose. "You're right. Sounds best left alone. Although…if you slipped some of it to the king, I bet he'd cease to be so opposed to you marrying Niklaus."

"Thalia!"

"What? I'm only trying to help."

Calida looked down at the steaming mug of tea and picked it up. "I'd better get this to the king before it goes cold."

"Yes, I imagine that would please him to no end," Thalia muttered dryly. "Don't let me stop you."

Calida walked briskly, as though trying to leave behind her thoughts along with the room. But Thalia's insinuation, though unpleasant, was not so easily dismissed.

A small part of Calida was tempted by the suggestion. The rest of her was appalled, but there was no denying the temptation was there, ready to take root.

* * *

Niklaus went to see his father after the dinner had ended and Calida had given him his nightly dose of rainleaf. It was later than usual, not a good time for a conversation with the king, but Niklaus wanted to strike while the memories and impressions of the dinner were still fresh in his mind.

The king had changed into his robe, but hadn't yet gone to bed.

Niklaus kept his hands behind his back. "I thought the dinner was a success. Calida did well."

Perhaps if he could get his father to acknowledge that fact, he could do as Calida had asked and press his advantage.

The king grunted. "Did she?"

It wasn't the answer Niklaus had been expecting. "What? Of course she did. You were there, Father. Did you see something different?"

"Yes, I did," the king snapped. "I am not blinded to the girl's flaws the way you seem to be."

"And what flaws are those?" Niklaus asked, an edge of irritation creeping into his voice in spite of himself. The slight to Calida had rattled him.

The king turned to face him. "To put it bluntly, she is not fit to be queen and I think if you look closer, you'll see it too."

"What are you talking about?" Niklaus exploded. "She's done everything you asked of her. We've had no complaints about the servants, no high turnover rate and those that do leave are quickly replaced. If there was something wrong with the menu she chose for tonight, I'd like to hear it." He stood there waiting with his arms crossed, knowing he was on dangerous ground now, but unable to contain his temper.

The king, for his part, did not seem phased by his son's outburst. "I have no complaints about tonight's dinner," he said softly, "because Calida did not prepare it."

"What?"

"It has been brought to my attention that Calida has been neglecting her duties for some time now. She is no longer managing the servants or preparing a budget, seeing to the household or even approving the menu. She has passed on such responsibilities to her sister. Her sister about which, I might add, I have heard much praise. More than one of my guests tonight made a point of telling me before they left how much they enjoyed the selection of food and a few even went so far as to inform me that Thalia made a delightful addition to the party. Why, one guest was even under the mistaken assumption that she was the hostess! An assumption that could be easily made."

Niklaus could only stare at his father in mute shock.

"It was clear from Calida's conduct that she made only the barest effort when it came to conversing with the other guests. She put no thought into what she said. Thalia, on the other hand, was gracious, humorous, and charming. She made a lasting, favorable impression, which cannot be said for Calida. The guests that came here tonight will remember Thalia, not her sister. Your fiancée, as good of a healer she may be, would make a poor queen."

"You don't know that," Niklaus protested, finding his voice. "She makes me a better man."

"She might make you a worse king. I've seen the type before. She put no effort into making tonight a success, yet she seemingly reaped all the rewards. She is lazy, Niklaus. She enjoys the finer points of royal life, the horse races, the fine food, the pretty clothes, but she isn't willing to put forth the work. She might be good company, she might be pretty to look at, but when you need her the most, you will find her unreliable."

"You're lying. You just don't want to accept her. You're letting your own prejudice cloud your judgement. You've been against her from the start!" Niklaus exclaimed, speaking faster until the words were nearly tumbling out.

"You're right, and now you know why. Ask her yourself, if you truly think I'm lying to you. Ask if she delegated her duties to someone else. Ask if Thalia is responsible for the success of tonight's dinner."

"I will," Niklaus retorted but though his voice did not lack conviction, he wasn't sure he wanted to do it.

What if his father *was* right about Calida? What did that mean for their impending marriage? For the kingdom?

"Niklaus." The king crossed the room and laid a hand on his shoulder. "I cannot dictate who you can marry. Once I am gone, you are free to do as you wish. I only want what is best for you and the kingdom and I know how difficult this must be for you. Think on what I have said. That's all I ask."

Niklaus nodded numbly, not knowing what else to do. He could certainly think it over. And he trusted Calida, didn't he? What sort of relationship did they have if he couldn't ask her a simple question?

He would ask her and she would tell him that the king was making the whole thing up or at the very least, exaggerating. After all, he was the only one with reason to lie about such a thing. He didn't like her and by his own admission, never had. How exactly, then, could he be expected to remain unbiased in his assessment of her?

The king just didn't want to admit he'd been wrong. Calida's performance tonight had proven just that and he resented her for it.

Niklaus wouldn't trouble Calida with such things tonight. Tomorrow would be soon enough.

CHAPTER 19

The next morning, Calida went out riding with Niklaus, their horses strolling along the beach, guards behind, carefully keeping their distance. The outing had been Niklaus's idea and she knew he wanted to talk to her, but she refrained from asking, waiting patiently for him to speak. She cast a glance up at the sky. It was mostly blue for now, but she could see gray gathering in the distance, threatening rain, and she hoped he didn't take too long.

"I think the dinner last night went well," Niklaus finally said, breaking the silence. "My father agrees."

Calida looked up in surprise. Had she finally managed to do something that the king approved of?

But Niklaus hadn't finished. "However, he alleged the dinner was a success in spite of you rather than because of you…"

"What is that supposed to mean?" she demanded, her earlier elation already vanishing.

Niklaus fidgeted in the saddle, clearly uncomfortable. "He said you weren't responsible for the menu or managing the servants anymore or any of the rest of it. He said you'd delegated those tasks to your sister." He turned to face her. "Is that true?"

She hesitated. She hadn't told Niklaus, or anyone else, about her decision but she didn't see why it should matter. "It's true."

Niklaus reined his horse to a halt and Calida was forced to stop as well. "What were you thinking? Those duties were assigned to you. They were *your* responsibility."

"I know how to do them," Calida protested. "Isn't that what matters?"

"What matters is that you were supposed to be proving yourself capable in order to change his mind, remember?" Niklaus snapped. His blue eyes, usually calm, now glinted with anger. "How exactly are you going to win his favor by shirking your duties and handing them over to someone else who's better at it than you?"

Calida stiffened. She knew Thalia handled things differently than she had but that didn't make her any better at it. "What's the point? Your father has no intention of ever changing his mind. He's been set against me from the moment you informed him of our engagement—and you know it. Why should I continue to slave away and all for what?"

"For us," Niklaus hissed. "For our marriage."

"We'll be married anyway. We just have to wait until the king's dead, that's all. He's not going to change his mind, Niklaus, and so there's no point in trying to please him. Queens delegate tasks to others. Why can't I?"

"Because you're not the queen yet! And if my father has his way, you never will be. He doesn't think you're fit to be queen, Calida, and you've done nothing to dispel that notion."

She glared at him. "And what do you think?"

He sighed. "I don't know. I think if you applied yourself—"

Calida cut him off, anger surging through her. "Well, perhaps you should have your father tell you what to think, since you can't do so on your own."

She spurred her horse, more viciously than she'd intended, and the animal leapt forward, churning up sand in her wake. She heard Niklaus call to her, but she ignored him.

How could he think so little of her? The king didn't think she was fit to rule, but he'd always felt that way and no amount of persuading or proving herself would ever change a mind that didn't want to be changed. Why couldn't Niklaus see how biased his father was? The king didn't want to see a witch on the throne, that was all there was to it. She was an interloper, intruding where she didn't belong and wasn't wanted, upsetting everything along the way.

Surely Niklaus didn't agree that she wasn't fit to rule. But he hadn't said either way. How could he not come to his own conclusion? How could he agree with the king? He had chosen her, he had asked her to marry him, knowing exactly who and what she was and claiming he hadn't cared. Why was she the one being punished for it? Why should any of them be surprised that she failed to live up to their standards?

She'd only been at the palace for a few months. How much could one expect of her in such a short amount of time?

Calida glanced over her shoulder, but she had left Niklaus and the guards far behind. None of them had chased after her, the prince likely not wanting to get into trouble along with her—and she would be in trouble once the king learned she had abandoned her escort.

She didn't care. She'd meant what she'd said to Niklaus. Why should she bother trying to please a man who refused to acknowledge or approve of any of her efforts? He probably gleaned some sort of sick amusement from watching her scurry around, doing his bidding, knowing it was all for naught.

It should have come as no surprise that she had failed to prove herself to the king. But then a darker thought intruded upon her mind, unwelcome and horrid in its implication. What if she had failed to prove herself to Niklaus as well? She wouldn't have thought she had to. Hadn't she done so already?

Was that where his doubts came from? His lack of faith in her stung, cutting deeper than Thalia's initial doubts had. She'd thought they were a team.

She shook the thought away, the wind streaming past her cheeks as she urged the horse on. Niklaus would either love her as she was and if he didn't, then perhaps he had never really loved her at all.

The skies opened up above her, rain pouring down and soon she was soaked to the skin, hair plastered to her forehead, water running down her neck, but Calida didn't care. The rain was cold and miserable, but it suited her just then. And at least she was free. All of her responsibilities and the pressure of royal life would still be waiting for her when she returned, but for now, she could pretend it was possible to outrun them.

* * *

Coming out of the conservatory where she'd gone to pick a few more flowers, Thalia nearly ran into the prince and she let out a cry.

Upon seeing who it was, she gave a small curtsy. "Oh, Your Highness. I'm sorry. I should pay more attention."

His hair and clothes were slightly damp, as if he'd been caught out in the rain, and there was a frown etched deep between his brows.

"You're all right," he murmured, making to brush past her and then seemed to think better of it. "Have you seen Calida?"

"No. I thought she was with you."

"She was. Until she ran off."

Calida had run away? "Is something the matter?" Thalia asked tentatively.

He sighed. "You're her sister. You must know her better than just about anyone," he said, stepping into the conservatory.

Thalia followed. "I suppose so."

"I've learned that you are the one responsible for the menus and all the rest, not her. That she's delegated such things to you."

"That's right. She expressed frustration with her duties, once she'd gotten the hang of them and they no longer provided a challenge, only dull and monotonous work. I offered to do them for her."

"Well, you're doing a fine job. You are a credit to your kingdom."

"Thank you, Your Highness."

"Niklaus, please. We are friends, after all."

Thalia inclined her head. "As you wish."

"The truth is, Thalia, I'm having a bit of a hard time with Calida at the moment. I don't know how to make her understand how important all of this is. She's shirked her duties and doesn't seem to understand why that's a bad thing. She says the king will never approve of her, so why should she even attempt to do as he wishes?"

"My sister can be terribly stubborn," Thalia murmured.

"I think I'm beginning to see that."

She smiled at him. "I don't know if she's right about your father, but I do know that if she doesn't want to put her time and energy into what she deems menial tasks, then she won't—and you'll be wasting your time trying to convince her otherwise."

"But it's her duty," Niklaus protested. "How can she be expected to be a good queen if she shirks her duties the moment they become inconvenient?"

"I don't know," Thalia said honestly. "Perhaps she can't. It's one of the things Calida has struggled with her entire life. It is, I think, one reason why she found it so difficult at the monastery, forced to commit to just one thing. She always spoke to me about fate and how we have no say in any of it, as witches. I think, given the chance, she will try to forge her own path, rather than doing what is expected of her." She glanced at Niklaus. "I hope, of course, that I am wrong."

He sighed again, coming to a stop in front of the rainleaf plants Calida had grown. "I'll talk to her again, see what can be done. If she comes back, that is. I don't know where she's gone."

"She'll come back," Thalia replied. Of that, at least, she was sure.

Niklaus nodded. "We'll work this out," he murmured, almost to himself. "We'll find a way."

He turned to leave but stopped as Thalia called after him.

"Just remember, Calida finally escaped the monastery. You'll never make her go back again."

* * *

When Calida returned, over an hour later, the storm outside had not let up. Niklaus was fully prepared to set aside their previous disagreement and try again. They were both adults, after all. They would find some way to make this work. And perhaps he had judged her too harshly.

But the moment he saw her, stalking through the halls, dripping water onto the polished floor, his anger resurfaced and he strode over to her.

Her skin was paler than usual, her red hair made darker by the moisture, hanging in damp, tangled clumps. He ignored her full lips and the way the water made her dress cling to her figure, accentuating her curves. He was too angry for any of that.

"Look at you," he hissed. "You're a mess. Is this the way the future queen of Alara conducts herself? And you're trailing water all over the floor, making more work for the servants. They'll have to clean it up—and clean your dress." She'd somehow contrived to splash mud on the hem. "You were in charge of managing them at one point; you know how much work they already have without you adding to it."

She had the grace to flush but he didn't miss the flash of indignation in her gray eyes. "I wasn't thinking of them."

"No," Niklaus said, aware he was being waspish. "You never think of others, only about what you want in the moment." The words were harsh, as he'd intended them to be. "Now get cleaned up and make yourself presentable for dinner."

Calida shot him a glare and moved past him, head still held high.

In spite of himself, Niklaus glanced over his shoulder and watched her stalk away. She was at once empathetic and vexing. His heart ached with his feelings for her, but now there was something else there as well, that hadn't been before—a twinge of doubt.

She may have understood him in a way no one else ever had, she may have made a good partner, but that didn't necessarily mean she would make a good queen. And he needed that in a wife as much as anything else.

* * *

Dinner was a subdued affair. Calida refused to look at Niklaus and any conversation was stilted. Thalia made a valiant effort to lighten the mood. Calida, usually thankful for her sister's efforts, wished she wouldn't bother and thankfully she soon realized it was hopeless and gave up.

Calida had expected Niklaus to apologize upon her return to the palace. She'd expected him to feel guilty at seeing her disheveled state, knowing that his unkind words had upset her, leading her to run off in the first place.

But he hadn't apologized at all. He'd reacted with more anger, as if he were the offended party and she'd insulted his sensibilities by appearing in such a state. She supposed he would have preferred her to stay out in the storm.

After dinner, she gave the king his dose of rainleaf, expecting him to say something about her abandoning her guards. He said nothing, yet she marveled silently at his ability to so effectively convey displeasure with nothing more than silence. He didn't have to utter a word for her to know he wasn't pleased with her actions.

Well she was determined not to care. He may have been the king, but she was no longer interested in trying to appeal to him.

She retreated to her room and a knock sounded on the door a few moments later, too soft to be Niklaus. "Come in," she called, knowing already who it was.

There was a part of her that desperately wanted it to be Niklaus even though it wasn't, for him to come to her and say what he should have said earlier, tell her how sorry he was and take her in his arms.

Instead, Thalia came in, shutting the door behind her. "I heard you ran off earlier."

"I don't want to talk about it," Calida said, sinking down onto her bed.

"Are you sure?"

"No." She sat up. "Niklaus accused me of being unfit to be queen." Calida was unable to keep her voice from shaking as she allowed the full hurt his remark had caused to wash over her.

"That's rather unfair of him," Thalia said, crossing the room to sit beside her. "Why would he say that?"

"Because I delegated what was supposed to be my responsibility to you."

"Well, I told you the king would never change his mind. He's determined to dislike you and even if you did everything perfectly, he would still manage to find some fault with it. So why should you even bother wasting your time?"

"Exactly!" Calida cried. "That's what I told Niklaus, but he didn't understand. I think he thinks I'm lazy." Her vision blurred with tears. It was the first major argument they'd had and it hurt more than she cared to admit.

"You're not," Thalia said fiercely, wrapping her arms around her sister. "Niklaus has to love you as you are. You shouldn't have to change who you are and he has no right to ask that of you."

"You're right," Calida murmured, returning the embrace. "You're always right."

Thalia pulled back. "You can have your duties back if you want. I don't mind."

"No, you're doing a good job. Besides, you were right about what you said. Why should I waste my time?"

* * *

After dinner, Niklaus went to speak with his father in his study, knowing he owed him an apology for accusing him of being untruthful. He hadn't been lying about Calida's duties and instead of putting his mind to rest, Niklaus's conversation with her had only muddled the waters further.

Perhaps his father had been right and he'd seen something in Calida that Niklaus had been willfully blind to. Either way, he deserved an apology. Niklaus was man enough to admit when he was wrong.

His father was sitting behind his desk when he came in, still fully dressed. His cup of rainleaf tea sat before him, half finished. "I heard your fiancée ran off earlier today, leaving her guards behind, and returned to the palace in a lamentable state."

There was no point in denying it. "Yes," Niklaus admitted. "I asked her about what you said last night. We argued and she became angry with me. Perhaps I handled the situation poorly, as I did during our own conversation last night and for that, I apologize. You were right. Her sister has indeed taken over responsibility for her duties."

The king rose to his feet. "It gives me no joy to be right in this instance," he murmured. "But I felt that you should know. What is it about this girl that first drew you to her? It can't simply be her looks. She's beautiful, make no mistake, but her sister is even more so."

It had, in fact, been her looks, but Niklaus thought better of saying so. It was shallow and that was precisely how it would sound.

So instead he chose to go with the other reason. "She spoke to me as if I were nothing special. No one had ever treated me like that before. I know that must sound disrespectful to you, Father, but I felt like she saw me for who I was as a person and not just my titles. Outwardly, socially, we couldn't be more different. One day, I will have to rule a kingdom whether I want to or not. I have no say over my own fate. And neither did she. When witches reach a certain age, they are taken from their families and brought to the Erlohn monastery to train and learn how they might best serve the kingdom. It's never about what they want to do with their life, always about what they're best at. I saw a part of my own situation in that. No nobleman's daughter ever understood me like that."

"But does she understand your duty?" the king asked, his voice quiet still. "You were right; you can't change your fate. But I think that's precisely what Calida has been trying to do, ever since she came to the palace. She wants to change what she feels is her destiny. She wants something different. She doesn't want to share in your burden, her own fate being tied down by yours, and so it is my fear that you will be left to shoulder it on your own."

It was eerily similar to what Thalia had previously told him. And she was Calida's sister, who knew her better than anyone. If the king could see it so clearly, why couldn't he?

Was it true that Calida would tire of him, the way she had tired of the rest of palace life, once the shine had worn off?

Oh sure, she liked the fine food and the entertainments, just as she must have found him fresh and exciting. But when that gave way to the inevitable reality of life, to the harder, less pleasant aspects that no one found enjoyable but that needed to be done, would she still be there to support him?

Or would she leave him alone, to succeed or drown on his own?

It was an unpleasant thought and Niklaus felt guilty for even considering it. But letting such a thing come to pass would be even worse. Ruling entirely alone would be far more preferable to ruling with a partner who did not support him.

He needed to be careful, to make sure that his decision was the right one, that he hadn't been wrong about Calida, and to do everything in his power to ensure that such a fate did not come to pass.

"I love her, Father," he said simply, trying to ignore the niggling doubt in the back of his mind, that had taken root like a recalcitrant weed, always growing back when he thought it had finally been plucked. *At least I think I do.*

"But does she love you?" the king asked. "Or does she love what you represent? What you can offer her?"

Niklaus wanted to say that of course she loved him. Why would she treat him as if he were ordinary, as if she didn't notice or care about his titles if that was, in fact, all she cared about? Or had she only changed her mind once he had proposed to her?

He swallowed. "She loves me." But his voice lacked conviction, even to his own ears.

His father drained the last of his tea and turned to face the window. "Sometimes love is not enough."

* * *

Calida waited for the outrage to die down and for things to return to normal. They did, slowly. Things became easier between her and Niklaus, but not as they had been before

289

and she began to wonder if they ever would. Nothing more was said about her duties, for which she was grateful, but she was still aware that he did not approve.

It seemed everything she did was overshadowed by a sort of sorrow, an awareness of something lost, possibly never to be regained.

More time slipped away and still the old king clung stubbornly to life. Calida had no way of knowing just how effective rainleaf would be when she'd first suggested it, but it had exceeded all of their hopes and expectations.

The more time that passed, she despaired further of ever being able to marry Niklaus. She didn't think he would change his mind about her, but the waiting was nearly as difficult to bear as his disapproval.

Still, she made no effort to please the king or win his approval. At some point, she even stopped going to the frivolous events that had been planned for her. If she didn't need to please the king, why bother trying to please and amuse the nobles? She wasn't some novelty to be gawked at for their entertainment and refused to be treated as such.

Niklaus seemed to know better than to confront her over such things again, but she didn't realize how upset he was by it all until one morning he announced he was going out riding.

"I'll come with you," she offered. Even if they no longer spoke as often, there was still a certain enjoyment to be found in each other's company.

"No," Niklaus retorted. "I'm going alone."

Calida stared at him, stung by the rebuff. Even though she didn't always accompany him, he'd never outright refused to let her go with him.

She followed as he strode away, toward the stables. "Niklaus!" She grabbed his sleeve, forcing him to stop, but he did not turn to look at her. "What's the matter?"

He whirled on her then. "You weren't present at the luncheon yesterday with Lord and Lady Pemberly."

Calida blinked. She'd forgotten all about it. Ever since she'd stopped going, she hadn't bothered to remember when such events were taking place. "I never go to such things."

"Yes, and that's the problem, isn't it? It's one thing to neglect your responsibilities and quite another to be an embarrassment to me."

She let go of his sleeve, taking a step back. "An embarrassment?"

"Yes! We were supposed to be there together and instead it was just me. How do you think that looks to the nobility? You made me look like a fool, Calida."

"I'm sorry," she murmured, feeling a rush of guilt wash over her. Even though his words hurt, she hadn't meant to wound him in such a way.

Niklaus shook his head, brows drawn close together in an expression that looked more exasperated than angry. "I'd ask you to do better, but I don't think you have any intention of doing so," he said quietly and somehow, his disappointment cut deeper than his ire. "You make no effort to be courteous and make people like you."

"I don't care if they like me or not," Calida protested. "Besides, they don't want to like me anyway."

"You don't know that. And you do need to care." He raked a hand through his golden hair. "I know you don't care about pleasing my father, but what about me?"

He turned away then and she let him go.

* * *

That night, Calida retreated to the conservatory early, not wanting to be disturbed by anyone. Few people rarely came in here, including servants. She knew Niklaus wasn't afraid to venture within, but she doubted he wanted to see her just then. That suited her just fine.

She tended to her two rainleaf plants, wanting to put off preparing the king's medicine for as long as possible. Just thinking about him made her jaw clench. Her temples ached from the tension. She plucked a few leaves that were yellowing and tore off a few healthy ones as well, to set aside for drying later on.

Both plants had grown quite large, big enough that she doubted she would have been able to carry their pots now. Soon, she would be able to grow a third plant if she wished. It was the prudent thing to do, but Calida was tempted not to bother.

She rang for a servant to bring the tea and when it arrived, she poured it herself, the liquid piping hot. With a sigh, she withdrew a single dried leaf from her bundle. The bright blue leaves turned a dark shade when severed from the main plant and it crumbled easily in her grasp. Calida dropped the pieces into the tea and stirred, her thoughts a million miles away.

She thought of Jeremy, how long it had been since she had last seen him, and wondered what he thought of her and her absence. He still didn't know about her engagement.

Calida sighed again, still stirring, the dark liquid swirling hypnotically. How excited she had been to share her news with him at first. Now, that excitement had dulled, much like the dried rainleaf. Would it, too, dissolve into nothing?

The spoon clinked against the side of the cup, breaking her out of her thoughts. She found herself staring at the *bellavexis* plant. She'd been eying its velvet, petal-like leaves, and black-red berries without realizing it.

She frowned, the spoon ceasing its movement as she thought back to Thalia's suggestion. Silk snare, as the plant was more commonly known, wasn't lethal. There was no risk of overdosing on it; the plant's danger lay elsewhere.

Would it really be so wrong if she slipped some to the king? If it made him more docile, more agreeable and compliant, that could only be a good thing.

Was it really so easy? Was the problem standing in her way so easily solved?

If the king became more agreeable, perhaps he could be persuaded to allow the marriage to go ahead. Once married, the doubts that had been plaguing Calida would be no more. There would be nothing for her to worry about. She could finally be happy—her and Niklaus both.

Calida felt a sudden pang in her chest, the longing so strong it nearly took her breath away. She wanted it so badly it hurt.

There was no harm in trying and if she succeeded, she would have everything she wanted.

Her fingers reached toward the plant, for the deceptively small berries. She plucked a single one, the plant's strong perfume wafting over her. She could always take more next time, should the need arise.

Crushing the berry in her palm, Calida squeezed the juice, the color of freshly spilled blood, into the tea, and stirred quickly. She knew the juice had no taste, its presence undetectable aside from the smell.

That done, she hurried across the room to one of the faucets. Her hand looked stained with blood, as though she'd cut her palm. She scrubbed her skin beneath the stream until it felt raw, the evidence vanishing down the drain.

Calida straightened, wiping her palm on her skirt, taking a deep breath as the full realization of what she had done struck her.

No, what she was about to do. She hadn't done it yet. It wasn't too late. She could step back from that precipice. She didn't have to do this.

Briefly, she wondered what Niklaus would think if he knew.

It didn't matter.

He would never know.

Calida walked back to the table and lifted the cup of rainleaf tea, now tainted with devil's blood.

Without hesitation, she ran toward the precipice and hurled herself over the edge.

If the king smelled any hint of the presence of the newest ingredient in his tea, he didn't show it. She didn't even need to encourage him.

He drank it down to the very last drop, until there was nothing left but dregs.

CHAPTER 20

Niklaus wanted to believe that Calida would change her behavior, but he knew better than to hope. She'd shown no such inclination thus far.

He sighed to himself in frustration. What was wrong with her? Didn't she love him enough to do these small things for him? He didn't particularly enjoy meeting with other nobles himself. It was quite dull and either patronizing or sycophantic and there were a hundred other things he could think of that he'd rather be doing.

But duty came before any of that. It was what separated a good ruler from the bad. He knew that. He'd been born to such things, having them drilled into his head his entire life. But Calida hadn't been. Was he being too hard on her? How could she ever fit into a world where she didn't truly understand the gravity of such things?

He would need the support of the nobility when he ascended the throne but if they hated his wife, how could he expect their support?

Such power was a heady thing and he knew the throne was coveted by more than one member of the nobility. Changes in power were always trying times and he didn't need to give any of them an excuse to see him removed, forcibly or otherwise.

Niklaus received word that Daera was sending delegates to meet the future queen of Alara, to see for themselves the woman Niklaus had chosen. Currently, Alara was on friendly terms with their neighbor to the north and he wanted to maintain the easy relationship between the kingdoms. Calida would need to prove herself.

But on the day the delegates were set to arrive, she was nowhere to be found. Niklaus went looking for her, striding down the corridors, swearing under his breath. She wasn't in her room, nor the conservatory or the royal infirmary or any of the other likely haunts where she could usually be found at any given time.

With a sinking feeling in his stomach, he made his way down to the stables and asked the groom if Calida had been by recently.

"Aye, Your Highness," the groom replied. 'She took a horse out not quite an hour ago."

If she had gone out riding, there was no telling where she would be by now and it was not likely that she'd gone down to the docks to greet the Daeran delegates personally.

Niklaus closed his eyes, a wave of disappointment sweeping over him. In that moment, he realized Calida would not change. Not for the king, not for the kingdom, and not for him.

The realization hurt. The first two he could have borne, but the last was simply too much.

But he had no time to dwell on it now. He couldn't allow himself to be made to look a fool in front of a foreign kingdom. They would not take him seriously as a king if it appeared that his wife did not respect him enough to even show up. It made him look weak.

He straightened his shoulders, trying to think of a way out of this predicament. Perhaps he should say that she had taken ill, but there was always the risk that the rumor would spread and someone, somewhere, who knew the truth would disprove it.

No one from Daera had yet met Calida and so they didn't know exactly what she looked like. He strode back into the palace, descending into the servants' quarters until he found Thalia, overseeing the preparations for that night's dinner.

There was no time for preamble. "I need your help," he said, voice pitched low so as not to be overheard by any of the staff.

"What is it?" she asked.

"The Daeran delegates are on their way here to meet Calida and she's run off to skies know where. I know it's a lot to ask, but would you fill in for her? Do you think you can do that?"

"Of course," she replied, all poise. If she was at all surprised or intimidated by his request, she gave no indication.

Niklaus breathed out in relief. "Thank you."

Thalia retreated to her room to change and style her hair in a manner appropriate for the alleged future queen of Alara. When Niklaus met up with her again, it was obvious she had taken great care with her appearance, but it hadn't made her late.

"Ready?" Niklaus asked her before they headed in together, announced by servants.

His heart fluttered uncomfortably in his chest, distracting him, aware of each beat. If their ruse were discovered, he would feel even more foolish than if he had simply admitted that Calida had stood him up.

Thalia was skilled and undeniably gifted, but was she up to the task of impersonating her own sister, the future queen of Alara?

He needn't have worried. She played her role better than Niklaus could have ever hoped, asking after her guests' comfort and answering their questions. She did not fidget, as

Calida had done when she still bothered to attend such meetings, obviously eager to be gone. If she wished the meeting to come to a swift conclusion, Thalia did not show it.

More than once, she glanced over at him with a warm smile that matched her eyes, the two of them presenting the very picture of a young couple in love. Niklaus felt his unease and misgivings fade away.

Thalia was all of the things Calida should have been: patient, gracious, confident but not condescending, and charming when the situation called for it. When the delegates had left, Niklaus felt as though a great weight had been lifted from his shoulders.

Thalia turned to him. "How did I do?"

He was surprised she didn't already know. "You were perfect. Thank you."

She simply smiled and returned to her duties. After that performance, she deserved some time off and yet she went straight back to her responsibilities. Niklaus was struck by the difference between the two sisters.

Even in this, Thalia was better at being Calida than Calida was.

Niklaus kept a watch out the window for Calida's return to the stables. She approached on foot, leading her horse, hair a wild mass of tangles, her feet bare. He took a deep breath, not looking forward to what was about to happen. He didn't want to argue with her, but he didn't foresee the conversation going any other way and something had to be said. They couldn't continue on this way.

She was still beautiful to his eyes, in a wild, untamed way—like one of the horses she so cared for—but also unapproachable.

He walked out to meet her as one of the grooms took her horse. "So good of you to join us. The Daeran delegates just left."

She paled, as though recognizing the severity of the situation, but it was too late. It wasn't as though he hadn't informed her. "I forgot," she murmured. "I'm sorry."

She looked ashamed, but he knew it meant nothing. She always did and yet she always went right back to her old pattern of behavior. If she were truly repentant, she would have changed. And yet, she never did.

"Ah, yes, you forgot," Niklaus replied, aware that his voice dripped with sarcasm, but unable to hold back his frustration. "I suppose it's difficult to remember such things, what with everything else you have demanding your attention."

She flushed, but he thought it was with anger now. Her eyes narrowed, but she wisely said nothing.

"I handled the situation, but you should have been in there with me and instead, you're out here, running about barefooted like a wild thing."

"I was on the beach—"

"It makes no difference to me where you were," Niklaus retorted, voice rising. "You weren't where you were supposed to be." He turned away in exasperation, running his hands over his face. "I wonder if we didn't think this engagement through. Maybe we rushed into things."

"What are you saying? You can't mean that!"

"I wish I didn't. But I can't help but wonder."

"You should love me as I am, not for what you'd like me to be," Calida snapped. She didn't move, but in her gaze he could see her withdrawing from him all the same. "Or else you don't really love me at all."

"I *do* love you, Calida," he said softly. "But do you love me?"

"How can you say that?" She shook her head in scoffing disbelief. "This is your father's doing! His words are poison. He's turned you against me!"

Niklaus opened his mouth to explain that while his father may have initially suggested it, he had come to feel that way himself. He wanted to explain why, but she pushed past him.

"Calida!"

She ignored him and broke into a run, but not before he heard a sob, abruptly cut off.

* * *

Calida raced through the palace, her vision so blurred with tears that she could hardly see where she was going, but she knew the way to her sister's room by heart. Thalia was seated in front of her dressing table, unpinning her hair when Calida burst in, tears streaming down her face. She hated being so weak, showing this part of herself in front of her younger sister, but there was nowhere else to turn.

Thalia glanced at her in the mirror. "What did he say this time?"

"How do you know it's because of him?" Calida asked feebly. "I might've received bad news from home."

"We never receive word from home. He's the only person who can make you cry like that."

Calida stifled a sob. Thalia had no idea how right she was about that. The one person who could lift Calida's heart to new heights could also bring her crashing down and crush her.

Love was a greater weakness than she knew.

Briefly, Calida told her what Niklaus had said, about him accusing her of not loving him and questioning if they had entered into their engagement prematurely.

"How can he say that? I thought he knew I loved him. I didn't think I had to prove myself to him, too. I thought he understood me, but maybe he can't, fully. Maybe he understands and loves me only as far as a prince can."

"Maybe," Thalia said softly. "He's not like us, after all. He's lived a life of luxury, born to a sense of duty and responsibility he now wants to project onto you. It must be hard to let all of that go when it's all you've ever known."

"I suppose so," Calida murmured, beginning to feel she'd been unfair.

"Still, he knew saying those things would upset you. I think he was feeling hurt over the Daeran delegation and wanted to inflict a little pain in return. It was wrong of him."

Calida sat on the bed, drawing her knees up to her chest. "I know I shouldn't say such things…but I wish the king were dead. Then we could be married and stop all of this."

"It's natural to feel that way," Thalia replied. "The king hasn't been kind to you either." She turned back to face the mirror, her voice quiet. "It's hard to fit in where you're not wanted."

"It's just that I'm the one keeping him alive and he's the one standing in the way of my happiness."

"It's like I told you, Calida. Kings don't live forever."

"Maybe," Calida murmured. "But how long will I have to wait?"

Thalia had no answer to give her.

Calida glanced around the room and then leaned closer, lowering her voice conspiratorially even though it was only the two of them. "I took your advice and snuck the king some of the *bellavexis*."

Thalia turned, blue eyes wide. "You didn't!" A slow grin spread across her face. "Have you noticed any change?"

Calida shrugged. "He seems more distracted than before. But he hasn't warmed up to me any."

"Give it more time, maybe." Thalia sat back on her stool, leaning against the dressing table. "I'm impressed. You're not afraid to reach for what you want, that's for sure."

Her praise warmed Calida. Why shouldn't she reach for what she wanted, when it had been denied to her for so long? If nothing ever changed, if the king had his way, it would be denied to her forever.

Things needed to change. Niklaus had promised to help her bring that about. So why now did he expect her to fall in line when they had both agreed to break the mold?

Calida knew what else she wanted and she had waited long enough for it. She sent Horus out and when he had returned with his answer, she was resolved.

That evening, before dinner, she found Thalia again and told her of her plans.

"I'm going to see Jeremy."

"Are you sure that's wise?" Thalia cautioned.

Calida didn't think so. It wouldn't earn her any more points in her favor or make Niklaus any less disappointed with her, but she needed to talk to Jeremy. It had been too long since they had seen each other and if she didn't do this now, she didn't know if she would ever see him again.

"Yes," Calida said simply. She knew Thalia wouldn't tell anyone where she'd gone.

"How do you plan on losing the guards?"

"I have an idea for that." The guards were the only thing really standing in her way and they could be taken care of easily enough.

"All right," Thalia conceded. "Just be careful."

Calida made her way to the stables when she should have been heading to dinner, an escort of guards following her. They mounted up and she set off at a leisurely pace, giving no sign of trouble. Rather than heading directly for the town where Jeremy would be waiting, she slipped into the forest as though intending to return to the monastery.

It seemed like a lifetime had passed since she'd last set foot there and she wondered if it still looked the same. *How could it not? Nothing ever changed there.*

But the monastery was not her destination, though she was strangely tempted to ride past and catch a glimpse of it. As soon as they ventured deeper into the trees, the branches overhead blocking out the rays of the dying sun, and the sound of the towns fading behind them, Calida made her move.

She urged her horse forward into a sudden gallop. Such speed was risky in the forest, with the densely packed trees and undergrowth that could tangle a horse's legs. She heard her guards let out a cry of surprise and begin to chase after her, but in seconds, their pathway became blocked by intertwining tree limbs, roots, and brambles, stretching out to bar the way.

Calida glanced over her shoulder and, satisfied by what she saw, faced forward again. The guards would have to find a way around the roadblock and by that time, she would be halfway into town. Only when she was sure that they were still far behind did she slow her horse's pace. She saw no further sign of her escort and trotted into town without incident.

Part of her felt slightly guilty at the position she was placing the guards in. They might be reprimanded for failing to stay with her. No doubt they would search in the growing darkness, trying in vain to find her, before admitting defeat and returning to the palace alone. Calida didn't want to get anyone else into trouble, but there was no other way.

She dismounted, tethering her horse outside the tavern. There was always the chance the guards would recognize it if they spotted it, but she didn't think they would venture into town. No one knew she had any reason to be there aside from Thalia.

Calida stepped into the tavern, but a quick glance revealed that Jeremy wasn't in. Horus had said that the *Sea Witch* was at the docks so perhaps he had chosen to remain on board.

As she turned away, an old fear resurfaced. Horus had only seen the ship, not Jeremy himself. In the long months since she'd last seen him, anything could have happened.

Her stomach clenched at the thought of never seeing him again, that she had lost her last chance being trapped in a life of luxury up at the palace. She shoved the thought away and hurried down the line of ships until she reached the *Witch*.

To her immense relief, Jeremy came to the railing, peering down at her. "I saw Horus fly by earlier and thought you might be stopping by. Come aboard, firebrand."

Calida smiled, her relief making her giddy. It had been too long since she'd heard that nickname. She mounted the gangplank and was soon standing beside him on the deck, the ship shifting beneath her gently, never completely still.

Jeremy jerked his head back toward the helm and the door that led to the great cabin beneath it. "We can talk privately in there."

She followed him inside and he shut the door behind her. The back wall of the cabin was entirely made up of windows and Calida looked through them at the Atlas Sea stretching out endlessly behind. A small bed was set to one side and there was a table in the middle of the room, nearly hidden beneath clutter, but not much else aside from a few sea chests.

Jeremy stepped forward, lighting one of the hanging lanterns. "Sorry about the mess." He strode to the table, strewn with maps and charts—some rolled, others not— instruments that must have been used to plot a course, a pistol, and a sheathed cutlass. He bundled them into his arms and dumped them unceremoniously onto the bed.

Without asking, he uncorked a bottle of some dark liquid and handed it to her, taking a seat at the table. "It's been a long time."

"A very long time." Calida grimaced, joining him. "How are you?"

He shrugged. "Same as ever. Building up the coffers. Haven't yet managed to find me a bigger ship, but I'm not sure I want to. The *Witch* here has been good to me. I take it you don't need any more rainleaf? How are the plants doing?"

"Fine. I managed to grow a second one—almost ready for a third. I don't imagine I'll run out again."

Jeremy nodded, then got to his feet and fetched a second bottle for himself. "And how are you, Calida?"

Calida. Not firebrand this time.

She took a deep breath, already knowing that this was a conversation that would require fortification from whatever drink he'd plied her with. She took a swig of it and winced at its sharp burn. It was an unpleasant sensation but the warmth that followed wasn't.

"I haven't been able to leave the palace or I'd have come much sooner."

"I got your note. It said you couldn't leave but it didn't say why."

"I didn't want to put it into writing." She looked down at the grooved wood of the table. "The prince asked me to marry him."

Jeremy stared at her for a long moment. "Ah," he said finally, rejoining her at the table. "I take it you said yes."

"I did."

His keen brown eyes were still watching her. "You don't look happy, Calida."

"I'm not," she said, the words slipping out without thinking, but she was surprised at how true they were. "I was, but I'm not anymore."

"Tell me," he said simply and she did, explaining the intricacies of life at the palace and all the things that were expected of her.

How inadequate she felt and unaccepted and most of all, how she did not feel accepted for who she was and her refusal to change. By the time she had finished, her bottle was nearly empty, but she felt much lighter having confessed such things to him. She could always go to Thalia, but even Thalia knew what court life was like. Jeremy had no idea. He was an outsider who might view her circumstances differently.

"I don't know what to do," she finished. "I suppose I thought it would all be different. That life at the palace, as the future queen, would be some sort of dream come true. But it isn't. I thought that if I could heal the king, he would be so grateful that he'd give me whatever I wanted. When it became clear that would never happen, I thought maybe if I became queen, I could have the life I always wanted."

"I don't know what to tell you," Jeremy admitted. "Is being queen what you want?"

"I just wanted to be able to live my own life. To not forever be told what I could or couldn't be. Now, I just want Niklaus to accept me for who I am, but that's not up to me, and I'm suddenly not sure he can." She felt tears prick her vision and turned away.

Jeremy was right; she wasn't happy and it was obvious enough that, even after their time apart, he'd noticed.

She changed the subject, holding up the bottle, the last of the liquid sloshing in the bottom. "What is this anyway? I quite like it."

"Rum," Jeremy replied, getting to his feet. "From Indris. Takes some getting used to, but once you've acquired a taste, there's no going back." He reached into one of the chests and withdrew another bottle, offering it to her. "Have another."

"Don't mind if I do."

* * *

Niklaus wasn't surprised to find Calida absent from dinner. His father said nothing. Niklaus tried to catch his father's eye more than once, expecting to see precisely what he was thinking written across his face, lips thinned to practically nothing. But there was no reaction to be found.

The food was excellent, as usual, selected by Thalia, but that fact only made him more acutely aware of the reason for his misery and he ate very little. Afterward, he pulled Thalia aside and asked if she would walk with him in the gardens, hoping the fresh night air would soothe his nerves and keep his temper in check.

She walked beside him silently, the silk of her dress sliding over the cobbled path. The stars twinkled overhead in a cloudless sky, the humid tropical air clinging, but the heat of the day had mostly gone.

"I don't suppose you know where your sister has gone," Niklaus remarked. "She didn't deign to dine with us again this evening."

"She confides in me often, but I'm afraid not in this matter."

Niklaus stopped walking and so did she, looking up at him with her dark blue eyes. His father was right. She was more beautiful than Calida.

"I don't understand how to get through to her. I don't understand why she insists on tormenting me."

"She told me earlier that you wondered if your engagement had been too rushed."

Niklaus winced. The words had been true, but he regretted them all the same. "Wouldn't you feel the same, if you were in my position?"

She pursed her lips. "I would."

"She insists that she loves me, but she has a funny way of showing it," Niklaus muttered, unable to keep all of the bitterness out of his voice.

But he valued Thalia's honesty and it made him want to be honest in return.

"Perhaps she doesn't," Thalia suggested.

"What do you mean?"

"I don't doubt that your feelings were genuine, but the engagement was rushed. You were obviously grateful to her for what she's been able to do for your father—and that's only natural. But think about how it must have appeared from her perspective. She's a witch, in a kingdom where the only value a witch has is based on what he or she has to offer. We do not come from a wealthy family, Niklaus. Our parents were farmers. If she loses her place at the palace, what does she have to go back to? What does she have to look forward to? Where will she go?"

Niklaus understood what Thalia was implying and felt a weight settle in his stomach like lead. "You're saying that she accepted my proposal because it was advantageous to do so, not out of any sense of love."

Thalia spread her hands. "I can't know for sure, but wouldn't you have been tempted to do the same, in her place?"

Niklaus couldn't say with any sort of certainty that he would have behaved any differently. He understood Calida's motivations, her hopes and fears—and that galled him. Understandable though it may be, she had used him.

It made a horrible kind of sense. If she had never loved him in the first place and had only used him to secure her position and future, it made sense why his pleas seemed to fall on deaf ears. She didn't love him; she had no desire to please him.

In her mind, she had already gotten what she wanted. Because his feelings for her were genuine, even if hers were not, she felt her position was safe, even though they weren't yet married. If he truly loved her, she didn't believe the engagement could possibly be in any danger.

Niklaus looked up, brought back out of his thoughts. Thalia was fidgeting and looked deeply unhappy. "Is there something else?"

"I don't know if it's my place to say, but Calida told me that she wished the king would die, so the two of you didn't have to wait any longer and could finally be married. I'm not sure she meant anything by it—she was probably just speaking out of frustration—but I thought you ought to know."

Niklaus wouldn't have thought it possible, but his mood darkened even further.

He hadn't liked being made to wait by his father either, but he had been willing to do so. Calida, it seemed, was not. Difficult as the king could be, he was still Niklaus's father and it was an incredibly callous thing for Calida, the woman tasked with healing him, to say, knowing how much such an event would hurt Niklaus.

"You did the right thing in telling me," he murmured, reaching out to take Thalia's hands in his own. "Thank you. You've given me much to think on. I know that can't have been easy. Calida is your sister and even if you don't agree with her, you will always have that bond. You owe me no loyalty, apart from that you would give a sovereign, but you still chose to confide in me."

She peered up at him. "I think you are a man who does not receive the support he should." She ducked her head suddenly, as though embarrassed.

"Thalia," Niklaus said abruptly. "Am I being too hard on Calida?"

It seemed a ridiculous thing to say, after what he'd just been told, but some part of him still cared for her. None of this could be easy for her and he could never understand what it must be like for someone who was an outsider. He wanted to give her the benefit of the doubt.

Thalia met his gaze, her eyes rueful. "She will try to convince you that you are. Don't let her. She's the one being unreasonable, refusing to listen or consider things from your point of view. You have given her many chances, skies know, but she does not respect you."

He nodded. He certainly had. "Thank you," he said again.

He squeezed her hands and left her there, the moonlight shining on her red hair.

* * *

Thalia watched until Niklaus disappeared and then stepped back inside the palace. So far as she knew, Calida had not yet returned and she didn't expect her to any time soon. Still, she checked Calida's room and the infirmary before making her way to the conservatory.

In the hall outside, she lifted one of the torches from the wall. No open flames were kept within the conservatory; the danger it presented to the plants was obvious. With the entire room surrounded by tall, thin windows and a glass dome, daylight easily streamed in, rendering artificial light needless. Clear nights like this one were no exception; moonlight poured in effortlessly, like liquid silver.

She took a deep breath, inhaling the mingling scents of the plants within, and began walking over to where Calida's two rainleaf plants stood waiting. Thalia could feel the heat from the flame on her hand, knowing all the while that each step was one she couldn't take back.

Surrounded by plants that only an earth witch could control, this was still the room that made Thalia feel the most powerful. Here, she had full unrestricted access to her power, no longer trapped behind cold stone walls.

It was a terrible risk, but a necessary one. The conversation with Niklaus had confirmed it—the time had come. Slowly, Thalia lifted the torch, bringing the flame close to the exposed bright blue leaves.

Was it her imagination or did they seem to shrink before the heat?

She touched the flame to the rainleaf, first one plant and then the next, stepping back and watching as the fire caught. Within moments, the leaves had shriveled, turning black and curling in on themselves. The leaves soon burned away to nothing but twiggy stems, the trunk of the plants dark with ash.

Lifting a hand, Thalia cut off the fire's oxygen, choking it. It had burned long enough; the rainleaf plants were useless now. Calida would no longer be able to harvest leaves from them, crumbling them into a tea for the king. And if the plants themselves died, so too did her source.

Thalia watched as the flames dwindled, shrinking before her eyes like a dying candle. And then, in an instant, they were gone, fading away to nothing, as if they had never been, were it not for the scorched wreckage they had left behind.

Slowly, Thalia turned, taking in every inch of the conservatory that she could see, searching for any sign that she had been there.

Satisfied, she made good on her escape. There was no one in the corridor as she stepped out, replacing the torch. No one had seen her enter and there was no one to see her leave.

She drew herself up and unhurriedly made for her room.

CHAPTER 21

Darkness had fully engulfed Alara by the time Calida returned. Clouds had rolled in from the sea, partially obscuring the moon, and she hoped that her return would pass mostly unnoticed.

She hadn't meant to stay so late, but neither had she wanted to leave until she absolutely had to. She hadn't seen Jeremy in so long, even the time she'd had tonight didn't seem like enough.

But he had insisted that he needed to go. He and his crew had already spent too long at the dock as it was and as disappointed as Calida was, she didn't want to put them in any more danger than she already had.

No one knew where she had gone. No guards had caught up to her and she suspected she'd been right about them returning to the palace without her.

Tired, she stepped inside wanting nothing more than to go to bed. Her head ached and her steps were slightly unsteady, making her suspect she'd had too much to drink. But she needed to give the king his rainleaf first.

Wearily, Calida trudged her way up the stairs toward the conservatory, mentally bracing herself for the hell she would catch for leaving it so late.

Despite her muddled thoughts, on the way back, she had thought long and hard about the things she had told Jeremy and what he'd had to say.

She had come to the conclusion that perhaps Niklaus hadn't been wholly wrong when he accused her of not loving him.

She'd insisted that she did love him—and she did—but she had come to realize that while she did love him, she loved something else more.

Her freedom.

And she wasn't going to be forced to change, to be forced into a box, to become something she wasn't. Not for anyone. Not even him.

Calida stopped short, all thought fleeing from her head, the effects of the rum evaporating, at the sight before her.

Her two rainleaf plants were blackened and withered, burned beyond all use and recognition. She wouldn't have known these were her plants at all if not for their position, planted right beside the *bellavexis*, completely unharmed, its terrible berries glittering in the moonlight.

A cry sprang from her lips and she rushed forward, as if eliminating the distance would somehow change what had happened.

She reached out, touching one of the shriveled stems where once there had been leaves. It crumbled to ash at her touch and she jerked her hand back as if burned herself.

This couldn't be happening. It had to be a dream or the effect of too much rum. Calida squeezed her eyes shut so hard it hurt, but when she opened them, the plants remained ruined.

She clenched the edge of the table until her knucklebones pressed against the skin. She gasped in deep, uneven breaths, the room around her seeming to narrow and threatening to close in on her.

How had this happened? Who would do such a thing?

"Calida?" a soft voice spoke behind her.

She whirled to see Niklaus standing in the doorway. His expression was one she had become tragically familiar with over the past few months—lips tightened, eyes narrowed, the furrow between his brow.

Some of her horror must have shown on her own face because his expression morphed at once, becoming one of concern.

"Calida?" He stepped closer. "What's wrong?"

She wanted to shout at him not to come any closer, but that would have been absurd and her throat wouldn't work anyway. She tried to block his view with her body, but she couldn't stop him from laying eyes on the horrible sight.

He sucked in a breath, eyes growing wide in horror, as he stared down at the ruined rainleaf.

"What have you done?" he breathed.

Calida blinked at him, mouth agape, her shock giving way to anger, the sudden shift in emotion leaving her reeling.

"I didn't do this!" she exclaimed, finally finding her voice. It was high and strained. "Why would you think I did this?"

"Why do you think?" he retorted, his eyes burning with a feverish mixture of anger and fear. "Why do you think I'm here? I came to ensure you still intended to give my father his medicine. It would seem not."

"Why the hell would I do this?" Calida demanded.

"Perhaps you didn't intend to wait any longer," Niklaus said darkly. "I know how you felt about my father." He grimaced. "You reek of alcohol."

"How could you accuse me of such a thing? *Regicide?* You know as well as I do what that rainleaf means to the king and what will happen without it. Do you really think I'd do something so brazen or that I'd allow myself to be caught like this if I had done it?" Her voice kept rising until it was a roar and she paused, steadying herself and purposefully lowering her tone. "Do you think that would allow me to marry you sooner? I'd be a traitor!"

He seemed to realize he'd gone too far and paled beneath his flushed cheeks. "I don't know what to think," he said, voice barely a whisper. "Who would do something like this?"

"I don't know. Someone who wanted the king dead, clearly. Anyone could have done it." She crossed her arms, looking at him, hurt more by his lack of faith in her than anything else. "How could you think even for a moment that I could have done this?"

"I don't know." He shook his head, echoing her earlier words. "I don't feel like I know you anymore, Calida. I don't know what to think. I'm sorry."

She stared at him, at the doubt that lingered in his gaze, and said nothing.

"Do you have any rainleaf left?"

"A little," she answered. She had only what she had dried ahead of time and once that ran out, she had no way of getting more.

"But I'll get more," she added, more confidently than she felt.

Jeremy had been in town. She prayed he hadn't left yet. If she hurried, she could race back down to the docks and tell him what had happened, pleading with him to get her some more rainleaf, as he once had.

It was the best chance she had, but there was no way to know how quickly he could get her the herb, and that was only provided he hadn't left yet. If he had, her fate, and that of the king, was all but sealed.

"I can get some more," she repeated. "But I need to go now."

Niklaus jerked his head. "Go."

He didn't apologize for his earlier accusation and Calida shoved it out of her mind for now. She had to focus on the task at hand before it was too late.

She raced down to the stables, commandeering Niklaus's own horse, the chestnut. There was no time to waste with tack and she hauled herself up onto the horse's bare back, hands gripping its mane as she urged it toward town as fast as its legs could fly.

The trip seemed to take longer than normal, when she had made it at a slower pace, on a different horse, though she knew that was impossible. Calida was able to keep the unwanted thoughts at bay for the time being, concentrating on not falling off at such high speed.

For the second time that night, she arrived at the docks. The horse staggered to a halt, tossing its head in displeasure as Calida slid to the ground and raced forward, stopping short. The spot where the *Sea Witch* had been berthed was empty and the ship was gone. Calida could see no sign of her out on the ocean through the darkness.

The full sense of her failure descended and she returned to the horse, wrapping one arm around its neck for support as the tears came, obscuring her vision.

In her panic, she hadn't even thought to send Horus to check. If she had, she would have saved herself the trip and the disappointment, though part of her doubted she would have accepted that Jeremy had already gone unless she'd seen it with her own eyes.

If she had thought to send Horus, could she have caught Jeremy in time? Most likely not, but the other part of her would always wonder.

If she had known this would happen, she would have asked Jeremy to take her with him. She wouldn't care where they went so long as it was far away from here and she never had to return.

What would she do now? She had no rainleaf left to give the king, save that which she had already prepared and it would run out soon enough. Niklaus was expecting her to return with more. She stared across the water toward where she knew Amberleigh sat, hidden in the dark.

She could send Horus with a note, asking Jeremy to get her more rainleaf as soon as possible, but there was no telling when the hawk would manage to find the *Witch* or when Jeremy could meet her again.

Still, she had no other option. It was the best she could do and pray in the meantime that her remaining supply held out long enough.

Turning the horse back toward the palace, Calida now rode at a slower pace. There was no point in hurrying. On the way back, the unwanted thoughts assaulted her, no longer able to be ignored.

Niklaus had accused her of destroying the rainleaf plants on purpose. Granted, it didn't look good, her standing over them, but he had to know her better than that. She would never do such a thing, no matter how strong her disdain for the king. She loved Niklaus too much for that and if she were caught, it wouldn't help her achieve her goal.

She would be thrown into prison, perhaps executed for essentially murdering a monarch. And it would have been murder. Without rainleaf, the king would die, much sooner than anticipated.

And for a moment, Niklaus had thought her responsible. That stung, cutting deep, in a way no other hurtful thing he'd ever said had. There was no going back from that. How could they continue on with their relationship as if nothing had happened? How could she look at him and pretend he hadn't accused her of being a murderer?

Why and how could he think that of her? She had felt that she wanted the king to die so that they could be married, but she hadn't meant it. Not really. Certainly not to the point of taking action.

But then…who had done it? Anyone in the palace could have, but Calida could think of no one who hated the king—

or her for that matter—enough to do such a thing. She could think of no one who wanted to see her fail. Even the king, for all his disapproval, supported her efforts in this matter, so beneficial was it to him.

Niklaus was still waiting for her in the conservatory when she returned. He'd been sitting on one of the benches but he stood up at once. "Do you have it?"

She shook her head. "I couldn't get any now. But I *will* get some."

"Yes, you will. You will remedy this mistake."

"I told you, I didn't do this!"

"If I thought you did, do you really think I'd be giving you a chance to make this right?" he asked coldly. "I don't want to think you are responsible and I hope you're telling the truth. But regardless, we cannot go on this way, Calida. You're always running off, doing whatever it is you want, without regard for what *must* be done. You're never where you should be. You're never there to support me. I need to seriously consider the future of Alara and who I will marry, especially given how things stand now." He gestured toward the decimated rainleaf.

"What are you saying?" Calida demanded.

"I'm saying my father was right. You may be a suitable partner, but you're not a suitable queen."

She recoiled. "How can you say that? I thought we understood each other and yet you betray my trust."

"Betray you?" he scoffed. "You're never there when I need you, Calida."

"You said you would marry me!"

"I did, but now I'm not so sure. I have to do what is best for the kingdom. Unlike you, I cannot escape or run away from my duty. Ultimately, this isn't about what I want. I would have thought you, of all people, would understand, but it seems not. Thalia is much more suitable to be queen."

"Why don't you marry her, then?" Calida snarled.

She could feel rage boiling up inside of her, rising like a flame. She knew she should be careful and keep control of her temper, but at that moment, she didn't care. She wanted to hurt him as much as he was hurting her.

"Perhaps I will!" Niklaus snapped, his own temper responding in kind. "You frustrate and vex me at every turn. I love you, but I cannot marry you." Beneath the anger, she could see pain of his own shading his eyes. "If you truly loved me, then perhaps you would understand. I have already given up much to marry you, Calida. It was unconventional, and perhaps unsuitable, but I was willing to do it anyway, to risk my father's wrath. And when I ask you to behave more like a proper lady, at least outwardly, for everyone else's sake, you don't put forth any effort. You refuse to make any allowances for me. I'm sorry, but I *must* think of Alara." He lowered his voice, the anger slipping away, leaving behind only disappointment. "I'm releasing you from our engagement." He glanced at the rainleaf plants. "Because I care for you, I'm willing to allow you to stay at the palace and make this right."

She watched him walk away, her form still shaking with anger. In the span of one night, everything she had carefully built had come crashing down.

Calida whirled on one of the rainleaf plants, seizing its burned remains and yanking them from the soil. They snapped off, angering her further, and in her frenzied rage, she tore at the plants, screaming in frustration, raking the soil with her bare hands until she, and the floor around her, were spattered with dirt. Grabbing the empty pot, she heaved it up, with no small amount of effort, and hurled it to the floor, where it smashed into pieces.

She would have thought she'd used up all of her tears on the trip back to the palace, but it appeared not, as more trailed their way down her cheeks. She wiped at them impatiently, smearing soil across her face.

If only she had done things differently, all those years ago, things would have been different. She would have never been asked to serve as a healer at the palace. She would never have met Niklaus, much less allowed herself to feel more for him than she had any right to.

If only she had done as Master Kallias asked and killed that criminal in the forest, she could have been a soldier instead of a healer and none of this would have ever happened.

Her heart wouldn't be breaking now.

Footsteps sounded on the marble floor and Calida looked up, through blurred eyes, to see Thalia standing in the doorway, taking in the scene of destruction before her.

"I heard something break…I came to see if you were all right. What happened?"

Ordinarily, Calida would have rushed to her sister's side and told her everything, but now she had not the strength to care.

"Leave me," she murmured, glancing down at the front of her dress, smeared with dirt. "I want to be alone."

She was suddenly ashamed at her outburst of anger, at her appearance, at how she must look. Hair, made wild by her frantic flight to the docks. The dirt across her face and dress, covering her hands, lodged beneath her nails.

She looked down at the scattered shards of the pot she had smashed. It had accomplished nothing except to create more destruction. The pot had had a beautiful glaze on it and it seemed a shame to have ruined something so beautiful. The plants had been beyond salvaging, but she hadn't needed to destroy something else, too.

The thought only made her cry harder. She sank down and began trying to scoop up the scattered pieces, but her blurred vision made it hard to see and she cut herself on the jagged edges.

Thalia sighed and came over to help her, her clear vision and delicate fingers picking up the pieces with much more care.

"Niklaus broke off our engagement," Calida blurted, no longer able to keep quiet.

She couldn't see her sister's expression, but her voice remained soft. "What happened?"

"Someone destroyed my rainleaf plants. Niklaus accused me of doing it. I went back to the dock, to ask Jeremy for some more, but he had already gone. What am I going to do, Thalia?"

Calida supposed she should have resented Thalia at least a little for Niklaus's remark about her being infinitely more suitable to be queen, but she couldn't bring herself to do so. That was Niklaus's opinion, after all, not Thalia's fault, and she had done nothing wrong.

"You'll think of something," Thalia replied, touching a hand to one of Calida's dirtied cheeks. "You always do. First, let's get this cleaned up and then you can see to your hand."

Calida nodded through her tears. She would finish picking up the pieces, wash away the dirt, bandage her hand, and send Horus out immediately with a note, hoping it reached Jeremy quickly. It was all she could do.

The cut on her hand stung horribly, but it was nothing compared to the pain tearing through her chest, threatening to suffocate her.

She didn't know of any herb to treat this sort of wound.

CHAPTER 22

After leaving the conservatory, Niklaus hovered in the hallway, lingering outside his father's door. More than once, he reached for the handle, before pulling away, not wishing to disturb his father, but wanting to know that he was still, for the moment, all right.

After dawdling what felt like an impossibly long time, Niklaus, at last growing frustrated with his cowardice, gripped the door handle and slowly eased it open. It swept across the floor with a whisper, revealing the king's bedchamber.

There was no fire lit and all the candles had been extinguished, but the curtains remained open, allowing moonlight to filter in. Niklaus blinked, eyes adjusting to the darkness, as he made out the form of his father beneath the blankets.

His face was a still mask of sleep, appearing as he always did. Cheeks slightly sunken, skin papery thin, but alive. Very much alive. Though for how much longer, it was impossible to say.

Niklaus swallowed, watching the rise and fall of his father's chest, listening to the soft sound of his breathing, his own breath hitching whenever there was a pause, fearful that the king had breathed his last.

He wondered if his father had ever stood outside his own door, watching over his only son and heir, fearful for the future, wanting to protect him and knowing there were so many ways in which he could not.

Was the death that they all feared, that they once believed so imminent, finally lurking, waiting just around the corner? They were not out of rainleaf yet, and Niklaus truly believed Calida would do everything in her power to get more. It was to her benefit just as much as it was the king's. But if not…

Niklaus had to be hopeful but realistic.

He forced himself to turn away, the day's events weighing heavily on him as exhaustion settled in. He should try to sleep, even though it would likely prove impossible. He seemed to have a sixth sense for such things.

Retreating to his own room, Niklaus undressed and climbed into bed, but thoughts of Calida followed, tormenting him.

She had given him joy and a cause for hope unlike anyone else, but she had also cut him to the core in a way no one else ever had—or possibly could. He had given her that power over him by allowing himself to care too much.

It had been a mistake to allow himself to form feelings for her, he saw that now. If he had kept things to their proper place and station, they would not now be in this mess. Calida should have remained a healer, never anything more. But the damage had been done.

Niklaus felt tears wet his eyelashes, threatening to break free. If this was what love felt like, how quickly it could sour, he didn't want it. The euphoria of the greatest height was nothing compared to the depths of the valley below, the gut-wrenching despair he felt now.

With a sigh, he climbed out of bed, shrugging on a robe. Perhaps a brief stroll would help, as it had in the past. Even if it didn't, he would walk the entire length of the palace, if only to have something to do. Anything was better than simply lying there, feeling the slow eternity of every second slipping by, waiting for an end to the nightmare that might not come.

His footsteps echoed in the silent halls, his shadow cast by the sconces his only companion. He stopped in front of one of the balconies that overlooked the garden, thrusting the glass doors open and inhaling deeply of the fresh air, only now realizing how suffocated he felt within the palace walls.

A steady breeze was blowing, likely coming off the sea, carrying with it a faint tang of salt, but also sweeter scents from the flowers arrayed before him.

"Your Highness?"

He turned, not having heard her approach. Thalia stood behind him, draped in a long, gauzy nightgown that revealed far more of her figure than he had any right to see. She held a candle in one hand to light her way.

Niklaus swallowed. "Thalia."

She came closer. "I couldn't sleep, worrying about Calida. I suppose you couldn't either." She grimaced. "Of course not. Skies know my situation is nothing compared to what you must be going through. Forgive me. You probably think very little of me given the circumstances."

He looked at her, brow furrowing. "And why would I do that?"

"Calida is my sister and…" She trailed off but Niklaus could imagine what she had intended to say. *And she destroyed the rainleaf. Or at least, the rainleaf was her responsibility. And she wanted the king to die so the two of you could be married.*

He sighed, closing his eyes. "I shouldn't have accused Calida of destroying the plants."

"Do you believe her guilty?"

"I must have believed it at the time, or else I never would have said something so daft…" But the damage had been done, much like that which had befallen the rainleaf plants themselves. He could not take back the accusation. He could not repair their fractured relationship.

He turned to face Thalia, the moonlight silver against her hair. "You know her better than anyone, Thalia. Do you think she would be capable of such a thing?"

Her lips thinned, her brows drawing together, as she looked up at him with large blue eyes. Eyes that said more than words ever could, wishing he hadn't asked such a question, but more than anything, wishing she could give a different answer.

"I don't know it it's my place to say…I feel stuck between two people that mean a great deal to me. But if I were honest, ever since we came here, I hardly recognize Calida anymore." Thalia lifted the candle holder, setting it down on the balcony rail, watching the flame gutter in the wind. "This place has changed her. I think she values her position here a great deal and, much as I hate to admit it, I don't know that there's anything she wouldn't do to keep it. It's really no secret that there's no love lost between Calida and the king."

The wind picked up for a moment, the fragile flame winking out of existence.

Niklaus took a deep breath. "Thank you for your honesty, Thalia. It can't have been easy, but I appreciate it more than you know."

He turned to go, thinking he might give sleep one more chance. Thalia reached out, silently laying a hand on his arm. It was a gesture of solidarity, of comfort, and Niklaus covered her hand with his own, her skin smooth and cool against his.

Suddenly, irrationally, he wanted to ask her to come with him, not wanting to be alone. How much more comforting would it be if she took him in her arms, if he could pour out his soul to her? It had been so long since he'd last felt the reassuring touch of another person. That, too, was denied to him.

But he knew, as much as his heart might yearn to give in, he could not. It was a vulnerability and a luxury he could not afford.

He forced himself to move, to break the contact, and head back inside. He felt her eyes on him as he left her standing there. Did she feel the same? Was she even now silently willing him to turn back?

Morning seemed a long way off.

* * *

Horus returned the next day, having delivered Calida's letter and obtaining an answer from Jeremy. *"He says he'll do his best,"* the hawk reported, as he swooped through the window Calida had left open for him in her room. *"But he doesn't know when he'll be able to get it to you."*

It was what Calida had feared but the best she could hope for.

Days at the palace seemed to pass slowly now, and yet all too quickly. Calida spent most of her time consumed in misery, wondering who could have destroyed the rainleaf plants, worrying about the king as she watched her remaining supply dwindle, the pain of Niklaus's betrayal still aching.

She did her best to avoid him, no longer going down to dinner in the evenings. She had meals sent up to her room instead. She thought back to the first dinner they'd shared together at the palace. He'd seemed to like the fact that she didn't follow palace etiquette then. Why then, knowing what she was, had he asked her to marry him? And why had she accepted?

Calida still checked on the king twice each day, doing what she could for him, reducing each dose ever so little, trying to stretch what she had left and make it go as far as she could.

And still there was no word from Jeremy.

Desperate, Calida considered sending Horus to the island of Amberleigh to fetch some rainleaf himself. He wouldn't be able to carry much and he certainly couldn't bring her a live plant, but Calida would take anything she could get.

Despite her best efforts to make the rainleaf last as long as possible, Calida came to her final leaf one evening. With heaviness in her heart, knowing this marked the beginning of the end without some intercession from Jeremy, she crushed the leaf into a cup of tea.

Without a steady stream of rainleaf to keep his illness at bay, the king quickly deteriorated. The fever returned within days, along with the fatigue that kept him bedridden. Without rainleaf, he returned to the state she had found him in when she'd first come to the palace and now there was nothing she could do for him.

It was painful to witness, her sense of failure acute.

A sort of hush had fallen over the palace, as though everyone were holding their breath, waiting for something to happen. No one said as much, but Calida knew the end was imminent.

She wondered what would happen to her once the king was dead, now that she no longer had the security of her engagement. Niklaus would not marry her, that much was plain, and he would have no further need of her services as a healer. She would be cast out to find another placement elsewhere and she conceded that perhaps it was for the best.

It was the way things should have been from the beginning. She should never have come here, hoping against all odds that she, of all people, could heal the king and that he would be so overwhelmed with gratitude that he would grant her whatever she wished.

She snorted to herself now at the thought. How naïve she had been. How foolish. Even with the improvement of the king's health, he had not been sufficiently grateful to give her what she wanted. He hadn't given her and Niklaus permission to marry and now it was too late.

Maybe if she left the palace and all its painful memories behind, her heart could begin to heal. Her placement had always been elsewhere. She didn't belong here.

* * *

Niklaus spent most of his time with his father. It made it easier not to accidentally encounter Calida in any of the corridors. He knew what time she typically came to see to his father, though she could do little now that the rainleaf had run out, and so he made sure to step out whenever she stopped by.

He didn't need her opinion as a healer to know that time was short and that he should make the most of whatever remained. He had accepted that now, as his father seemed to. There was no point in fighting it, raging against the fading light. It would change nothing and Niklaus didn't have the strength.

On that particular morning, his father was awake and alert, the fever having broken late last night.

"It won't be long now," the king murmured. "I can feel it."

Niklaus turned in his chair from where he'd been staring out the window. There wasn't much for him to do and that left him with plenty of time to think, which he didn't particularly care for; his thoughts had taken a dark turn of late. But he wasn't going to leave his father's side unless he had to.

He'd already told his father what had happened to the rainleaf plants and that he'd broken off his engagement with Calida. He knew his father must have been pleased to hear that he'd finally seen sense, but he hadn't crowed about it, likely knowing Niklaus already felt terrible enough about the way things had turned out.

He reached out and took his father's hand. The king wore a frilly white nightshirt, open at the collar. His skin appeared more sunken than ever, clinging to the bones beneath.

Though the fever had broken, his skin still felt clammy and there was an unhealthy sheen to his eyes.

Niklaus looked down at his father's hand, clasped in his own, the blue veins visible through the thin skin. Once those hands had been so strong, the man himself seeming larger than life. Niklaus had looked up to him in a way only a son could. His father had been so full of life, he'd been sure nothing bad could ever happen to him.

How wrong he'd been. He'd been wrong about a lot of things.

"I don't feel ready," he whispered. He wasn't ready for any of it, but claiming the crown as his own least of all. And now he was once again alone, with no future queen at his side to help him through, the way his father had intended.

"No one ever is," the king replied. He frowned. "I don't want you to be alone, my boy."

"It seems I will be," Niklaus replied.

A sudden emotion swept over him, clawing at his chest, stealing the breath from his lungs. It was not a feeling with which he was intimately familiar, but he knew it for what it was.

Guilt.

"You were right about her, Father. I should have listened. If I had never brought her to the palace, none of this would have ever happened. Forgive me." He leaned forward, curling over the side of the bed, beside his father. This time when the tears came, he made no attempt to stop them. "I was a fool."

Someone had destroyed the rainleaf plants. Whether that someone was Calida, Niklaus remained uncertain. He didn't want to think such a thing of her, but he couldn't forget what Thalia had confided to him. Calida had expressed a desire for the king to die. Even when denying the destruction of the rainleaf, Calida didn't deny that.

That admission alone hurt. If she had gotten to the point where she was tired of waiting and wanted the king dead, who knew what steps she might be tempted to take. Perhaps she had thought to take matters into her own hands, no longer content to let nature take its course in its own time.

If she was guilty, then Niklaus also shared in that blame, for bringing her to the palace in the first place, giving her access to the king, and most certainly for allowing himself to feel more for her than he should have.

He felt his father's hand alight on his head, stroking his hair. "We're all fools when it comes to love. But duty is what matters now. Of the two sisters, I know you were fond of Calida. But I am willing to give my permission for you to marry Thalia."

Niklaus pulled back, looking at his father in surprise. "Thalia?"

The king nodded. "We both know that she is infinitely more suited to the role of queen. She has done a magnificent job handling the duties that should have been Calida's. I understand that you may not feel the same way toward her that you did with Calida, but I believe she will support you in a way her sister did not. And perhaps you could come to care for each other. I don't want you to be alone. We must think of Alara."

Niklaus knew the wisdom of his father's words. He had seen for himself how capable Thalia was. She had never once complained, never once abandoned her duties; even when she deserved a break, she always put them first.

She had even been willing to impersonate her own sister so that he would not be made to look a fool in front of the delegates from a foreign land. She had done more for him than Calida had when she didn't have to.

He wasn't sure he loved her—certainly he didn't feel the same about her as he had Calida—but he thought he might be able to.

Still, the decision would have to be hers. Perhaps she didn't want such a life for herself. Niklaus didn't know what he would do if she refused his offer, but he would respect her choice. Everyone who could deserved to have a say over their own fate and perhaps, despite the pain she had caused him, that was why he couldn't completely fault Calida.

"Very well. I will think about it, Father."

The king looked as though there was something more he wished to say, but the look in his eyes grew distant and he withdrew into himself, sinking back against the pillows, staring out without really seeing.

The conversation was over, as if it had never been.

For the rest of the day, Niklaus thought over his decision carefully and then that evening, before Calida came to check on the king, he left his father's side and went in search of the younger sister.

Niklaus found her standing on the balcony in her room, the doors opened and curtains flung aside. Her arms were resting lightly on the railing, her head tilted back to look up at the night sky, the warm evening air brushing past and stirring her long hair. Her fox familiar, seldom seen during her time at the palace, rested by her feet, and it raised its head at his approach.

Thalia turned before he could say anything, as if sensing his presence.

"I need to speak with you," he said simply.

She moved over at the railing, making room for him to join her. At her side, like an equal.

Niklaus did so, fingering the rough stone of the rail, wondering how to begin. His offer would not have the same emotional plea or impact as his proposal to Calida, so perhaps it was best to simply say what he had come to say and be done with it. She would either accept or she would not.

If she did not, he didn't think he would be terribly hurt by it. The hardest part would be the realization that he was still on his own and that he might not ever find someone who would stand beside him. If he was forced to choose from among the nobility, as originally intended, his chances seemed bleak.

And besides, perhaps it was best this way. If what he felt for Calida was love, Niklaus had come to the conclusion that he didn't much care for the way love weakened him. Perhaps it was better to bind himself to someone he felt friendship for and nothing more.

"My father, in all likelihood, has little time left to live. It is his wish that I find myself a bride before that time comes, who will support me and help me do what is best for the kingdom. I thought that woman was your sister, but I was mistaken."

He looked directly at her. "Thalia, you have been there every step of the way, always doing more than what was asked of you, with both poise and efficiency, never wavering. I believe you have the makings of a great queen and my father agrees. He has given his blessing for us to be married, if that is what you wish and you accept the offer."

She blinked slowly. "You're asking me to marry you?"

"I am. I believe you will do what is best for Alara, as a good ruler should. You have proven yourself selfless, putting the tasks that need to be done and the needs of others above your own desires. But the choice is entirely yours and I will respect whatever decision you make."

"It is a great honor," she said softly and Niklaus was sure she was about to refuse. Instead, she sank down onto one knee, head bowed. "I know I was not your first choice, but I will endeavor to prove myself, to you and the people of Alara. And perhaps also, in this way, I can try to make up for my sister's shortcomings."

"Then you accept?"

"I do."

Niklaus offered her a hand. "Then rise. You will be my queen, my equal. Your place is by my side, not at my feet."

She took his hand and allowed him to help her stand. There was none of the elation that Niklaus had seen in Calida's expression. Thalia's face remained grave. She understood the gravity of the situation and what was being asked of her.

Niklaus nodded, pressing a kiss to the back of her hand. "Thank you. You have taken a great weight off of my shoulders—and the king's as well. Perhaps he can rest more easily now."

He turned to leave and return to his father's side, but Thalia called after him and he glanced back at her.

"Niklaus? I know you do not love me as you do my sister, but I will try to be a good queen."

He gave her a small smile. "You will be."

CHAPTER 23

Two days later, the king was dead, the kingdom of Alara plunged into mourning. Only then was Niklaus's engagement to Thalia announced. If there was any confusion or surprise among the nobility at the sudden proclamation, they knew better than to show it.

Jeremy never had returned with a supply of rainleaf and now there was no need for it. Calida roamed the halls, expecting any day to be told to leave the palace, her services and her stay at an end.

But instead, the engagement was announced. Niklaus had asked Thalia to marry him. Part of Calida wasn't surprised; Thalia was capable in everything she did and therefore an obvious choice, especially since Niklaus's biggest issue with Calida had been what he deemed her lack of responsibility.

The other part of her was floored by the announcement. Thalia hadn't confided in her. Calida had known nothing about it. She'd found out the same time as everyone else and that stung, but not as much as the news itself.

The petty, jealous part of her that still hurt over Niklaus's betrayal thought Thalia should have refused his offer, knowing how much it would hurt her sister. She should have rejected him, as a show of solidarity with Calida.

Thalia didn't love him, after all, and even though Calida now doubted how much Niklaus had ever truly loved her, she knew he didn't love Thalia. It was a marriage of convenience, nothing more.

If Niklaus had questioned whether or not their engagement had been rushed, this one certainly was. He didn't know Thalia the way he knew Calida.

But the other part of her, the part that was thinking with logic and not emotion, knew that Thalia had done them both a great service by accepting. They could both stay at the palace, her position as Niklaus's wife secured, and Calida allowed to remain as her sister. They would not be cast out into the unknown, out of a world that had seemed so strange at first, but had come to be so familiar.

Still, she should have been told.

After the announcement had been made, Calida went to find her sister and found her in her room, studying what appeared to be a map of Alara. She'd had even less training and time than Calida had and she would need to make up ground quickly.

"Why didn't you tell me?" Calida asked, knowing Thalia would know what she meant.

Thalia looked up from the map. "I wanted to discuss it with you first, but there was no time. He wanted an answer from me. I suppose I could have said that I would think about it, but it seemed cruel to make him wait, not knowing how long the king had left. I did what I thought best for both of us. I know there's no need for a healer now that the king is gone, but I'll see that you can stay at the palace as long as you like."

"That's very generous of you," Calida replied, sinking down onto one of the chairs. How very like her sister to know the fear that lurked in the forefront of her mind. "When Jeremy returns, I'll have to tell him that I won't be needing any more rainleaf. I wish I knew who had destroyed the rainleaf plants."

She hadn't been able to figure it out and it had bothered her ever since that fateful night. Thinking about it brought back painful memories of Niklaus's accusation, so she didn't like to dwell on it. She preferred to pretend that he had never said those things at all, but there was no taking it back.

Looking back, it had been the moment any hope of their relationship had died. He couldn't take back his words. The damage had been done, their relationship destroyed as surely as the rainleaf plants had been.

And he had thought she might have done it. Calida couldn't think of why he'd suspect such a thing, other than the careless remarks she had made about wishing the king dead. But she hadn't said those things to Niklaus. It would have been a hurtful and stupid thing to say.

She had only spoken such desires to one other person.

Calida looked up, across the table, at her sister sitting opposite her.

If she herself hadn't told Niklaus about her frustration, and only one other person knew, then there was only one way he could have learned of it. In the aftermath of the rainleaf plants' destruction, the panic of trying to find more of the herb, and witnessing the king's declining health, helpless to do anything to stop it, Calida hadn't thought much about it.

But she should have. She saw that now.

Calida gripped the arms of her chair. "You told him, didn't you?"

Thalia was still engrossed in the map. "What?"

"You told Niklaus what I said about wanting the king dead so we could be married, didn't you?"

Thalia looked up then, a crease between her brows. "Why would you think that?"

"Because I didn't tell him. I told you. The only way he could have found out what I said was if *you* told him. The night the rainleaf was destroyed, he accused me of doing it because of what I said and how I felt about the king!"

Thalia sighed. "Yes, I told him. I thought he deserved to know."

Calida leapt to her feet. "I told you in confidence!"

"And I told him in confidence! When you told me, by your own admission, you said you knew you shouldn't say such things. And you were right. You shouldn't have," Thalia retorted.

Calida felt heat cascade over her skin. "That didn't give you the right to tell him."

"There's no point arguing about it. It won't change what happened. We both know he was bound to break off the engagement sooner or later."

"What else have you been telling him?" Calida demanded.

Thalia glared at her but did not answer.

It was a warning to drop it, to not push any further, to go back while she still could. Calida suddenly felt she was standing on the edge of a cliff, teetering. One more step and she would fall, unable to take it back. Nothing would ever be the same.

She could step back, walk away, pretend everything was as it should be, as it had always been. But she had seen too much. Nothing was how it had always been—or rather how she had perceived it to be.

And so she took that step.

"No," she said softly. "You didn't tell him because you thought he ought to know. You told him because it was to your advantage to do so. This is what you've wanted all along, isn't it? Why you so readily volunteered to do my job for me? You weren't offering out of the kindness of your heart, you were using it to your advantage. To make me look bad and yourself glowing in comparison. This whole time, you were outshining me, showing how capable you were, how charming, the picture of a proper lady, and I thought you were supporting me. Every single thing I told you, you ran off, armed with it, to Niklaus. I shudder to think what you told him!"

Suddenly, everything made sense. Niklaus's slow withdrawal from her, the souring of his mood, his judgement and condemnation of her.

It wasn't her and her actions—at least not wholly. He had been poisoned, slowly turned against her, not so much by the king, as Calida had thought, but by her own flesh and blood.

Slowly, Thalia rose to her feet, dark blue eyes stormy. The air practically crackled with tension and Calida wondered if it was some subtle manifestation of Thalia's power.

"I didn't do anything the two of you hadn't already done for me. If you had done what was expected of you, none of this would have ever happened. But instead, you grew bored with your responsibilities, once they were no longer a challenge, and appointed me to take care of them instead. Turns out, I'm better at them than you. But that's not my fault, Calida. Yes, I took advantage, make no mistake. But you *gave* me the advantage."

"But how could you?" Calida exclaimed. "You're my sister. I trusted you! I thought you were supporting me… We've always done everything together…"

But even as she said it, she knew the words weren't true. They had ended up in the same place, yes, but they had taken different paths to get there. From the moment they first passed beneath the monastery archway, the bond that they had shared for the first twelve years of life began to crack.

"Do you think I didn't want something more from life?" Thalia sneered. "That I was content to manage servants and plan menus for the rest of my life, always in your shadow, when I could do a better job than you ever could? Do you remember what I told you all those years ago, when you asked why I let Arin bully me? I told you that I was always being underestimated and that's why I would win. You're no different, Calida. You're too blind to see what's in front of you. You landed a placement that no one like us has any right to even *dream* of. *I wasn't going to let you squander it!*"

"You destroyed my rainleaf plants!" Calida exploded, pointing an accusing finger at her sister. "You set me up to fail because it was what you wanted." She headed for the door. "I'm telling Niklaus what you've done."

"He won't believe you," Thalia said calmly and Calida froze, her back still to her sister. "As you said, I've proven myself nothing but capable. Why should I do such a thing? If you go to him, throwing around wild accusations, you'll only look petty and jealous. You're still upset over him breaking off your engagement. You can't bear to see him with anyone else, least of all your own sister, so you'll do anything to smear my reputation and convince him to take you back. You've proven yourself to be both unreliable and unreasonable, dear sister, while I have been by his side every step of the way, offering support and comfort. Which of us do you think he'll believe?"

Calida knew her sister was right. Niklaus would not want to believe her. She could tell him the truth and it wouldn't matter. She shut her eyes tightly against the threat of tears, still refusing to turn around. She would not let Thalia have the satisfaction of seeing her cry.

She had thought Niklaus breaking off their engagement had been painful, but it was nothing compared to the anguish she felt now at Thalia's betrayal. Niklaus hadn't betrayed her. Her own sister had.

The sister she had shared every experience with, who had gone to the monastery with her, who came from nothing and sought to make something of herself. Well now she would be queen of Alara, having risen all the way to the top, and Calida would be nothing.

How could their relationship, everything they had gone through together, mean so little to Thalia that she would throw it all away for a chance at power and prestige, securing a life of luxury for herself?

Skies, could Niklaus even guess at the depths of the treachery of the woman he had bound himself to? Beneath the anger, some small part of her that still cared for him, that had always cared for him, lurched in fear.

Calida left the room before she had the chance to do something stupid or lose what fragile hold she had on her emotions.

Thalia had said that she was still welcome to stay at the palace, but she could not. Calida had only one idea as to where she might go, and she had to try. Anywhere was better than here, stuck with the two people who had hurt her the most and being forced to live each day pretending as if everything were all right.

She had nothing more to say to Thalia. She needed to find Niklaus.

After that, Calida never wanted to see either of them again.

She found him in his father's study, seated behind the desk. It looked as though he'd been flipping through paperwork that had been left behind, the desk's surface covered with scattered papers. But now he stared at them without really seeing, head in his hands.

Calida felt momentarily sorry for him. He had broken off an engagement, lost his father, and then become engaged to a woman he didn't love in short order.

Calida might have wanted the king dead, but she had never wanted the pain it would cause Niklaus.

She forced herself to recall how much his decisions had hurt her and how much she did not approve of them, her sympathy fading.

He looked up as she entered, no doubt wondering what it was she wanted.

"I need a favor," Calida told him without preamble.

She didn't want to have to ask him for anything, but there was no other way she could find out the information she sought. And she hoped that he would feel guilty enough over the way things had ended between them to at least grant this one request.

He blushed slightly, as if realizing what she was thinking. "What is it?"

"I need to know where my friend Lorelei received her placement. She graduated the same year I did. She's a midwife. I assume you have ways of finding out."

"I could, yes."

She nodded. "Thank you."

If she didn't intend to remain at the palace any longer, she would need somewhere else to stay and Lorelei was the only friend she could think of who might take her in. It had been so long since they'd last seen each other and they had a lot of catching up to do. Any number of things might have happened since they'd parted ways. A lot had certainly happened on Calida's part.

She waited for Niklaus to get back to her with the information, avoiding both him and her sister. She hoped she wouldn't have to wait much longer. Every moment spent at the palace did nothing to relieve her mood or change what had happened. Not even riding held the same appeal as it once had.

Thalia's betrayal hurt the most. Calida tried not to think about it, but she couldn't keep the thoughts away for very long. She felt just as angry as she had upon first realizing the depth of her sister's treachery, resentment taking root inside of her.

At last, Niklaus finally returned with the information Calida sought. Lorelei was staying at an address in Brisban, the capitol of Alara. Apparently, she'd done quite well for herself and established a profitable business as a midwife, her services much in demand.

Calida thanked Niklaus for the information stiffly and went immediately to pack her bags. She still had very few belongings that were actually hers. That much hadn't changed from when she had prepared to leave the monastery. Ultimately, nothing much had changed. She was back where she had started, only perhaps worse off than she'd been even then.

Her plans did not go unnoticed. "You don't have to do this," Niklaus told her. "You're welcome to stay."

No, I don't think I really am. "I can't stay here," she said simply, shoving her dresses down and closing her pack. She thought perhaps she ought to tell him that she hoped he and Thalia were happy, but it would have been a lie and so she didn't say anything.

"I'll call a carriage for you," he offered.

"No. I'd rather walk."

It was a long trip to make on foot, but manageable, and she didn't want to accept or need anything more from him. She'd reach Lorelei's door by the end of the day if she set out now.

He nodded then, taking a small step back. "You're right. Perhaps it's for the best."

She had never seen him look so defeated, his blue eyes so dull. She wanted to reach out and comfort him, but that was a duty that no longer fell to her.

"Goodbye, Calida."

"Goodbye, Niklaus. I am sorry, for whatever it's worth."

She thought Niklaus might insist on seeing her to the palace steps, but he remained behind and watched her go. It did not escape her notice that Thalia didn't see her off at all.

Calida forced herself not to look back as the palace faded behind her. She wondered if Thalia stood at one of the high windows, watching her leave, smug in her satisfaction. She gritted her teeth, hefting her pack higher, and increased her pace, eager to be gone, Horus perched on her shoulder.

Her feet ached horribly by the time she reached Brisban, the largest city in Alara, the cobblestone streets far more uncomfortable than grass. She stopped in front of the address Niklaus had provided, no doubt obtained through discreet inquiries at the monastery, and looked up at the building before her.

It was a modest two-story house, the bricks worn. The curtains were drawn and it suddenly occurred to Calida that her friend may not be home. She had no idea how long she might be forced to wait.

But her knock was answered and the door swung open to reveal Lorelei standing there, looking much the same as she always had. There was something immensely comforting in that.

"Calida," she said in surprise, eyeing the pack she carried. "What brings you here?"

"It's a very long story," Calida said wearily, resigning herself to the fact that she would have to relive it all over again. But Lorelei deserved to know.

"Well I've been summoned, so I must go. Make yourself at home in the meantime. We can talk when I get back."

She moved aside, allowing Calida to pass and she stepped into a small, clean kitchen, the walls painted a dark blue-green. Lorelei collected her bag and was gone, leaving Calida along with Horus in the unfamiliar house.

She set her pack on one of the wooden chairs and sat down at the kitchen table. Horus perched on the back of the chair next to hers. A clock on the wall ticked softly, but there was no other sound.

Calida sighed, running her fingers through her unruly hair. "How could Thalia do this to me?" she asked her familiar.

Horus had no answer for that particular question. "*What are we going to do now?*"

It was a good question. They couldn't stay with Lorelei forever, taking advantage of her hospitality. Eventually, they'd have to move on and make their own way in the world. But Calida was too tired to even consider that.

The hours ticked by and Lorelei had yet to return. Calida rummaged around in the cabinets and brewed herself some tea, before finally collapsing on the sofa in the next room and taking a nap.

She awoke to the sound of the door opening and she sat up, coming back into the kitchen as Lorelei shuffled into the room, looking harried. Some of her brown hair had escaped its pins, but there was a look of satisfaction in her gaze.

"Success," she said with a smile. "Sorry it took so long, but babies come when they're ready and not a moment before."

"Looks like you found your true placement, then," Calida said. "Do you like it?"

"I love it. It's meaningful work. My mentor died a year ago and now I've taken over. Keeps me busy, but I like it that way. But let's talk about you, while I rustle up some dinner. What have you been doing?"

Calida sighed and launched into the story of how the prince had visited the monastery, asked her to come to the palace and try to heal the ailing king, and all that had inevitably followed.

By the time she had finished, Lorelei was done cooking dinner—a fresh fillet of fish and some potatoes—and was halfway through with her meal. Calida hadn't much touched hers, so busy telling her story.

It was good, the fish seasoned perfectly, the potatoes buttery, but she didn't have much of an appetite.

"I can't stand to stay there with the two of them," she finished, pushing a piece of potato around her plate. "I couldn't think of anywhere else to go, so I came here. But I understand if you're busy. We don't want to cause you any trouble, so we'll be on our way if—"

Lorelei waved the suggestion away. "Nonsense. You're more than welcome to stay, the both of you. Truth be told, it gets a bit lonely here whenever I'm not working."

Calida remembered that Lorelei had no familiar to keep her company. She glanced across at Horus, still picking at his own piece of fish. Lorelei had even thought of him.

"What will you do now?" Lorelei asked, echoing the hawk's earlier question.

"I don't know," Calida replied honestly. "I'll find something. In the meantime, I can always help out around the house, do whatever needs to be done."

The two of them fell into an easy routine. Lorelei could be called away at any time, all hours of the day. Calida saw to the shopping, making sure that the essentials were always well-stocked. She did the laundry and most of the cooking and cleaning that needed to be done around the house, but Lorelei shared in the chores whenever she had time.

Still, Calida did most of it. It was hard work, but she didn't mind. She had no source of income and she was well aware that she was living in Lorelei's house for free. The charity didn't bother her, but she wasn't going to take advantage and certainly wasn't going to make a nuisance of herself.

All the work reminded Calida of the various tasks she had been expected to do at the palace and how she had ignored them, doing only what *she* wanted to do instead. She felt as though she had been forced to learn some sort of painful lesson the hard way.

She wasn't opposed to hard work now. Perhaps if she had felt that way a little sooner, things would have been very different. But there was no going back now. This was her life and she had to make the best of it.

Lorelei returned one evening with news that Niklaus had officially ascended to the throne and that he was king now. "It's all anyone in town is talking about," she remarked.

Calida grunted. She didn't go out into town for any reason other than errands. She still sent Horus out every evening to search for the *Sea Witch* but so far, Jeremy had not returned. She had no idea what the latest bits of gossip were and so any news was brought to her by Lorelei.

Unsurprisingly, shortly thereafter the announcement was made that Niklaus and Thalia had been married. Her sister was now queen of Alara. Calida felt a stab of jealousy at that, though she tried to tell herself that she should have been over it by now.

But she wasn't.

Her mood remained sour for the rest of the day and Lorelei noticed as she picked at her food. Calida didn't consider herself a bad cook—she knew how to effectively use herbs to bring out flavor—but it was still nothing compared to what the palace had to offer.

"If you don't want me to tell you things I hear about them, I won't," Lorelei offered, shifting uncomfortably in her chair.

"No, it's all right," Calida replied. Some part of her still wanted to know, for whatever reason. She didn't care to examine her motives too closely.

"All right," Lorelei said. "But…maybe it's not healthy. Maybe you should let it go."

Calida said nothing. She knew it was the smart thing to do, but she didn't think she could do it.

She didn't want to.

Less than two months after the marriage announcement came the news that Calida had been expecting, but dreading all the same. It was the natural course of events, but she had hoped…

"The queen is expecting their first child," Lorelei said quietly.

Calida kept dusting the mantel as though she were unconcerned. *Their first child.* As if there would be more. And why wouldn't there be? Part of her was, simply, surprised by the news. Niklaus and Thalia didn't love each other, but she supposed love had nothing to do with it. Duty came before all; no doubt they had approached this part of life the same as any other.

They needed to have an heir.

Calida tried not to think about it as she had with everything else, but the harder she tried, the more she did the very thing she was trying not to do.

She lay awake at night, long after the house had fallen silent and Lorelei had gone to bed, her hands clenched into fists. That child should have been hers and Niklaus's, not Thalia's. It was yet another thing her sister had taken from her.

She lay there, imagining the two of them entwined, laying in each other's arms, her rage building. No doubt Thalia had pretended in that, the same as with everything else.

Calida thought of punishing Thalia for all of the pain and suffering she had caused and wondered how she might go about it. Feeding her resentment and imagined retribution were the only things that seemed to lessen the pain. She was still angry as ever, but having a plan of action, a way to channel that anger, was better than fury alone. Impotent rage did no one any good, but perhaps there *was* something she could do.

Thalia had betrayed her trust and taken everything from her. She deserved something in return.

Late one afternoon, while Lorelei was out, Calida left the house. She went alone, not taking Horus with her. It was evening by the time she reached the palace on foot and was confronted by the guards at the gate.

"Tell the queen that her sister is here to see her," Calida instructed, speaking as though she had the authority to give these guards orders. She'd had such authority once and should have had it still.

She didn't know if Thalia would agree to see her, but Calida thought she would, if only out of some perverse sense of triumph, to fully crow now that her position as queen was secure. In her mind, there was nothing Calida could do now to threaten it.

She was taken to a sitting room and left to wait for her sister to grace her with her presence. At this time of night, the palace had settled down and was mostly quiet. Perhaps Thalia and Niklaus were just sitting down to dinner.

Thalia wouldn't tell him that Calida was there. She'd come alone, for her own amusement, to see what had brought her sister back after all this time.

Calida looked up as the door opened softly and her sister stepped inside. She looked radiant in her gown of blue silk, her hair styled in soft waves. She was not yet far enough along in her pregnancy for her condition to show, but Calida had heard the news. She knew the truth.

Calida glared at her, unable to keep her emotions hidden. Her sister was carrying Niklaus's child.

"Have you finally come to beg that we take you back?" Thalia asked quietly.

"Hardly," Calida growled.

"My, my. That's no way to speak to your queen."

"You're no queen of mine."

Thalia smiled, as though amused by her sister's disrespect, rather than upset. "Why are you here, Calida?"

Calida looked again at her sister and let some of her hurt show. "How could you do this? How could you turn Niklaus against me and take him from me?"

"You made it so easy."

Calida knew that she had. She wished she had listened to Niklaus. She wished she had done what had been expected of her. She wished she could have been the person he needed, but it was too late for any of that now.

"Why this?" she gestured to Thalia, at the stomach that had yet to grow round. "You didn't have to—" She bit off the words. What Thalia had already done had been bad enough. She hadn't had to take it a step further.

"Sleep with him?" Thalia asked bluntly. "It wasn't so hard. I pretend when it comes to everything else. Why should that be any different?"

The casual, callous way she spoke enraged Calida. Niklaus didn't deserve a woman like this, who was only using him to get what she wanted as much as she had used Calida.

"You don't love him!" Calida exploded, taking a step closer. How could she be expected to love his child?

"What does love have to do with it?" Thalia sneered. "The king must have an heir. Do you think I will enjoy this?" She gestured to her stomach. "I can't wait for it to be over."

Calida shook her head. "You won't love that child. You don't deserve that child. Or Niklaus! You're using him, just like you used me. And you'll use your child, too!" She felt the threat of tears burning against the back of her eyes and she pushed it away. Not now. "That child should have been mine! Everything you have should have been mine. And it was, until you took it from me!"

She lunged forward. Her powers were useless here, but that didn't mean she was powerless. She grabbed at Thalia, scratching, clawing and tearing at any exposed flesh she could find.

Thalia took a step back, reaching up to try and defend herself, but Calida's rage leant her a strength Thalia did not have. Thalia pressed a hand to Calida's stomach and a moment later, she was thrown back by a sudden gust of wind.

Calida slammed into the stone wall behind her and slid to the floor with a gasp. Moonlight streamed through the open window to her right, falling upon the floor.

Thalia could still use her power here.

The sky witch stood there for a moment, panting, her hair and dress in disarray, blood oozing from the cuts on her cheek where Calida's nails had bit deep. Then she whirled around and threw open the door. Calida faintly heard her calling for help. Any moment now, she would summon countless guards and Calida would be trapped.

Who knew what would happen to her then? Thalia would probably have her thrown into the dungeon beneath the palace.

Calida scrambled to her feet and raced out the door. She remembered her way around the palace well enough to find her own way out, ducking behind columns or into doorways to avoid groups of guards, their footsteps pounding on the marble floors.

She raced outside into the darkness, skirts billowing around her legs. It had been foolish to come here tonight. What had she hoped to accomplish? Niklaus knew where she had gone to stay when she had left the palace. What if they came looking for her and didn't let her go? She had attacked the queen, after all. She might get Lorelei into trouble for harboring a fugitive, but she had to go back. All of her belongings were there.

Some of the guards shouted at her, shaking her out of her thoughts. She had been seen and they had followed her.

Now outside, Calida had full access to her power and she called upon it now, summoning roots to trip the guards up, wrapping around their bodies until they were incapacitated.

She did not stop running and she did not look back. It was too far to run all the way back to Brisban and she might be run down on the road if she continued. Instead, she ducked into the forest that would take her back to the Erlohn monastery, seeking shelter beneath the trees.

She encountered no one and took a circuitous route, making it back to Lorelei's house the long way. It was late by the time she returned, the dark of midnight having come and gone, but at least she was safe.

She approached the door hesitantly. Through the window, she could see a light had been lit within. Were the guards here, waiting for her?

Chiding herself for being paranoid, Calida pushed open the door and went in.

Lorelei had been sitting at the kitchen table, Horus beside her, but she sprang to her feet immediately. "Where have you been?" she demanded. "Palace guards stopped by, demanding to know where you'd gone and I told them I had no idea."

"Are they still here now?" Calida asked, her adrenaline spiking once more.

"No, they left hours ago. What happened?" Lorelei inquired, her expression a mixture of irritation and fear.

It was the sternest Calida had ever seen her friend and she felt a stab of guilt for putting Lorelei in such a situation.

"I'm sorry," she said, sinking down into one of the chairs. Her muscles ached from exhaustion. Now that the imminent danger had passed, the fear faded, leaving her with no strength to keep going. "I went to visit my sister. Or perhaps confront would be a better word. I've made a mess of things."

Lorelei sighed. "I don't have to ask if the two of you reconciled. There wouldn't have been guards banging on my door in the middle of the night if you had."

"I'm sorry," Calida said again. "I didn't mean for it to go so wrong. I lost control and attacked her."

"You attacked the queen of Alara? Calida, what were you thinking?"

"I don't know!" Calida cried, her voice nearly rising to a wail as the earlier tears she had held back threatened once more.

"If you stay upstairs and don't go into town anymore, people might think you've moved on. If the guards come back, I'll tell them you never returned, though if they insist on searching the house, I don't know that I'd be able to stop them. And given what you've just told me, I'd be surprised if they're not having the house watched."

"No," Calida said, nearly overwhelmed by her friend's loyalty. Even after what a fool she'd been, Lorelei was still willing to let her stay, even if it meant putting herself at risk. "It's too dangerous. I won't have you punished for my mistake. I'll go."

"But where will you go?" Lorelei asked.

"I don't know. I never planned for any of this to happen. I'll find something." She felt hopelessly adrift. She'd felt that way ever since leaving the palace.

"Fine. In the morning, then. You may as well stay here tonight."

But Calida shook her head. If the house was indeed being watched, there was no time to lose. "I should go now, while there's still a chance. Thank you, for everything you've done for me."

Lorelei smiled, but it didn't quite reach her eyes.

Calida went upstairs to her small bedroom beneath the eaves, and began gathering her few possessions.

Perhaps she would ask Jeremy to let her sail away with him after all.

CHAPTER 24

"A re you all right?" Niklaus asked, peering at the cuts on Thalia's face. He reached out as though to touch them and then let his fingers fall. "Should I fetch a healer?"

She was aware of the irony that her sister could have healed the wounds better than anyone, certainly better than the healer that had replaced her.

"There's no need," she replied. "It's just a scratch." But she made sure to let a slight tremble enter her voice, a trace of fear show in her eyes.

She didn't add that Calida couldn't truly hurt her. As a sky witch, Thalia was infinitely more powerful and perfectly capable of defending herself. She'd had more combat training than Calida had, after all.

The ferocity of the attack had taken her by surprise. In that moment, Calida had looked more like a crazed beast. And in doing so, without meaning to, had provided Thalia with yet another opportunity.

"Skies." Niklaus sank down onto the floor beside their bed.

He had come running, having heard her cries, and ushered Thalia to the safety and privacy of their bedroom, where they could discuss what had happened without fear of being overheard. Starlight filtering through the open window bathed his pained expression in silver as Thalia joined him.

"I suppose it was foolish of me to agree to see her," Thalia said quietly. "But she's my sister. I never thought…" She paused as though composing herself, taking a deep breath. "But it's like I told you. I don't recognize her anymore, the person she's become. I wasn't afraid for myself or what she might do to me. But…our child…"

"She really did kill my father," he murmured, almost to himself. "I miss him," Niklaus added, the misery he felt plain in his voice. "I wish he were here. He wasn't always the kindest, but he loved me, in his own way."

Thalia leaned her head against his shoulder, pressing up against him, lending warmth and the comfort only the touch of another person could bring.

"I wish he were here," Niklaus repeated. "And he would be if not for Calida. She killed him as sure as if she'd done it with her own hands. She found a cure and didn't like to admit it. She wasn't content to wait and so she killed him. And now she wants to kill our child."

Thalia gripped his arm, letting some of the ferocity she felt show in her eyes. "I won't let that happen."

He covered her hand with his own. "Of course not." He turned away again, staring straight ahead. "If Father were here, he'd know what to do. But he's gone and I'm all alone."

"You're not alone," Thalia reminded him. "I'm here."

Niklaus gave her a wan smile. "Yes. And a good thing, too. I'd be lost without you."

"What's to be done about Calida?" Thalia asked. "She'll lay low, if she knows what's good for her, but we can't take it for granted that she won't try something like this again."

He sighed. "The punishment for regicide is execution. But I can't do that to her. There's some part of me that still cares for her—or rather the woman I thought she was. I can't completely forget or overlook that part. And I don't think you could either."

"Then what? We can't sit back and do nothing."

"No," he agreed. "We need to find her. And then she needs to be banished from Alara. I know where she's staying—or at least where she went to stay when she left here." He paused, considering. "Do you think Lorelei knew what she intended?"

Thalia shook her head. "No, I know Lorelei. She was at the monastery with me. She's not one to take risks. I can't say the same for the other witches, though."

"You think she would seek refuge with her fellow witches? That they would harbor her?"

"Where else would she go? I think she would find many an ally among the others. You know how unsatisfied she was with the life available to a witch. The monastery and what comes after, never being able to choose for yourself. She was lucky, all things considered, but so many aren't. I know there are others who feel the same way. I saw it at the monastery. I know how much Calida resented the monarchy, believing it was your fault, that you put the system she hated in place."

Niklaus took a deep breath. "We'll find her. With any amount of luck, she'll still be at Lorelei's."

But she wasn't. The guards reported conducting a thorough search of Lorelei's quarters, but Calida was not to be found. Others reported witnessing Calida flee into the forest after absconding from the palace, in the direction of the monastery. But a search of the grounds there revealed nothing and if any of the witches there, student or instructor, knew where she'd gone, they refused to say.

Niklaus sent out increased patrols of guards, thinking Calida couldn't have gone far, but a week passed by without word of the red-haired witch. He became increasingly frustrated, sullen, and withdrawn, hardly eating.

Thalia was aware of the anxious glances he shot her, fearful for her safety and that of the child she carried, whose presence was just beginning to make itself known.

"We should have heard something by now," he said one evening, drumming his fingers on the table, the discarded remnants of dinner scattered around them.

"Someone knows where she is," Thalia said softly, raising her eyes to meet his. "They must."

"Are you sure Lorelei knows nothing?" Niklaus asked, leaning eagerly over the edge of the table.

"She and Calida were always friends, but I don't think my sister would risk putting her in danger. Either way though, it wouldn't hurt having her brought to the palace. I'll have need of her services soon enough and she's one of the best."

* * *

A sharp, insistent pounding sounded on the door in the middle of breakfast, making Lorelei freeze, looking up in alarm.

These days, she didn't know who to expect at her door. Was it a frantic husband, come to say that his wife was in labor and to come right away? Or had the guards returned to question her once more about Calida?

It had been over a week since Lorelei had laid eyes on Calida, but her friend had managed to send word to her that she was safe, sending the letters and any replies Lorelei wished to give via Horus.

She'd heard rumors that other witches who had graduated around the same time as Calida had also been questioned. What they could possibly tell the crown, Lorelei had no idea, but it gave her an uncomfortable, twisting feeling in her gut.

Steeling herself against whatever might be waiting for her on the other side of the door, Lorelei rose and answered the summons.

And a summons it was, as confirmed by the guard who stood on her step, red livery scarlet in the sun. She had been summoned to the palace by the queen, who had requested her services.

"I'm to take you there directly," the guard added.

Lorelei felt herself stiffen. She was in no position to deny Thalia anything, but it felt wrong. There were any number of midwives she could have chosen and Lorelei was needed here.

"I can't leave," she told the guard. "What if one of my clients needs me?"

"Then they can find another midwife," the guard said brusquely. "The queen asked for you and it's you she shall have."

Lorelei felt her jaw clench. How much of this was a genuine need of a midwife and how much nothing more than a means of keeping an eye on her, to try and weasel out of her what she might know about Calida?

She wanted to shut the door in the guard's face. Instead she said, "Give me a few minutes to pack my things."

Hastily, she scratched off a quick letter to Calida, telling her where she'd be. She slipped the folded piece of paper beneath the window, securing just enough of the corner that it wouldn't blow away, but that Horus could tug it free easily enough.

The hawk would be able to find her at the palace and get word to her there, of that she had no doubt.

What a clever and useful familiar, Lorelei thought, feeling the familiar ache in her chest whenever she thought of Penny.

Penny wouldn't have been able to help her now, though.

* * *

Calida's first instinct upon being forced to leave Lorelei's had been to flee to the tavern where she had always met Jeremy. But Thalia knew of the existence of that tavern, even if she had rarely ventured there. It was too much of a liability and as much as it pained Calida to pass it by, she couldn't risk it.

Instead, she found herself at a different inn, unfamiliar to both of them. By the end of the first day, she had gotten herself a job as a barmaid there.

As part of the agreement of her employment, some of her pay would be deducted toward room and board. She had taken a small room on the second floor, with a tiny, dingy window. It was cramped, the mattress old and lumpy, and the food was even worse than what the monastery had offered, if that were possible. But at least she had somewhere to stay.

That evening, she sent Horus with a note for Lorelei, telling her where she was staying. She left the window in her room open so he could come and go as he pleased. Otherwise, he had to remain in the room; he couldn't be seen by anyone downstairs and she knew he grew bored being cooped up.

It was hard work at the inn, with long hours on her feet, and by the end of her first day, her arms ached with all the carrying she'd had to do.

Every evening, she sent Horus to keep an eye out for the *Sea Witch*, but there was no sign of the ship or Jeremy.

Despite the less-than-ideal living conditions, the measly pay, and the grueling labor, Calida strangely enjoyed it in a way. It was the first time she had ever felt truly normal. Here, no one gave her a second glance, and if they did, it was only because some sailor found her attractive, not because anyone knew she was a witch.

Her whole life, she had been treated as nothing but a witch. It had come to define her very existence and value. It felt strange to shed that burden. She hadn't even realized just how much it weighed her down until it was gone.

Here, she was no one. Here, she could blend in and disappear.

A note came from Lorelei just over a week later. Horus had found the letter Lorelei had left for them, wedged in the window sill, and Calida had since directed any missives to the palace. She didn't want to write too often, fearful that the letter might fall into the wrong hands.

In the privacy of her room, by flickering firelight, Calida hastily read Lorelei's words, dread growing with each one.

I've heard gossip among the other servants. They're looking for you. They've begun rounding up other witches and questioning them as to your whereabouts. I wouldn't stay in any one place for too long, if I were you. This is serious. You also might want to consider dyeing your hair.

It wasn't signed. Neither of them ever bothered; they both recognized each other's handwriting and Horus delivered each letter personally. Lorelei also didn't spell out the identity of the people hunting for Calida, but she didn't have to.

Horus returned to Calida with another letter just two days later.

Rumor is you've been exiled. To where and for what, I don't know, though I could guess. If they find you, they'll send you away. Though if you ask me, that's only if you're lucky. I wouldn't trust them.

Exiled? From Alara? Calida lowered the letter. But that was her home. If Thalia had her way, she would take that away from Calida as well.

And where would she be exiled to? The pirate haven, Amberleigh, dumped and left to fend for herself among criminals and other exiles? Perhaps that was one reason why people became pirates. Indris, to slave away on a sugarcane farm or hunt wild boar with the buccaneers? In many ways, life on Indris would be even harder than Amberleigh.

She didn't think Daera took exiles from Alara. Calida crumpled the note in her hand and threw it into the fire. Thalia could make all the decrees she wanted. That was fine. Calida so hated to disappoint her, but she wasn't going anywhere.

The next day, Calida took Lorelei's advice and left the inn that had become her home, not wanting to linger too long. Before leaving, she asked one of her fellow barmaids to help her dye her hair an ugly mud brown. She didn't know how long it would last, but there was no denying that it drastically altered her appearance.

From within the palace, as Calida hopped from one tavern or shop to the next, finding work and shelter where she could, Lorelei kept her apprised of news from the outside world. A world Calida could no longer show her face to.

They're not merely questioning witches now. I heard one interrogation turned violent last night. Niklaus is convinced that someone knows something. That our fellow witches are harboring you.

Calida shook her head as she read. It was not Niklaus behind these developments, she knew, but Thalia. It bore the mark of Thalia's design as she no doubt manipulated him still.

She wished there were a way to free him from Thalia's influence, but he likely wouldn't thank her for it.

At last, one evening, Horus reported that the *Sea Witch* had been spotted in the harbor. Calida took off work and raced as fast as her feet could carry her to the tavern where they always met. She knew, in the back of her mind, that it was foolish to return to old haunts, but this was an opportunity not to be missed. She hadn't seen Jeremy in months, since that awful night everything fell apart.

He looked momentarily startled as she rushed up to his table, before his expression cleared. "I almost didn't recognize you, firebrand—though I suppose I can't call you that anymore. I'll need to find something else."

"It's a long story," Calida replied, keeping her voice low. She wanted to say that she barely recognized herself these days.

He frowned, rising to his feet. Their distance and time apart had done nothing to lessen his ability to know when something was wrong. "A story for another setting. Come on."

To her relief, he led her along the dock to where the *Sea Witch* waited, appearing as she always had. Something about the ship's unchanging appearance lightened Calida's heart. She followed him into the great cabin, where they had spoken the last night they had seen each other.

Jeremy lit a few lanterns and turned to face her. "I've heard stories—so many stories. I don't know which ones to believe."

Calida sighed. "Suffice to say that Niklaus broke off our engagement and Thalia betrayed me. She turned him against me. I couldn't bear to stay at the palace with the two of them any longer and so I left."

He nodded. "I heard the various announcements. The coronation and the engagement. Word travels fast. I wondered what had happened. I wanted to come to you, just like I wanted to bring you the rainleaf, but it wasn't safe. There are naval ships everywhere. And, well, then I heard the king had died and I figured you probably didn't need it anymore."

"No," Calida agreed.

"I'm sorry. I'm sorry I couldn't get it to you fast enough. If I had…"

"It doesn't matter now." She didn't want him feeling guilty. If anyone was to blame, it was her. Thalia hadn't been wholly wrong when she'd said she hadn't done anything that Calida hadn't already done for her.

She had laid the groundwork and Thalia had built from there.

"Why the increase in naval ships?" Calida asked suddenly, worried that she was responsible for this, too.

Had Thalia ordered an increase in naval patrols as part of her search? In case Calida tried to flee? She had suggested once, all those years ago, that they simply sail away. Perhaps Thalia remembered and thought her sister might try now.

"I don't know." Jeremy shook his head. "But it's a dangerous time to be a pirate—and a witch, from what I've heard."

"Why?" A chill spider-walked down her spine. "What have you heard?"

He crossed his arms. "That they're rounding up witches—or anyone suspected of being a witch. Not ten minutes before you arrived, I overheard a man say that he'd been brought in for questioning. They were asking him about *you*, firebrand. He's got a birthmark over half his face, but he's no witch. It didn't seem to matter."

"What did they do to him?"

"Asked him a few questions." Jeremy shrugged. "Then let him go when it became clear he didn't know anything. He said he was one of the lucky ones."

Calida swore. "This is all Thalia's doing."

"I don't know what's going on, firebrand, but it's ugly." Jeremy held a hand out toward her. "Come with me."

Calida hesitated. At last, she was being offered what she had yearned for, for so long. A way to escape, to leave her past behind and start anew elsewhere. More than anything, she yearned to reach out and take his hand.

But she shook her head. "I can't. I have to..."

To what? Stop this? Fix it? Save Niklaus from Thalia? Punish Thalia for what she'd done?

All likely impossible tasks. But running, tempting as it was, felt like letting Thalia win.

"I can't leave things like this," Calida finished.

"I can't say I understand. But if that's what you want..."

He withdrew his hand, but not before she caught a glimpse of a tattoo on the inside of his forearm, only part of it visible, the rest disappearing beneath his rolled-up sleeve.

She didn't recall seeing it before and wanted to ask him what it was and if it had any special significance to him.

But now was not the time.

"But know if you ever find yourself in need, just send word. I'll be there."

"Thank you," Calida said, the words more heartfelt than any she could remember uttering lately.

She didn't know what she could do, if anything, and maybe it was foolish to even try, but she couldn't leave other witches—witches like Lorelei and Daniel, wherever he now found himself in the world—to suffer because of her.

Somehow, this needed to end.

* * *

Weeks turned into months and there was still no word on Calida. Thalia could no longer hide her condition. As the child within her grew, so too did Niklaus's paranoia.

He'd become convinced that the witches were conspiring against him to hide one of their own, a notion Thalia did nothing to dissuade.

She knew most of the witches that were questioned knew nothing, but even if they had, even if they had never met Calida and logically had no reason to defend her, they would never admit to it. Their hatred of the crown ran too deeply to betray one of their own, even one who was a stranger.

It had been her suggestion that the interrogations change from mere questioning to something a little more persuasive.

Niklaus had hesitated at first, believing there no need for violence. After all, not all witches could be bad. She herself was proof enough of that. She had proven it with her actions.

"Not every witch hates the crown," Thalia explained. "Some are loyal. They would serve you well. And a witch might be more willing to confide in one of their own."

Yes, she could think of at least one who would serve well…and be well rewarded for it.

"Perhaps you're right," Niklaus conceded.

For the first time since leaving the monastery, Thalia found herself face-to-face with Mordred. It had been easy enough to pull a few strings, find out where his placement had taken him, and summon him to the palace.

He had filled out even more since she had last seen him, his lanky black hair growing long, his shoulders broad. Dressed head to toe in black, standing out starkly against his pale skin, he was the perfect inquisitor to lead the hunt for Calida.

There was one other who possessed the cold, detached cruelty needed for the task at hand and Thalia was not above letting the past lie where it belonged. She sent word for Arin as well and felt no small amount of satisfaction when he bowed before her, ready to receive his instructions.

Who was the powerful one now?

But she would not gloat. She could easily have Arin disposed of for what he'd done to her all those years ago and if the roles had been reversed, he might have done it. But she hadn't gotten to where she had by giving in to every impulse.

He was useful to her and that was all that mattered.

Before leaving the throne room, Mordred looked at her and smirked. "I always knew you'd end up on top."

Thalia felt a smug sense of satisfaction at his words. There was someone who remembered what she'd done for him. Remembered and was grateful. He, too, was useful to her, just as she'd predicted he would be.

Niklaus seemed happy enough to leave such matters to her. Perhaps he realized that she was more experienced, being a witch herself. Or perhaps he didn't want to get his hands too dirty; at least this way he could claim ignorance. Either way mattered not to her.

But Niklaus had conceded that if the witch-hunt became violent, Calida might turn herself in, in order to put a stop to the persecution of her fellow witches.

They were to be disappointed.

"How can she do this?" Niklaus exclaimed one night as they were sitting before the unlit fire. "How can she stand to let others take the fall for her?"

"Now you see her as she truly is," Thalia replied. "As she always was. Selfish, above all else."

Niklaus didn't bother trying to deny it, staring where the flames should be and she wondered if he was seeing them within his mind. "Perhaps we should stop. Try something else. This isn't working."

It wasn't the first time he had expressed such doubts.

"Don't forget who the real enemy is. Witches have been told their entire lives that all the power in this world belongs to the crown. Yet the witches are the ones with magic. Once they realize that they hold all the power, what's to stop them from turning on us?"

What's to stop them from turning on me? From coveting my position, wanting what I have? From trying to take it from me?

"They are a threat, Niklaus," she said softly. "You didn't see Calida that night. I saw the hate in her eyes. Hate I'd seen before, at the monastery."

"Calida was right about one thing," he murmured, glancing at her. "Perhaps it is time for things to change."

CHAPTER 25

When the time came, Thalia knew that the moment had arrived, and yet she had no idea what was happening to her body. It was terrifying. She knew only what she'd been told, never having witnessed it personally.

She'd been the second to be born and so she hadn't witnessed Calida's birth. Even her sister likely didn't know what to expect; she would have only been a year old by the time Thalia herself arrived.

She snapped at one of the guards to send for the midwife at once. As she waited, the pain subsided and she began to wonder if it had been a false alarm, only for it to return sooner than she would have liked, rolling through her, wracking her frame.

Then Lorelei was suddenly at her side, helping her into bed and she remembered very little after that, lost in the all-consuming pain that followed.

"Go ahead and scream," Lorelei instructed. "It will help."

Thalia did, giving voice to all her agony and fury, that this was what she must endure. But endure she did, until the pain finally subsided and she heard Lorelei telling her that it was over. She collapsed back against the pillows, exhausted.

Lorelei stood at the foot of the bed, holding the squalling baby. The sound grated against Thalia's already frayed nerves.

"It's a son," Lorelei told her. "With a good pair of lungs. He appears perfectly healthy; there's nothing physically wrong with him."

There was only one thing that concerned Thalia at the moment. "Give him to me," she demanded.

Lorelei obliged, handing over the baby, who was still crying.

Thalia looked down at her son and began searching. With his small body, it didn't take long to find. There, on the back of his right hand, was a witch-mark, identical to the one on the small of her back.

She allowed herself a genuine smile. Her son was a witch. Time would tell what type he was, but he had inherited some form of power from her.

"Take him," she said, offering him back to the midwife.

Lorelei looked surprised. "What's to be his name, Your Highness?"

"Later," Thalia sighed. "We'll deal with that later." She was much too tired to think of that right now, much less deal with the crying infant.

Blessedly, Lorelei took him away, leaving her in peace.

* * *

It was only a matter of time before the next fateful announcement came down from the palace. Calida had tried not to keep an ear out for it, knowing it would only cause her more misery, but she couldn't help herself.

She needn't have bothered, anyway. It would have been impossible to ignore. It was the talk of the town when word came. The queen had given birth—to a son. The next heir to the throne had been secured.

She received another note from Lorelei that day, finding it waiting for her where Horus had placed it on the nightstand beside her bed.

You probably already know that you're an aunt, Lorelei wrote. *But what you don't know is that the little prince has a witch-mark, on the back of his right hand.*

Calida felt an uncomfortable sensation in her chest, as though her heart had just lurched. Thalia's son was a witch. The son who should have been hers, Calida couldn't help but think.

No doubt that pleased her sister to no end.

Calida lay awake that night, thinking over what Lorelei had told her and its implications. She knew she should put it out of her mind and get some sleep. Her next shift would be difficult enough without a sleepless night on top of it.

But she didn't let it go and by the time dawn arrived, she had begun to formulate the beginnings of a plan.

Thalia had taken everything from her. It was only fair that she take something back.

Early the next morning, Calida sent word to Lorelei, asking her to meet her as soon as possible. Until then, she could only wait and so she went about her duties, part of her mind always thinking about the plan she had concocted. The more she thought about it, the fonder she became of the idea.

Lorelei came into the tavern that evening and Calida sent her upstairs to her room to wait for her until she had finished her shift. They couldn't very well discuss things downstairs. Even with all the noise, there was the risk they might be discovered and Calida wouldn't chance it.

Exhausted after finishing her work, Calida wanted nothing more than to collapse into bed, but this must be done first. It was too important. She hadn't gone through what she had and planned her revenge for nothing.

"There you are," Lorelei hissed as Calida came into the room, shutting the door behind her. The shutters were already drawn across the windows, blocking out the light. "I don't know how long I can stay. Someone might miss me back at the palace. I'm responsible for taking care of the prince, you know."

"I'll be brief," Calida interrupted, her voice pitched low. They were already taking a risk, meeting like this, and what she had to say could not be overheard by anyone.

She took a deep breath. Once spoken, the words could not be taken back, and she prayed Lorelei would agree to help her. Without her, there was no chance.

"The prince is the reason I called you here. I want to take him from Thalia and I need your help to do it."

Lorelei stared at her, aghast. "You can't be serious."

"I am. You're in the perfect position to help me—"

"Do you realize what will happen to us if we're caught?"

"I don't intend to be caught."

"I am not risking my position, much less my life, for this scheme of yours, Calida! I'm sorry."

"Please," Calida begged. She hated pleading, but she needed Lorelei on board. "Thalia took everything from me. I want to take something back. And more than that, you know what kind of a mother she would be. I don't want my nephew growing up with her as a mother. She doesn't deserve that child. She'll turn him into a monster, just like her. He'll never know love or kindness, only manipulation and cruelty and what kind of future king would that make? Even worse, you said he's a witch. Think of what she could do with that kind of power in addition to her own. Think of what she's already doing to our kind."

Lorelei sighed. "All right, I'll listen to what you have to say. But I make no promises. How exactly do you plan to smuggle him out of the palace?"

"That's where you come in. You'll need to put him in something that Horus can carry—a basket, maybe. If you leave him out on one of the balconies, my hawk can come collect him and bring him to me."

"That's all very well and good, but someone will notice he's missing. And we both know who will take the fall for it."

Calida shook her head. "Obviously we can't just take the baby. I don't intend for Thalia to ever realize anything's wrong. We'll have to replace him with another baby."

"You're forgetting the witch-mark," Lorelei pointed out. "How are you going to fake that? You can be sure Thalia will notice if it's not there. It's all she cared about; she made a point of looking for it almost immediately."

"What does it look like? Tell me exactly."

"Show me your mark," Lorelei instructed.

Calida withdrew her left foot from her shoe.

Lorelei nodded. "Like yours. It's just like yours."

Like hers and Thalia's.

"I've got an idea for the mark, but I'll still need to find a baby who looks similar to the prince. What does he look like?"

"He's got his father's fair hair and blue eyes, but light, not like Thalia's. How are you going to find a spare baby that no one wants?"

"Leave that to me. If I can't manage it, then the plan's off. All you need to worry about is getting the prince out on the balcony when the time comes."

Lorelei moved toward the door. "I can't stay any longer. Send word if you've managed to work out the rest of the plan. I'm still not convinced, mind, but there's no point in moving forward with the rest of it until then."

"This isn't just about my own revenge, I swear. It's for the best." Calida reached out, grabbing her friend's arm. "Lorelei, if you go through with this, you do realize we'll both have to leave. I'm already an exile. I can't stay here once this is done and neither can you. If something goes wrong and they realize what we've done, you'll be in danger."

Lorelei swallowed. "But where would we go?"

Calida shrugged. "Daera, maybe? I've got an idea for that, too."

Her friend shook her head. "You really have thought of everything, haven't you?" Without waiting for a reply, Lorelei pulled the door open and disappeared down the stairs into the darkness.

Calida closed the door again and leaned against it.

Lorelei still might refuse, but regardless, Calida had to move forward with the next part of the plan.

* * *

The birth of his son had an immediate effect on Niklaus. He marveled over the tiny child, marveling at how fragile he was. Thalia was relieved at his attention, both because it saved her the trouble of having to give the child more attention than she wanted, and because it was the most animated and alive she'd seen the king since the death of his father.

Despite acknowledging the vulnerable state of the kingdom and the fragility of their son, Thalia knew that while Niklaus had come to see the witches as more of a threat, he would never sanction the destruction of the monastery.

And until the monastery was gone, it would continue to conscript more young witches into its ranks with each passing year, each one a rival for her power and position. Perhaps, given enough time, Thalia could have convinced Niklaus to take that step, but time was a luxury she could not afford. She had been patient thus far. Now it was time to take matters into her own hands and act.

She summoned Mordred, knowing he held no love for the Erlohn monastery in his heart either, and gave him his orders. Accompanied by armed guards, he set out.

Thalia waited before setting out after them.

She did not wish to participate, but she wanted to be there when it happened, to witness the destruction. From the sounds of screams and the smell of smoke carrying on the wind, reaching her before she'd even arrived, she knew Mordred had been successful. But nothing could have prepared her for the sight.

Thalia reigned her horse to a stop, her breath catching as she beheld the monastery, wreathed in flames. The stone buildings would not burn, but they could blacken. The wind shifted slightly, blasting a wave of heat over her.

With a flick of her hand, a mere gesture, she stirred the air, feeding the flames, watching as they roared, orange demons capering, sweeping higher.

The thatched roofs, garden plots, and flowerbeds were not so lucky, going up in moments. Surrounding the keep on all sides were the contingent of guards Mordred had brought, with instructions to run down any who attempted to flee.

As Thalia watched, several witches, covered in soot, staggered toward the main archway, only to find their path blocked. When the guards gestured that they turn around, that they get back, a few hesitated, hanging back, unwilling to risk their wrath.

The others, with the flames beckoning behind, darted forward, their movements borne of desperation. Quickly, they were shot, brought down with rifles and pistols or trampled beneath the horses' hooves.

Thalia urged her horse closer, despite the heat and the smoke choking the air, stinging her eyes. She should have felt horror at the sight before her, knowing she had played a part in it. That she had set this into motion. She had made it happen.

Instead, she felt exultant as she watched the flames devour the place that had stolen her childhood.

Through a gap in the flames, she saw one witch stumble, succumbing to the smoke. Coughing, the witch raised her head, her eyes meeting Thalia's, and she recognized Ayani, her old combat instructor.

A moment later, a gust of wind sent the flames soaring higher, blotting Ayani from view. Thalia did not see her again.

Slowly, she turned her horse around and began making for the palace. She hadn't seen Mordred, but she knew he was here, faithfully carrying out her orders, as he had each time she'd given them. She would return, when the flames had died, but the blackened stone still radiated warmth, to see what remained.

Niklaus was horrified when he learned what had happened and Thalia did her best to appear contrite, already having thought of what she would tell him.

"How could this happen?" he demanded. "My scouts reported there were very few survivors."

Thalia felt a flicker of irritation at that, but it couldn't be helped. It was unreasonable to think that they could stop every single witch from escaping.

"It was an accident," she replied. "Our inquisitors went there to perform an interrogation. You know how tensions have been rising lately and they finally boiled over. Guards were called in to deal with the riot, but the situation spiraled out of hand. I don't know how the fire started, but once it did, the high winds made quick work of it. After that, it was nothing but panic. A tragic loss of life, but one that sadly could have been avoided."

Niklaus frowned. "Rumor going around says you were seen. What were you doing there?"

Thalia spread her hands. "I grew up there. And I am a sky witch. I thought perhaps my powers could help, but by the time I arrived, the place was too far gone."

He rubbed at his brow. "These…interrogations are going a bit far, don't you think?"

She hung her head and said nothing to contradict him.

But that night, he was still upset over what had happened. Reports had rolled in all day about the great loss of life at the monastery and Thalia had discreetly dispatched Mordred to hunt down any survivors. It would be good for him to stay away from the palace for a while.

She approached Niklaus after dinner, armed with an apology and a glass of wine.

"You were right," she said softly. "I should have informed you that they would be going to the monastery, especially in light of recent events. With tensions running so high, things were bound to boil over. It was wrong of me. But know that everything I've done, I've believed to be right and for the good of this kingdom….and our son's future. We have to look to him now and think about what kind of world we want him to inherit."

Niklaus sighed, his eyes softening at the mention of their son. "You're right."

She smiled, handing him the wine glass, and poured one for herself. "To a better world," she said, clinking her glass against his and watching as he brought it to his lips.

If he suspected anything amiss, he did not show it. But Thalia had decided to follow her own advice and she watched as he drank down the concoction, oblivious to the devil's blood within.

Three days later, Thalia received word from Mordred that he had tracked down one of the remaining survivors. A witch named Kallias, whom he'd found wounded and recovering at an inn. Mordred had offered to help attend to the man's wounds, but sadly, he died of his injuries.

* * *

The letter from Lorelei was brief, containing only three words, but Calida knew what she meant.

You were right.

She didn't have to ask what had caused Lorelei's change of heart. It was the talk of the town, possibly the entire kingdom. The Erlohn monastery had burned, killing almost all within.

The news had sent chills down Calida's spine. It was true that the arch was the main way in and out of the monastery, but there was more than one exit. They should have been able to escape before it was too late.

Even without the rumors that royal guards had surrounded the place, ruthlessly mowing down any who attempted to flee, Calida knew Thalia was responsible. The whole sordid mess reeked of one of her plots. And now, Lorelei could no longer deny what the queen was. She saw her for who she really was and the danger she posed to all witches.

Alara was no longer safe.

With Lorelei on board, Calida knew they needed to act quickly. She sent Horus out with a message for Jeremy and waited anxiously for his reply. If she was wrong and this wasn't possible, the whole plan would fall through before it even began.

His reply came quickly, again passed on verbally by Horus.

"He says there's a member of his crew that's skilled at tattooing and that she's done it for several other members. He doesn't know if tattooing a witch-mark would work, but the design is simple enough."

A tattoo was the only way Calida could think to put a fake witch-mark on the baby that would replace the real prince. You were either born with one or you weren't and even if Calida could find a child who already had one, it wouldn't be identical to the one she shared with Thalia.

Now all she had to do was find a baby similar enough in appearance that Thalia wouldn't be fooled. This was easier said than done. Calida couldn't simply walk up to another woman and ask to be given her child, even if he did have the right appearance. And an orphanage seemed too risky. Calida wanted a child that was untraceable, abandoned, that no one wanted and no one would miss.

During her time off, she began wandering the streets of the poorer neighborhoods—taking care to ensure her hair remained dyed—where times were hard, looking for a suitable baby that might have been abandoned because the parents were either dead, didn't want the child anymore, or simply couldn't afford to take care of it.

The task took far longer than she would have liked. Every time she stepped out of the tavern, she was aware of each pair of eyes on her, aware that any one of them could be one of Thalia's inquisitors looking for her.

More than once, Lorelei wrote to her, asking if she had given up on the idea and Calida wrote back saying that she hadn't and needed more time. But if she couldn't find a suitable baby, she would have to admit that the plan wasn't likely to happen.

It wasn't as though she couldn't find *any* abandoned children. She found several during her travels, but they were always the wrong age, had the wrong eye color, or were girls. She found it sad, but there were far more abandoned girls than there were boys.

It had been weeks since Lorelei had stopped by and Calida was almost ready to give up when she finally stumbled upon one she thought might work. She would have missed him entirely if not for the pitiful wails that had led her there.

The baby had been left in an alley, in the shadows between buildings. His hair was a fiery red, nearly the same shade as Calida's own and his eyes were a dark blue. It was almost startling to look at them. They were so like Thalia's that Calida could have believed they were, in fact, her sister's eyes.

This child did not have blond hair or the right shade of blue eyes, but Calida knew it was likely as close as she was going to get. It was already uncanny enough. The baby would resemble Thalia rather than Niklaus, but perhaps Thalia wouldn't notice the difference. Lorelei had said the only thing she cared about had been the witch-mark, so perhaps she hadn't bothered to take in the rest of the baby's appearance.

And hair color did change, especially when a child was young. If Thalia neglected her son, she might not even notice the difference by the time she next deigned to favor the child with her attention.

Calida would have to count on that and pray the rest of the plan worked. If not, at least she and Lorelei would be well away by the time Thalia realized anything was wrong.

There was a part of Calida that almost wished Thalia would realize what they'd done after the fact. She could imagine the pain and outrage her sister would feel at having lost her only son—and a witch at that. She wanted to inflict that pain as it had been inflicted upon her.

But perhaps the crueler, more painful thing would be for Thalia to unwittingly raise a false son for years, never realizing she'd been deceived. Her knowledge of the fact did nothing, ultimately, to change what Calida had done. She would be victorious regardless.

Calida bent down, scooping up the abandoned baby in her arms. He was heavier than she'd anticipated and slightly malnourished. The baby had been here for a little while. She wasn't taking a child that had been temporarily left there by his parents. In all likelihood, she was saving his life.

She took him back to her room at the tavern and gave him bottles of milk. She knew it probably wasn't what he needed, but it was the best she could do. Calida sent Horus off again to find Jeremy, telling him that she needed to see him urgently and to come as quickly as possible. As an added incentive to get him there as fast as possible, she added that he could anchor off the coast somewhere if need be and she could meet him there.

The reply came swiftly. He agreed to meet with her, off the eastern coast which faced Amberleigh, under the cover of darkness.

Calida knew she had to act quickly. Taking the child with her, she left the tavern, no longer concerned about fulfilling her shifts. If all went according to plan, she would soon have no further need of her room above the bar. She would be long gone.

Following Horus's directions, Calida set out on foot, careful to avoid any guards patrolling the area. If they were local, they wouldn't likely realize who she was, but she took no chances, having come this far.

It was a long trip on foot. Her feet hurt and her arms ached from carrying the baby by the time she arrived. The baby was a particularly fussy one and she tried, mostly without success, to soothe him, worried his cries would attract unwanted attention.

She could see the *Sea Witch* anchored off the coast, barely visible in the darkness. She might not have known it was there at all if she hadn't been looking for it and spotted the small lanterns that had been lit on deck. Standing on the beach, she sent Horus on to tell Jeremy that she was here, waiting, once again thankful that a winged familiar had chosen her.

As she watched, a longboat was slowly lowered into the water, a lantern at its prow, and began making its way toward her. Jeremy jumped onto shore and approached her as the boat was tugged up onto the sand.

He took in the baby in her arms. "Do I even want to ask?"

"It's not mine," Calida said indignantly.

"Looks like it could be."

"That's the point. I plan to steal my sister's son and put this baby in his place." There was no point in claiming otherwise and she knew she could be honest with Jeremy. He'd kept her secret all these years, after all. "But her son is a witch and so I need a false witch-mark tattooed on this baby or she'll realize he's not her son."

Jeremy inhaled deeply. "So you're involving us in kidnapping a member of the royal family now, are you?"

"You're pirates," she pointed out. "I doubt one more crime on your record will matter much."

He grinned suddenly. "No. If we're caught, we're all dead men, regardless of whether we help you kidnap the prince or not. All right, we'll do it here. The movement of a ship is too unpredictable for tattooing and I imagine you want this to be as precise as possible."

"Yes. I also have a reference for what it should look like, if that helps."

"It would help tremendously." Jeremy turned to one of the members of the crew that had come with him. "This is Esme."

A slender young woman stepped forward. Her sleeves were rolled up, revealing many intricate tattoos along her forearms. In the dim lighting, Calida could make out flowers, skulls, and written characters.

"You're a girl," Calida said before she could stop herself.

For some reason, she hadn't imagined there were any female pirates—not with the conflict it could cause between the other crew members and the superstition that women brought nothing but ill fortune.

Esme smiled knowingly. "And the best tattooist on the Atlas Sea." She reached into the longboat and removed a small chest. "I brought everything I should need, although I admit, I've never tattooed an infant before…"

In a matter of moments, Calida was sitting in the sand, the baby in her lap so she could keep him from squirming. Esme warned her the process could be painful. Calida had removed the shoe on her left foot, her own witch-mark visible. Esme sat in front of her, taking the baby's right hand, her chest of supplies open on the sand beside her.

Jeremy stood over them, holding the lantern so Esme had enough light to see by. The other pirates milled around, keeping an eye out for anyone who might try and approach, but the beach was deserted and Calida didn't think they would be disturbed.

"Thank goodness it's a full moon," Esme remarked, leaning close. "I usually do this in daylight."

Calida watched as she went to work with her needle, glancing every now and then at Calida's own mark as she emulated it on the baby. He let out cries of protest as the needle pricked his skin and Calida felt a prick of her own, guilty that she was doing this to him.

But then she remembered the reason why and hardened her heart. She tightened her grip on the child, preventing him from moving.

The design was simple but the process was slow. Calida's muscles soon felt cramped and one of her legs had fallen asleep. She thought Esme must feel the same way, but the girl remained very still, completely focused on her work. She had a dark green cloth wrapped around her forehead, keeping her hair out of her face. Jeremy had already shifted his weight multiple times and she knew his feet must be bothering him.

At last, the task was done. The first hints of dawn were beginning to stain the sky. It had taken longer than Calida thought, but Esme had been meticulous.

Esme sat back. "There. It will take some time to heal."

Calida looked down at a perfect replica of her own witch-mark on the back of the baby's right hand. He had eventually worn himself out and fallen silent.

"Thank you." Calida reached into a pocket of her dress and withdrew a small bag of coins. "I have a little money saved up. Take it."

She thought if it had been Jeremy she was offering it to, he would have refused, but Esme had no such qualms. She was an artist and expected to be paid for her work.

Calida stood stiffly and looked up at Jeremy. "When this is over, I'm afraid I'll need your help again. I'll have to leave Alara."

He nodded. "You can't very well stay, having kidnapped the prince. Just send word and we'll meet here again." He frowned, hesitating. "But I hope you know what you're doing, firebrand. For your sake."

She assured him that she did, but as she made her way back, she began to doubt. There was so much that could go wrong, and yet no other path forward that she could see.

Back in her room at the tavern—Calida hadn't realized she would need it much longer—she mixed up a healing salve and applied it to the baby's tattoo. It would speed up the healing process, ensuring she didn't have to wait as long, but it would still take longer than she'd like.

At this point, anything longer than the immediate was too long.

Only when all signs of redness or swelling had gone down, and the tattoo looked completely natural, did Calida send for Lorelei.

I'm ready. It's time.

She half expected Lorelei to protest some more, or back out now that the time had come, but the reply surprised her.

Send Horus to the palace. I will meet you at the tavern when it's done.

Calida inhaled deeply. This was it. There would be no going back. As instructed, she sent Horus to the palace and then sat on the edge of her bed.

All she could do now was wait.

* * *

Lorelei crept out onto the balcony, her heart in her throat. She kept looking all around, thinking she would be discovered any moment and be commanded to give an explanation of what she was doing. But there was no one there. And if there were, she doubted all the suspicious glancing around would make her look any less guilty.

She'd had a devil of a time finding a basket large enough to hold the little prince, but she'd finally found one, stashing it away in her room. She'd half hoped that she would never need it, never hear from Calida and that her friend would have forgotten all about this plan, but she hadn't.

And she knew, dangerous though it was, this was the only action they could take. Thalia had crossed a line, gone too far, in destroying the monastery. It was as good as declaring open war on her fellow witches, leading the kingdom down a dark path.

This is going to get us all killed, she thought, even as she stepped forward, clutching the basket. Lorelei tilted her head up, shielding her eyes with a hand, but she didn't see any sign of Calida's hawk.

She'd just have to trust that he was coming. She set the basket down in the middle of the balcony and then adjusted it so the sun wouldn't be in the baby's face. Thankfully, he was being very quiet, looking up at her with those bright blue eyes. She was the one who cared for him, not Thalia, and he no doubt felt safe in her presence.

It wouldn't do to linger. "Goodbye, little one," she whispered and ducked back through the open doors, shrinking down behind a piece of furniture to watch.

She would look utterly ridiculous if she were caught and there would be no explanation she could give. Lorelei supposed if that should happen, then she'd have to fling herself over the side of the balcony.

Moments later, as she watched, Horus swooped down, landing on the basket handle. The hawk peered down at the baby within, cocking his head as one small hand reached up toward him. Then he lifted into the air.

Lorelei watched, heart in her throat, hoping the basket wasn't too heavy for the bird and that he didn't drop it. Come to that, she should have asked Calida more questions just to be sure.

What did she intend to do with the baby once she had him? She knew nothing about caring for them. Surely she didn't intend to harm him. What would be the point of having the hawk bring the baby to her if that were her intention? It would have made more sense to drop the basket along the way.

Or perhaps that was the plan all along. Lorelei felt a stab of terror. But it was too late now. She resisted the urge to abandon her post and rush forward, demanding the hawk bring the child back. He would be long gone by now.

After what felt like an eternity, the hawk returned, carrying the basket again. He left it on the open balcony, exactly as he had first found it, and flew away.

Cautiously, Lorelei crept forward. The baby within had red hair and dark blue eyes. What had Calida been thinking, choosing this baby for the replacement? They looked nothing alike. But then she looked at the back of his right hand and her eyebrows rose even further.

However Calida had managed it, the witch-mark looked perfect. No one would suspect the mark of being fake and why would they? Perhaps she was counting on that to make Thalia overlook the discrepancies. That, and her own inattention.

It was too late to back out now. Calida would never return the real prince now that she had him. Lorelei needed to act. Thalia thought the prince was in the nursery, having his afternoon nap. It was why Lorelei had decided to act now, knowing the queen wouldn't ask for the baby any time soon.

In all actuality, the queen never really asked to see her son. She probably wanted to wait until he was older and therefore more useful to her. A baby was helpless and what good was that?

Lorelei snatched up the basket, heading for the nursery. She would place the false prince there and then make good on her escape.

* * *

Horus had a difficult time maneuvering the basket through the small window in Calida's room and she had to help him, taking the basket from him, the bird following after.

She looked down at the child within. He stared up at her with bright blue eyes—Niklaus's eyes.

She'd been somewhat prepared to dislike the baby on principle. He represented everything Thalia had taken from her, everything she'd been denied.

But he was also the child of the man she had loved and Calida found she could not bring herself to dislike the baby. Gingerly, she lifted him from the basket, glancing at his witch-mark. It was nearly identical to the fake one and she thought it would do.

She picked up the false baby and placed him in the basket, wrapping him in the white blankets Lorelei had included.

She turned to Horus. The poor bird was panting from the exertion, but she knew he would not fail. "You know what to do."

Calida handed him the basket out the window and watched as the bundle began its journey to the palace. Then she turned back to the bed and took her nephew in her arms. She wondered what kind of man he would become under her guidance instead of Thalia's.

She knew one thing for certain: he would never know his true identity.

She realized she didn't even know his name.

Horus returned before Lorelei arrived and though she knew he was exhausted, Calida sent him to inform Jeremy that they would soon be needing him. He had not yet come back by the time Lorelei arrived, breathless.

She let out a sigh of relief upon seeing the baby in Calida's arms. "Oh skies, he made it safely."

"And the other?"

"In the nursery when I left."

"Were you followed?"

"No. No one knew anything had happened when I left, though I can't speak for now."

The two of them waited in silence, sitting beside each other on the edge of the bed, for Horus to return.

The hawk's report was brief. "*The* Sea Witch *will wait for you along the eastern coast, as before.*"

"Perfect," Calida stood. "Let's go."

Horus hopped onto her shoulder and she and Lorelei made their way down the stairs of the tavern for the last time, Lorelei carrying two small bags of belongings, the only things they would bring with them into their new lives.

Clutching her bundle to her chest, Calida felt the weight of what she had done. She was holding the prince of Alara in her arms and no one knew. Still, she felt the weight of the eyes watching her as the people they passed briefly glanced their way. They couldn't possibly know anything but that did nothing to stop her nerves. Her heart was pounding and she fought the urge to run.

"Skies, I can't believe we're actually doing this," Lorelei gasped.

Calida knew what she meant. Everything was happening too fast. It suddenly felt like just yesterday she had left the palace of her own free will. Just yesterday Niklaus had broken off their engagement. Just yesterday she had shared that kiss with him the night of the party. Just yesterday she had crossed beneath the archway at the Erlohn monastery for the last time...

Darkness had once again fallen by the time she and Lorelei reached the beach, and it was all they could do to stay upright. The longboat had been rowed out in preparation so they didn't have to wait this time.

Lorelei stiffened as they approached and Calida thought she was thinking back to another evening on a beach, years ago, when she had lost her familiar.

"You didn't tell me these friends of yours were pirates," she hissed.

"We can trust Jeremy," Calida replied. "He's known I'm a witch all this time and kept my secret."

Jeremy was standing by the prow of the longboat, hands in his pockets. "So this is the little prince. You managed to pull it off."

"Well, not quite," Calida replied. They were still in Alara. A land she was exiled from, a land her sister ruled, and a land the baby in her arms would have one day ruled, if not for Calida's meddling.

If she had her way, he'd never lay eyes on this shore again. And neither would she.

Jeremy nodded. "Let's shove off. I won't feel safe until we're out of Alaran waters."

He helped Calida and Lorelei into the waiting longboat. They settled themselves and within moments, the boat had been pushed off into the water and they were rowing toward the waiting *Sea Witch*.

The longboat pulled up alongside the ship. Ropes were lowered and attached and then the boat was hauled up until it was level with the deck. The pirates disembarked and once again, Jeremy helped Calida and Lorelei, the footing treacherous.

Calida looked around as she stood on the deck. She could hear Jeremy shouting orders, but she wasn't really listening. The anchor was hauled up, adjustments made to the canvas above her head and then they were moving through the water, not merely sitting in it.

She staggered slightly. The movement of the ship would take some getting used to. It seemed she would be sailing away with Jeremy after all. She smiled to herself at the thought.

He reappeared at her shoulder. "Where would you like us to take you?"

She would have liked to stay on board, despite the dangers of such a life, but she had her nephew to think of now and a pirate ship was no place for an infant.

"Daera," she replied. It was the only option. Perhaps they'd be safer there and be able to build a new life.

Jeremy Lussard nodded and returned to the helm.

Calida was left standing beside Lorelei as the midwife gripped the railing and sailors bustled past, going about their tasks. The sea stretched out endlessly before them, the shore of Alara, the only home Calida had ever known, shrinking in the background.

Calida looked down at the baby in her arms. "I didn't ask. What's his name?"

Lorelei shook her head. "I think you should give him a new one. His old life is gone. He is no longer who he used to be."

Calida nodded. No, she would not use any name her sister had chosen for this child. She thought of what name she would have liked to give him if he had been her child instead of Thalia's, and knew what she would call him.

"Benjamin," she decided, gazing over the waves at the kingdom they'd left behind. "His name is Benjamin."

Thank you for reading!

When I was twelve, I decided that my dream was to become a published author. I have since achieved that dream, but an author is nothing without their readers. So thank you, reader, for giving this book a chance.

If you enjoyed this book, it would mean the world to me if you would consider leaving a review on Amazon or Goodreads. Reviews are essential for authors. They help our books get seen, they help our book get promoted, and they can be the difference between whether or not another reader decides to take a chance on a book.

While it may sound cheesy, you are literally helping make my dream come true. So thank you again for your support and happy reading!

ABOUT THE AUTHOR

Rachel Terry grew up in a small town where nothing much ever happened, dreaming of grand adventures and far-away places, which she found between the pages of books. When not writing, she can be found reading, making YouTube videos, gaming with friends, or indulging in her love of history. She currently resides in the Midwest with her family and a cat named Crinkles.

Visit her online at: rachel-terry.com

YouTube: RachelTerryAuthor

Instagram: rterrywriter

Facebook: rachelterryauthor

THE PHOENIX AND THE CROWN

THE PHOENIX AND THE CROWN
Atlas Sea Book 1

A pirate with a deadly secret.
A princess desperate to save her dying kingdom.

LIGHTBRINGER

LIGHTBRINGER
The Guardians Duology Book 1

When an old wrong leads to war, one girl finds herself in the middle of it all.

www.ingramcontent.com/pod-product-compliance
Lightning Source LLC
Chambersburg PA
CBHW020343010826
48973CB00005B/1246